Dangerous Shores

Jessica Blair

PIATKUS

PIATKUS

First published in Great Britain in 2007 by Piatkus Books

North Lanarkshire Council
   Motherwell Library
Hamilton Road, Motherwell
   MOT

7 777536 08	
Askews & Holts	14-Dec-2012
AF ☒ PBK	£6.99
MOT	297630

No part of this publication may be reproduced, stored in a retrieval system, or transmitted, in any form or by any means, without the prior permission in writing of the publisher, nor be otherwise circulated in any form of binding or cover other than that in which it is published and without a similar condition including this condition being imposed on the subsequent purchaser

A CIP catalogue record for this book
is available from the British Library

ISBN 978-0-7499-0928-4

Typeset in Times by Phoenix Photosetting, Chatham, Kent
Printed in the UK by CPI Mackays, Chatham, ME5 8TD

Papers used by Piatkus Books are natural, renewable and recyclable
products made from wood grown in sustainable forests and certified
in accordance with the rules of the Forest Stewardship Council.

Mixed Sources
Product group from well-managed
forests and other controlled sources
www.fsc.org Cert no. SGS-COC-004081
© 1996 Forest Stewardship Council

Piatkus Books
An imprint of
Little, Brown Book Group
100 Victoria Embankment
London EC4Y 0DY

An Hachette Livre UK Company
www.hachettelivre.co.uk

www.piatkus.co.uk

FOR
JILL
WHOSE MAGIC INSPIRED
ME TO KEEP GOING

Acknowledgements

I thank all those people, many of them unknown names, who were involved in all aspects of this book from the first word to the last and beyond to bring it into the hands of you, the reader.

I must make special thanks to my daughter Judith who read the manuscript as it developed, advising and correcting me. Also my thanks to her twin, Geraldine, who checked the manuscript in its entirety. I must also thank Anne, my eldest daughter, and my son, Duncan, for their continued support and interest.

I make grateful thanks to my wonderful editor Lynn Curtis who has been involved with all my Jessica Blair novels. I owe her a great debt.

I also thank the whole team at my publisher, Piatkus, particularly Gillian Green who oversaw it all.

Dangerous Shores

Chapter One

'We have a problem.'

Eliza looked up from the smiling eyes of two-year-old Abigail, wriggling pleasurably in her cradle, to see her husband John come striding into the drawing room. His voice was serious but, she thought, not too serious. Whatever the problem was, it could be dealt with satisfactorily, though it obviously needed thought and attention.

Eliza was always flattered when he chose to consult her, as he did on most matters. Many men she knew made such judgements without even mentioning them to their wives. She appreciated that John looked beyond the convention of 1782 and considered her an equal partner in his life. His love for her was deep and sincere, and she returned that love in full measure. She showed an interest in all he did, especially the running of the small estate he'd inherited from his father, on the Yorkshire coast, four miles south of the thriving port of Whitby. It was there that his father had made his money as a ship's chandler, and where John continued to run the business that enabled him and Eliza to enjoy the peace and tranquillity of Bloomfield Manor, a medium-sized Georgian house with views of the sea.

'What's the problem, love?' Eliza asked when John reached the window. 'I suppose it has to do with the papers in your hand?' she added as she rose from her chair and came to join him.

'It's a wonderful view, isn't it?' was all he said in answer to her questions.

'Wonderful,' she replied, and waited patiently for him to explain what troubled him.

How often they had stood here, gazing across the terrace and over the lawn to the cliff edge beyond overhanging a tiny bay where at this moment the sea lapped lazily. No matter what the season, no matter what the weather or the tumult of the sea, this view always entranced them and inevitably their fingers entwined as they enjoyed it together.

'Well, what is it?' she prompted quietly. 'What has that piece of paper to do with the view?'

John turned to her. As ever she saw love and adoration on his handsome face, but she also saw from the shadows in his deep blue eyes that he was troubled.

'Maybe we'll leave it,' he said quietly, letting go of her hand and running his hand through his thick dark hair; a worried gesture.

'What?' His statement evoked disbelief in her. She stared at him, her eyes wide with shock and curiosity. 'Leave Bloomfield Manor. Why?'

He hesitated as if searching for the right words. 'This,' he said, holding up the papers.

Eliza took them. The top one was a letter written in immaculate copperplate handwriting; obviously executed by someone used to producing clearly legible documents. Her eyes skipped over the words quickly. The shock she received caused her to sink on to the window seat to read the letter more carefully, making sure she had truly understood the contents at first glance. When she knew that she had she looked up slowly to meet John's anxious gaze.

'Well?' she said.

He tightened his lips and shrugged his shoulders. She noticed his quick glance out of the window but could not interpret whether he was deliberately redirecting her attention to the view they both loved and silently saying: 'This is what I want.' She stood up and placed a comforting hand on his arm. Her blue eyes met his, asking him to say something, for whatever he wanted she would agree to.

'I wish Uncle Gerard hadn't done this, then we wouldn't have been faced with a decision that could affect our lives and even Abigail's.'

'Well, he has. We cannot get away from that. I don't think we can walk away from his immense generosity either without considering it carefully.'

'I suppose not. But I hardly remember him. He left Whitby when I was a child. Under a bit of a cloud, I believe. He was twelve years older than my father. Never set foot here again. Sailed the seven seas and, it was rumoured, made a fortune. He finally settled in Cornwall.'

'And now he's died,' added Eliza when her husband hesitated, 'and left everything to, as it says here, "John Mitchell, my nephew and only male relation". According to these figures it's a considerable fortune in money and land.'

'Yes, but note the proviso. I will have to take up residence in his property, and he stipulates that I must reside there for twelve years otherwise everything I inherit will be forfeit. If I were to leave within that time then I would have to make good the estate's worth to its present value.'

'Or you could refuse the bequest,' Eliza pointed out.

'Are you saying that's what I should do?'

'No. I am just pointing out that there is an alternative.'

'And if I do, the whole of my uncle's estate will pass to the government.'

'Do I detect from your tone of voice that you would not like that to happen?'

'It would seem as if we were throwing his kindness back in Uncle Gerard's face. After all, though I have barely met him since childhood, it seems he did not forget me.'

'True. It looks as though he forgot Martha, though, which is strange considering your sister is four years older than you.'

'What would he know of her, not having been in touch with the family? He probably assumed she'd be married with a husband to provide for her by now.'

'He could have bothered to find out. If he had, he'd have known she lost the love of her life when he was drowned on a whaling voyage in the Arctic,' Eliza pointed out.

'Maybe he was planning to. That letter says my uncle died suddenly.'

'It also states he had drawn up his will two years ago; if he had planned to consider Martha, he would have had time.'

'Well, we will never know his reasons for leaving everything to me, but we have a decision to make.'

'I think before we do so you had better go to Cornwall and view the situation and prospects there. After all, it may *sound* very enticing but we don't want to give up everything here and find later we have made a bad move with poor future prospects.'

'You are always the one with the common sense.' John gave a little smile and tenderly reached out to stroke her dark hair and let it run through his fingers, allowing the copper tint to catch the light.

'Will you tell Martha?' she asked.

'Of course, when she gets back from Scarborough in two days' time. I'll have to or she will wonder why I am going to Cornwall. After all, she is living with us and will be affected by our decision.'

'I wonder if she will take kindly to a move, if that is what we decide?' mused Eliza.

'Should that colour our decision?'

'Not really, but she is close to us both and she adores Abigail, so if she feels her roots are here and does not want to move with us, it could be traumatic for her to see us go.'

This worried them both and a thoughtful silence fell until Eliza wisely said, 'This has come as a shock to us and there are a lot of things to consider. Too many for us to reach a quick decision. We really should wait until you have been to Cornwall before we discuss it further.'

'True,' he agreed. 'I know it will be on our minds but let's not worry about it now. There are a couple of maps with that letter, let's have a look at those instead.'

They went to a table and spread them out.

'That must be the house.' John pointed to a couple of rectangles occupying a position close to the coastline.

'It could have as good a view as this one,' remarked Eliza, running her finger along the boundary line to the south of the house.

4

'Could it ever match it?' commented John wistfully.

'You'll be the judge of that. I suggest you arrange to leave the day after Martha's return. It's no good hanging about in these matters. A decision will have to be made sooner or later. I know your uncle has stipulated that it has to be done within three months – I think, the sooner the better. It would be unfair to keep Martha on tenterhooks.'

The following morning Eliza was already sitting in the dining room over breakfast when John came in.

'I hope our dilemma did not keep you awake?' he said as he sat down at the table after helping himself to a bowl of porridge from the tureen on the oak sideboard.

'I pushed it from my mind,' replied Eliza. 'I saw no point in worrying about it at this stage. What about you?'

'When I woke this morning I had a solution to part of our problem.'

'What was that?' Eliza raised an eyebrow.

'Well, we have a fine house here. The estate, though not big, is well run, and the chandler's business in Whitby comfortably profitable.'

'Which sounds as though you will regret getting rid of it?'

'Yes, I would, in a way. But that would only happen if we *all* moved to Cornwall. If Martha does not wish to leave it throws another light on our situation.'

Eliza looked a little puzzled. 'What are you getting at?'

'If it is to our advantage to move and Martha does not wish to, I will sign over this property and the business in Whitby to her, with the proviso that if at any time in the future any of us wishes to return, we can do so. I think Martha would agree to that.'

Eliza's eyes brightened. Her sister-in-law's position in all this had troubled her, especially if she did not want to leave Whitby. 'And Martha's capable of managing both?'

'She certainly is,' agreed John. 'She has always taken an interest in both aspects of the business, particularly after Jos was killed. I was pleased she did at the time; it gave her something to think about. Now it might pay off.'

5

'When will you put this to her?'

'Not until after we have told her about the move. I would not want it to influence her decision.'

When the carriage that Martha had hired in Scarborough turned into the drive of Bloomfield Manor, she breathed a sigh of contentment. It was good to be home.

She was thankful that she and her brother John, four years younger than she, were close. They had had their childhood arguments and differences but if anything this had strengthened their loyalty to each other. They'd been thankful for that when their parents died in an epidemic, and Martha was deeply grateful for her brother's support when her sweetheart Jos, whom she was to marry on his return from a whaling voyage, was reported lost with five others in a whale boat while chasing their quarry. John and Eliza had insisted that she come to live with them at Bloomfield Manor and after that the relationship between them inevitably strengthened. Forward-looking like her brother, Martha was not one to sit back and waste her life. Once her period of mourning was over she took a keen interest in the estate and business, something that John was now pleased he had encouraged.

Hearing the crunch of the wheels on the gravelled drive, John and Eliza were at the door by the time the coachman helped Martha from the carriage. Greetings were exchanged with unfeigned pleasure and then Eliza linked arms with her sister-in-law and they walked into the house together while John took charge of two valises.

'You had a good journey?' queried Eliza.

'I did indeed. A most helpful and attentive coachman.'

Who could resist Martha's charm? thought Eliza. Her deportment, elegant without being showy, naturally caught the attention. Coupled with her warm ready smile, it hooked and held the onlooker's deference and brought her many friends. Her deep brown eyes sparkled with the joy of being home again; the touch of her long thin fingers, resting on Eliza's arm, spoke of her love for her sister-in-law.

'Good. And your friend in Scarborough, was she well?'

'Yes, in very good health.' Martha called over her shoulder as John caught them up, 'I got us some business through her husband. He happened to remark he was not satisfied with a quotation for fifty barrels for the ship he was fitting out. Without knowing what the quotation was, I gave him a price. He was astonished we could supply him from Whitby and still undercut a rival.'

'So it's settled?'

'Signed and sealed. The documents are in my bag.'

John chuckled. 'You certainly aren't one to miss an opportunity.'

'The business is important to me.'

They had reached the front door and as Martha went in she did not see the meaningful glances that passed between husband and wife, nor could she realise how significant her last remark was to them.

'I'll take these to your room,' said John, heading for the stairs.

'You refresh yourself and I'll order tea,' said Eliza. 'Evening meal at our usual time.'

Martha hugged her sister-in-law. 'Thank you, Eliza. It's so good to be back. I shan't be long. I expect Abigail is having her afternoon nap. May I look in on her?'

'Of course.'

'I won't wake her,' Martha promised as she hurried after her brother who was halfway up the stairs by now.

When John came down a few moments later he hurried straight to the drawing room to find Eliza.

'What do you think?' he asked.

'It's going to be difficult. You saw how pleased she was to be back and how enthusiastic about the business.'

John nodded. 'I know, but it's better to tackle the problem now rather than wait.'

'You'll have to if you are to go to Cornwall tomorrow.'

Two maids arrived with the tea then and just as they were leaving Martha entered the room. 'Oh, this is nice,' she said, eyeing the tray of scones, but continued over to the window. She stood for a moment, looking out, before she said,

'There's no view like this.' She turned away slowly, as if reluctant to leave the vista, put a scone on a plate and sat down beside a small table on which John had placed a cup of tea poured by Eliza. 'Abigail looks well,' she commented. 'How have you both been while I've been away?'

'Very well,' replied Eliza, and shot a glance at her husband.

'We have something to tell you,' he said.

Martha gave a small frown as she looked at her brother. 'It sounds serious.'

'It is. We have a decision to make which will affect us all.'

'What? We three, you mean?'

'Plus Abigail and all the staff.'

'What has happened?' asked Martha, concern in her voice as she glanced from brother to sister-in-law.

'I have received a letter from a solicitor in Cornwall to say that Uncle Gerard has left me his entire estate. It comes to a considerable sum. In fact, a small fortune.'

For a moment Martha was struck silent by the shock of the news. 'What? Father's black sheep brother? But you hardly knew him. I certainly have only the faintest recollection of him, and you are younger than I.'

'I know. I can hardly picture him either, but there it is. He has remembered me, though why I don't know.'

'Does the solicitor say anything about him?'

'Only that he sailed the seven seas, made money, chose to settle in Cornwall where he speculated in tin, made more money and bought an estate, Penorna, which along with his ready money and his interests in a copper mine he has left to me.'

Martha raised her eyebrows expressively. 'Lucky for you. I'm delighted. You'll never have financial worries now, and nor will Abigail.' She saw that her brother's expression was still serious and filled with doubt, as if there was something he wasn't telling her. 'I can see it doesn't please you entirely. Come on, tell me why?'

'There are certain stipulations to my inheritance.'

'Oh?' Martha looked askance at Eliza. 'And you don't like them?'

'Well, they are not insurmountable but . . .'

'All right, John, what are they?'

'I have to take up residence in his Cornish property and live there for at least twelve years. If I don't agree I get nothing, and if I leave within that time I have to make good the value of the estate.'

'Oh, I see,' said Martha quietly, pausing for a moment after that. 'Have you reached a decision?' she asked finally.

'Not yet.'

'We wanted to wait until we heard what you thought,' said Eliza.

'But it has nothing to do with me.'

'You are very much a part of the family.'

'You are very kind to me, always have been, I couldn't have wished for a better sister-in-law. But this decision is for you and John to take.' Martha added in a cautionary tone, 'How much do you know of this place?'

'The house and land holdings are substantial. The solicitor sent us this map.' John rose as he was speaking. 'Come and see.' He went to the table and rolled it out. Martha and Eliza joined him. He pointed out the boundaries to his sister.

She studied the map and then commented, 'It certainly is substantial, and it looks as if the estate has a wonderful coastline with cliffs and small bays.'

'This is the house.' John tapped the map.

'I thought it must be. It looks as if it will enjoy a wonderful view. What about these?' She pointed to some markings grouped closely together near the western boundary.

'I can only conclude they are the village of Penorna from which the estate takes its name.'

'You must be tempted?' said his sister.

'Yes, but I have suggested that John goes to Cornwall and looks the place and its prospects over first. It is no good deciding now and then finding it's not what we expect,' Eliza put in.

'That sounds a sensible idea,' agreed Martha. 'How soon must you decide?'

'We have three months, but would like to proceed as soon as possible. I have arranged to leave for Cornwall tomorrow,' her brother told her.

'So soon?'

'It's best to get on with things.'

'Of course.'

'I shall take a coach to Scarborough and another to York. I will stay there the night and arrange my onward journey there.'

'How long do you expect to be away?'

'It may take eight to ten days each way.'

'And there is the time John will be in Cornwall,' added Eliza.

'How long that will take God only knows, but I must be certain about everything.'

That night, lying in her husband's arms, Eliza said, 'John, if there is a decision to be made while you are in Cornwall, make it. I will agree with whatever you want to do.'

'Thank you my love. That eases my mind.'

'Hurry back. I'll miss you.'

'I'll miss you too, dearest.' He kissed her neck.

She shuddered. 'Love me again,' she requested with quiet temptation.

Ten weeks later John arrived home to a rapturous welcome. Eliza had heard the carriage wheels and gave a whoop of delight when she saw her husband descend from the vehicle. She flew from the room, flung open the front door and was down the terrace steps and into his arms almost before he had thanked the coachman. They hugged each other amidst much joyous laughter and then lost themselves in a welcome home kiss. Finally, with arms wrapped round each other, they started for the house. As they stepped on to the terrace, Martha came out.

In her room on the first floor she had heard Eliza's shout and judged that John must be home. As keen as she was to welcome her brother back she delayed a few moments in order to let him and Eliza enjoy their own private greeting.

10

Now she held out her arms to him and brother and sister exchanged hugs of greeting.

'You've been away longer than I expected,' commented Eliza. 'I hope it was all worthwhile?'

'Tell you when I've got the grime of travel off me,' he teased.

'We want to know now, don't we, Martha?'

'We do,' she agreed.

He tried to slip away but they grabbed his arms.

'Now!' said Eliza determinedly.

He laughed. 'All right. You'll have to wait for the fine details but it's all arranged. We go as soon as I can settle things here.'

Silence fell briefly on them. Eliza was filled with astonishment, charged with excitement at the prospect of this new venture alongside her husband. Martha's heart sank with disappointment. She did not want to leave Whitby. She loved it here; had thought she was settled for life, and now that old certainty was being thrown into upheaval. But she could not detract from the joy that was emanating from John and Eliza and tried to show some excitement, for their sake.

'Oh, John!' cried Eliza. 'I'll order some tea. You go and freshen up; and then come and tell us all about it.'

When they entered the house he went straight upstairs. Eliza started for the kitchen but was detained by Martha. 'I'll order the tea, you go to John.'

'Thank you.' She gave her sister-in-law a hug.

A quarter of an hour later, as soon as John and Eliza walked into the drawing room, Martha poured the tea. John got comfortable in a chair facing the two young women who were both anxious to hear his account.

'Well?' promoted Eliza, eager for him to start.

'It is a wonderful place. The scenery is magnificent along the coast . . .'

'Better than ours?' queried Martha tartly.

'Well . . .' John drew the word out in an expression of doubt.

11

'There, I knew it!' Martha seized on her chance, but before she had time to express any more favourable opinions on the Yorkshire coast, Eliza intervened.

'Go on, John. Where did you stay?'

'A local inn in Sandannack. It was somewhat primitive but comfortable enough with good basic food. The locals were a bit suspicious of me, especially when it became known that I was the new owner of Penorna. Seems my uncle was well liked, so of course they wondered if the new owner would be up to his standards. They feared change; just wanted to go on in the way they always had, with no outside interference. It was almost like being in a foreign country. I soon settled their doubts, especially after I had seen the solicitor and he had briefed me on all aspects of the estate.'

'And what is that like?' asked Eliza.

'Wonderful,' replied John with enthusiasm. 'Uncle Gerard turned some rough meadows into good farmland. He allowed the villagers . . .'

'Then the village is ours too?' Eliza broke in. 'Is that Sandannack?'

'Yes. Twenty families live there. They were afraid I might rescind the rights my uncle had given them, such as access across his land to the sea so that they could pursue their fishing. That is only a part-time occupation for most of them as the majority, along with others from neighbouring villages, work in the copper mine.'

'Ours too?'

'Yes. And we also own several houses in Penzance.'

Martha, who had listened in silence, said, 'From the sound of it you could do no other than accept such an inheritance. The only thing that could have kept you here is your love of Yorkshire.'

John looked grave. 'I must admit it still exerts a strong pull, and finding myself so far from home I nearly refused to have anything to do with Penorna, but then I thought it would be wrong not to keep and expand upon what my uncle worked so hard to achieve. And these people had looked up to him as a just and kindly landlord. What might happen to them if I refused to take on the responsibility?'

'Quite right,' approved Martha. 'Uncle Gerard would have been proud of you. Besides, you are making a more secure future for Abigail.' Her voice caught in her throat. 'I will miss her, I will miss you all.' Her eyes dampened, but, being one who had learned to control her feelings in public since losing Jos, she held back the tears. They could flow later in the privacy of her room.

'But you'll come with us?' gasped Eliza.

'You must,' said John.

Martha shook her head slowly. 'No. It's a new life you are making for yourselves. I could not share it fully while my heart is set on the Yorkshire coast, and more specifically Whitby.' She raised her hands to stem the protest and persuasion she saw coming. 'No, don't. You'll never talk me into it. I thought about it a lot while you were away, John, realising that you might take up your inheritance, while there was no way that I could be persuaded to uproot myself from Yorkshire. Here in Whitby I still feel close to Jos. Don't say any more about it. I will move out of the house as soon as I can find somewhere else to live.'

John glanced at his wife and he saw her almost imperceptible nod of agreement and approval.

'Well, Martha, I'm sorry you won't come with us. We will miss you. But there is no need for you to look for anywhere else to live. You must stay here.'

Martha's eyes widened as she tried to grasp what her brother was doing. 'You mean, here in Bloomfield Manor?'

'With what my uncle has left me, I have no need to sell this house or my business. I will assign them both to you. You shall not want, and I will be happy in that knowledge. You are capable of running the estate yourself but get a manager in if it helps, or promote the foreman, Giles Smithers. We've got a loyal staff in the chandlery business and you have a great aptitude for that. Mind you, you might meet opposition from some of the other businessmen in Whitby, but I think you are strong enough to outface them.'

Martha smiled through the tears in her eyes. 'I look forward to the challenge. John, Eliza, thank you, I don't deserve such consideration.'

'You can come and visit us whenever you like, and we can come north to see you,' said Eliza.

Martha gave a wan smile. 'It's a long way.'

Chapter Two

'Have you got the roof sorted for Ben Fowley?' Eliza asked, as she and John rose from the breakfast table.

'The repairs should have been finished yesterday. I'm going to the village this morning to check.'

Eliza glanced at the window. 'You've nice weather for the walk.'

'Wouldn't have gone if it had been any other,' he replied with a grin.

'Come and say goodbye to Abigail before you go.'

'Wouldn't miss that either.' He took Eliza's hand and they went to the nursery together.

When they entered the room, Abigail sprang from her chair and with a five-year-old's shouts of glee rushed to them: 'Mama! Papa! She flung herself at her mother who swept her into her arms and lifted her high, then hugged her tight as they laughed together. From her mother's arms she turned a bright loving smile on her father. John tweaked her cheeks and she giggled. 'How's my favourite girl?'

'Had all my breakfast,' Abigail responded.

Eliza glanced across at the eighteen-year-old governess, Dorinda Jenkins, who gave a nod confirming the child's statement.

'Good girl. Coming to see Papa off?'

'Yes! Yes!'

Eliza allowed her to slide from her arms to the floor, whereupon she took hold of her father's hand.

John selected a Malacca cane from the stand beside the front door, struck a little pose with it and raised a questioning eyebrow at his wife.

'You look very elegant.' Eliza smiled. 'You always do,' she added, admiring his long tailcoat with its high velvet collar. A full-length waistcoat opened at the neck to reveal a white embroidered cravat tied neatly at his throat. Corn-coloured breeches, buttoned below the knee, came to the top of his brown leather boots.

Abigail ran to a chest, opened it and took out a hat. 'Hat, Papa, hat!' she called, running to him.

'Thank you. Be a good girl while I'm away.' John turned to Eliza and kissed her. 'I hope there are no other problems in the village to hold me up. I want to see how the new tenants are settling in at Croft Farm.'

Eliza and Abigail followed him on to the terrace and watched until he reached a bend in the drive where he stopped and waved to them.

Eliza felt a surge of pride. Though, three years ago, she had harboured some doubts about coming to Cornwall, she had kept them to herself when John had returned from his first visit full of enthusiasm. She had known they would be embarking upon a different life from that they knew in Yorkshire, but seeing John's tact in engaging the confidence of his tenants, especially the miners who worked his mine, she soon realised that her worries had been unfounded. It was the same story with the landed gentry of the county, and though she knew that John did not always agree with them over land policies and their treatment of tenants, he was sub-tle enough not to attract outright enmity. She knew she had played her part in this, too, and in their acceptance into local society. Eliza was quick to observe and note the local eti-quette and soon entertained on an equal scale. They were set-tled in Cornwall now and had a good life here.

She was the one who wrote to Martha, knowing that John, no matter how close he had been to his sister, would not will-ingly take up a pen. Or had she spoiled him by taking up this correspondence when they first arrived in Cornwall? Gradually the frequency of the letters had dwindled and there had been no exchange at all during the last year. It seemed that lives in both Cornwall and Yorkshire had become too full.

Reaching the end of the drive, John paused. He had two choices: a walk across country or the longer coastal route. He decided on the latter. The day was one of glorious sunshine, with a slight nip in the air that brought sharp clarity to every view. The scenery along the coast, the soaring cliffs, land sweeping down to the sea, bays and coves, had woven its magic spell on him and today he could not resist such a call.

The path took him close to the cliff edge and he could not help but stop frequently to admire the view. Outcrops of rock with the sea foaming round them stood sentinel in some of the bays; in others virgin sand was touched by the lazy waves that scarcely bothered to break. Gulls squawked overhead and plunged like stones to find precarious footholds on the jagged cliffs. Cormorants lurked there, eyes fixed on some prey, before plunging at speed into the sea to emerge triumphant. Two fishing boats dragged their nets while in the distance a three-master beat its way along the Channel. In the three years he had been here John had never tired of the scenery along this coast.

The path swung away from the cliff edge but he knew that after about a hundred yards it would return above a small cove of untouched sand sheltered by towering cliffs on three sides. Here he was brought to a sudden stop. Today footprints marked the sand below. He could not believe it. Whose were they? How had they got there? Then he saw her emerge from the shadow of the cliff to his right: a thin waif of a girl who strolled casually along the water's edge, allowing the waves to lap over her bare feet. She held her dress so that it would not get wet around the hem, then seemingly irritated by having to do so let it go, flinging her arms high in a gesture of freedom and joy. She did a little jig and skipped a few steps before pirouetting on and on along the sward of sand and in and out of the water, ignoring the splashes that wet the thin cotton, causing the dress to cling to her, emphasising the curves of her lithe body.

John's whole attention was drawn to her. He was filled with curiosity and a desire to know more about her. He had to find out. All thoughts of his mission were driven from his mind.

He looked for some way down but could not find one. Then he turned his attention back to the cove. She had disappeared. His eyes swept the bay. She was nowhere to be seen; only the footprints in the sand remained as evidence that she had ever walked and danced there. If she had clambered round the headland on the rocks, had he missed her in its shadow? It was the only conclusion he could come to. Annoyed, his lips tightened with frustration, he resumed his journey.

Throughout the rest of his visits his attention kept drifting back to memories of the girl on the sand. He wondered who she was and if he would ever see her again. But as he turned for home in the afternoon he tried to thrust all such thoughts away. What had commanded his interest anyway? The fact that she was on a beach that he'd thought completely isolated? Was it purely the magic of seeing someone give way to such carefree abandon? Irritated with himself, he spoke out loud, 'Fool! You'll probably never see her again.'

Nevertheless, during the next fortnight, he walked that way every day but saw no one. He began to think she had been a figment of his imagination.

'John, are you ready? Benson is bringing the carriage to the door.' Eliza turned from their bedroom window.

'Coming, love.' He appeared from his dressing room, stopped and stared in loving admiration at his wife. 'You look wonderful.'

'Like it?' she asked, doing a turn so that he could appreciate her full simple dress of white satin with a low round neck and elbow-length sleeves embellished with tiny ruffles. The new fashion of wearing a slightly higher waist than had been usual allowed the dress to fall more naturally in sweeping folds while maintaining the slimmer effect. Her only ornament was a pink belt at the waist and a soft fichu of the same colour around her neck.

'I'm pleased you kept it as a surprise,' John said appreciatively. 'Such elegance suits you.'

Eliza came to him and kissed him on the cheek. 'Thank you for treating me to a new gown. And might I say that you too

18

look very elegant?' She stood back, admiring his dark blue tailcoat cut high at the waist and matching well-fitting trousers.

'I like this new fashion of trousers, especially for evening wear,' she commented.

'So do I,' he agreed, 'though breeches can be more practical throughout the day. What about the rest of me?'

He wore a white waistcoat with six pearl buttons, and a slightly starched linen cravat tied neatly at his neck and held with a pearl pin. His black shoes shone like mirrors.

'Impeccable, as always.'

He smiled his appreciation. 'I'll wear my beaver hat,' he said. 'You?'

'I'm just going to have my kerchief, the one with three pheasant's feathers.'

'Good, then let's go, we don't want to be late.' He opened the door for her.

She glided past him and down the stairs to the hall where she picked up a shawl as a protection for her shoulders against the sharp evening air.

When they emerged on to the terrace Benson jumped down from his seat on the box and opened the coach's door for them. Once they were settled, the coachman took his place again, gathered the reins and sent the horse on its way to Trethtowan Manor, a matter of five miles further along the coast to the west, where their neighbours Selwyn and Harriet Westbury had lived for ten years since their marriage after his father had bought them the run-down estate. Now, through Selwyn's diligence and hard work, the estate and one copper mine provided them with a high standard of living. Harriet had worked hard too, overseeing the renovation of the old house until it was acknowledged as one of the most attractive along the south Cornish coast. Her gift as a hostess made the lavish parties at Trethtowan Manor the talk of Cornwall and gentry would vie for an invitation. This was not such an event; just a friendly evening with neighbours to whom the Westburys had taken immediately. They were eight years older than John and Eliza with two children, James aged nine and Juliana eight. The family had known John's uncle and were delighted that his nephew had decided to come south and run the estate. John and Eliza had found their advice valuable and it had made their transition to their new life much easier. Now they looked forward to a pleasant evening in good company, with good food and easy conversation.

Benson turned the coach expertly through the stone pillars where the ornamental iron gates had already been opened by the gate-keeper who had been warned of the time of the Mitchells' arrival. Benson liked these visits. He knew the servants at Trethtowan Manor well and expected his own entertainment in a warm kitchen where he would enjoy Cook's hearty fare for the servants, washed down by some of the best ale in the county. He drew the horse to a halt in front of the imposing façade and was quickly to the ground to open the door for Mrs Mitchell.

As they climbed the four steps to the covered stone veranda that stretched the full length of the façade, the large front door swung open and a liveried servant stood beside it to greet them with an inclination of his head and a quiet, 'Good evening, ma'am. Good evening, sir.'

John and Eliza accepted the greeting and moved into a spacious, marble-floored hall where two maidservants were standing by to take their outdoor clothes.

'Eliza! John!' Selwyn held out his hands to them as he came from the drawing room. His broad welcoming smile almost hid the scar that marked his left cheek, supposedly the result of a chance encounter with a would-be thief on the lonely moor as he returned home late. Privately he still suspected there might have been more to it than that. Though he could not prove it, he believed it was the result of the disagreement that festered between himself and Jeremy Gaisford of neighbouring Senewey Estate. Tonight, however, Selwyn's eyes sparkled with delight as he kissed Eliza on the cheek and shook John's hand.

Petite Harriet, who seemed to glide across the marble floor, expressed her own pleasure at seeing them and as she escorted Eliza to the drawing room admired her guest's dress, an observation that was heartily reciprocated. On reaching the room, Eliza stepped away from her hostess to admire Harriet's simple white muslin gown that fell in neat folds to her dainty feet. She had dispensed with the usual ruffles on the sleeves, preferring them plain and ending tightly at the wrists.

After seeing his guests comfortably seated, Selwyn went to the decanter and glasses on the sideboard and was pouring Madeira for them all when the door opened slowly and a young lady stepped tentatively into the room.

'Ah, Lydia, my dear,' cried Harriet, rising quickly. 'Come and meet our guests.' She hurried to the newcomer's side and took her arm.

John had already jumped to his feet. He fought to control the gasp of surprise on his lips. The young woman from the beach! It must be. He surely wasn't mistaken even though he had only seen her from a distance. His heart and mind raced. That lithe body he had seen splashing joyfully through the water could not be disguised by a plain pink dress simply cut with a square neckline. The silk shawl that covered her shoulders complemented the beauty of her ivory-skinned oval face. Pale blue eyes sparkled from it in a lively fashion.

'Eliza, I would like you to meet Miss Lydia Booth. Lydia, this is Mrs Mitchell of whom I have spoken.'

The young woman took the hand Eliza extended. 'I am pleased to meet you, Mrs Mitchell. Mrs Westbury spoke of you in enthusiastic terms.'

'I am delighted to meet you too, Miss Booth. You have the advantage of me. My friend has not mentioned you to me.'

'After a brief visit two weeks ago, I only arrived here yesterday.'

As Harriet turned Lydia towards John he realised why he had not seen her since that day on the beach. 'Lydia, this is Mr Mitchell. John . . . Miss Lydia Booth.'

He took the hand she offered and raised it to his lips as he made a slight bow, never taking his eyes off hers. 'It is a pleasure to meet you, Miss Booth. I look forward to hearing more about you.'

Lydia gave a small smile. 'There is little to tell, Mr Mitchell.'

He was unable to make any further comment as Selwyn brought over a tray with five glasses on it. With the wine taken and everyone seated, Harriet offered an explanation.

'Lydia's family were very close friends of mine when we lived in Oxford. Her mother died a year ago and her grieving father just three months ago.' The murmurs of sympathy from Eliza and John were accepted by Lydia with a slight inclination of her head. 'Lydia has a brother, Samuel, whom I'm sorry to say refused to take responsibility for her, leaving her with no home. Selwyn and I talked it over and decided to offer Lydia the position of governess here to our children. She will live as part of our family.'

'It was a most kind and generous offer,' put in Lydia when Harriet paused, 'and I will be ever grateful to Mr and Mrs Westbury.' Her eyes dampened and her voice caught in her throat as she glanced at them.

'Lydia paid us a brief visit a fortnight ago before returning to Oxford to clear out what had been the family home. Her brother now lives in Wales. She only arrived back here yesterday.'

'I am sure you will be very happy with Mr and Mrs Westbury,' said Eliza with a pleasant smile. 'And James and Juliana are delightful children.'

'From the little I have seen of them, I agree with you,' returned Lydia. 'I am looking forward to teaching them.'

'You have done this sort of work before?' asked John.

'No, Mr Mitchell, I have not, but I have had a good education myself including painting and the pianoforte,' she replied, a little coolly, as if detecting an implied doubt of her ability.

If anyone else noticed they made no comment, but John was aware of the reproof in her eyes as she met his gaze in a manner that forced him to look away.

'Have you any children, Mrs Mitchell?' Lydia asked, turning her attention to Eliza.

'One. A little girl of five named Abigail.'

22

'A nice-sounding name.'

'You must come and meet her and her governess. The children often meet and play together.'

'That is kind of you, Mrs Mitchell. I look forward to it.'

'I don't like leaving things in the air, so should we say next Wednesday at three o'clock?'

Lydia glanced questioningly at Harriet as she replied, 'If Mrs Westbury is in agreement?'

'Of course, Lydia. I'm sure James and Juliana will enjoy the outing.'

Ten minutes later a manservant appeared to announce that dinner was served. Selwyn offered his arm to Eliza and started for the door. John turned to Harriet. As she placed her hand on his arm, he glanced at Lydia who had hung back, prepared to bring up the rear on her own. He offered his other arm to her, which she took with a smile of gratitude.

His gesture made her feel accepted on an equal footing by the Mitchells. Maybe her first opinion of him had been wrong, though nothing in the subsequent conversation had softened her judgment, but now ...

John was seated opposite her at the table. Throughout the meal, as conversation flowed, Lydia was aware that his eyes frequently strayed to her and felt that she was being assessed and judged.

'Your artistic talent, Miss Booth, was that inherited? Were your mother and father that way inclined?' His questions startled her. She had barely followed the direction of the general chatter, lost in memories of the beautiful beach she had visited on her last trip to the Manor.

Embarrassed by her own distracted manner, she dabbed her lips with her napkin. As she replaced it on her lap she said, 'My mother was an excellent embroideress and made her own designs.'

'Then it must have come from her.'

'My painting could not compare with her talent,' Lydia demurred.

'Did you keep some of your mother's work?' asked Eliza.

'Indeed I did, ma'am.'

'I should like to see it. Embroidery is an interest of mine. Would you care to show it to us?'

'I would be proud to, Mrs Mitchell.'

Eliza glanced at her hostess. 'After dinner, Harriet?'

'Of course, my dear, while the gentlemen have their port and cigars.'

'Oh, but we must see Miss Booth's painting alongside her mother's embroidery, to make a comparison and assess the source of Miss Booth's talent,' said John. He glanced at Lydia. 'I presume you have a painting you can show us, and are willing to do so?'

She felt her cheeks redden for she sensed there was something of a challenge about this request. 'I have, Mr Mitchell. You shall see both, if you wish.'

John inclined his head. 'Thank you, Miss Booth, we will look forward to it.'

As the meal continued Lydia wondered if Mr Mitchell had a genuine interest in art and if so how good a judge he would be of workmanship and talent? She began to feel twinges of apprehension.

When the men rejoined the ladies in the drawing room, Harriet suggested that Lydia bring the embroidery and painting right away. She took the opportunity to compose herself in the quiet of her room, straightened her dress and patted her hair into place. Satisfied with her reflection in the mirror, she selected a tablecloth and a runner for a sideboard that she judged to be among her mother's best work. She had rescued them before her brother got his hands on them, for she knew he would only sell them to get what he could to appease his drinking habit. She turned her attention to the four paintings she had also brought with her. She pondered and then, a decision made, picked up a watercolour of the Isis with the spires of Oxford in the distance. Taking a deep breath, she left her room.

Selwyn had poured some wine and had placed a glass for Lydia on a side table. She thanked him and sat down, being careful to keep her painting from view. Settling herself, she caught a glint of amusement in John's eyes as he asked, 'Are you keeping that a secret, Miss Booth?'

Lydia's lips tightened but quickly relaxed; she must show no hostility to a guest. 'Not at all, Mr Mitchell. I thought you should see the best work first. I did not want my poor contribution to be in your mind when you saw my mother's.' She started to unwrap the tablecloth.

Harriet got to her feet. 'I think I'd better take one end and then we can hold it up before laying it on the floor as we haven't a table big enough in here.'

'Thank you, Mrs Westbury.'

As they unfolded the cloth Eliza gave little gasps of delight. Finally, when the full extent of the design was exposed, Eliza cried out, 'That is exquisite. Simply wonderful! I have never seen embroidery so beautiful. It must have taken your mother hours and hours of painstaking work.' She was on her feet examining the cloth more closely, murmuring her admiration all the time.

Pride surged in Lydia. How she wished her mother could have heard such praise. 'Thank you, Mrs Mitchell, you are most kind.'

'Not at all, my dear, I mean everything I say.' She glanced at Harriet. 'Don't you think it's just beautiful? You'll have seen it before?'

'Only when Lydia's mother was working on it, never in its entirety. Hold this end, Eliza, so I can see the whole cloth.'

'Of course.' She took over from Harriet.

Their hostess stood silently, concentrating on the exquisite depiction of intertwined flowers, mostly roses, that bordered the cloth. The centrepiece was a mass of foliage, a blending of many shades of green that in parts was extended as if to embrace the roses. 'It is a truly imaginative work, beautifully executed. Selwyn, John, come and have a closer look.'

The two men rose to their feet and joined Harriet. Lydia watched them closely, trying to interpret their reactions, but found herself wondering more about Mr Mitchell's than Mr Westbury's.

After a few moments Selwyn spoke. 'It is truly magnificent.'

'There can't be a stitch out of place,' commented John as he bent closer to the cloth.

'There will be one,' said Lydia. 'Mother always made one slip, and beside it would turn a stitch in the pattern into her initial, W, just to show that it truly was the work of one person.'

'How forward-looking. That would make the cloth all the more valuable should it ever come up for sale.'

'I could never sell it, Mr Mitchell.'

'No, I don't suppose you could. From all I have seen and heard tonight, I can tell how much you loved your mother. You must have been very close.'

'Indeed we were, Mr Mitchell. I wish you and Mrs Mitchell could have met her.'

'I wish we could too, Miss Booth,' he returned quietly. Seeing the dampness in her eyes he said more brightly, 'now we must see your painting.'

Thankful for the change of subject, she gave a small smile and reached for her painting. She stood so all could see it when she turned it round. Silence filled the room as the four friends studied a delicate watercolour of a river with the spires of Oxford hazy in the distance. The whole scene was brought alive by her use of the late light, and the flowing water seemed to invite the viewer to follow it towards those distant spires and uncover the mysteries that lay concealed along its banks.

'A truly accomplished work, Miss Booth! You see colours where other people would not.'

Lydia inclined her head in acknowledgement of his praise. 'Thank you, Mr Mitchell. The greens of the leaves and the grass contain many other colours within them.'

'And you have a subtle way of catching them, Miss Booth,' commented Eliza.

'Thank you, Mrs Mitchell. You and your husband seem to have some knowledge of painting. Are you painters yourselves?'

'Not really, but we were both interested in the work of local artists and bought some after we first married.'

26

'We were fortunate in that there was a small school of painters in Whitby where we then lived. We were able to study their techniques at first hand.'

'You were fortunate indeed.'

'We like to think it developed our appreciation of art.' John turned to his host. 'What about you, Selwyn? And Harriet? I know from our previous conversations that neither of you are artists, but with such a talent as Miss Booth's under the same roof you must develop your interest.'

'Lydia is certainly very gifted, we can see that. But we'd never pretend to be experts in the matter.'

'What really counts, Mr Westbury, is that a painting pleases you,' said Lydia, 'and that you can live with it, day after day.'

'Well, I could certainly live with yours. Couldn't you, Harriet?' He turned to his wife, whose eyes had never left the painting during these exchanges.

'Though I can't pretend to understand all the finer points, I would receive pleasure from that work every time I walked into the room where it hung,' she replied in a voice that reflected how much it had moved her.

'Then, Mrs Westbury, you shall have it,' offered Lydia.

'But I couldn't!'

'You can. Please, in grateful thanks for all you have done for me.'

Harriet spread her hands. 'What have I done? Given you a position as governess.'

'You have given me a home and welcomed me to it when my future looked extremely bleak. It is yours, Mrs Westbury.'

'Well . . . Thank you, my dear. I will always treasure it.'

'Where will you hang it?' asked Selwyn.

'There is just the place in the hall. I will see it every morning when I come downstairs, and during the day when I pass that way. Visitors will see it, too. Who knows, Lydia? It may result in further commissions for you.'

'And Eliza and I will be the first to place one,' put in John.

'I had no intention of taking up painting on that basis.' Lydia gasped at this turn in her fortune. 'I don't really think I'm good enough, but I'll certainly paint one for you.'

'You shouldn't hide or belittle the talent I can see in that picture,' Eliza told her. 'And you must put a fair price on any painting you do for us.'

'But Mrs Mitchell, I couldn't . . .'

'You must. I insist.'

'Then I must paint the subject you request.'

John looked thoughtful for a moment. 'What about a section of the coast nearby? Is that a good idea, Eliza?'

'Delightful,' she agreed.

'That would be pleasant to undertake and would allow for various interpretations,' Lydia agreed.

'I have a place in mind. It is a little bay that has always attracted us.'

'Where would that be?'

'Difficult to explain to you as you are new to the area, it would be better if I could show you. We will arrange it some time.'

Lydia took that last statement as a dismissal of the subject and wondered why a time could not be arranged now, until she realised that in her eagerness she had overlooked etiquette. Arranging a meeting between a man and a woman, strangers until this evening, would be frowned upon unless they were chaperoned.

The thought came back into her mind as she lay in bed that night. She began to wonder if Mr Mitchell had deliberately avoided a firm arrangement. Maybe he did not want to be encumbered with a chaperone? She chided herself for having such a thought, for with it had come the realisation she would like to see him alone on such an occasion. It would be easier to discuss what he wanted with no one else there – but was that her real reason? Good heavens, what was she thinking? Still, there had been something attractive about him. His deep blue eyes, so alert to everything. His full mouth with laughter lines about it. There were many things about him she'd become aware of as the evening wore on, not least his astute mind and gift for intelligent and penetrating conversation that nevertheless could turn to lighter matters and be amusing. There was something decidedly attractive about him, Lydia

28

decided. Stop it, girl, he's a happily married man who wouldn't give you a second look she told herself. But hadn't he cast glances in her direction very often when his attention might have been directed elsewhere? Just imagination, she decided. Best dismiss all such fanciful thoughts and get to sleep.

Chapter Three

'I am so pleased that they have taken to each other,' observed Eliza as she and Harriet, sitting at the drawing-room window, watched the two governesses playing with the children on the lawn at Penorna. 'From what we saw of Miss Booth the other night, I am sure you have found a gem. Such talent ... I do hope she will be able to pass it on to your children. She's charming too, and today has confirmed her ease of manner.'

'Yes, I am highly delighted,' agreed Harriet. 'And so pleased we could help her. But you are fortunate, with Miss Jenkins.'

'Indeed. Abigail took to her immediately.' Eliza gave a little laugh. 'I must say I felt a pang of jealousy, but I soon realised that Dorinda was careful to prevent Abigail from switching her affection away from me entirely. She knew just where and when to draw the line.'

'Good. Where affection is concerned, there is always a danger that the governess will get most of it. I have seen it happen before, and even destroy a marriage in one case where the father received all the parental love and the governess what should rightly have been the mother's.'

'But surely the parents could have intervened?'

'They should have done. It is not easy, however, when the governess becomes possessive but is skilful at disguising it while appearing the model employee.' Harriet looked in the direction of the children busy chasing after a ball as the two governesses encouraged them while keeping the play within bounds. 'I don't think we have any such worries.'

Eliza laughed as she saw Abigail fall, roll over and spring quickly to her feet again with a merry laugh. 'I don't think we have. They are a happy group.' She turned away to accompany Harriet to the sofa. 'Are you thinking of giving Miss Booth any free time?'

'Selwyn and I were discussing it only last night,' replied Harriet. 'We agreed it was the correct thing to do. After all, she shouldn't be tied to the children all the time.'

'That was the attitude we took ourselves when we engaged Dorinda, and it works well,' explained Eliza. 'She appreciates having complete freedom for one day a week, and Abigail enjoys a full day spent with me. I was going to suggest, having seen today how well Dorinda and Lydia have taken to each other, that if you had the same idea we should agree to give them the same day off and then the two of them could meet if they wished.'

'That's a splendid suggestion. I'm sure Lydia would welcome it, particularly as Dorinda is a Cornish girl who knows these parts and people in Cribyan and Sandannack. If I remember correctly she always has Thursday off?'

'Yes, and we allow her some time on a Sunday afternoon to visit her family in Penzance. Her father is a shopkeeper there and had the foresight to give his daughter as good an education as possible. We were indeed fortunate to find her.'

'Then I shall allow Lydia the same free time. She knows no one in this area so a friendly relationship with Dorinda might help her to settle, though she has an independent streak.'

'I'm sure Dorinda will welcome her companionship.'

The two girls were delighted when, over tea with the children, Eliza and Harriet explained the arrangements. As they were leaving, Dorinda told Lydia that if she walked to Penorna Manor on the Thursday of the following week, she would take her into the village of Cribyan.

As she lay down that night Lydia blessed her own good fortune. She felt sure that she had found a good friend in Dorinda and that she would be happy in Cornwall, though her new life here was in marked contrast to that she had led in Oxford.

The day she was to meet Dorinda dawned bright. By the time she was ready to leave clouds were gathering, though they did not seem threatening. Nevertheless Lydia put her cloak round her shoulders; during the past week she had experienced the way a Cornish wind could bring a chill, even on a warm day, to the exposed cliff-walk. She kept to a brisk pace, enjoying the views of the sea crashing onto the rugged coast and beating on the rocks far below.

She had walked about a mile when her steps faltered and she finally stopped to gaze down on a small bay. Joy at the sight surged within her for it recalled the day during her first short visit when she had discovered this very place and had skipped across its sand and splashed in the sea as it ran around her bare feet, in the sheer ecstasy of having been given a new chance in life. She had thought of it then as *her* bay, and still thought of it as that now. It was special to her and always would be; marking a turning point in her life. She smiled and felt the bay embrace her. Her footsteps were light as she went on her way.

As she approached Penorna she saw Dorinda sitting on a garden seat under the front portico with Abigail beside her.

Seeing the new arrival the five year old jumped from her seat and, face wreathed in smiles, ran to meet her. 'Miss Booth! Miss Booth!' she shouted. 'Have you come to play with us again? Where are Juliana and James?'

Laughing at such enthusiasm, and pleased that she had been accepted, Lydia took Abigail's hand. 'No, I'm sorry, I'm not here to play today. Miss Jenkins and I have a free day and she is going to take me to Cribyan. I've never been before.'

'Can I come?'

This last remark had been overheard by her mother who had come from the house on realising that Lydia had arrived.

'No, you can't,' said Eliza gently. 'This will be a special day like every Thursday. It's the day on which Miss Booth and Miss Jenkins can do as they please.'

'Whatever they want?' Abigail's eyes widened in disbelief.

'Yes,' smiled Eliza.

'I wish *I* could.'

'You will one day, love.' Eliza placed a reassuring hand on her daughter's shoulder. 'Now, let them get on their way.'

Dorinda smiled at her mistress. 'Thank you, Mrs Mitchell, we'll be back by six.'

Eliza nodded and stood with Abigail, watching the two governesses walk down the drive. They fell into step, relishing their freedom and the chance to talk freely. By the time they had walked the four miles to Cribyan they knew a great deal about each other.

Lydia told her new friend how she had lost her parents and of the way her brother had failed her. She had felt herself fortunate when the Westburys, family friends from Oxford, had offered her the position of governess.

'Are you settling in?' asked Dorinda.

'Yes. The Westburys are very kind and treat me well, but I know when they want to be on their own or to be alone with special guests.'

'I am not in quite the same position as you, not having known Mr and Mrs Mitchell before I was employed by them.'

'How did you get the position?'

'The previous governess was from Bristol. Though she was with the family two years she never really settled and eventually decided it was best to leave. I heard of it and applied for the position, as it would bring me nearer home. The Mitchells saw the sense in that too and gave me a chance.'

'How long have you been at Penorna Manor?'

'Eighteen months.'

'And it's worked out well for you?'

'Oh, yes.'

'What will you do when Abigail no longer needs a governess?'

'I'll cross that bridge when I come to it. A lot can happen between now and then.'

'Best way of looking at it,' approved Lydia. 'Mr and Mrs Mitchell aren't from these parts, are they?'

Dorinda smiled. 'No. It's pretty obvious from their accent. They came from Whitby in Yorkshire.'

'Good heavens, so far?'

'Mr Mitchell was left the Penorna Estate by his uncle.'

'Lucky him! What's he like?'

Dorinda eyed her friend with a little smile twitching at her lips. 'Handsome, isn't he?' Her smile broadened when she saw Lydia blush. 'Ah, you've noticed.'

'No one could miss that,' replied Lydia, trying to put on a disinterested attitude.

'Those deep blue eyes sometimes give him a brooding aura but he's a kindly man, considerate, good with children and adores his wife. He would do anything for her.'

'And her?'

'Well, you've seen her – beautiful, wouldn't you agree?'

'I suppose she is.'

'Suppose?' Dorinda looked horrified. 'You know she is! That perfectly shaped face with its high cheekbones. Eyes like cornflowers, and the copper tint in her dark hair makes it so striking.'

'But what is she like as a person?'

'Good to work for. She is always willing to exchange ideas about Abigail's upbringing and education, and expects me to do the same. She is gentle and kind, casts an aura when she comes into a room. Didn't you feel that when they dined with you?'

'Well, I was aware of her but not in the way you are implying.'

'I suppose you were thinking more of him,' commented Dorinda, still with a teasing twinkle in her eyes.

'Not at all,' replied Lydia indignantly. She stopped talking then, thankful that she could change the course of the conversation without seeming to do so deliberately. 'Is that where we are going?'

They had come to the top of a rise. The land ahead twisted down a hillside to a wide shallow valley in which stood a group of about forty houses, mostly of golden flint and thatch. They straddled a stream and extended along its banks. The lazy curling smoke from several chimneys gave the scene an atmosphere of tranquillity.

'How beautiful,' commented Lydia.

'It is, but don't be disappointed when you see that several of the cottages are falling into disrepair. We're now on the

Senewey Estate, owned by the Gaisford family, who are not too particular about living conditions for their tenants. They keep repairs and improvements to a minimum but still extract high rents.'

'So why don't the tenants leave?'

'And go where? They are farm workers or miners. A few might find work elsewhere but there isn't sufficient for them all. And they might even find worse conditions under harsher landlords. Better the devil you know than him you don't.'

'I've only been here a short while but I can't imagine Mr Westbury or Mr Mitchell being like that.'

'They aren't, and thankfully there are others like them nowadays. But come on, let's away down.'

Dorinda started down the slope. Lydia paused a moment, lost in her thoughts, then caught up with her friend and fell into step with her.

'Hello, Dorinda!' a voice boomed across a field to the left.

Dorinda waved to a man carrying a scythe over his right shoulder. 'Mr Telfrey,' she explained. 'Paid a pittance as odd job man to the Gaisfords. Five children under the age of twelve, but he and his wife are always cheerful.'

They'd reached the first cottage by now. As they proceeded along the street, Lydia saw that some of the houses showed signs of needing attention: thatch was thinning, or hanging loose in some places; stones in the walls slipping. 'I see what you mean about repairs,' she commented.

'I thought you would,' Dorinda responded. 'In most cases where a property is in good shape, the repairs will have been done by the tenants themselves. Those who can take the attitude that as they are living here, they may as well keep their home as comfortable and as weather-proof as possible.'

'What about the materials?'

'They'll scrat around to find what they want. Sometimes, out of the goodness of his heart, old man Gaisford will graciously provide them – that way he gets his property repaired for nothing.'

'Exploitation,' hissed Lydia, disgusted by what she was hearing. 'Who are these Gaisfords?'

'The largest landholders in the county. They also own several mines to the north. Present head of the family is Mr Miles Gaisford. He has three sons, Mr Jeremy, Mr Charles and Mr Logan. They're all married. Mr Charles and Mr Logan spend a lot of time in London. Don't know what they do there but I'll tell you this – when they come home all hell is let loose. Parties here, there and everywhere as others in the county catch on to their coat-tails as you might say. Mr Jeremy is as wild as they are, if not worse, and encourages them. He'll inherit one day and I dread to think what the estate will be like then. Or how his brat Luke will turn out in the future.'

'They sound a charming family.'

'Steer clear of them is what I say. Ah, here we are.' Dorinda opened the door to a cottage. When Lydia had followed her in she found herself in a shop. The room was not big but it was full of all manner of things: ironmongery, crockery, cloth, clogs, shoes, and food, with open sacks of potatoes, sugar and flour standing against one of the walls. Lydia gazed in amazement at the variety of goods in such a small space. There was not room for a counter for the shopkeeper to stand behind; instead he stood beside a barrel on which he had balanced some scales.

'Good day, Miss Dorinda,' he said with a cheerful tone and a broad smile.

'Good day, Mr Hollis. This is my new friend, Miss Lydia Booth. She's governess with the Westbury family at Trethtowan.'

'Pleased to meet you, miss.' He touched his forehead with a finger.

'And I you, Mr Hollis.'

'Job not arrived yet?' Dorinda asked.

'I'm expecting him any time. It's a wonder you didn't see him on the way in.'

'I'm afraid we didn't. Something will have delayed him – trouble with the cart or maybe his horse; shoe off or something.' She turned to Lydia to explain. 'Mr Hollis gets his supplies from my father in Penzance. They are due in today. I send a letter to my parents via Job.' She pulled an envelope from the pocket in her cape. 'I have it here, Mr Hollis.'

He took the letter. 'I'll see he gets it. Now, are you going through to have a bite to eat with us? Mrs Hollis will be disappointed if you don't. She'll want to catch up on all the gossip and to meet your new friend.'

'Thank you, Mr Hollis. We can't disappoint Mrs Hollis, can we?' Dorinda gave Lydia a wink and made for the inside door.

A rosy-cheeked buxom lady welcomed them as if they were prodigal daughters returned home. When Dorinda had received her welcoming hug she introduced Lydia who received the same greeting. Mrs Hollis fussed around them, making sure they were comfortably seated, then bustled off 'to get that bite to eat'.

Lydia looked around and saw a room that was obviously under the care of a house-proud lady. The furniture was highly polished, the cushions on the hide sofa and chairs fluffed up and placed just right. Brass candlesticks on the mantelpiece shone; the mirror over the fireplace dare not have a speck of dust on it.

Dorinda noted Lydia's wandering gaze and whispered, 'Not all the cottages are like those dilapidated ones we saw. Many others are cared for like this even though it is a struggle sometimes on the wages most of these people earn. That does not stop them from taking a pride in their homes and making them as comfortable and presentable as they possibly can. Mr and Mrs Hollis have the advantage of having their own business, though I suspect the Gaisfords exact a higher rent because of that.'

Mrs Hollis reappeared carrying knives and forks and started to lay the table. She stopped, looked at Dorinda and said, 'You'll be wondering about Colin.'

'I am. Is he not around today?'

'Sorry, my dear, he's not. He's away to the fishing, trying to supplement his pittance from the fields.'

'I'll not see him, then?'

'No, lass, you won't. Maybe next week.'

Disappointment clouded Dorinda's face as Mrs Hollis left the room.

'Is Colin your sweetheart?' asked Lydia.

Dorinda nodded. 'He's generally around when I come on a Thursday, but he's been saying for a while he might go to the fishing.'

Lydia sympathised with her friend, but no more was said then as Mrs Hollis reappeared with some plates. She stayed for a while chatting and then disappeared back to the kitchen. This was repeated many times over the next hour during which time she brought them glasses of home-made elderflower wine. Finally she stood surveying the laid table, giving a little nod of satisfaction as if to say, I've thought of everything. She heard a bolt being shot in the shop door and knew that as usual she had timed the meal to perfection. Mr Hollis appeared and his wife greeted him as if he had been away to work.

'I'll just wash my hands,' he said.

Lydia recognised that this whole scenario was one the couple played out every day. She smiled to herself at such eccentricity but then thought, What does it matter? If that routine makes them happy and appreciate each other there's nothing wrong in it.

When Mr Hollis came back, he was rubbing his hands in eager anticipation of the food that was coming. 'Please be seated, young ladies.' He indicated the places at the table where he wanted them to sit.

After the meal, which passed off with pleasant chatter, the two girls insisted on helping with the washing up while Mr Hollis went to reopen the shop. With the clean pots stacked, Dorinda indicated that they should be going.

'I want to show Lydia the rest of the village and then take her back a different way,' she explained. 'We have enjoyed your cooking. Mrs Hollis, thank you for the meal.'

'You are indeed a good cook, thank you for having me,' added Lydia.

'Any friend of Dorinda is a friend of ours. You will be welcome here any time.'

As they left the shop, Dorinda collided with a man who was hurrying past, deep in thought. She was sent spinning backwards and bumped into Lydia who would have fallen but for the wall.

In a split second the man had stopped in his tracks and was staring at them. Anger flared in his eyes briefly. It was gone just as quickly when he saw the two young women. 'My apologies.' His hand went to his hat. 'I'm so sorry, I . . .' The words died away to be replaced by an expression of surprise. 'Why, Miss Booth! Dorinda! Are you both all right?'

The two girls had got their breath back. 'Yes thank you, Mr Mitchell,' spluttered Dorinda. She glanced at Lydia who was aware that Mr Mitchell's enquiring gaze had settled on her.

'Oh, yes, I'm unharmed, thank you.'

'I'm so sorry. I was lost in thought, not looking where I was walking. Are you sure you are not harmed?'

'Certain, sir,' replied Dorinda.

'Your cape, Miss Booth, the wall has marked it.'

'It will brush off, Mr Mitchell. Think nothing of it,' Lydia replied.

'I apologise again.' He doffed his hat. 'I hope the rest of your day is pleasant.' He started to turn away, then stopped and turned back to Lydia. 'I have thought of the place I would like you to paint. I will have to show it to you. That is, if you still want to do it?'

'I would love to. It will spur me on to resume painting.'

'Very well then! I will arrange to show you the view I would like.' With that, he turned sharply and hurried away.

The girls stood in silence watching him, then Dorinda placed a hand on Lydia's arm and turned her round. 'Your back's a bit of a mess from the wall,' she said. 'I'll see if Mrs Hollis has a clothes brush.'

While Dorinda re-entered the shop on her quest, Lydia stared after Mr Mitchell. Her thoughts were in a whirl. Had she really read interest in his eyes or was it a figment of her own imagination? She reined in her thoughts. She should not be giving way to such fancies. Mr Mitchell could have no interest in her – he was a happily married man. She certainly

39

should not be entertaining such ideas which could only lead to ignominy and disaster.

They were driven from her mind when Dorinda emerged from the shop triumphantly brandishing a clothes brush. With a few deft sweeps across Lydia's back the dust and grime were banished.

'There!' she said. 'As good as new.' She was in and out of the shop in a flash, grabbed Lydia's arm and started along the street. 'What was all that about?' she asked eagerly, sensing a story.

'What?' returned Lydia in feigned innocence.

'You know very well what I mean. The painting Mr Mitchell referred to.'

'Oh, that,' said Lydia, as if it was of no consequence.

'Yes, that,' insisted Dorinda.

'Mr Mitchell wants me to do a painting for him.'

'I didn't know you painted?'

Lydia knew that Dorinda would persist in her curiosity so told her how she had taken up painting, and what had happened when Mr and Mrs Mitchell had visited the Westburys.

Dorinda listened intently with only a few 'Ohs' and 'Ahs', but when Lydia had finished she added, 'So what are you to paint for him?'

'I don't know. You heard him, he's going to show me.'

'Ah!' This time her words were laden with innuendo and accompanied by a teasing twinkle in her eyes which changed to doubt as she warned, 'Be careful. Don't get involved in anything you might regret – he's a handsome man.'

'Don't worry, Dorinda, I won't. I'm only going to paint a picture. For all I know he might forget about it.' But Lydia hoped he wouldn't.

'Oh, I wonder what's going on there,' said her friend as she and Lydia turned through the church gate. She indicated what appeared to be a serious conversation between two men standing at a cottage door further along the street.

'It's Mr Mitchell again,' said Lydia.

'I know, and I'm wondering what he's doing at Ben Lowther's cottage.'

'Shouldn't he be?'

'It's a free world, or so we like to think,' replied Dorinda with a shrug of her shoulders. 'But Ben Lowther recently got the sack from the Gaisford mine for laziness and belligerence.'

'Bad character then?'

'Not really. He's decent enough at heart. Rumour has it that Jeremy Gaisford was pestering Ben's wife, an attractive lass. Ben got wind of it and tackled him, giving him a bloody nose.'

'And you don't hit the boss's son and get away with it.'

'Right. I wonder what Mr Mitchell is doing there?'

Lydia started along the path to the church.

'Wait a moment.' Dorinda drew her back. 'There's something going on.'

They saw Mr Mitchell and Ben Lowther shake hands, then before Mr Mitchell could turn away, Mrs Lowther appeared.

'She's crying,' commented Lydia.

'Aye, but through a smile. And look how she's grasping Mr Mitchell's hands. If that isn't gratitude, I don't know what is. I wonder what's been going on?' Dorinda paused and then added with determination, 'I'll find out before we leave the village.'

They spent a little while in the church. When they reached the gate to leave Dorinda said, 'We're in luck. That's Ben's brother just come out of the cottage.' She turned in that direction. 'Hello, Jules,' she called pleasantly as they neared the young man who was walking towards them with a jaunty step. 'You look pleased with yourself?'

His smile broadened as he stopped. 'Hello, Dorinda.'

'Lydia Booth,' she said by way of quick introduction.

Jules only nodded his greeting because Dorinda was already asking, 'Well, what's pleased you? You look like the cat who's got the cream.'

'Aye, I do. Ben's been offered a job and a cottage, and I can go too.'

'What? Leave Cribyan?'

'Aye. And glad we'll be to get off Gaisford land and away from that bloody family!' He glanced sheepishly at Lydia. 'Pardon me, miss, but if you knew them you'd agree with me.'

'Where are you going?' Dorinda asked eagerly.

'Sandannack.'

'Village on the Penorna Estate,' Dorinda explained.

'Mr Mitchell's just seen Ben. He'd heard of the trouble and Ben's sacking. He's looking for a few new workers and has four vacant cottages. Ben jumped at the chance to get Jessie away from the pawing hands of Mr Jeremy. My brother asked if there was a chance for me too and when Mr Mitchell said there was, Ben sent young Alec to find me. The deed is done – we're moving out tomorrow. Sal will be glad too. Well, must be off. Maybe we'll meet again, Miss Booth.' He touched his forehead to her and was gone.

'There you are, Lydia, told you I'd find it all out,' said Dorinda with a triumphant grin. 'Seems our Mr Mitchell is a knight in shining armour. And maybe he'll need that armour. The Gaisfords don't like interference and will regard this as just that.'

'But surely Ben is free to choose where he goes and who he works for, and Mr Mitchell who he employs?'

'Oh, yes, but the Gaisfords still won't like it. And accidents can happen . . .'

'You mean, they could make trouble for him?'

'Aye. As I say, they don't like what they regard as interference and will stop at nothing to teach an opponent a lesson. You've seen the scar on Mr Westbury's cheek?'

'You mean, they were responsible?' Lydia looked shocked.

'Rumour has it.'

'And you believe them?'

'Rumour never lies.'

Chapter Four

Three weeks later Thursday dawned bright with the promise of a settled day. Lydia stood at her window, trying to decide what to do. Dorinda had sent her a note yesterday saying that, unlike the previous Thursdays, she would be unable to meet her as she had been called to Penzance where her father was unwell. Lydia hoped that it was nothing serious and at this moment said a prayer for her friend's father's speedy recovery.

With the weather so tempting she decided that she would get Cook to make her a small picnic, take her pencil and sketch-pad, and walk along the coastal path until a suitable scene took her fancy. Half an hour later she left the house and paused for a moment on the veranda, drawing in a deep breath of the breeze that rolled in from the west, bringing with it the salt tang of the wide Atlantic. She stepped down from the terrace and headed for the garden gate where she took the path leading to the cliff edge.

Her mind drifted over the events of recent weeks and she thanked her own good fortune at the way life had turned out for her. She was now truly settled at Trethtowan Manor where the Westburys regarded her as part of the family and were delighted that James and Juliana had taken so readily to their new governess. Yes, she thought, life is good and I am so lucky.

Her spirits were high when she reached the cliff edge and stopped to gaze across the vastness of the calm sea that for once was not in vicious contest with the rocks and cliff face far below. Her mind wandered as she mused on what lay far beyond the horizon and allowed herself to conjure up magical places. She smiled at her own flight of fancy but, coupled with her skill with pencil and brushes, it at least meant her life need never be dull.

How long she stood day dreaming she never knew but suddenly she started out of her reverie. Her fingers itched to put the pencil to work. But where? She glanced around. Maybe a little further along the coast. She had only moved a few steps when the enchantment of the tiny bay she had visited on that first visit to Trethtowan came back to her mind.

She walked for half a mile keeping close to the cliff edge, marvelling at the panoramas continually unfolding beneath her; jutting rock had been eroded to leave arches through which she caught glimpses of the sea; cliff faces were sheered away, leaving precipitous drops softened by sea pinks and stone crop. She loved this coast and saw much that she could paint here but did not cease her stroll until she was looking down into the tiny bay where she had celebrated her change in fortune. Even now she could feel the same exhilaration and joy at the sight. She was lost in her thoughts, oblivious to anything but what she had come to regard as her place.

'Good day, Miss Booth.'

A voice close behind her made her jump. She swung round, a startled expression on her face. 'Oh, my goodness!' she gasped. Then, seeing Mr Mitchell, she quickly gathered her thoughts.

'I'm sorry if I startled you,' he apologised.

Lydia felt her face glow. She felt a strange pleasure in the closeness of his dark blue gaze that seemed to draw her into closer contact. What was in his thoughts as he looked at her? She felt a stirring in her breast. What did she want him to be thinking? Did his thoughts match her own . . .?

'Oh, no, it's perfectly all right,' she spluttered.

He came nearer. 'I think I did, and I apologise. I would not wish to cause you any distress.' His voice was soft and caressing.

Her thoughts swam. How she envied Mrs Mitchell, listening to this man every day. She stiffened herself. She should not be thinking like this. It was with mixed emotions that she heard Mr Mitchell continue speaking, thankfully breaking her own chain of thought.

'You seemed to be lost in contemplation of the bay?' It came as more of a question than a statement. 'It is beautiful, isn't it?'

'It is. This coastline has cast its spell on me.'

'And on me, but I think this place especially.'

'It is charming,' she conceded without revealing her true feelings.

'Strange that we should meet here,' he went on. 'You remember I asked for a painting to hang in Penorna Manor?' She nodded. 'And said I would arrange to show you the view I wanted?' Again she nodded. 'Well, there it is, this bay.'

'Oh.' Her bay! The unexpectedness of it made her start.

'Is that not possible? Too difficult?'

'Oh, no,' Lydia was quick to reply. She did not want any doubt casting on her ability. 'From here?'

'No. There are different aspects all along this cliff path as you will no doubt have seen. All of them are attractive but there is one place that Mrs Mitchell and I especially like. I'll show you. It's a few yards further on.'

Silently she fell into step beside him. John did not hurry, carefully assessing the exact position. Finally he stopped. 'There, looking towards the swing of the cliff that protects that end of the bay. The various rock strata are particularly picturesque and mark this bay out as something special. The cliffs give way to a fine strand of unmarked sand that is especially beautiful just after it has been washed by the sea. And of course there is the water itself which according to its mood can alter the atmosphere of the bay too.'

'And which mood would you want me to paint it in, Mr Mitchell?'

He looked thoughtful as if weighing up exactly what he wanted. 'Well, I think a tranquil mood. That would emphasise the exhilaration exuded by the figure I think should be placed splashing ankle-deep in the sea, arms stretched above her, clearly expressing the pleasure she is feeling.'

Lydia was stunned, unable to speak. Conscious of his eyes fixed upon her, she reddened. Embarrassed that the feelings she had experienced on that particular day were no longer her own, she could only whisper, 'You saw me?'

He nodded and said quietly, 'I did, from this very spot.'

'I did not see you.'

'You were lost in your own world of happiness. I wondered then, and did until we came to dine at Trethtowan Manor, who you were and why you felt such joy.'

'Do you really want me to put a figure in that scene?'

He laughed. 'Not really. In fact, I think any painting of the bay would be more effective executed from the beach itself,' she heard him saying, 'but alas I know of no way down. You must, though?'

'I do.' In her confusion the admission was out before Lydia realised it.

'Well?' he prompted.

'Seeing this view seemed to symbolise my luck that day. I felt I just had to find a way down. I explored and found one. I can understand why you have never found it, though. It is rather obscure and almost hidden by the fact that you have to climb so far down an awkward fissure in the rock face. But I was determined that day.' Lydia made no move towards it, though.

'Well, Miss Booth, aren't you going to show me?'

She hesitated. 'I don't know if I should . . .' She felt bolder now that she was in possession of knowledge he was not. 'Maybe I like having a secret.' The twinkle in her eyes teased him.

'Miss Booth, if you are to paint in the bay itself on my behalf, I must know if it is possible for you to get down there encumbered with equipment without endangering yourself.'

'Though ideally I would like to paint the scene out of doors it is, as you rightly presume, a hazard to take equipment down there. But all I would need is a pad and pencil to draw the scene and make notes. The painting itself could be done in my room.'

'If it is in any way dangerous, I could not countenance your risking your person on my account. Show me, Miss Booth, and let me judge for myself.'

She hesitated a moment and then said, 'Very well, follow me.'

Lydia retraced their steps for about twenty yards and turned into some undergrowth that ran to the very edge of the cliff. She started into it.

'Miss Booth!' called John with alarm in his voice.

She stopped and smiled over her shoulder. 'It's all right, Mr Mitchell. Now you know why you never found the way down.' She went two more yards and then, stooping, pushed aside the undergrowth. 'There you are, Mr Mitchell.'

He came to stand beside her and found himself looking down into a fissure in the cliff that extended downwards for about six feet before it appeared to stop at a solid rock face.

'Follow me,' she said brightly. 'There are good footholds to either side of this shaft, but pick them out carefully and don't slip.' With that she lowered herself down and he followed.

At the bottom of the shaft he was surprised to find there was a ledge wide enough for them to stand on side by side. Though it was gloomy he realised that light was coming not only from above but also from the right. The ledge ran on in that direction and then widened. Lydia started along it and from there the descent became easier with a lessening of the gradient until, with a final turn, it gave on to the beach.

John stopped in wonder. The beauty of the bay, attractive from above, was almost overpowering from here and embraced him with the feeling of entering another world. Towering cliffs swung in both directions in a protective curve, as if saying, This belongs to you two alone. Though he knew Lydia's feet had once marked that stretch of virgin sand, the sea had washed all evidence away and returned its purity. She started forward now. He stopped her. 'Don't spoil it, paint it from here.'

She turned to question his decision but, seeing in his eyes a powerful love for the scene, did not speak. She could tell that this place moved him on many different levels and felt it would be wrong of her to query this. Whatever was going through his mind was his to know, and his alone, unless he chose to share his thoughts. She did not move until he broke the spell.

'Getting down was not as bad as I feared. I can see why the path is difficult to find and I don't suppose anyone else ever will unless they have your determination. I am glad you showed it to me, though, and think it wise I should know. At least I will know where to look if ever you go missing.'

Lydia smiled. 'I suppose that is a comforting thought for me too. I won't end up a skeleton in an unvisited bay. You're sure this viewpoint will do?'

'Yes, it is very similar to the one I described but I would like to be reminded of the first time I saw it from here. Now, I think we'd better go.' He would have liked to linger; to share more time with this young woman whom he was finding more and more fascinating, but common sense dictated he shouldn't. When his wife came to mind he realised his love for her had no bounds; she was the mother of his child, the pivot of his life. She'd supported him in everything he had ever done. He could not repay her by giving way to the first attraction he'd felt towards another woman.

John started for the cleft in the rock. Lydia watched him go, struggling with her emotions. Why did she feel a stirring that she had never felt before? A yearning? A need? Had the change in her situation enabled her to look for things out of life she had never hoped for before? He was a handsome man and those magnetic blue eyes drew her to him as they seemed to penetrate to her very soul, but today she had seen a gentler side to his nature and the mixture only added to his fascination for her. He was leaving; she must go too. She followed and insisted on leading the way so she could point out the best footholds, especially in the final six foot of rock.

Once at the top John thanked her for showing him the way. 'What do you intend to do now?' he asked with casual interest.

'I have brought a picnic.' She tapped the bag she had over her shoulder. 'I'll probably do some sketching.'

'You are going down again?' She thought she detected a hint of concern in his voice.

'No. I'll do drawings of my bay from up here. They will help when I start the real canvas.'

'*My* bay, you said.' He fixed his eyes on hers, daring her to look away. 'Shouldn't that be *our* bay?' There was only a slight pause before he added, 'Good day, Miss Booth.' He raised his hat and strode away.

She watched him go, his words ringing in her mind 'Our bay.' Did she mind the intrusion? No, rather she was pleased. She shared something with him. Before her thoughts could drift further along the wrong path she reminded herself that she could hardly mind. After all, the bay was along the stretch of coastline he owned. She was really the intruder.

She saw Mr Mitchell stop and turn. He took a few steps back towards her and then paused. 'Miss Booth, when you have something ready, you must bring it to show my wife and seek her approval.'

'I will, Mr Mitchell.'

He nodded and resumed his walk.

Had that last instruction been a reminder to her that he was married? Had she unknowingly given a hint of her interest in him, causing him to issue a veiled warning?

John's mind was still on Lydia as he turned away from the cliffs and headed towards Sandannack. He had intended to be there already to see if the Lowther families had settled but was not annoyed at the delay. He had been in the presence of a charming person, one with whom he felt comfortable and moreover one who had shown him a means of reaching the bay that had attracted him and Eliza since the first day they had walked this coast together. He must tell his wife of this discovery but doubted he would ever persuade her to take that first precarious climb down. She had no head for such things. Miss Booth had not flinched, nor appeared to see any danger. He admired that side of her personality.

Maybe her exuberance when he had first seen her had resulted from having found a way down that was known to her alone. But now she had shared it. Deliberately? Or had the invitation slipped out accidentally? Had he really detected a personal interest in him? He chided himself for vanity, and for besmirching an attractive young woman's mind. But try as he would to thrust such thoughts away, he could not deny that he had felt a spark of attraction towards her. His musings only stopped when he heard the sound of a galloping horse. He looked round to see the hard-ridden animal turn in his direction.

John stopped walking and his nerves stiffened when he recognised Jeremy Gaisford. He saw that the animal was heaving and sweating, but that was typical of the way Gaisford treated his horses. He himself was dust-covered; his jacket unbuttoned to reveal a grubby white shirt worn open at the neck where the cravat hung loose. He was bareheaded and his red hair had been blown into disarray. He pulled the animal to a lurching halt, yelling at it to obey and settle down, sending dust swirling over John.

Gaisford pointed his riding crop at him. 'Lure any more of our tenants away with false promises and you're in trouble,' he yelled, grey eyes fixed angrily on John.

'Those weren't false promises,' he replied, quietly but with undeniable force as he met Gaisford's gaze without flinching. 'There'd be no need for me to offer a man a job if you treated him right.'

'The way I handle my tenants is my business, not yours! Tread warily, John Mitchell! You're still an outsider here, don't start crossing swords with me now.' The menace in Jeremy Gaisford's tone was not lost on John.

There had been an undercurrent of animosity between them ever since the Mitchells had arrived in Cornwall and John had openly criticised the Gaisford's land policy and treatment of some of their tenants. Now it seemed his latest move had angered Jeremy Gaisford to the point of open threats.

'Heed what I say!' Gaisford deliberately wheeled his horse around so that it struck John and sent him sprawling heavily to the ground, driving the breath from his body. For a moment he struggled to get up, but realising that Gaisford was already galloping away he lay still until he'd recovered.

'You look a bit out of sorts, John,' observed Eliza as she crossed the hall to meet him. 'Was everything all right at the Lowthers'?'

'Oh, yes, they're getting settled. He'd already been to the mine with my message. He and Jules are starting tomorrow.'

'Good. They'll be glad. So what's wrong?'

John scowled. 'I had a run in with Jeremy Gaisford. He threatened me and ran me down with his horse.'

'What?' Eliza showed concern. 'Are you all right?'

'Just a few cuts and bruises. I need a wash and a brush down.' He started towards the stairs.

'What was it all about?' she asked, accompanying him up the stairs.

As he washed, she laid out fresh clothes for him and he told her what had happened.

'This is the first trouble we have had from the Gaisfords since we arrived,' she commented, 'though I must say they have never gone out of their way to be friendly and the Westburys did warn us what they could be like.'

'Selwyn was always suspicious about that attack that left him scarred. He thought then, and still does, it was retaliation for the time he stopped Jeremy from beating a young boy who had accidentally scared his horse.'

'Be careful, John. It's better to keep clear of them. Don't forget they have quite a following.'

'Young moneyed brats who think if they emulate the Gaisfords they can ride roughshod over everybody else. They're the curse of the county.'

She saw he was getting worked up and taking it out on the cravat he was having trouble tying.

'Here, let me do that.' She came to him with a smile and gave him a peck on the cheek as she took hold of the cravat. 'Calm down. Forget Jeremy Gaisford.'

He gave a little grunt and raised his chin so that she could see what she was doing.

'There,' said Eliza with satisfaction as she stepped back to survey her handiwork.

'Thank you, my dear.' He picked up his jacket and as he shrugged himself into it, said, 'By the way, something more pleasant occurred before Gaisford appeared. I came across Miss Booth along the coast path. She had her sketch-book and pencils and was thinking about the picture we mentioned when we dined with the Westburys.'

'Oh. She was on her own?'

'Yes.'

'Of course, Dorinda's in Penzance.' Eliza's thoughtful expression vanished as she remembered. 'Had she decided what she would paint?'

'That pretty little bay we liked so much the first time we saw it.'

'She'll have to paint it from the cliff top then. There's no way down.'

'I think that is what she intends to do.'

'I'm sure she'll do a good job but I don't know when she will get time to do it. James and Juliana will keep her occupied.'

'Busy people always make time.'

'There's truth in that,' his wife agreed.

It was only later, when Eliza was seeing Abigail to bed and he was alone, that John wondered why he had not told his wife that Miss Booth had shown him how to reach the bay and together they had enjoyed its beauty and solitude. It was as if he wanted to share it with no one but pretty Miss Booth.

The knock on the drawing-room door at mid-morning the following day drew Eliza's attention. She'd been watching seagulls using eddies of warm air rising from the face of the cliffs to glide upon with barely a sweep of their wings. These birds were much the same as those she had watched on the cliffs near Whitby except that Whitby birds had a more distinctive screech, which she still missed. Hearing gulls always raised a touch of homesickness in her and a desire to visit Whitby again, both of which she kept hidden from John. He had settled here quickly, had thrown himself unsparingly into running the estate and soon shown his tenants that he was a tolerant and helpful landlord. He had made friends quickly among the local gentry and been accepted by most. Eliza had never worried that the Gaisfords had not extended the hand of friendship, that was their affair, and she knew their relationship with some of the other local landowners was no better. It seemed they kept to their own cronies, as she would call them, and if that was how they wanted it then so be it. But now, after John's run-in with Jeremy, she was worried. She knew of the young man's reputation and his hot-headedness. Her husband's compassion for the plight of others had led him to help the Lowther brothers which had stirred Jeremy Gaisford's hostility. Cross one Gaisford and you crossed them all.

It therefore came as a surprise when a maid appeared carrying a small silver salver on which there was a letter.

'This has just been delivered, ma'am,' the maid said as she crossed the room.

'Thank you, Jane.'

As she took the letter, Eliza glanced at the writing. She did not recognise the scrawl etched across the paper but could make out her own name. She would have said it was the writing of an older person. Her attention was drawn back to Jane.

'Ma'am, Miss Jenkins has just returned. She said to tell you she'd be with you in a few minutes.'

Eliza gave a little nod. 'Thank you, Jane. Will you pass me the letter opener from the desk, please?'

'Certainly, ma'am.'

Eager to assuage her curiosity Eliza had the letter opener in her hand before Jane had left the room. She unfolded the sheet of paper and read:

The Gaisford family

Request the pleasure of your company

At their Annual Ball

on 8th August

at Senewey Manor

Carriages 1a.m.

R.S.V.P.

53

Eliza stared disbelievingly at the invitation and re-read it to make sure.

There was no mistaking it, this really was an invitation to the Gaisford Ball. She had heard of it as being *the* event of the county; it outshone every other which would inevitably be compared unfavourably with the Gaisford Ball. She also knew that those attending this particular event always showed off their new dresses and brought out all their most valuable jewellery, vying to be seen as the most opulently dressed and dazzling person there. A sense of achievement seemed to wash over her then – though they had made many friends in Cornwall, it now seemed they had been fully accepted in the county at last. Maybe she and John had read more into his clash with Jeremy Gaisford yesterday than there in fact was. With Jeremy in mind, she recalled that she had heard how before the ball was over, he, his brothers and their friends always ran riot, passing off whatever devilment they got up to as just good fun. Be that as it may, she felt a surge of pride: she and John had been invited. She was eager to tell him, but that meant being patient until he returned from visiting two of the farms. Her thoughts were interrupted by a knock on the door and the appearance of Dorinda.

'Come in, my dear,' Eliza said brightly. 'I did not expect you back today. I told you to make sure everything was all right with your father.'

'I have, ma'am,' she replied, and went to the chair indicated by Eliza.

'How is he?'

'He had slipped and fallen in the shop, scraping his leg rather badly. The doctor was called and has attended to him. Father is to rest it for a few days and when he does get up must only stay on his feet for a few hours at a time.'

'What about help?'

'He has good neighbours who have kept an eye on him since Mother died. They had called the doctor and seen to him but then thought I had better know. They said there was no need for me to stay longer.'

'You are happy with all the arrangements.'

'Yes, ma'am.'

'If you are called back at any time, you must go.'

'Thank you, ma'am. I'll go on my day off next week, and probably also on Sunday, if that is all right, ma'am?'

'Of course it is. Families are important, especially parents.'

'Thank you, ma'am. I'll go to Abigail now. I looked in on her before I came down. She seemed happy with what she was doing and I told her I wouldn't be long.'

Unable to settle to anything, Eliza waited for an hour impatiently before she heard the front door open. She was out of her chair in a flash and across the room. She flung the door open. 'John, come here!' she called excitedly, holding out her hand as she went to him.

Startled by the crash of the door, he looked at her askance, surprised by such exuberance in his wife. 'What is it?'

'Come!' She had him by the hand and was hurrying him towards the drawing room. With the door closed she turned to him and held out the invitation. 'This arrived just over an hour ago.'

He took the letter from her and silently read it then looked up. 'I don't believe this. This is the first time since we came to Cornwall, and I certainly wouldn't have expected it after what happened yesterday.'

'Well, there it is,' said Eliza, excitement dancing in her eyes.

'But this must be from his father, not Jeremy.'

'Yes. Jeremy may be hot-headed but from what I hear he has to toe the line at home.'

John gave a little grunt. 'His father can't be at his side all the time. And he'll support a son against any outsider. Don't you think it strange this should come just after I cross swords with Jeremy?'

'That did strike me, but I thought it might be a peace offering from the family.'

'You could be right,' agreed John, but his voice held a note of doubt.

'There's only one way to find out.'

'Accept the invitation?'

'Of course. I never entertained the thought of not doing so, and hope you agree with me?'

'Though I have my doubts about the motive behind it, I do agree. We must go, to heal any rifts that have occurred.'

Chapter Five

Jeremy Gaisford tapped his left palm with his riding crop as he strode down the long stone corridor to the great hall of Senewey Manor. Though he lived here with his wife Hester and his five-year-old son Luke, it was still his father's home and he ruled it. Jeremy envied the freedom experienced by his brothers who each had their own smaller estate in another part of Cornwall. He as the eldest would inherit Senewey but meanwhile was tied to it by his father's inflexible command. The fortune that would one day be his outweighed the lack of freedom, for Jeremy liked money and the power and influence it gave him. He especially liked to exert his superiority over the young bucks of the county, who were only too eager to exploit his generosity.

Today his lips were tight with the annoyance that his morning ride would be delayed. On his way to the stables he had been stopped by one of the servants who had run from the house to tell him his father wanted to see him in the study immediately. Summoned that way, Jeremy knew it meant *now* unless he wanted to upset his father and he did not want that.

'Father! Father!'

The child's shout did not halt him. He saw his own son Luke slip his hand from his governess's grasp at the top of the stairs. The eight year old soon reached the hall, ran to his father and grabbed at his breeches.

'Where are you going?' demanded Luke.

'To see Grandfather.'

'Can I come?'

'No! And leave go!' Jeremy snapped, giving his son a little tap with his riding crop.

'Why can't I come?'

'Because I say so!'

'But . . .'

Jeremy glared at the governess who had now reached the bottom of the stairs. 'Can't you keep him under control?'

'Sorry, sir! Luke, come here.'

'No!' he screamed at her.

'Come here.' she said more firmly.

Luke's grip on his father's leg tightened. Jeremy's face darkened, his square jaw setting. 'Let go!' he snarled, and with a rough push sent the boy tumbling to the floor. Luke instantly started to cry. 'Stop your snivelling! Be a man!' The governess was crouching beside the boy, trying to comfort him and help him to his feet. She felt like pouring out a tirade at Jeremy but dare not. She knew it would be difficult to find another position in the county if she openly criticised him. With ailing parents to support she dare not lose this position. As Jeremy strode away he called over his shoulder, 'Toughen him up!'

She made no reply. Her glare after his retreating figure gave her some satisfaction. Couldn't he see that his son already was tough; that his crying now was not because he had been pushed to the floor but because his father had not given him even one second of his time? Had he done so the boy would have been overwhelmed with happiness. She knew Luke was sturdy with a hardy streak. Tears very seldom came to his eyes even at the roughest of falls, and there were many of those in the way he played, given his love for adventure and daring. 'Come, Luke, your father's busy, we'll go out and see what we can find to do.'

With that he was on his feet, tears dry and a new light in his eyes. He loved it when they went outside. There were trees to climb, animals to stalk, streams to splash in, and a hundred other things to do.

Jeremy tapped on the thick oak door of his father's study and walked in. Even now there was something awe-inspiring about this large room with its dark oak panelling. Here he had received the first vicious scolding and heavy punishment meted out by his father when he was seven. It had had no physical effect on him; in fact he'd gloried in the fact that he felt little pain, but whenever he entered this room now he recalled his own determination one day to sit in his father's chair where he'd watch the heavy old panelling around him torn out, piece by piece, and with it every memory of Miles Gaisford.

Now Miles sat behind his large mahogany desk facing the door. Though he was of medium build he possessed a force of personality that was felt wherever he was. Jeremy, though used to it, always experienced it, just as he did now walking towards the desk. The thick carpet muffled his steps. He would have preferred to hear them; the sound would have given him some confidence, whereas the silence seemed to be imposed by his father and implied that only he could break it. Miles knew how to dominate men who were much stronger than him physically. Every time he looked at his brutish son he revelled in that thought.

'Sit down,' he ordered curtly.

Jeremy knew he was in for a tongue lashing, but for what reason he did not know.

Miles watched his son closely with eyes that were sunken in a sharp, pointed face. Those eyes missed nothing, quick to sum up a situation or a person, particularly one he was meeting for the first time. More often than not his instant judgement was right.

Born the second son in a middle-class family of minor merchants in the north of the county, Miles had shrewdly courted Rowena, the only child of the owner of the Senewey Estate, knowing it would pass to her on her father's death. He set himself out to show his father-in-law that he would be capable of running such a possession. Delighted by his son-in-law's nimble brain, quick learning and aptitude, Rowena's father gave him more and more responsibility and Miles turned that to greater and greater account as he expanded the assets of the estate. The marriage was no love match but it was convenient for both him and her. Rowena wanted for nothing and knew before her father died that he was satisfied that it was so. She produced three healthy sons and knew that pleased her husband. He ignored the shortcomings in her looks and was not averse to finding satisfaction elsewhere to which Rowena, not wishing to upset the situation, closed her eyes.

As he stared at his bull-like son Miles admired him but would not let him know it. He knew Jeremy was tough, a hard man, quite capable of looking after himself with pistol, sword or fists. A skilful horseman, he rode hard, a trait that his father, a lover of fine horses, frequently criticised. Miles wished he could instil some judgement in his son so he might consider situations carefully before taking action, whether they concerned the running of the estate, their other enterprises, or his personal dealings. He also wished that Jeremy could control the hot temper that went with his red hair.

'What was the meaning of the fracas you had with John Mitchell?' Miles's voice was low but incisive.

Jeremy was surprised. He had never mentioned it. How did his father know? He moistened his lips nervously. 'Mitchell stole two of our employees.'

'Stole?'

'He took the Lowther brothers to work for him.'

'Were they employed by us?'

'Yes.'

Miles's eyes narrowed. 'You sure about that?'

'Yes.'

'Hadn't you sacked them?'

'Er . . .'

'You were conveniently trying to forget that, I see.'

Jeremy said nothing.

'So if they weren't employed by us, there was nothing to stop Mitchell hiring them?'

Jeremy looked uncomfortable. 'I suppose not,' he muttered.

'Yet you threatened him. Oh, yes, I know about that, don't ask me how. And don't think it was Mitchell who told me because it wasn't. Why don't you think before you act?' His father's eyes blazed. 'It's better to have friends among the other estate owners rather than enemies. You'd better mend some fences. You can start by being polite to Mitchell and his wife at the Ball.'

'You've invited them?'

'Yes. They've been here since '85, three years, it's time we were on better terms with them and inviting them to the Ball is a first step.'

'Anyone else coming I should know about?'

Miles gave a small smile. 'Yes, the Westburys have been invited also.'

Jeremy raised his eyebrows. 'I thought after three refusals you crossed people off the list?'

'I know, I know, I've gone against pattern there. The Westburys used to come and, as you point out, would automatically have been left off the list this year, but it has come to my notice that they are very friendly with the Mitchells, so as it is their first time I thought it would be more comfortable for them if their friends came too.'

'Are you up to something?' Jeremy dared to ask, knowing his father could be a devious man and did little unless it was to his own advantage.

'It pays to be on good terms with all the gentry of this county, so see you are polite to the Mitchells and never cross swords with them again. Or, before you do, make sure you are in the right. Don't blunder in as you did on this occasion when you were clearly in the wrong. They have a sizeable estate, a profitable mine, close to the Westbury mine, and own a stretch of coastline. They'd be better friends than enemies. Off with you now and have your ride.' Jeremy took the dismissal obediently and started for the door. 'And treat your horse kindly,' his father called after him.

Two days after they had received their invitation Eliza and John rode over to the Westburys and were delighted to learn that Harriet and Selwyn had also received one.

'We were surprised,' added Harriet.

'Why?' queried Eliza.

'We haven't been for three years,' she said, and went on to explain about the Gaisford rule. 'So this gave us a shock.'

'Tell us more about it?' Eliza urged. Though she was easier in her mind now she knew their friends were going, she realised she would be more so if she had some prior knowledge of what was expected.

The days leading up to the Senewey Ball became more and more hectic but Rowena was in her element. She loved it all and frequently recalled the days when as a little girl she used to peep down from the landing to watch the elegant guests arrive. Then came her own first Ball, and memories of that were always recalled as the day of the latest one drew near. As Mistress of Senewey Manor the burden of organising it fell upon her. She recalled all that her mother had taught her and what she had observed for herself throughout the years. She was thankful that Miles was generous with the amount he set aside for provisions. Like her, he always wanted the celebration to be better than last years.

More servants were brought in. Rowena divided them into groups and placed one of her regular servants in charge of each one to which she assigned a special role for the evening. She paid particular attention to the floral decorations and personally supervised the laying of the tables in the dining room so that the buffet meal could be served to best advantage and guests not be kept waiting. She made sure that every servant knew the part they were playing and made it sound as if the success of the whole rested on that particular task. That way she engaged everyone's interest and made them keen to see that nothing went wrong. Miles oversaw the wines and put two male servants in charge of the cellars. He gave one last look to the estate workers who were to see to the parking of the carriages and that the grooms and their horses were looked after.

As the minutes ticked away towards the arrival of their guests Rowena grew more and more anxious about the weather. When he saw her go out on to the stone veranda for the umpteenth time in the last fifteen minutes, Miles followed her outside.

'Will you stop worrying, Rowena? It's a perfect autumn evening,' he said in a comforting tone.

'Yes, but you know how easily the weather can change and if it rains there could be chaos.'

'It won't rain, the weather is settled, there's barely a hint of wind. It's ideal and will put all our guests in a good mood. Everything is ready.' He took her hand. 'As usual you have done a splendid job, I just know this is going to be better than ever.' He smiled and her mind flew back to the first time he had smiled at her all those years ago – it seemed more than a lifetime. She could still remember it and in that moment had thought, This is love. Of course, in a matter of days she knew it wasn't, and never would be, and that their relationship would instead develop into a mutual respect and understanding that was all they expected and wanted. She had derived a certain type of happiness from it over all these years, and suspected Miles had too.

'Come inside, sit down. your dress is beautiful and suits you as you suit it. Relax with a glass of wine,' he told her. 'Jeremy and Hester will be down in a few minutes. Charles and Emma, and Logan and Fanny, won't be long. They always arrive early for the Ball to have a few words with us before the guests arrive.'

'You're right,' she conceded. 'I can't do any more and I've no control over the weather. I just want everything to be right for you. I know you set great store by our Ball, helping to create and maintain good relationships throughout the county.'

'And tonight we have the Mitchells from Penorna for the first time. I know you'll see they are made most welcome.'

'Why have you never invited them before?'

'I wanted to see how they fitted in first. Mr Mitchell's uncle did so very well but that wasn't to say his nephew would. And they were coming from Yorkshire. Cornwall's a world away – so different. They may not have settled and we Cornish folk may not have taken to them. But they do seem to have integrated well, from what I hear.' They reached a small room off the main hall and took a window seat from where they could see the first arrivals.

Ten minutes later Jeremy and Hester came into the room. Miles frowned upon seeing his son already with a tankard of ale in his hand and wondered how much he had drunk already, but not wanting to start the evening badly for the sake of the ladies, he held back from open criticism. He would have a sharp word before long, though. Leaving the ladies admiring each other's dresses, he poured them a glass of Madeira each. As he was doing so he heard the scrunch of hooves and wheels on the drive. Glancing out of the window, he saw the light from lanterns strategically placed near the entrance to the house reveal two coaches he recognised. 'Charles and Logan are here,' he called over his shoulder.

Jeremy put his tankard down and hurried from the room, ever ready to exchange back-slapping greetings with his brothers and joke with his pretty sisters-in-law whom he knew were not averse to responding flirtatiously.

Family greetings were exchanged heartily, dresses admired, children's welfare queried, wine distributed, the thirty minutes together setting the tone for the start of the evening.

'You look very becoming, my dear.' John, who had had some misgivings about this evening after his altercation with Jeremy, was assiduous with his compliments nevertheless and his eyes reflected his approval of Eliza's dress for he knew she put great importance on her attire and sensed she needed reassurance tonight.

This evening she had discarded her old stiff silks and had had a dress made in the newer cotton that was pouring out of the Lancashire cotton mills. Lighter and less ostentatious, it incorporated discreet padding to give the slimmer female figure a gentle bustle. The dress, of a pale yellow fabric with a small light blue flower motif, fell with only a slight flare from a high waist. Eliza preferred the sleeves long and tight to the wrist, and around her bare shoulders had set a silk shawl, with the simplest of silver necklaces sparkling against her skin. She had been pleased with her own appearance and her husband's praise, returning it when she saw he had replaced his fussy embroidered waistcoat with a severely elegant one of light brown silk. He wore a long jacket, left open at the front, with a high collar and a stock of muslin wound several times round the neck. His matching pale grey trousers came tight to his calves, below which he wore white stockings that were reflected in his highly polished evening shoes adorned with small silver buckles.

Even Benson was bold enough to offer his congratulations on their appearance when he saw them into the coach before leaving Penorna Manor. They drove to the Westburys' as pre-arranged for they preferred to travel on together. Greetings and compliments were made when they arrived and news exchanged over a glass of wine.

As Harriet and Eliza came from the drawing room into the hall with laughter on their lips, Lydia was coming down the stairs.

'Are the children settled?' Harriet asked her.

'They are, Mrs Westbury. Good evening, Mrs Mitchell. I hope you have a pleasant time,' Lydia said, pausing two steps from the bottom.

The two men came into the hall then and she had to stifle her reaction on seeing John.

'Good evening, Miss Booth,' he said pleasantly.

'Good evening, Mr Mitchell,' she replied. Her heart lurched when his eyes met hers. She thought she had detected a hidden interest as he passed her by. She stood still, her mind pounding. He looked so handsome. Then he was gone. She gazed at the closed door, wondering what it would be like to dance with John Mitchell. She was sure he would be an elegant and accomplished dancer. She pictured herself in the most wonderful gown, matching his steps with hers, feeling his hand on hers, his touch on her waist as he whirled her round: the most elegant couple on the floor.

With the sound of the first carriage arriving Miles and Rowena took up position to greet their guests. Servants were on hand to take cloaks, coats and hats while others hovered with trays of welcoming punch. Their three sons and their wives welcomed the guests after their parents and saw that they mingled to create the convivial atmosphere expected at the Gaisford Ball.

'Oh, good, there are a number of people here already.' Eliza expressed her delight as they came in sight of Senewey Manor. She had not wanted to be the first to arrive at this, their first Gaisford Ball.

The coach was directed to its position and the new arrivals escorted to the house where they found people already milling about in the hall and the babble of conversation coming from rooms beyond.

They were greeted by a liveried footman who politely enquired their names, announced them in a loud voice, and directed them to Mr Miles Gaisford and his wife who were amiably receiving their guests.

'Ah, Mr and Mrs Mitchell, how delighted we are to see you. Welcome to your first Gaisford Ball.' Miles took Eliza's hand and raised it to his lips as he made her a small bow. Then he took John's hand in a firm grip.

'It is a pleasure to be here, Mr Gaisford,' replied John.

Miles raised his hands in protest. 'Miles, please. We are near neighbours.'

John signalled his acknowledgement with an exchange of his own Christian name. Eliza thanked Miles for his invitation and when he had said, 'Enjoy yourselves,' she passed on to Rowena's friendly and warm greeting.

As they moved away they were offered glasses of punch. They lingered a while in the hall, wondering which direction they should take, while looking for any familiar faces and awaiting the Westburys who were now being welcomed by Miles and Rowena.

Raucous laughter from a group of men across the hall attracted their attention and at that moment John caught a look from Jeremy Gaisford that he could not read. He saw him speak quickly to the others around him and leave them to come over.

'John!' He extended his hands in greeting and smiled with unexpected warmth. 'It *is* good to see you, and I must apologise for that unfortunate incident a few days ago. I was in the wrong, accusing you of stealing the Lowthers from us. They were perfectly free to move.' As he had been speaking he had

66

shaken hands in what could only be described as an obsequious manner.

Taken aback by what seemed to be genuine contrition, John could do nothing but respond in like manner, particularly as he was a guest. 'Think nothing of it.'

'Good man.' Jeremy slapped him on the shoulder and turned to Eliza. 'Mrs Mitchell, welcome to our home and to your first Ball. May it be one of many for it will be our delight to have your charms continue to adorn it.' He bowed, took her hand and raised it to his lips, all the while concentrating his gaze on her.

She smiled in return and thanked him for his welcome. 'It is a pleasure to be here.'

'Please enjoy yourself, and such an exquisitely dressed lady must reserve a dance for me – that is,' he cast a glance at John, 'if you will allow me the pleasure?'

He inclined his head in agreement.

'Then let me book the second one. The first must be your husband's. Now you must come and meet my brothers.' He led them to the group he had left and made the introductions quickly but without undue haste. They were made to feel at ease, and as the group around them gradually split up with the arrival of more guests found themselves being shown round the house by Charles and Emma.

A large room to the right with chairs set against three walls was to be used for dancing. As the evening was warm the doors had been opened to allow guests on to the veranda that ran along three sides of the house. In a similar room to the left of the hall, again with access to the veranda, tables had been laid with the most tempting array of food. Smaller salons with access from both these main rooms were open for use, and in one of these Emma suggested they sit down while Charles went in search of replenishments for their glasses.

'It is a sizeable house,' commented Eliza.

'Indeed it is,' replied Emma. 'It has been in the family for many years but it was Charles's grandfather who expanded the building, partly with the idea of being able to establish these Balls as a means of cementing relationships within the county.'

Charles caught that last remark as he returned with a maid carrying a tray of wine glasses.

'It worked,' he added, 'and I hope in the present case it is successful. This is your first time, I believe?'

'And enjoying it,' replied Eliza.

'I'm so pleased,' said Emma. 'I hope you continue to do so. The night is still young, there are many hours of enjoyment left.'

As the two ladies fell into conversation, Charles turned to John. 'I'm sorry about that run in you had with Jeremy. He can be impetuous at times.'

'You heard about it?'

'Naturally. I don't condone everything he does but at heart he's a good brother.'

'He's made his apologies and the incident is now forgotten as far as I'm concerned.' Even as he spoke John was wondering if there was an ulterior motive behind these niceties. Apologies seemed so out of keeping with what he had heard of Jeremy and yet the Gaisfords were acting in a friendly manner that could not be faulted.

All thoughts and conversations were interrupted when they heard the musicians strike the first notes to inform everyone that dancing would take place in a few minutes. As the gentle strains continued, the buzz of chatter raised its pitch in anticipation of the pleasure to come.

'We had better take the first dance with our wives,' said Charles with a wry smile, 'but, Mrs Mitchell, may I claim one later?'

'Shall we say the fifth, Mr Gaisford?'

'My pleasure,' he replied.

'Then I shall be bold enough to ask you for that dance too, Mr Mitchell,' put in Emma quickly, a twinkle in her eyes, daring him to refuse. 'I would guess that you are an excellent dancer,' she added, allowing her gaze to run over his figure.

He responded with a little inclination of his head and said, 'I look forward to it.'

As they walked to the room set aside for the dancing, Eliza whispered, 'Brazen flirt! Watch your step, John Mitchell.'

'I'll certainly be careful not to step on her toes,' he replied, amused by her unintended pun. 'What do you think of the Gaisfords efforts to be charming?'

'Perhaps they are; perhaps we don't know them well enough.'

'Their reputations say otherwise.'

'Reputations are often exaggerated.'

'Well, we shall see.'

People were milling after them and quickly taking their places for the dance. An atmosphere of enjoyment charged the room from the first note and the guests swung into their first steps. The swirl of dresses sent cascades of colour around the room; every eye observed the better dancers, attractive ladies or handsome men, even as they wove their way in line across the polished floor.

Halfway through the first dance, as they passed each other, Eliza whispered, 'You are being watched.'

'I know,' John replied with a small smile that showed he was enjoying the flattery.

Their positions changed and he found himself opposite Emma.

Her eyes rested invitingly on his. 'You dance well,' she said quietly. 'We must try the waltz,' she added, knowing that during that dance they would stand close together. 'You are familiar with it?'

'Yes, I have danced it, though it is not generally performed in this country.'

'But it is so daring and exciting!' Her eyes twinkled mischievously.

She had been bold enough to make the suggestion and had cornered him so neatly he could hardly refuse. 'It will be my pleasure,' he replied as they moved apart.

'Has that minx got her claws into you?' Eliza quipped as they came together again.

'If dancing the waltz is any indication, yes,' he replied.

Eliza raised her eyebrows. 'The waltz! She must have planned that. You be careful, John Mitchell. I notice you have also been the object of other scrutiny.'

'You shouldn't have married such a handsome man,' he teased.

The dance finished but almost before the floor had cleared the musicians started the second. Jeremy was beside Eliza.

'May I claim my dance, Mrs Mitchell?'

'Indeed you may, Mr Gaisford.'

He led her on to the floor and she was surprised to find that, for a big solid man, Jeremy was light on his feet and an impeccable dancer. They floated around the floor and Eliza felt lost in another world where every other dancer was clumsy.

'You dance divinely, Mrs Mitchell,' he said.

'I could say the same for you, Mr Gaisford.'

'I enjoy it, as I'm sure you do?'

'Yes, I do, and regret that the opportunities rather fell away after we moved from Whitby.'

'That has been our loss, but I'm sure that after tonight opportunities will become more numerous. Other people who give Balls will have noticed you and your husband and the charm you are lending to this occasion.'

'You flatter us, Mr Gaisford.'

'I do not. And I regret that my father did not invite you before. I also regret I caused trouble with your husband, for it must have distressed you?'

'It did, but we have put that behind us.'

'I am pleased to hear it.'

When the dance finished he escorted her back to her husband, who had been dancing with Harriet.

'Thank you,' Jeremy said quietly to her, and then looking at the others as Selwyn joined them, 'I hope you are enjoying yourselves and will continue to do so.' He moved away to speak to some other guests.

John raised a querying eyebrow at Selwyn.

'He's being exceptionally pleasant.'

'Beware of the fox in disguise.'

'Oh, come on, you two,' put in Eliza. 'I think you read more into things because of his reputation for hard riding and hard living. Mr Gaisford was politeness itself, considerate, and a divine dancer.'

'Put on for this evening,' replied Selwyn. He allowed his voice to trail away as he saw Miles and Rowena approaching them.

'And how are our new guests enjoying themselves?'

'Very much,' replied John. 'Indeed, it is a splendid occasion.'

'I like to set the standard for the whole county. I hope it makes for good relationships and helps in many other ventures.'

'I'm sure it does, Mr Gaisford,' put in Selwyn.

'You have been here longer than Mr Mitchell and had time to observe us. I believe you should think again about some of the propositions I have put to you in the past which you chose not to take up. Consider how you could have benefited from them. Tell Mr Mitchell about them.'

'Miles! We said no business this evening. Well, certainly not in front of the ladies,' Rowena admonished.

'I am sorry, my dear, and I apologise to you too, ladies.' Miles's eyes swept over Harriet and Eliza. 'And may I add how delightful your dresses are? You both sparkle among so many beautiful gowns.'

'You are a flatterer, Mr Gaisford,' said Eliza. 'I can see from whom your eldest son inherits his charm.'

Miles smiled. 'I saw you dancing with Jeremy. I hope his steps were to your liking?'

'Indeed they were.'

'Then please go on enjoying yourselves.'

The Mitchells and the Westburys made sure that they did. They danced, mingled, and dined from tables laden with every kind of savoury and sweetmeat. The Mitchells were pleased to be introduced by their neighbours to other county gentry, but in the course of conversation through odd words and expressions John was constantly reminded of just how much influence the Gaisfords wielded in the county. It made

71

him wonder why Miles Gaisford had never approached him before this evening, until he realised from other snippets he heard that he had been giving John time to settle and see if he was going to stay permanently in Cornwall. Had he finally reached a conclusion about that? It seemed so, from what he had said to Selwyn earlier. John wondered what propositions he had been referring to and why exactly Selwyn had turned them down? He meant to find out but tonight was not the time.

Chapter Six

'I am going to ride over to see Selwyn,' he announced at breakfast the next morning.

'Curious about those propositions Mr Gaisford mentioned?' queried Eliza, looking up from her scrambled egg.

'Better to be forearmed. After what I heard last night, I reckon the Gaisfords wield more power in this county than we ever imagined.'

'Maybe. You would hear more than I – male talk – but I found them all charming. Did you not, or was your attention focused more on Charles's wife?'

'She certainly went out of her way to flirt.'

'And you enjoyed it.'

'And you'd think there was something wrong with me if I didn't,' he teased. 'Well, I must be off.' He rose from his chair, came round the table to kiss her and headed for the door.

The groom soon had his favourite horse saddled and John put it to a steady pace along the cliff top. The sharp air helped to clear his head of a slight hangover. He was in no hurry. He would enjoy the ride. The sun shone but he eyed the clouds to the west with suspicion; they could spell rain later in the day. He admired the coastal scenery that kept unfolding but nothing charged him with real emotion except the little bay that brought memories flooding back as he automatically halted his horse to take in its beauty. After a few moments he slid from the saddle, tethered his mount, and moved closer to the cliff edge. He stood easily, legs astride and hands clasped behind his back. Relaxed, he felt the bay call to him, offering itself, seeming to say there was more than peace and tranquillity to be had on its shore. He stepped towards the hidden path but stopped. This was foolish. He was letting emotion run away with reason. What more could the bay offer him? He started to turn back to his horse but was halted by a movement far below.

She stepped out of the shadow of the cliffs and waved to him.

He stood transfixed by the unexpected sight. Then he found himself hurrying to find the way down. He moved cautiously, at first, finding foothold after foothold. Eventually emerging on to the strand he found she had moved to a position from which she couldn't be seen from the cliff top.

He walked towards her, his mind in a whirl. What was he doing here? Hesitancy overcame his steps. He felt her eyes on him. Did he read a challenge there or was he giving way to an over-active imagination? A shaft of sunlight moved over her. She stood perfectly still; a thing of beauty.

'Miss Booth.' His mouth was parched, his throat dry. 'I did not expect to see you here.'

'Nor I you, Mr Mitchell.'

'I was on my way to Trethtowan to see Mr Westbury.'

'He was at home when I left. It's my day off, you know, and you require a painting,' she offered by way of explanation.

'Ah, yes, of course,' he stammered.

'Mr and Mrs Westbury told me it was a splendid Ball.' She seemed to be trying to find something to say rather than let a charged silence stretch between them. It was as if she dared not trust herself if that happened.

'Yes, it was.'

'I am pleased.'

'Thank you.'

'I . . . er . . . if I may say so . . .' She hesitated.

'Yes, Miss Booth?'

'Er . . . when you called at Trethtowan on your way to the Ball, I thought you most elegant.' The words escaped despite her better judgement.

'Thank you.' So she *had* noticed. He was surprised by the wave of pleasure that sent through him.

'And Mrs Mitchell, of course.'

The mention of his wife's name shattered John's complacency. What was he doing talking to this young attractive woman in the privacy of a place he had dubbed 'their own'?

'I had better be going.' He turned abruptly and hurried away.

Lydia watched him go, her heart thumping, cursing herself for having reminded him that he was married. She wanted to reach out and stop him. Instead a tear ran down her cheek. He disappeared from her sight. Her mind raced. Oh, why had she fallen in love with this man, a love she must keep secret even from him?

She bit her lip to drive back the tears of regret and picked up her pencil and pad. The resulting painting would be a labour of love.

Reaching the top of the cliff, John paused to get his breath and look back, but Lydia was not to be seen. Regretfully, he swung himself into the saddle and rode slowly to Trethtowan Manor, his thoughts full of the girl on the beach. Certain emotions threatened to overwhelm him and jeopardise the life he loved with Eliza and Abigail.

When he swung from the saddle in the Trethtowan stable yard and handed his horse over to one of the stable lads, he pushed the haunting thoughts from him and hurried to the house where Selwyn greeted him warmly. Once they were ensconced comfortably in his study and had exchanged brief comments about the Ball, John came straight to the reason for his visit.

'Nothing could have served better to cement local relationships than last night's Ball but I still have a nagging suspicion of Gaisford's intentions. We have been here three years and this is the first friendly approach from any of the family. He referred to propositions that you'd turned down and hinted you had been unwise. You never mentioned them to me.'

'Before your time here, John, so there was no point in telling you. I thought Gaisford had given up on me, but from what he said last night, I see he has ideas again.'

John looked puzzled. 'What exactly are you saying, Selwyn?'

'Look, you must have realised that the Gaisfords are powerful in Cornwall. They're the most prestigious family in the county and have accumulated land and wealth over generations though Miles's origins were not exalted. Nevertheless many of the gentry run with him rather than oppose him. If they do oppose the Gaisfords, they don't do it openly, careful not to cross swords with them.'

'Not like I did with Jeremy.'

Selwyn gave a little smile. 'Exactly. That run in could have cost you.' To emphasise his meaning he ran his finger along the scar on his cheek.

'You mean, the Gaisfords were behind that?'

'Happened before your time, as I said. I could never prove anything. The attack appeared to have been by footpads, but it came soon after I had finally refused one of Miles Gaisford's propositions.'

'What was that?'

'He was keen to buy a large parcel of land including my mine from me, and when I refused suggested we go into partnership together to raise more sheep. I knew he really had an idea that there were good copper deposits beneath that land and the terms he was suggesting for the partnership contained a clause about other possibilities for development that was very much in his favour. It was complicated so he thought I would not notice how it was angled.'

'And were there copper deposits?'

'Oh, yes, good ones. I knew that though but he didn't know I knew it.'

'But why not exploit them, if it would have made you money?'

'Money isn't everything, John. I had plenty and still do. We live comfortably already and a large section of our land would have been spoilt by further mining. I didn't want that, but Gaisford did not like my refusal.'

'And you think he tried to persuade you?' John indicated the scar.

'Yes.'

'Did he try again?'

'Oh, yes. I had a horse killed from under me, though it was made to look like an accident. And Harriet was molested by a couple of thugs in Penzance.'

'What?' John expressed his shock.

'Snatched her bag, knocking her down in the process. She ended up with two black eyes and cuts to her forehead and knees, plus of course the shock. She gave as good a description as she could of her attackers but they were never caught.'

'And you think Gaisford was behind that as well? Surely he wouldn't sink so low as having a woman attacked?'

Selwyn shrugged his shoulders. 'Well, it's only my suspicion but all the events occurred when I was not going along with Miles's propositions.'

'There were others?'

'He wanted to buy some facilities I have in Falmouth but I refused, knowing he would try to force me out. I also have two fishing vessels I refused to sell him.'

'So what made him give up?'

'My stubbornness, but really he never gives up because he refuses to be beaten. After what he said last night, I think he has something else in mind, either for you or me or both of us.'

'What can I possibly have that would interest him?'

'Who knows? Look to your assets. I know he was at your uncle several times but Gerard was a wily old bird, if you don't mind my saying so. He outfoxed Gaisford on several occasions and he didn't like it. Your uncle was a very popular man, though, and could have raised a great deal of support, you might almost say an army, if Gaisford had moved against him. Could be that you might become a fitting target to satisfy his need for revenge.'

John grimaced. 'Thanks for the warning but I don't ...'

'Don't underestimate the Gaisfords. They'll band together if it suits them, and the younger wives are not averse to helping either. Be very wary of their wiles.'

Selwyn's words occupied John's mind for a few days but, as the weeks progressed in the peacefulness of everyday life, they gradually faded from his memory until they were brought sharply back to mind one day in the spring of the following year.

He had set off walking on his weekly visit to the mine. He was halfway there when a rider broke the horizon and came towards him. It was not long before he recognised Jeremy Gaisford who for once was moving at a slow, considered pace. He halted his mount a few yards in front of John.

'Good morning to you, Mr Mitchell,' he called, steadying his horse with a firm hand.

'And to you, Mr Gaisford,' replied John.

'I was just coming to see you.'

John's expression betrayed surprise. He had seen none of the Gaisfords since the Ball. Why should Jeremy be on his way to see him?

'Father would like you to call on him.' The tone Jeremy used was more like a summons than a request. John bristled.

'What's he want?'

'It's his business to tell you. He would have come to see you himself but he's not well.'

'I'm sorry to hear that.' John calmed his tone. 'Maybe it would be better if I waited until he was recovered?'

Jeremy grimaced as he shook his head. 'If Father says now, he means now.'

'You mean, today?'

'Yes.'

'But I have other things to see to, I cannot . . .'

Jeremy did not allow him to finish. 'Look, Mr Mitchell, I wouldn't normally plead with you, but as I said, Father is not well and there is something he would like to get settled with you. So not only he but I would be obliged if you could pay him a visit before the day is out.'

This was a new side to Jeremy Gaisford, one he had never heard of. His father must be far from well for Jeremy to put the request in this way. John looked thoughtful for a moment then he nodded and uttered a brusque, 'All right. I'll be at Senewey within the next two hours.'

'I'm obliged, Mr Mitchell,' replied Jeremy, and without another word turned his horse and put it into a gallop the way he had come.

John watched him for a few moments with a puzzled frown. What could this be all about? What was so important that it couldn't wait until Miles Gaisford had recovered? He turned on his heel and walked back home where he instructed his groom to have a horse saddled. All was quiet as he entered the house by a side door but on reaching the hall he heard voices coming from the drawing room. Entering the room, he pulled up short.

'Mrs Gaisford.' He bowed politely to Emma who acknowledged his greeting with a radiant smile.

'Mr Mitchell. It adds pleasure to my visit to see you,' she replied.

John turned to his wife. 'I did not know you were expecting a visitor.'

'Naughty of me, Mr Mitchell,' Emma put in quickly. 'It was my spur of the moment whim to come visiting. I had seen nothing of you or your wife since the Ball and thought it ought to be rectified. I am going to hold a small dinner party and hope you will be able to accept an invitation when I make the arrangements?'

'That is very kind of you, Mrs Gaisford. I will leave the decision to my wife. You must excuse me, I have an appointment.'

'I thought you were on your way to the mine?' said Eliza, curiosity in the glance she exchanged with her husband.

'I was but had to change my plans.' His expression told her to ask no more.

'Will you be back about the same time?'

'I should be no later.' He turned to Emma. 'Forgive me.'

'There is nothing to forgive, Mr Mitchell. Appointments must be kept.'

As John went for his horse he wondered how much she knew of her father-in-law's summons and whether that forthcoming dinner party was all part of another Gaisford scheme. But to what end?

When he reached Senewey Manor a groom appeared to take care of his horse. Inside the house he was taken quickly to Mr Miles Gaisford's study.

He received a shock. Miles was propped up by pillows and cushions in a large armchair positioned so that he could receive all the warmth from the fire. He was dressed but had a rug around his knees. His skin had a yellowish pallor and his eyes seemed even deeper set in his gaunt face. He was far from the hale and hearty man who had graced the Senewey Ball.

'Mr Gaisford, I received a message from your son.' John glanced in the direction of Jeremy who was standing beside the large mahogany desk. 'And may I say how sorry I am to see you are not well?'

Miles gave a little dismissive wave of his hand. 'Something I picked up when I was in the Indies. It recurs once a year and is not pleasant when it does. There are times when I fear . . .' He gave an even firmer wave of his hand. 'But let's not talk of that. However, I decided I must put a proposition to you before it is too late. Jeremy could see to it but this is something dear to my heart and just in case this illness moves for the worst, I thought it best to deal with the matter now. I thank you for coming so quickly.'

John noted his words carefully. Was Miles trying to play on his sympathy?' 'I cannot envisage that anything concerning me would interest you, Mr Gaisford.'

'Ah, now that is where you are wrong, Mr Mitchell.'

'Well, I can make no comment until I hear of your interest and proposition.'

'Quite right.' He looked in the direction of his son. 'Where are those drinks?' he snapped. 'Don't keep our guest waiting.' Miles lowered his tone as he asked John, 'You will take a glass of Madeira with us?'

'Thank you.'

'Do sit down.' Miles indicated one of the two chairs that had been placed to face his.

John sat down, judging that the other was for Jeremy, who arrived with a tray on which there were three glasses of wine.

John took one, making his thanks as he did so. Jeremy turned to his father. 'Do you think you ought to, Father?'

The older man bristled. 'Don't mollycoddle me. When did a glass of good wine harm me? Give it here. And that decanter's nearly empty. Get some more.'

Driven by his father's sharp tongue, Jeremy started for the door.

Miles savoured his drink and then said, 'You have some land that I would like to buy.'

John's instinctive reaction was to say no and point out firmly that he was not in the market to sell anything, but he suspected Miles had more in mind than just buying a piece of land. He wanted to know more about this interest.

'Which piece of land would that be?'

'Map.' Miles waved a hand irritably at his son.

Jeremy turned back from the door, pushed a small table towards his father, plucked a map from the desk and left the room.

'Come nearer,' Miles said.

John shuffled his chair so that he could see the complete map and immediately noted that it covered the section occupied by the Senewey, Trethtowan and Penorna Estates.

'That is the parcel I would like to buy from you.' Miles pointed to a tract someone had marked on the north side of the Penorna Estate.

John made a thoughtful sound. 'Why that particular section, Mr Gaisford, it doesn't border yours?'

'I've bought land north of it and would like to enlarge it so I can run a larger flock of sheep.'

John felt sure there was more to it than that. He had noticed that the western edge of this section bordered the land Gaisford had previously tried to buy from Selwyn, and that was connected with the supposed existence of a rich vein of copper. He wondered if Gaisford was speculating that it ran through to Penorna land as well?

'I'll give you a good price for it. Three hundred.'

John looked thoughtful. His mind was racing. That certainly was a good price. It confirmed that what he suspected was true. There was more to this than acquiring more grazing. 'I don't know, Mr Gaisford,' he replied. 'I'm not sure that I really want to sell any land. You see, my uncle left the estate to me and I'm sure he would want me to keep it intact. Did you, by any chance, offer to buy that land from him?'

'No, I did not. I did not have the land to the north in Gerard's day. It has been a recent acquisition.'

'I am flattered by your offer but I don't really think so.'

Miles's lips tightened in a sharp line. He did not like to be beaten. 'Three hundred and fifty.'

'No, Mr Gaisford, and please don't offer more, it will be a waste of time. I am adamant – I won't sell.'

'A great pity. What about a partnership then?'

'Partnership? Just to run more sheep? Come, Mr Gaisford, that seems an unlikely idea.'

'All right, Mr Mitchell, I'll be honest with you but you can't blame me for trying. I illegally had a survey done. It shows signs of a rich vein of copper running from my land, through Mr Westbury's and into yours. The three of us could form a partnership to exploit our joint assets. Developing together could substantially reduce our costs.'

John's lips tightened. 'May I remind you that by carrying out any survey on my land you were breaking the law. I could take you to court over this.'

'But you won't. It would be no advantage to you to do so, and would only bring down antagonism towards you from many of the local gentry if you sullied the Gaisford name. So you have a chance of making a fortune.'

'Have you approached Mr Westbury?' he asked tersely.

'Some time ago. He wasn't interested but now you are involved he might change his mind. We will . . .'

'Don't presume,' John cut in roughly. He stood up and fixed his gaze on Miles. 'I have no intention of selling land to you, nor will I ever go into partnership with you. I don't think that would be as straightforward as you try to make out. You endeavoured to get me to sell on the pretext of running sheep, hoping I'd fall for it and you would get a much better deal than you were prepared to pay for. Any dealings I have, I like to be honest and above board.'

Miles's lips tightened. His face began to colour from the neck up. 'You damned whippersnapper! How dare you speak to me like that?'

'I speak to people how I find them.'

'Why, you . . .' Miles's face was a mask of fury.

'Good day to you,' John cut in and strode towards the door.

'Jeremy! Jeremy! Get yourself in here!' Miles's shouts reverberated round the room. 'Jeremy!'

The door was flung open just as John reached it. He did not stop but strode past an amazed Jeremy.

'Throw him out! Throw him out! Get rid of that insulting cur!'

Unsure what to do, Jeremy's step faltered. Should he do as he was bidden or go to his father and try to calm him? Alarm gripped him. He was shocked to see his father's face turning purple with rage. 'He's going, Father. Calm yourself.'

'He wants horse whipping!'

Jeremy heard the front door crash shut behind John.

'He's gone. He's out of the house. Just calm down. It's not good for you to get so worked up.'

'Worked up! Worked up! You weren't here. You didn't hear what he said. As good as called me a cheat. Me! Miles Gaisford! How dare he insult me? And I offered him a fortune, too. Ungrateful runt turned me down and insulted me while he did it.'

'You want me to act on that?'

'Act on it? Do you have to ask? Gather your wits about you. That man insulted a Gaisford. Insult one and you insult us all. You hear that?' Miles's voice had risen with fury. His hands and arms were shaking. 'If I'd been younger I'd have thrashed him within an inch of his life.' The words started to come spasmodically. 'I . . . would . . . have taught . . . him . . . a . . . le . . . sson.'

Alarm struck Jeremy with the stark realisation that something was dreadfully wrong.

'I . . . I . . . w . . . would . . . I . . .'

'I know, Father.' He was on his knees, trying to pacify him.

His father stared at him as if he didn't know him. Then he clutched at his chest and fell forward and would have fallen out of the chair if Jeremy hadn't been there.

'Help! Help!' Jeremy's shout echoed beyond the door.

Two manservants burst into the room. They sized up the situation in a moment and were quickly helping Jeremy.

'Better get him upstairs.'

The commotion brought others hurrying to the scene. Rowena, after the initial shock of seeing her husband hardly able to hold his head up, took charge.

'Jeremy, send a rider for the doctor and you'd better send news to Charles and Logan also.'

He ran from the room.

'Hester,' Rowena went on to her daughter-in-law, 'see that the house servants go on with their duties, reassure them that nothing else can be done until the doctor arrives. Inform the governess and see that Luke's all right. No need to tell him what has happened.'

She supervised the servants carrying Miles to his bedroom. As they laid him gently on the bed he groaned and opened his eyes.

'What? What?' the words spluttered their way out. His eyes moved as if he was trying to recognise his surroundings.

'Lie quiet,' Rowena soothed. Satisfied that they could do no more, she signalled the servants to leave the room. She turned back to her husband, who had closed his eyes again, and ran her fingertips gently across his forehead. She felt a little relief when she saw Miles respond with the faintest of smiles for a brief moment. She pulled a chair close to him and sat watching him closely. His breathing was shallow but had settled into a regular rhythm for which she was thankful.

A few minutes later an anxious-looking Jeremy hurried into the room. His mother signalled him to be quiet. He came to stand beside her and placed one hand on her shoulder.

'How is he?'

'Quiet and stable,' she whispered. 'We'll let him be still until the doctor comes.'

It was an hour before he arrived, having been out on another call that had taken him to a remote part of the county. In that hour Miles had remained peaceful, though not responding to any questions from his family. Hester had assured Rowena that the household was operating as near normally as was possible, though a tense atmosphere and concern permeated it. Charles and Logan, accompanied by their wives, had arrived by now to see their father and were perturbed by his inability to show any sign of knowing they were by his bedside.

Still anxious to know the full story of what had happened, Rowena noticed her eldest son signal to his brothers and saw them follow him from the room. She left her daughters-in-law with her husband and hurried after her sons.

Coming on to the landing, she saw them striding purposefully towards the staircase. There was something about their attitude she did not like.

'Wait!' The command came from her like a whiplash.

All three stopped as one and swung round to face their stern-faced mother.

'Drawing room,' she ordered, and swept past them on to the staircase.

They eyed each other but each knew they dared not defy a direct order.

Rowena stood imperiously in the centre of the room, facing the door. 'You seemed to be busy about something,' she said coldly as the door closed.

'Jeremy wanted to tell us some news,' replied Charles lamely.

'I suspect it was to do with what happened to your father and I think he had already dropped a hint to you as soon as you arrived.' She eyed her eldest son. 'Jeremy, you were there. I too want to know what happened.'

'It was that bastard John Mitchell!' he replied with all the venom he could master.

Rowena, knowing his short temper, stared coldly at him. 'That tells me nothing.' Her icy words forced him to get the better of his rage.

'There was a dispute.'

'Explain,' she snapped, irritated by his fencing. 'And don't try to fob me off. I'll know if you are.'

He knew only too well that she would. None of them had ever been able to deceive their mother. He went on to tell them all exactly what had happened when Mitchell visited Senewey at Miles's request.

'So you see, Mitchell is to blame. If he had agreed to a proposition which was highly beneficial to him this would never have happened. He deserves to be taught a lesson.'

Charles and Logan muttered their approval.

Rowena, who had shown no reaction throughout this story, embraced her three sons with a gaze that was cold and penetrating. 'You will do nothing!' The words came with a deliberate emphasis that also indicated there would be dire consequences if they were disobeyed.

Though he had registered that, Jeremy had to voice a protest. 'Mother, our father is lying up there and we don't as yet know whether he will live or die or remain helpless. We *have* to do something about it.'

'Yes, you have, and that is support him, help in his recovery, and don't upset him by any stupid actions you will term revenge.'

'But Father raged against Mitchell!'

'Maybe, but I know your father. It would be a spur-of-the-moment temper. Miles is no hot head. How do you think he gets his way in the county? No, you *don't* use physical means and you *don't* do anything that will jeopardise your father's recovery. That is of paramount importance to us all. Don't any of you forget it!'

Chapter Seven

John was discussing the proposed changes to the garden at the front of the house with his head gardener when their attention was drawn by the sound of an approaching horse. A few moments later the rider appeared and John immediately recognised Selwyn.

'We'll continue this discussion later,' he said.

'Certainly, sir,' the gardener replied and headed for his greenhouse.

John waited for his friend. 'Good morning, Selwyn,' he greeted him brightly as the horse was brought to a standstill.

'Morning, John,' returned Selwyn, swinging out of the saddle. 'Have you heard about Miles Gaisford?' he added as he secured his horse to a rail set to one side for this purpose.

'Heard what?'

'He collapsed yesterday. From what I've heard it sounds serious.'

'What? But I was with him only then.'

'How did you find him?'

'He wasn't well, propped up in an armchair, looking pale, but he had all his wits about him. Dismissed his illness as nothing.' John had noted a questioning look come over his friend's face and knew he was expecting an explanation as to why he'd been at Senewey. 'Miles had summoned me.'

'Summoned you?' Selwyn's curiosity was heightened even more by this revelation.

'Yes. He sent Jeremy on purpose to ask me. I was on my way to my mine at the time but Jeremy was adamant I should go to see his father immediately. Seemed important so I went.'

'And was it?' prompted Selwyn.

'Well, depends how you look at it. Miles wanted to buy some land from me. I was thankful you had forewarned me about the propositions he made to you. After an illegal survey he believes the land contains a rich vein of copper. He got rather het up when I refused to sell and riled at me. You could even say I was verbally thrown out of the house with threats being hurled after me.'

Selwyn pulled a face. 'Miles has a temper but he's good at keeping it under control, though there's no mistaking his displeasure when he has not got his way. But he'll do things subtly to try to get what he wants. Now Jeremy, he'll charge in without thinking . . . but his father and mother generally keep him on a tight rein. If they've made an order he'll very rarely defy them unless he thinks they won't get to know.'

John frowned in concern. 'I hope his altercation with me did not bring a worsening of his condition. I think I'd better go and see how he is. Will you come with me?'

'Of course! He is my neighbour and it is only proper to show concern.'

Recognising the two men as near neighbours of the Gaisfords, the footman who had answered the door met their request to see Mrs Gaisford by showing them into the small reception room close to the front door.

'I will let the mistress know you are here,' he said politely.

A few minutes later, when they heard the door open, both men turned from the paintings they were examining.

'Gentlemen,' Rowena greeted them as she came into the room, allowing the door to swing shut behind her. She held herself erect, perfectly in control of herself and the situation.

'Mrs Gaisford.' They both spoke together. Selwyn glanced at John, acknowledging him as their spokesman.

'We are terribly sorry to hear of your husband's illness. We hope it is nothing serious.'

'His collapse caused us all alarm and anxiety but I am pleased to say that the doctor has diagnosed nothing serious. However, he will require a lot of rest and in future will have to curtail some of his activities. He must not become as angry as he did yesterday. You may remember him becoming so, Mr Mitchell?' She turned cold, questioning eyes on John.

'I do, Mrs Gaisford, and am sorry if our conversation was to blame for what happened.'

She gave a little shrug of her shoulders. 'Who can tell?'

'Indeed,' he agreed, though he knew Jeremy would fully have reported his meeting with her husband and no doubt embellished certain aspects of it. 'Business propositions are not worth getting worked up about.'

'I agree. Mr Gaisford generally does not do so. I can only assume that being indisposed as he was at the time did not help.' As if that was the end of the matter she added, 'I will give him your commiserations.'

John bowed his acknowledgement as Selwyn said, 'And our good wishes for his speedy recovery.'

'Thank you, gentlemen.' She went to the door.

The two men followed and in a matter of moments were riding away from Senewey.

'Did you see Jeremy watching us from the window?' asked Selwyn as they put their horses to a trot.

'I did. I could feel the ice in his stare from that distance.'

'Then beware. He'll blame you for what happened to Miles, particularly if he doesn't make a full recovery. Their father and mother may dominate the Gaisford sons but they can't always be in control of them. The three of them, especially Jeremy, are not averse to using underhand methods that can't be traced back. Watch yourself, John. This dispute has become more than just a suggested land purchase.'

John heeded his friend's words but when nothing untoward happened over the next three weeks he began to lower his guard, especially when word got round that Miles Gaisford was up and about again. Though he would never be the same man, his wiry stamina and natural determination had stood him in good stead. His mind and speech were not impaired and he was, therefore, still able to rule his family with the same authority he had always done. So it was that he curbed Jeremy when his son came to him with the opinion that John Mitchell should be taught a lesson for what he had done.

'Raise one finger against him and you'll have me to answer to! There are other ways of going about this that will not antagonise members of our community.'

Fuming at this rebuff, the second he had received from his father where John Mitchell was concerned, Jeremy nursed his grudge in private. Things would certainly be different when he took over the Senewey Estate, something he had seen coming sooner than expected until his father made an unwelcome recovery.

A month had gone by when, one evening, Jeremy swung out of the saddle at the Waning Moon, a wayside inn used by travellers on the northern edge of the Senewey Estate. Two other horses were tethered to the rail. He eyed them but did not recognise them. Jeremy pushed open the heavy oak door, lowered his head under the lintel, and stepped inside. The flagged floor was uneven and strewn here and there with grasses culled from the edge of the neighbouring moor. A rough wooden counter stretched the full length of one wall. Eight rickety oak tables of varying sizes occupied most of the floor space without crowding it. Sitting at two of them were eight unsavoury-looking characters who glanced in Jeremy's direction when he came in but then returned their attention to their tankards. His gaze swept over them as he went to the bar. He was satisfied with what he saw. The landlord, of ample girth and florid features, acknowledged him without mentioning his name, something Jeremy had banned him from doing, especially if there were strangers in the inn.

'Ale,' he said, fishing a coin from his pocket. He glanced at the two men leaning on the counter nursing their tankards. He did not know them. No doubt they were the owners of the horses he had noted outside.

One of them straightened, glanced at him, nodded and made a gruff, 'Good evening.'

Jeremy acknowledged it. He did not want to get involved in a conversation but to ignore them completely would only draw attention to himself. 'Strangers in these parts?' he added, making his statement a question.

'Indeed we are and glad to find this inn. We did not want to attempt the moor at night. Landlord has obligingly agreed to give us a room for the night. We'll continue our journey to St Just in the morning.'

'A wise move,' agreed Jeremy. 'There are treacherous places on the moor and if you don't know them you could be in trouble.' Though he made his tone amiable he was cursing to himself. He had banked on there being no strangers at the Waning Moon tonight. However, that was not an insurmountable problem so long as he was not seen to be associated with any of the other occupants of the room. A little more care must be taken and he knew that the plans he had instigated for any such situation would be observed.

Ten minutes later, after a desultory conversation that carried no significant information, one of the strangers stretched and said, 'We'll stable our horses, landlord, and then away to bed. We've had a tiring day.'

'No need to bother with your horses, Toby will see to them.' Without giving the strangers time to countermand this idea the landlord opened a door behind the counter and shouted, 'Toby!'

A few moments later a lad of about fifteen bustled into the room. 'Yes, Pa?'

'Stable these gentlemen's horses.'

'Yes, Pa.'

'Mind you give 'em a good rub down and feed 'em.'

The lad was gone at that. The landlord eyed the two men. 'I'll take you up now, if you wish.'

One of them yawned. 'Seems I'm ready.'

The landlord picked up an oil lamp and lit it from one of the candles that were burning on the counter. 'Follow me.'

The two men made their goodnights to all in the room and received a few nods in return while Jeremy put his into words.

As the door closed behind the strangers the men sitting at the tables turned their attention to Jeremy. They knew if Mr Jeremy Gaisford was here something was afoot – he wanted some of them for a job. One of them started to say something but he raised a hand, warning them to say nothing until he did. He listened intently to the footsteps on the stairs and crossing the floor overhead. He followed their progress, and was satisfied that the landlord was taking the men to rooms as far from the bar as possible. He grunted with satisfaction to himself. No one spoke until the landlord reappeared.

Jeremy eyed him. 'Settled?'

'Aye, they soon will be. I took 'em a glass of whisky each as a nightcap. Drop of something in it that'll make 'em sleep like babes 'til morning.'

'Good. Then fill up the tankards all round,' said Jeremy.

That brought good-humoured murmurs from all the men. He dragged over a chair to join them.

'I'll only need Davey and Con for this one,' he said, 'so the rest of you drink up and get off home.'

The other six knew better than to show their discontent for they had all been in the same position as Davey and Con at some time or other and knew their turn would come. They also knew that Jeremy preferred only the persons involved in a plan and the landlord to know what was going on; the landlord because he was the lynchpin, the Waning Moon being the place where messages could be left and sent.

Once the room was clear except for the landlord, Davey, Con and himself, Jeremy came straight to the point. 'I want John Mitchell roughing up.'

Davey and Con grinned at each other. This was just up their street and they would be well paid.

'Don't overdo it. I just want him taught a lesson that'll make him reflect. Make it look like robbery.'

'When?' asked Con.

'Any time, but you may want to study his movements before you proceed.'

Both men nodded. 'Leave it to us.'

Mitchell must be taught a lesson for what had happened to his father. Obtaining the land that could yield a good vein of copper could come later. For the present, revenge was all that mattered to Jeremy.

For three weeks Davey and Con kept John Mitchell's movements under scrutiny until it emerged that he visited his mine every Tuesday, his tenants in Sandannack on Wednesday, and those in outlying cottages and farmsteads on Thursday. He always walked to the first two, but because of the greater distance involved he rode to the others.

'It's misty,' commented Eliza, looking out of their bedroom window before going down to breakfast one Wednesday in early September. 'Will you still go to Sandannack?'

John, pulling on his jacket, came to stand beside her. He observed the weather before he replied. 'It looks thin; the sun will soon burn it up. It could turn out to be a pleasant walk.'

They went down to breakfast together, calling to see if Dorinda had Abigail ready to accompany them.

Unknown to them two men, pulling their jackets tighter against the rolling, chilling mist, were moving close to the house.

Con shivered and fished a bottle from his pocket, taking a swig. He smacked his lips as the whisky burned its way down. 'That's better,' he said and thrust the bottle at Davey who was munching a sandwich. He swallowed and then put the bottle to his own lips.

'Think he'll go today?' asked Con.

'Sure. This fog may delay him but it ain't going to last.'

'Then let's get it over with.'

Davey nodded as he took another bite at his bread. 'Aye, and then we can have more comfortable breakfasts.'

An hour later, with the sun winning its contest with the mist, Con gave the dozing Davey a sharp dig in the ribs. He was immediately awake, stifling a protesting grunt when he saw John Mitchell emerge from the house, pause on the veranda to observe the sky, kiss his wife and walk down the steps and along the drive.

The two men waited until Mrs Mitchell returned inside which she did when her husband was lost to sight round a curve in the drive. From previous weeks they knew which direction their quarry would take when he reached the end and so set off through the tree-covered ground to their right to be in position to pick John up on his walk to Sandannack.

'When are we going to take him?' asked Con.

'In the hollow, we decided, but on his way back.'

'Why not as he's going?'

'He'll be missed sooner if he doesn't arrive in Sandannack.'

'Think anyone there will bother?'

'They might. I hear he's liked in the village. Someone might be curious.'

Con grunted and nodded. He always let Davey take the lead.

Reaching the first house, they saw John start his rounds. When they were satisfied that he was following the usual pattern they headed for the inn, a small establishment on which, with John's financial support, repairs were being carried out. They called for some ale and took a corner seat where they spent time over their drink. Towards noon, after a second tankard of ale, they left the inn and strolled a mile out of the village to a small hillock that would keep them from view of anyone on the road they knew that Mitchell would take to return home. The day had turned out warm so, with a pie and some apples which they had brought with them, they lay down and satisfied their hunger.

Only three people drew their attention until, shortly before three o'clock, footsteps were heard crunching on the stony track. Their intended victim. They exchanged glances and nods, indicating that each knew what their next move should be. They waited until John had passed from sight and then rose to their feet. They cut away from the track into a little gully that they knew would obscure their presence. Moving swiftly to out-run John, they circled back towards the track. Two miles from the village it dipped into a hollow, each side of which was strewn with large boulders that had fallen from an outcrop of rock. Neither man spoke but Davey indicated that they should take up the positions he had indicated when planning their strategy. He would be on John's right when he entered the hollow and Con on his left; boulders would hide both men.

The air was mild and still and John's footsteps were unmistakable as he approached the hollow. His spirits were high. It had been a good day for him and it had been made special when several of his tenants expressed their gratitude for the repairs he was having done to their houses before winter. Satisfied tenants made good workers and he knew he would see their appreciation reflected in their work. His mind was far away when suddenly a broad-shouldered man confronted him. He had a neckerchief tied tightly around the lower half of his face and was brandishing a cudgel. The abrupt appearance of the man from behind a boulder startled John. His arms automatically came up to defend his face but it was the blow from behind that pitched him to the ground.

'Perfect,' muttered Con who had delivered the blow.

'Aye, now let's give him something to remember,' snarled Davey. He felt pleasure as he drove his foot hard into John's midriff.

'Hold it,' said Davey sharply, stopping Con who was stamping on John's thighs. 'Let's see if he has any money. It has to look like robbery.'

'Aye.' Con grinned at the thought of lining his pockets. He dropped to his knees and started rifling through John's pockets. He found some loose change and then, with a cry of triumph, held up a small leather pouch drawn tight by a leather throng. He pulled it open and spilled ten sovereigns into his palm. 'Look at these!' he yelled, springing to his feet.

Davey's eyes brightened when he saw them. 'Five for you and five for me,' he whooped and grabbed his share. Then he froze. 'Listen!' His fierce intonation and changed expression froze Con.

'What?' he whispered, seeing alarm come to Davey's eyes.

'A horse!' he said and then, realising the hoof beats were coming from the direction of the village, added, 'A rider! Let's get out of here!' He started running for the slope. Breathing heavily, the two men reached the top, flung themselves over the ridge, lay flat and twisted round so that they could look down into the hollow.

The hoof beats grew louder. When the track dipped into the hollow the rider came into view.

'A girl,' hissed Con, seeing a young lady riding side-saddle at a steady trot. 'Let's take her!'

Davey gripped his arm firmly. 'No! Do that and we'll be finished! Jeremy Gaisford will find out and then we'll be done for. No more jobs and no more money.' He knew that thought would hold Con in check. 'Lie still and watch.'

Alarm and apprehension shot through Lydia when she saw a huddled figure on the ground as she dipped into the hollow. Automatically she pulled her horse to a halt and looked anxiously around. This was a perfect place to be waylaid and footpads had been known to set one of their number lying prone as a decoy. She saw no sign of anyone else but there were plenty of hiding places behind the boulders. She sat still for a few moments, casting cautious glances around her and letting her eyes stray back to the figure lying face down on the ground. She could detect no movement. Maybe whoever it was was dead. Alarm and horror gripped her.

Then she chided herself for the way in which she was behaving. If this person was hurt he needed attention. She inched her horse forward, her eyes on the figure but alert for any movement to left or right. She drew her mount to a halt and looked down at the man, his face hidden. This was no decoy; there was an ugly gash in the back of his head and blood had made a stain in the dust and soil. She slid quickly to the ground and dropped to her knees. She gripped his shoulders and turned the man over. There were bruises on both cheeks, one eye was puffing and there was a deep cut on his forehead. But she recognised him at once.

'Mr Mitchell!' Alarm filled her when she saw who it was. What could she do? What should she do? Get help, but where? Ride back to the village? But that would mean leaving him here; she could not do that. Ride to Trethtowan Manor? That would take longer but ... her flying thoughts were interrupted by a groan from John. She felt relief at hearing it. He was alive! 'Mr Mitchell! Mr Mitchell! Can you hear me?' His eyes flickered. 'Oh, thank goodness!' She watched him, willing his eyes to open properly.

His eyelids fluttered and after a few moments settled and remained open. He stared towards the sky, seeming to be having difficulty in focusing his eyes, then he turned his head, winced at the pain, and looked at her. For one moment he seemed puzzled but he said, 'Miss Booth?' in a way that seemed to ask, 'What are you doing here?'

'Yes, it's me,' she replied gently. 'You are hurt. We must get you home.'

That idea pleased John but when he moved he winced and let out a cry as pain seared his side. He lay still and looked at her with querying eyes. 'What happened?' he mumbled.

'I don't know. I came across you as I was going back to Trethtowan. I would say you were attacked.'

That observation struck a chord with him. 'I was. A man confronted me but I was struck from behind, so there must have been two of them.'

'And it looks as though they did more damage than that blow on the back of the head.'

'It feels like it.'

'Maybe they would have done even more if I hadn't come along.'

'Thank goodness you did. Did you see them?'

'No. What about you?'

'Well, I saw the one who confronted me but he had a neckerchief over his face.'

Lydia was pleased that throughout these exchanges John seemed to be gaining strength. Now she ventured to make a suggestion. 'We have two options. Either I leave you here and ride for help, or we see if with my help you can get on my horse and I will take you home.'

'That's what I'll try. If you leave me here they may return and finish me off. 'Feel in my right-hand pocket, Miss Booth.'

She did as she was told. 'Nothing, Mr Mitchell.'

'Nothing? There should have been a leather pouch with ten sovereigns in it.'

'So it was robbery?'

'It looks like it.' Though John had agreed with her assessment of the motive for the attack, he privately wondered if there was a deeper reason for it, one that stemmed from Jeremy Gaisford. 'Now let's see what I can do.'

It was a struggle and very painful but with her help and his determination John got to his feet. She held him up while he steadied himself for a moment. His legs felt weak where they had been stamped on and his right side felt as if it was one massive bruise.

'I might have a problem getting on to your horse,' he said, gritting his teeth against the pain.

Lydia looked around. 'Do you think we could get you on to that slab of rock? Height might be an advantage if I bring the horse alongside you.'

'A good idea! Let's try.'

She assisted him to the rock and helped him on to it. A few minutes later, in spite of the pain and discomfort, John was successfully seated on the horse. Walking beside him, in case he needed her shoulder to steady himself, Lydia took the reins and encouraged the horse into a walking pace.

Once he had assumed as comfortable a position as possible he put the question, 'How did you come to be on this track and on your own today? It's not Thursday.'

'Mr and Mrs Westbury were taking the children to see their grandmama in Penzance and that left me free. A friend of mine has just come to Mousehole for a month, I haven't seen her for five years. She had asked me to visit. As I was free today, Mr and Mrs Westbury suggested I ride over. I was on my way back.'

'Lucky for me! I might have laid there for a long time, or else the robbers might have completed their job.'

Lydia shuddered at the thought.

'I think they probably heard your horse and left before you appeared,' said John, 'but let's talk of more pleasant things. I need my mind taking off these cuts and bruises. How is the painting coming along?'

'I am highly satisfied so far. I was going to contact you. I would like you to view what I have done so far, but I wanted to do that in the bay itself.' Lydia pulled herself up. Had that sounded too bold? 'But it will have to be put off until you recover. You cannot possibly scramble down until you are completely well again.'

'You are right, but the thought of what is to come will aid my recovery.'

Lydia's heart skipped a beat. Was there something behind that statement or was she letting her imagination run away with her?

John wondered if anything lay behind the fact that she was suggesting they should meet in the bay, albeit to view her painting.

Lost in their own thoughts, they both lapsed into a charged silence.

The clatter of the hooves on the cobbles as Lydia led her horse into the stable yard at Penorna brought a groom hurrying to see who was arriving. Startled by the sight of Mr Mitchell led on a horse, he reacted quickly when Lydia said, 'Get Mrs Mitchell, there's been an accident.'

The brief message brought Eliza in a high state of concern hurrying from the house. By the time she'd reached the stable yard Lydia and another groom had helped John to the ground and were supporting him to the back door.

'John!' Eliza's voice was filled with shock at seeing the cuts and bruises on her husband's face, and the state of his clothes. 'What happened?' Her eyes flashed from him to Lydia, wondering how she came to be with her husband. She was by his side at once, taking over from the groom whom she told to fetch a doctor quickly.

'I was attacked,' John replied, wincing as a sharp pain stabbed through his side.

'About two miles from Sandannack,' said Lydia. 'I came across him on my way back from Mousehole,' she added by way of an explanation for her presence.

John stopped in his tracks and grasped at his ribs.

Alarm coursed through Eliza. 'We'd better get you to bed.'

Each step up the broad staircase sent a pain through his ribs even though he had support on both sides. They reached the door of the bedroom.

'Thank you, Miss Booth, I'll manage from here.'

Lydia detected a touch of coldness in Eliza's voice and wondered what the other woman was thinking. She nodded and went to the stairs. She hesitated at the top and looked back down the corridor. Eliza was manoeuvring her husband through the doorway but managed to glance in Lydia's direction. Their eyes met for one brief moment but neither could identify the expression in the other's.

By the time she reached the bottom of the stairs, Lydia had come to a decision. She would wait to hear the doctor's report. If she didn't she would have an uneasy time until she learned of the extent of John's injuries. But what would Mrs Mitchell think if she did wait? But why shouldn't she? Surely it was only courteous and neighbourly? Lydia sank down on to a chair opposite the stairs.

She had been sitting there nearly ten minutes when a maid come into the hall and showed surprise on seeing her.

'Oh, Miss Booth,' she gasped, recognising her from her visits to see Dorinda.

'Sorry if I startled you.'

'That's all right, miss, but come and sit in the drawing room.'

'No, I'm all right here.'

'Would you like a cup of tea, miss? You look pale. From what I hear it must have been a terrible shock for you to find Mr Mitchell.'

'It was. I would love a cup of tea, if that would be all right?'

'I'm sure Mrs Mitchell would approve.'

The girl hurried away, leaving Lydia marvelling at how quickly gossip circulated among servants. The girl could only have known about Lydia's finding John from the remark she'd made in the presence of the groom as they were helping him into the house.

Twenty minutes later she was still sitting there but had finished two cups of tea from the teapot when she heard a door open and close upstairs and footsteps approach the top of the stairs. She saw Mrs Mitchell appear. Her step faltered for a moment when she glanced down and saw Lydia.

Eliza glided swiftly down the staircase, noting the tray set on a small table beside her. Reaching the hall she said, 'Miss Booth, I am so sorry. Forgive my bad manners. I should have ordered tea myself and told you to go to the drawing room, but I hope you will understand the distress I felt on seeing my husband in that state.'

Though there was every indication of friendliness, Lydia felt the explanation was not as warm as it should have been. 'There is nothing to reproach yourself for, Mrs Mitchell. I hope you don't mind my waiting? I was anxious to hear about Mr Mitchell's condition.'

'He has some terrible bruising on his body and legs, but how serious it is we won't know until the doctor has been. Do you want to wait until then?'

'If that is all right with you?'

'Of course.' Eliza felt she could do nothing but agree. 'It might be a good idea. You will be able to carry a full account to Mr and Mrs Westbury.' Besides, she thought, it will give me a chance to learn how exactly you came to find him. 'Do let us go to the drawing room. Mr Mitchell has settled and had drifted into sleep when I left him. We can only await the doctor.' She led the way into the room and when they were seated comfortably began: 'From the few words my husband spoke it seems it was lucky that you came along or his beating might have been worse, even fatal. He thinks you disturbed the robbers.'

'I am not sure about that, Mrs Mitchell. There was no one to be seen when I arrived and saw him lying on the track. I did not even know who it was until I turned him over. He was lying face down. It may well be true that my horse alerted them to my approach and they made off, otherwise I suppose they would have hidden your husband behind some boulders.'

'It sounds as though they had chosen their place well. Thank goodness you did disturb them! My husband may not have been found for days if they had concealed their handiwork. How fortuitous that you came along. You were alone?'

Realising that Mrs Mitchell thought it strange that she should be riding alone Lydia quickly offered her explanation.

She had just finished that when there was a knock on the door and a maid entered the rom.

'The doctor is here, ma'am.'

Eliza was on her feet immediately. Seeing Lydia began to rise also, she said as she headed for the door, 'Wait here, Miss Booth. I'll let you know the result of the examination as soon as the doctor has made it.' Then she was gone. Lydia sank back on her chair, reproved. Was Mrs Mitchell harbouring suspicions? Did she really believe that Lydia had been visiting a friend in Mousehole, or did she think that she was on her way to an assignation with John? Lydia pulled herself up sharply. This was purely the work of her own vivid imagining, surely?

How long she battled with these thoughts and others like them she did not know but they were banished quickly when the door opened and Mrs Mitchell walked back in. Lydia immediately jumped to her feet.

'It is not as bad as we feared, Miss Booth. There is a lot of bruising, especially around the ribs, but none are broken. It is the same with his legs. He'll have some pain for a little while but should be up in two days. He'll have to take things steadily for a while until the bruising and aches disappear. Though it is a bad gash on the head, the doctor thinks there is no concussion. The black eye and facial cuts will leave no scars.'

With every word Lydia felt more relief. She tried to control the tremor in her voice as she said, 'I'm so relieved. I will inform Mr and Mrs Westbury.'

'Thank you, Miss Booth.'

Eliza escorted Lydia to her horse and as she rode away stood watching her thoughtfully.

Was that young lady's story about being on her way back from Mousehole true? She could have chosen another route to Trethtowan Manor. She was attractive, too, something John had surely noticed. He had been very keen on her doing a painting . . .

Eliza, deep in thought, walked slowly back into the house.

Chapter Eight

'It's a pleasant morning,' said John, eyeing the sky as he and Eliza strolled on to the terrace after breakfast. 'I'll take a turn in the garden.'

'Are you sure?' she asked with concern, though she was pleased he wanted to make the effort. 'It's only ten days, John.'

'I feel a lot better.' He had become impatient with his slow recovery and this morning the aches and pains were so much less. 'I must try sometime. Walk with me?'

'Of course! We'll get our coats.' She turned to the door and he followed her. His request struck a chord with her. He wants me with him. I should never have harboured suspicions. It was only natural he should mention how Miss Booth helped him, and there has been nothing else to deepen my unfounded doubts.

'Had enough, John?' she asked after half an hour, detecting that even at this leisurely pace her husband's steps had slowed.

'I think so, but it's been very pleasant. I'll try to venture a little further every day.'

A week later he announced, 'I'll walk over to Trethtowan and have a chat with Selwyn today.'

'You do that. It will be a change for you.'

Though Selwyn and Harriet had visited John, the two men had never had the opportunity to talk privately about the attack and John was eager to compare notes with his friend.

'Ah, my dear John, it is good to see you've managed to walk this far,' Selwyn greeted him with great delight. 'How are you feeling?'

'Well,' replied John.

'Come inside, sit down,' Selwyn urged, considerate for his welfare.

'May we sit outside? It's such a pleasant September day.'

'Of course.' He started towards the seat on the canopied terrace that stretched the full width of the house. 'Drink?'

'Chocolate would be fortifying.'

'Certainly. I'll be back in a moment.' Selwyn hurried inside and returned in a few minutes accompanied by his wife.

'How good to see you here,' greeted Harriet with a broad welcoming smile. 'Don't get up. I hope you haven't tired yourself, walking this far?'

'No. I've been gradually working up to it. Today when I woke up I felt so much better, and here I am.'

The three friends relaxed in each other's company and chatted amiably over their chocolate.

When she had finished hers, Harriet rose from the seat. 'I'm sure you men would like to talk on your own. If you'll excuse me, I have some letters I must write to be ready for collection tomorrow.'

The two men got to their feet.

'Will you dine with us before you set off home, John?' Harriet asked. 'We have some fine cold beef.'

'That is kind of you and I appreciate being asked but I told Eliza I would not stay.'

'Very well. Why don't both of you come the day after tomorrow, about this time?'

'I'm sure Eliza would like that.'

'We'll see you then.'

When she had gone the two men settled back on their seats.

'Selwyn, I have never heard any details of the attack on you, but in the light of what happened to me recently, do you mind talking about it?'

'Of course not! I thought it was in the past and since there has not been a recurrence I was inclined to forget it. Now, after your experience, we should probably exchange notes.'

'You said you suspected the Gaisfords might be behind it, especially as it followed an offer they had made to buy some land from you that you turned down?'

'Yes, but I had no direct evidence to connect them with the attack.'

'But doesn't it seem strange the attack on me should follow a similar pattern? I had just turned down Miles Gaisford's offer to buy my land.'

Selwyn frowned. 'I did not realise it was such a close similarity. I thought the Gaisfords were blaming you for Miles's seizure because there'd been an exchange of words that grew heated. I'd no idea what the subject was.'

'My refusal to sell may well have sparked Miles's upset,' John commented.

'It's possible,' Selwyn agreed gravely.

'Tell me, did you see your assailants?' John asked.

'I saw one but could not recognise him again, his face was covered. While he confronted me I was struck from behind so there must have been two of them.'

'Exactly what happened to me,' John confirmed, a touch of excitement in his voice.

'So you are thinking they must have been the same two men?'

'It seems more than likely.'

'But you can't link them with the Gaisfords?'

'No. And even if I were able to confront them, they would deny it.'

'Most certainly, and the Gaisfords would then see to it that your name was blackened in the county. Accusing someone without proof does not go down well hereabouts.'

John's lips tightened in exasperation.

Selwyn saw it and said, 'Don't do anything rash, it's not worth it. They are a powerful family. But if you quietly take notice of what happened to you, though I know you won't like doing that, relations with the Gaisfords may move into calmer waters, like they did with me. Oh, they continued to make offers to buy the land but they eventually saw I was determined not to sell. I have no doubt they will approach you again, more than once. If you weaken, they will eventually put more pressure on me to sell. They want to link our land with theirs.'

'Selwyn, you have my firm assurance that I will not sell.' His friend's firm delivery left Selwyn in no doubt that he meant what he said. 'Now, I think I had better be going.' John rose to his feet. 'Thank you for your hospitality.'

'You are welcome any time. I'll see you the day after tomorrow.'

Before John had time to move James and Juliana raced round the corner in a game of chase. They were followed by Lydia, who was laughing joyously at something that had gone on before. She pulled up when she saw the two gentlemen and her merriment died away. The children ran to their father.

John and Selwyn laughed with them as they circled about shouting, 'Hello, Mr Mitchell! Hello, Mr Mitchell!'

'Oh, I'm sorry,' Lydia gasped. 'Children, calm down, calm down!'

'It's all right, Miss Booth,' said Selwyn. 'It's good to see them happy and enjoying themselves.'

'Good day, Miss Booth.' John's eyes met hers.

'Good day, Mr Mitchell,' she replied, embarrassed that she should have been caught with such a dishevelled appearance after her run with the children. 'How are you? I hope fully recovered from your ordeal?'

'I am, Miss Booth, and it is very remiss of me not to have thanked you myself before now for all that you did for me that day.'

'It was only what anybody would have done, Mr Mitchell.'

'Perhaps, but you did it with such care.'

Lydia blushed and could make no answer. Instead she turned her attention to the children. 'James, Juliana, come on, you've some art work to do.'

While James pulled a face and Juliana shouted, 'Oh good, good!' Lydia ushered them into the house, pausing at the door only long enough to look back at John and say, 'I trust Mrs Mitchell is in good health?'

'She is, thank you, Miss Booth.'

With that she was gone, but the look she had given him lingered in his mind as he walked home.

Two mornings later when John and Eliza were about to leave for Trethtowan, a letter was delivered to them.

'It's from Martha,' said John, recognising the writing. He broke the wax seal that held the paper and unfolded it. He smiled as he said, 'She's got her money's worth.' He held up the paper for Eliza to see the sheet cross-covered with close writing which carried the narrative back between the original lines.

'Read it to me,' said Eliza, who was choosing which bonnet she should wear for the walk to the Westburys, for they had decided that on such a pleasant day the exercise would do them both good.

Martha, in the first part of the letter, merely gave them news of herself and happenings in Whitby. Then their attention was caught and held as John read: '"And now I come to more serious things. Some problems have arisen within the business and I would value John's opinion on them. I do not want to set them down on paper and so would be grateful if he could visit me here. I do not wish to cause alarm, nor for him to set out immediately. The problem can wait certainly a week or two, but it could be advantageous for it to be solved within four weeks."'

John stopped reading and then added, 'That seems to be it. Then she send her felicitations to you and Abigail and trusts that we are all in good health.'

'You must go,' said Eliza without hesitation. 'It must be something important if Martha requires your assistance. When will you go?'

Let's talk about that on the way to Trethtowan.'

Although Eliza would have preferred him to go by coach because of the time of year he decided to travel north on horseback to make use of the freedom. As there were some matters that needed his attention at the mine and in Sandannack, which could not be left until his return from Whitby, he would leave in four days' time.

When the Westburys were informed of his intended visit to Yorkshire they reassured John that they would make sure all was well with Eliza in his absence, even going so far as offering her a place with them until his return. This she declined, thinking the upheaval too much apart from which, with Abigail, Dorinda, and all the servants, she certainly would not be alone.

'You will look after Mama for me, won't you?' asked John, squatting on his haunches as he took hold of his daughter's hands.

'Of course I will, Papa.' Abigail looked serious as she made her vow. 'How long will you be away?'

'I don't know. It depends on what your Aunt Martha wants, but I'll be back as soon as possible. Give me a hug to remember you by.'

Abigail flung her arms round her father's neck and hugged him tight. He kissed her on the cheek and, as she released her hold, straightened up and looked with loving eyes at his wife. 'You are sure you'll be all right?'

'Of course,' Eliza replied firmly. 'Don't worry about us. You concentrate on your mission. I hope the problem is easily solved. Give Martha our love, and hurry back.'

'I will.' He kissed her and would have lingered but she was more practical.

'Off with you or you won't reach your planned first stop before night fall.'

He swung into the saddle; Eliza and Abigail accompanied him out of the stable yard then went on to the terrace from where they watched until they returned his wave before he rode out of sight.

'Jeremy, a word after breakfast.'

He knew that was a summons and immediately feared a reprimand. But since Miles's recovery some of the snap had gone out of his criticism even though his mind and speech were still as alert as ever.

When Jeremy entered the study his father indicated a chair to him. Miles's gaze was cold and penetrating as ever.

'I may be less active than I was but I still have it all up here,' he tapped his head, 'and I have my sources of information. It came to my notice two days ago that Mr Mitchell had been robbed by two thugs a few weeks back. Had you anything to do with that?'

'No.'

Miles's eyes narrowed. He slapped the top of the desk with the palm of his hand, sending the noise ricocheting from the panelled walls. 'Don't lie to me! I can read you like a book.' Jeremy flinched under the whiplash of his father's tongue.

'Mitchell had to be taught a lesson for what happened to you!'

'He had not! I take some of the blame for your over-reaction on myself. I ranted and raved that day ... I shouldn't have done, but I was ill and hadn't all my wits about me at the time. I've told you before, there are ways and means other than violence to attain our objectives.' He paused to let the significance of his words sink in. Jeremy nodded, looking contrite. 'Now, it has also come to my notice that Mr Mitchell has gone to Whitby.'

'For good?' Jeremy was always surprised by his father's omniscience and wondered how he got to know such things.

'No, a visit to his sister.' Miles gave a little smile at the fact that he knew something that had escaped his son. 'You wonder how I know? When will you learn to quiz servants in a subtle way? They love to tittle-tattle about their employers and are only too ready to air their knowledge to their peers from other estates. You learn a lot that way. Not all of it's useful but sometimes one little fact can be.'

'And what do you make of the fact that Mitchell has gone north?' queried Jeremy.

'We made him a tempting offer for that section of land; let us make an even more tempting one to his wife in his absence.'

'You think she might sell without her husband's knowledge?' Jeremy showed his surprise.

'Few women will turn away from the prospect of money and jewellery.'

'What exactly have you in mind?'

'I'll get your mother to set up a little supper party for three with Mrs Mitchell as our honoured guest, a kindly gesture because her husband is away.'

Jeremy smiled. He remembered how his father had concluded the purchase of some land along the coast that included a useful haven for small vessels in a similar manner. 'You are a wily old bird.'

'I've told you before, there are more ways than one.'

'But what if she doesn't bite?'

'Then I will put another plan into action. In case that has to be implemented I want you now subtly to find out the situation at Mitchell's copper mine. Are they likely to employ more men? How is production? Any chance of opening up new workings? Whatever you can find that might be useful. I must have such facts as soon as possible so that if Mrs Mitchell refuses to act without her husband, my second plan will be in place when I judge the time to be right.'

'Ma'am, a rider from Senewey has just brought this.' The maid held out a silver salver on which there was a sealed sheet of paper.

Eliza took the paper as she asked, 'Is the man awaiting an answer?'

'No, ma'am.'

'Thank you.'

When the maid had left the room Eliza broke the seal and unfolded the letter to read: 'Mr and Mrs Miles Gaisford request the pleasure of your company at supper on Wednesday 3rd April at 5p.m.'

She turned the sheet over so that she could check how it was addressed. She saw it bore only her name. So the Gaisfords must know that John is away, she thought. Was this purely a gesture of good will? Near neighbours being solicitous for a woman alone? She let her reasoning run. Would John approve of her accepting? Was there any good reason why she should not go ... and would she be slighting the Gaisfords if she did not?

A week later Benson drove his mistress to Senewey. Eliza was welcomed there most effusively by Rowena and Miles and quickly realised she was the only guest.

Over a glass of Madeira the Gaisfords learned that John had gone to Whitby at the request of his sister who had some queries about her business there for which she required her brother's advice. The conversation continued to flow pleasantly across many topics throughout the lavish meal taken at this time of day, as was the custom for families of such standing. Eliza was impressed and remarked upon the succulent pigeon pie and the tempting orange cheesecakes. The meal was leisurely and lasted two hours. Finally, feeling well satisfied, she accompanied her host and hostess into their elegant drawing room where the curtains had been drawn, lamps lit, and the fire raised to a warming blaze. Once they were comfortably seated and the servants had withdrawn, Miles judged it a good time to put his proposition to Eliza.

'Mrs Mitchell, you may know that some time ago I offered to buy some land from your husband?'

'Yes, I do. He would not sell.'

'That is true. I am particularly anxious to purchase that land in order to extend my northern holding.'

'But our land does not adjoin yours, Mr Gaisford, so any extension would be limited by the fact that Mr Westbury's land lies between,' Eliza pointed out.

Miles knew now that he was dealing with an astute woman. Very few wives, his own Rowena excluded, would have been as interested in their husband's land management, or indeed in any other of his economic affairs. Such things would have been left entirely to the men. But it was now obvious to him that the Mitchells had a shared interest in business. That suited him for he could now discuss the matter further; an uninterested wife would have meant any pursuit of the matter would have been useless.

'Correct, Mrs Mitchell, but if I am able to purchase your land I believe it would give Mr Westbury more incentive to sell his to me. Being able to link both pieces of land to mine would enhance my property without in any way detracting from yours. Mr Mitchell and Mr Westbury are not using that land for any specific purpose.'

'At the moment,' put in Eliza.

'Do you think Mr Mitchell has plans for it?'

'Not that I am aware of.'

'Then let me make you an offer?'

'I think that had better wait until my husband returns.'

'Do you know how long he will be away?'

'No. That depends on the nature of the help his sister requires.'

'He could be away for a considerable time?'

'It is possible.'

'If that is so it may be too late to complete the sale of the land. You see, Mrs Mitchell, I must not and cannot leave the money I am prepared to use for this purchase idle. That is not profitable. If your husband were to be absent for long I could not wait. It is a case of acting on the offer I make you now.'

'That puts me in an awkward position. There are many matters on which my husband seeks my advice and I know would allow me to act upon.' She left a thoughtful pause but it was sufficient for Rowena to interject.

'Then you and I are fortunate in our choice of husbands, Mrs Mitchell, for Mr Gaisford involves me in his affairs even more than he does our eldest son who will eventually inherit. Mr Gaisford has talked to me about his proposal, and I can tell you it is a very generous and a lucrative one for you.'

'Let me put this to you, Mrs Mitchell, and then I will say no more. I will not press you now for a decision because you will want time to consider it, but I would like an answer within the week so I can make a good start to 1786,' Miles told her.

Eliza listened very carefully to his proposition. Though he made no comment, Miles was delighted by her attentive expression. When he had finished he sat back in his chair. 'There it is for your consideration, Mrs Mitchell. We will say no more about it now. After all, this was really a social occasion. I apologise for turning to other matters.'

'That is perfectly all right, Mr Gaisford. I will think about your offer and if I consider that I should act upon it, I will do so as there will be no time to contact Mr Mitchell by letter and receive a reply in the next week.'

'I leave matters in your hands, Mrs Mitchell.'

Rowena turned the conversation to the embroidery she was doing and had purposefully left in sight so that it could become a talking point if necessary. The evening continued pleasantly and Eliza found herself seeing the Gaisfords in a more favourable light.

When she took her leave and was being helped into her out-door clothes, Miles excused himself for a moment and hurried into his study. He returned a few moments later with a small red leather box. He held it out to Eliza. 'A little memento to express our thanks for sharing a most pleasant evening with us.'

She hesitated. 'I couldn't, Mr Gaisford. It is I who should be thanking you.'

'And we accept your thanks,' put in Rowena. 'But we would like *you* to have a tangible reminder of this evening.'

'The evening itself is sufficient.'

'Please?' From Miles's expression Eliza knew he would be offended if she did not accept. She took the box and opened the hinged lid to discover a string of pearls resting on a bed of red velvet.

She gasped then looked at Miles and Rowena in amazement. 'Mr and Mrs Gaisford, this is more than kind. I really don't know what to say.' Her words trailed away as she looked down at the shining pearls again.

'Then say nothing,' said Miles quietly.

'Enjoy wearing them,' said Rowena, and patted Eliza's arm.

She sat back in the carriage as it headed for the ornate gates at the end of the long drive. 'A bribe, more like,' she muttered to herself. Then her thoughts turned to the more than gener-ous offer which was almost double that which had been made to John.

It was uppermost in her mind the next morning when she woke and continued to occupy her while she dressed. By the time she was ready to go downstairs she had resolved to consult Selwyn. After all, the Westburys had told John they were there to help her if need be while he was away, and she could forewarn Selwyn he too was likely to be approached again by Miles.

She called for Abigail and waited while Dorinda tied a ribbon in her hair, then mother and daughter went down to breakfast.

'I'm going to see Mr and Mrs Westbury this morning, do you want to come and see Juliana?'

'Oh, yes, please.' Abigail's eyes lit up. She had got on well with Juliana ever since their arrival in Cornwall and they had become firm friends. James being older had always adopted a superior attitude but Juliana had told Abigail to take no notice; that was just boys.

'You go into breakfast. I'll be there in a moment.' Eliza rang the bell that stood on a table at the bottom of the stairs. A few moments later a maid appeared and was sent to inform Benson to have the carriage ready to drive to Trethtowan Manor, after which she was to tell Dorinda that they would leave in half an hour.

Whenever these outings occurred the governess looked forward to them for it meant an exchange of gossip with her friend Lydia.

The drive was pleasant and once they were at the Trethtowan Estate the two governesses, at the instigation of Juliana and Abigail, took the girls for a walk in nearby woods.

'I hope I am not interrupting anything,' Eliza apologised when her friends had welcomed her.

'Not at all,' replied Harriet. 'We are always pleased to see you.'

'Well,' said Eliza as they walked into the house, 'I have something to tell you and I want your advice.'

'Only too pleased if we can give it,' replied Selwyn as Eliza slipped off her coat and handed it, together with her bonnet, to the maid.

'That's a beautiful string of pearls,' commented Harriet. 'I have not seen them before.'

Eliza gave a little smile. 'They are part of my story.'

'Oh?' Harriet was puzzled and eager to know more. What did they signify, and how did they figure in this advice Eliza had mentioned?

Harriet and Selwyn looked at her enquiringly once they were seated in the drawing room. They listened to her story with obvious amazement as it unfolded.

'That is an extraordinary offer,' commented Selwyn when she had finished.

'And no doubt, from what Mr Gaisford said, you'll be getting one too.'

'It will be very tempting if I do . . .'

'Don't be hasty,' his wife warned.

'A pity John isn't here,' Selwyn muttered.

'It is,' agreed Eliza, 'but we can't wait until he gets back. I say *we*,' she added quickly, 'because I think we should act together on this.'

'Quite right,' confirmed Selwyn. 'We know it's all about the possibility of finding copper on our land. And on top of his offer, I reckon those pearls are something of a bribe.'

'Exactly what I thought,' said Eliza.

'Such a price for the land is very tempting, however,' commented Selwyn.

'John was adamant about not selling before,' said Eliza in a tone that conveyed he might still have the same attitude.

'Then don't sell,' said Harriet, picking up on her feeling.

'But what if he returns and wishes I hadn't missed such a good offer?'

'There is another way of looking at it,' pointed out Selwyn. 'If it is that valuable to Gaisford then it is just as valuable to us. If our land has good copper deposits we can exploit them together without the Gaisfords. But I was not in favour of despoiling the landscape and nor was John, so in spite of this very tempting offer why don't we stick by our principles?'

There was only a momentary hesitation before Eliza spoke again and when she did her tone was full of resolve. 'Then don't sell! Miles Gaisford won't like it but he'll have to live with it. I'll write to him when I get back home. And I'll return these pearls.'

'Don't do that,' warned Harriet. 'He'll take it as an insult, for he will know that you have seen it as a bribe, whereas to all intents and purposes it was merely a gift to commemorate a pleasant evening.'

Eliza nodded. 'I suppose you are right.'

With goodbyes said and Abigail and Juliana acknowledging that they had had a good time, Lydia stood with her hand on Juliana's shoulder watching the carriage drive away. But her thoughts were all on the news just imparted by Dorinda. Mr Mitchell had gone to Whitby and it was not known when he would be back. She felt that something had been snatched away from her for she had expected to arrange, somehow or other, to meet him in their bay to get his approval of the painting.

Rowena watched her husband with keen eyes as he broke the seal on the letter that had just been delivered from Penorna Manor. It could only be one thing – an answer from Mrs Mitchell. She saw Miles's scowl and the way it darkened. His lips set in a tight line as he flung the paper on to the table. It slid across the polished surface to Rowena. She picked it up and read the polite refusal of her husband's offer.

'Damn the woman!' he hissed. 'Why wouldn't she sell?'

'Because she doesn't want to,' replied Rowena calmly.

'We could have made a fortune out of the copper deposits on which the Mitchells and Westburys are sitting!'

'I know it's a setback to your ambitions but we are well off as it is. Don't go getting yourself worked up about it. You know what happened last time.'

'I won't.' She saw a glint in his eye. 'I have an alternative plan in readiness.'

'And what is that?'

'Better you don't know.'

Rowena gave a little inclination of her head. She knew that the Gaisfords had employed underhand methods in the past and, as her husband rightly said, it was better she did not know of them now.

'Where have you been?' Miles asked as Jeremy strode on to the terrace after handing his horse over to one of the grooms.

'Getting the information you wanted,' he replied, a touch of satisfaction in his voice.

'Well, what is it?'

'Tell you in a minute.' Before his father could say anything Jeremy was away into the house. He returned after a few minutes with a glass of whisky in his hand.

'You drink too much,' his father criticised. 'It'll be your downfall.'

'Something to celebrate.' Jeremy grinned and raised his glass.

Miles was irritated by this carefree attitude when important things were at hand. 'Well?' he snapped.

'Mitchell's mine is below production. They are looking to recruit miners but it seems there are few unemployed hereabouts. Fishermen and farmers won't go underground even though there may be more money at it.'

'Are they looking to expand?'

'Not at present. There has been talk of it in the past but since Mitchell came that seems to have been dropped. He doesn't seem interested in expansion but does like to keep present production to capacity.'

'So if that capacity dropped he may be forced to open up another seam. That could be made costly for him and . . .'

'. . . it might be better for him to sell that copper-laden land you want.' Jeremy finished for him.

'Exactly.'

'So what is the next move?'

'We wait until Mitchell returns.'

'Why until then?'

'Because he's likely to act on what I plan. After the way he proceeded when he learned about the Lowthers, I'm almost certain he'll do the same again.'

'You are going to plant someone on his workforce?'

'You are getting the idea. Details can be finalised later. What you have to do is to recruit one of our workers on whom you can rely.'

'Leave it to me.' Jeremy grinned.

'See that whoever you get is absolutely trustworthy and will never talk.'

'I shall.'

Miles eyed his son. 'Where did you get your information?'

Jeremy smiled with the pleasure of knowing he could out-fox his father on this one. 'That is for me to know and only me, but I'll tell you this: my sources are very reliable.' He raised his glass in mock salute then drained it, stood up and walked briskly into the house.

His father watched him, tight-lipped, and wondered what the future held for his eldest boy who would so often act without thinking. He almost wished Logan had been the eldest.

Chapter Nine

Nostalgia swelled in John and tightened his throat at first sight of Whitby. The feeling that he was home heightened as he neared the town and saw the red-roofed houses climbing the cliffside towards the old church and ruined abbey. He took the track that led to the East Side. He was thrilled to see the bustling activity on the quays below where ships were loaded and unloaded. As he was swept up into Whitby's life, once so familiar to him, he felt a little twinge of regret that he had ever left his birthplace for the other end of the country. But then he tightened his lips and stiffened his determination not to let such sentimentality get out of hand.

He rode along Church Street and turned into the yard of the White Swan. The clatter of hooves brought a stableman and boy hurrying from the inn's stable.

The man pulled up short on seeing John. 'Mr Mitchell!' he gasped in surprise.

'Aye, it's me, Bob,' replied John with a broad grin. 'You haven't seen a ghost.' He swung out of the saddle.

The boy had taken the reins and Bob took John's proffered hand. 'It's good to see you, sir,' he said, and glancing at the boy ordered, 'Charlie, take good care of that horse. Rub it down and feed it.'

'Aye, aye, sir.' Charlie waited until John had taken his saddlebags and rolled cape then led the horse away.

'Here for long, sir?'

'Not sure yet. I'll let you know when I want my horse again.'

Bob nodded. 'How are Mrs Mitchell and that nice little girl of yours?'

'Very well,' replied John, sensing a tug at his heart at the mention of them. 'Jake Thorburn still landlord here?'

'Aye, sir, he's just inside.'

'I'll have a word.'

'Do you want a fresh horse to go to Bloomfield Manor?'

'Please.'

'It'll be ready in a few minutes.'

John headed for the inn while Bob went to the stable to see that Charlie was giving due attention to the horse belonging to someone who had once been a good customer.

A short while later John swung from the saddle in front of the house that had long been his home. He had lived his boyhood there and later brought his bride to this place. Abigail had been born here, and they had all welcomed his sister here in her days of sorrow. It held so many memories, happy days, only a few tinged with sadness and anxiety. As he started up the four front steps the door opened.

'John!'

His face was instantly wreathed in smiles. 'Martha!'

Then they were in each other's arms. The intensity of their hug betrayed the extent to which they had missed each other.

'I saw you from the window.' Martha's eyes were damp as she stepped back to look at him. 'You look well,' she said. 'A little tired maybe, but that is only to be expected after your long journey. Whitby air will soon put you right.'

'It obviously keeps you young,' he said as they went into the hall pushing the door closed behind them.

'You see what you wish to see,' she laughed.

'Truly, you haven't changed,' he insisted while admiring her aura of serenity. Her taste in dress was simple but fashionable and she always wore the colour that suited her best – light blue emphasised by the darker hue of the thin shawl draped neatly round her shoulders. He was pleased to see she wasn't wearing her business troubles, whatever they were, on her sleeve.

He had dropped his saddlebags and cape on the floor of the hall and tossed his hat on to a chair. As he shrugged himself out of his woollen jacket Martha rang a bell twice and after a very brief pause rang it again three times in quick succession. The signals had the desired results. A footman and maid duly appeared.

'This is Mr Mitchell, my brother,' she said. 'Robert and June,' she added, turning to John who acknowledged the new servants as they paid him a respectful welcome. 'Robert, take Mr Mitchell to the room we have ready for him. June, tea in the drawing room in ten minutes.'

When John came down to the drawing room after he had restored himself he found it empty. His immediate action was to walk to the window. How many times had he stood there and looked out just like this? He felt his heart beat a little faster – the view still moved him.

'It is still a glorious sight,' said Martha quietly as she came to stand beside him.

He started. 'Oh, I didn't hear you come in.'

'You were far away. Is it the view?'

John gave a little smile. 'It's still wonderful.'

'Nothing to match it in Cornwall?' She turned her eyes to him as he continued to look out of the window.

There was a moment's hesitation before he replied, 'There's a tiny bay . . .' He sounded wistful.

She noted the tone of his voice and the dreamy look that had come to his eyes but made no comment. A little flutter of anxiety touched her, though. Was there more behind his expression than he was telling her? Could she still read her brother like a book? Her thoughts were interrupted when a knock on the door was followed by the arrival of tea.

Brother and sister sat opposite each other with a low round table between them. She poured the tea and he had already taken a scone, looking at it with relish. 'You still have Mrs Binns cooking for you, I see. How I used to enjoy her scones.'

'Well, now you can enjoy them again.'

He spread some butter and then raspberry jam on the scone. Before he took a bite he said, 'What's the trouble in the business?'

Martha gave a slight, dismissive wave of her hand. 'That can wait until tomorrow. It will be better explained at the

121

office where there are all the necessary documents. What I want now is to hear all about Cornwall.'

The rest of the afternoon and evening were spent in John's detailed description of his new life in the far-off county.

When she undressed for bed Martha thought about the many things he had told her and linked some of them to that wistful look she had noted shortly after his arrival. She would not question him about it but she locked the facts away in her mind.

'Right, Martha, tell me something about what is troubling you here,' prompted John over breakfast the next morning. 'I know the relevant documents will be at the office, but let me hear what you believe is wrong now.'

Martha hesitated, which struck him as being slightly strange, because his sister had always been one to come straight to the point. Something truly must be wrong if she had to consider how best to tell him. He knew that her sipping at her coffee was only a delay while she mustered her words. She glanced down at her empty bowl and then met his enquiring gaze. 'I have stepped into something we had never before contemplated and it has brought me only trouble,' she told him. 'I wish now I had never done it.' In the touch of guilt that had come to her voice there was also a cry for help.

'All right. Whatever you've done can be undone, or least a solution found,' he said reassuringly. 'Just begin at the beginning.'

'Business was going well. Oh, there were those who resented a woman moving into a man's world, but no one really acted against me in any tangible way. People undercut my prices, but that's to be expected in trade. I made sure our service was better than most. I also saw a way in which I thought we could give better service and maybe even expand our field. I decided to build a ship.'

John raised his eyebrows. This was a surprise but, not wanting to interrupt his sister's flow nor give her any inkling of what he was thinking, he made no comment.

'We pay for our goods to be transported and I thought if we could do that ourselves we would be more profitable. I thought if we built a vessel of the right size we could get into smaller harbours and expand our trade to places that at the moment are only supplied overland.'

John nodded. He could understand her reasoning.

Martha gave a small wistful smile. 'I also dreamed of sailing on her to Penzance and giving you a surprise.'

'You certainly would have done that! So what has gone wrong?'

'I went carefully into the costing and got Mr Smithers to check the figures.'

'So you still have Stewart. I'm pleased to hear it.'

'The ever-faithful manager! The business would not be the same without him.'

'So, you did the costing, Stewart checked the figures, and you were happy enough to go ahead?'

'Yes.'

'What is the size of the vessel?'

'A one hundred-tonne sloop.'

John nodded and pursed his lips thoughtfully. 'Big enough to sail the coast yet small enough to get into creeks and small waterways.'

'Yes.'

'How far has the building gone?'

'About halfway. That's the trouble . . . she should have been finished by now. She's six months behind schedule.'

'What?' John's expression of shock could not be hidden. 'And I suppose that is costing you money?'

'Exactly. At this rate the venture will never be profitable.'

'Who's building her?'

'Carson and Son.'

'Who are they?' John frowned.

'A new firm, set up eighteen months ago.'

'Why did you choose them?'

'I thought newcomers would be keen for business and want to show what they could do. Besides, they were recommended to me by Mr Wesley Horton.'

'Ah!'

'You sound as if you don't like him?'

'Never did.'

'But why?'

John shrugged his shoulders. 'Never could quite put my finger on it, it was just one of those feelings. He was always friendly enough on the surface but I believed he could be a bit underhand, though I had no real proof. Was it general knowledge that you were to have a ship built?'

Martha gave a little nod. 'I never kept it a secret. Our staff would hear of it. Friends knew of it, and you know how it is, things have a habit of becoming general knowledge in Whitby.'

'What has been Horton's attitude to you running a business? After all, he's in the same trade.'

'Yes. I can't say he has been helpful other than by recommending Carson.'

'And after a while things started to go wrong there?'

'Yes. You don't think Mr Horton could be behind the delay?'

'It's a possibility. He could be stealing your idea and having a ship built himself to go after the same trade.'

Martha's lips tightened at the thought that she might have been duped. 'What can we do?'

'First of all, don't become distressed about it. I'll look into the reason for the delay and tell Carsons to get on with the job.'

'I'm sorry about this, and for dragging you all the way from Cornwall, leaving Eliza and Abigail.'

'Think nothing of it. It is better this way than letting the situation here go too far. I would like to see all the documents relating to the building of the ship before I visit Carson's.'

'Very well! We'll go to the office whenever you are ready.'

Half an hour later John was exchanging greetings with Stewart Smithers. A few minutes later he welcomed the moment when his sister announced she had some paperwork to do and would be occupied for an hour. It enabled him to have a chat with her manager about the business and about the situation arising out of the slow delivery of the sloop. He saw nothing untoward in what Smithers had to tell him except that the manager did not trust the excuses made by Carson's, and the fact that they were ever-ready to demand more money to finance the work.

Studying the contracts and payments, John saw that the situation was at a point where it would soon be over-budget.

'You look very concerned, John?' commented Martha on her return.

'The situation is decidedly tricky but I'll say no more now. We'll go and take a light luncheon at the Angel.'

They left the office situated on the east side of the river and threaded their way through the hustle and bustle of the thriving port. John realised how much he had missed it. They crossed the bridge and were soon at the Angel.

'Where's Carson's yard?' asked John later as they left the inn.

'Farthest one, upstream on this side of the river.'

'There certainly seems to be plenty of shipbuilding going on,' he commented as the sound of hammers and saws heralded much activity. All the yards were extremely busy constructing every manner of vessel, in keeping with Whitby's high reputation in this trade. He stopped at Carson's yard. Three ships were under construction there. Workmen were laying the keel on one. A second had reached the stage of having its deck beams and carlings fitted, but there was no work being done on the third which had reached the stage ready for hold shelf-pieces to be fitted.

'Which is yours?' John asked.

'The one on which they aren't working.'

'And whose is the one of similar design but at a more advanced stage?'

'I don't know, but I do know it was started after mine.'

'If yours was first, it should be the more advanced.'

'I pressed Mr Carson on that and he told me that when the timber arrived for the next stage of construction it was not suitable. Said he would have to wait for a new consignment.'

'That seems to me a lame excuse and points to bad management. He should have had sufficient timber to swap between the ships under construction so there was no delay on either of them. Certainly yours should now be further ahead than it is.' John paused a moment in thought then added, 'Why don't you go back to the office and leave this to me? I'll see you there shortly.'

Martha, knowing her brother, did not press him for further explanations but agreed.

When she had gone John strolled further into the yard and passed himself off as a possible customer. He was examining Martha's ship when a voice made him turn to see a thin man of average height studying him with eyes John would have described as shifty, though he wondered if his assessment was being coloured by the fact that his sister's ship had not been completed on time.

'Can I help you, sir?'

At least the man was polite though his voice held a note of suspicion.

'Mr Carson?'

'Yes, that's me. You looking to have a ship built?'

'I might be in the market in a month's time so I'm looking around. I heard tell you are new in Whitby?'

'Yes. These are our first three vessels. Are you from these parts?'

'No.' John decided not to reveal any more just yet.

Mr Carson looked surprised. 'But yet you come to Whitby for a ship?'

'I'm exploring all possibilities, but knowing Whitby's reputation for building good stout vessels, I would not be averse to having one built here.'

'Was my yard recommended?'

John had been trying to lead him to put that question. Now he had. 'Yes, by Mr Wesley Horton.'

'You know him?' Mr Carson's voice levelled into a more amenable tone. 'That's his . . .' He stopped as if he should not divulge any more but John had noted the inclination of Carson's head in the direction of the vessel that had progressed quicker than Martha's.

'You don't seem to have the space to take on another commission.'

'You said you would possibly be interested in a month's time?'

'Yes.'

'Well, I can speed work up on that one and have it cleared to suit your timescale.' So Horton's ship was priority, John noted.

John nodded. 'And that one?' He indicated Martha's vessel. 'Is that an order or one you are building to sell?'

Carson pulled a face. 'It's an order but I can delay it.'

'I wouldn't want to step on anybody's toes . . .'

'I can fix it, sir. The order has been placed by a lady! Now I ask you, sir, what is trade coming to when a woman moves into a man's world? We don't want them so what's it matter if I do a little delaying? And with you knowing Mr Horton, I don't mind giving you priority. It's easy to make excuses for the delay on that ship, especially as the person in question falls for everything I say.'

'Really?'

'Oh, yes.' He gave a laugh that showed he thought he was conducting a clever campaign.

'Well, Mr Carson, I have a vested interest in that ship you are delaying.' John's sudden rapier-like tone startled Carson. 'I want her finished in a month and no longer else I can legitimately deduct sufficient from the payments due to you to recompense Miss Mitchell for the trade she has lost. I have no doubt you will report my visit to Mr Horton with whom you are obviously in cahoots.' John saw denial rising to Carson's lips and quickly put in, 'Don't refute it, Mr Carson, I'm sure I'm right and you may as well know now that I am Miss Mitchell's brother. Not only that, I myself have powerful trading connections. No doubt Mr Horton will assure you that's untrue but he does not know the extent of my new connections since leaving Whitby. So, Carson, you could face ruin. Finish our ship or else . . .' He let the threat hang in mid-air. 'I'll be back.' John did not wait for him to speak but turned and strode purposefully away.

Carson stood watching him in confusion. He knew determination when he saw it and that Mr Mitchell was the type of

127

man who would carry out his threat if the work was not completed in the time specified. He could well face ruin. But what about Mr Horton? Dare he upset him? He swung round and hurried to the Horton vessel. In a few moments the men working on it were relocating themselves on the Mitchell sloop.

Once out of sight of the shipyard John slowed his step. He smiled to himself when he heard the sounds of work behind him cease. He stopped, listening intently. When he heard the first hammer blow taken up by others he turned and moved quickly back to the yard. He stepped quietly up to Carson who was so intent on shouting new instructions to his workforce that he did not realise John was there until he said, 'That was very wise of you, Mr Carson.'

He started but John was already striding away, leaving the shipbuilder to ponder his words.

Martha looked askance at her brother when he walked back into the office.

'I don't think you'll have any more bother with Mr Carson,' he commented with a knowing smile. 'And I don't think Mr Horton will try to outsmart you again. By Mr Carson's actions Horton will know we have seen through his ploy.' He went on to tell her what had transpired at the yard.

'But won't Mr Carson just employ more men?'

'I doubt he'll be able to. You've seen that all the shipyards are working to full capacity. Carson won't find another skilled man in Whitby.'

'But what will happen when you leave?'

'I'll stay to see your ship launched. Let Carson see me around the town.'

Martha's eyes brightened. 'You will?' she asked in a voice filled with excitement.

'I'll write to Eliza tomorrow, tell her I'm delayed but will be home for Christmas.'

Pleasure surged through Eliza when a maid brought her a sealed sheet of paper and she recognised the writing as John's. She broke the seal with eager fingers and unfolded the letter. Her heart sank when she read that her husband would not be home for at least a month, and probably a week longer taking into account his travelling time. Though disappointed, she understood his reasons and only hoped that nothing else would happen to delay his return. This had been their first spell apart since marrying and she had not realised how much she would miss him. The days to his return seemed to stretch endlessly ahead.

Chapter Ten

Three days later Miles Gaisford was sitting on the terrace enjoying the sunshine as he gazed across the undulating fields that sloped to the distant edge of the cliffs. He felt deep satisfaction that he had turned his inheritance by marriage into one of the largest estates in Cornwall, and if he counted in the two estates assigned to his younger sons, though bought and financed through the wealth he had generated, the Gaisfords truly had become powerful and rich landowners. If only he could buy the land he so coveted from Westbury and Mitchell! He had seen his opportunity when Mitchell had gone to Whitby but had not reckoned on the inflexibility of Mrs Mitchell. Who would have thought a woman would resist so much money *and* a pearl necklace? Well, his second plan must be used and now, seeing Jeremy returning from his morning ride, was the time to implement it.

He pushed himself slowly from his chair, stepping over to the balustrade. With one hand on the stonework, he signalled to his son. Jeremy slowed his horse to a walk and turned it towards the terrace. Miles gave a little nod of satisfaction and returned to his seat.

'Morning, Father,' Jeremy called as he pulled his mount to a halt and swung from the saddle. 'How are you this fine morning?' he asked, striding on to the terrace.

'Been better, been worse,' returned his father gruffly, but Jeremy was pleased to detect an undercurrent of satisfaction, as if something had initiated a decision.

'What is it?' he asked, slapping his riding crop into the palm of his left hand as he flung himself down into a chair beside his father.

'Mr Mitchell is away for at least another month.'

Jeremy eyed him with curiosity. 'How do you know that?'

Miles's lips twitched with satisfaction. 'I've told you before, use your ears and cultivate gossip.'

Jeremy nodded, knowing it was useless to press for more information; he would not get his father to divulge his sources. 'So does this mean that we are going to . . .'

'Yes, it does,' Miles interrupted, knowing what his son was going to say. 'Now it's up to you to see that everything is in place by the time Mitchell returns.'

'The bait will be ready. Mr Mitchell will bite and be hooked,' said Jeremy with a smile of satisfaction.

'Good. See that nothing goes wrong.'

Undeterred by the threat of rain, Jeremy rode across the wild expanse of moor to the village of Cribyan. Most of its men were working in the Gaisford mine three miles from the village but some had been delegated three days ago by Jeremy to repair two cottages in the village. One of them was Jim Lund. As he rode past Jeremy raised his finger in a signal and knew from the nod he received in return that Lund had got the message. Jeremy rode on through the village and was on the moor again when the rain struck. He cursed the weather, booted his horse into a quicker pace and hunched his shoulders against the rain.

Twenty minutes later he dropped from the saddle in front of the wind-lashed Waning Moon. He hurried inside, sending the door crashing behind him. Water dripped from his clothes on to the stone floor as he threw his cape from his shoulders and sent spray across the floor when he shook his hat. At the same time his glance surveyed the room. The landlord stood behind the bar chatting with the only other occupant of the inn.

'G'day, Mr Gaisford,' greeted the landlord. 'Not so hot out there?'

'Far from it, Tom,' replied Jeremy. He turned his gaze to the other man. 'How are things at Creaking Gate Farm, Jos?'

'Exactly that, Mr Gaisford, creaking, and if I doesn't get myself back they'll be creaking all the more.' With that he drained his tankard and hurried out into the pouring rain.

131

Ten minutes later Jeremy was starting his third whisky when the door burst open, letting in a blast of rain-driven air that propelled a cursing Jim Lund into the room. He shook himself like a dog and spray flew everywhere.

'Cut it out, Jim,' snapped Jeremy, glaring at the new arrival.

Jim made no reply but threw off his rain-sodden jacket and slumped against the bar. Tom was already pouring him some ale.

'Give him a warmer,' called Jeremy.

''Preciate it,' called Jim. As soon as the whisky was in front of him he drained the glass and felt warmth drive down his throat and through his body. 'That's better,' he said, smacking his lips. He picked up his tankard, crossed the stone floor and sat down opposite Jeremy.

He had closely watched this strong, broad-shouldered young man every moment since his tempestuous arrival. Strong-framed and muscular, these attributes had been further honed by a rough, tough life and were evident in Jim's height. Though this was not a man he would care to tangle with physically, Jeremy knew Jim could take orders and carry them out to the letter. And his other great asset was that he would keep his mouth shut. He realised he was on to a good thing, doing unsavoury jobs for Jeremy Gaisford.

Jim met his searching gaze. 'The job you mentioned has come up?' he asked.

'Yes. Still want it?'

'I don't yet know what it is,' replied Jim cautiously.

'I'll tell you about it only if you decide to do it.'

Jim grunted. He generally knew what a job entailed before accepting it but when Jeremy had first mentioned the possibility of something big he had not divulged its exact nature.

'Well?' prompted Jeremy. 'It will pay well. More than the last one . . . considerably more because it will have to be done over a greater length of time.'

For a moment Jim looked thoughtful, then deeming it wisest to keep on the right side of Jeremy Gaisford, he agreed.

Jeremy gave a nod of approval. During the next two hours, over four tankards of ale and two whiskys each, the plan was laid and finalised, but only after Jeremy had agreed to Jim's recruiting two other men whom he vowed would follow him to hell if necessary and were as tight-lipped as he was.

Hearing the rattle of a horse's hooves on the drive, Eliza looked up from her embroidery to see a horseman appear from behind the avenue of trees that lined the early part of the drive.

'John!' she gasped, dropping her needlework on the seat and springing to her feet. Joy surged in her heart and she rushed to the steps of the terrace, calling to Abigail who was playing ball on the lawn with Dorinda. 'Abigail, Abigail! It's Papa!'

Startled, the child froze with the ball in her hand. She looked bewildered and then the significance of what her mother had said struck home. 'Miss Jenkins! Miss Jenkins! It's Papa!' She was already racing to her mother who had come down the steps on to the lawn. They held hands and hurried towards the rider. Smiles wreathed their faces as John pulled to a halt, jumped from the saddle and held out his arms to them both.

'John!' Eliza felt such strength and comfort in his embrace and experienced a welcome sense of being protected again.

'It's good to be home,' he replied huskily, then dropped down to hug Abigail. 'How's my girl? Been good? Looked after Mama?'

Abigail laughed with joy. 'Yes! Yes!'

John straightened up, kissed his wife again, picked up the reins and led his horse as they all walked towards the stables, happy to be together again.

From a distance Dorinda had watched the reunion. She wondered how Lydia would view Mr Mitchell's return, for she had wondered if there was more behind her friend's casual enquiries about him than merely wanting a decision on her painting.

Later, when John had refreshed himself and taken a meal, he answered all Eliza's questions about Martha's welfare and the

133

trouble in Whitby. At the end of his story he eyed her questioningly. 'Something's troubling you. Has anything gone wrong while I have been away?'

Eliza bit her lip.

'Begin at the beginning,' he prompted.

First she told him about the invitation to dine with Miles and Rowena.

He frowned when she mentioned the gift of pearls. 'You refused them, of course?'

'No. When I went to warn Selwyn that Mr Gaisford might approach him with another offer to buy his land, I told him about the gift and he and Harriet advised me to accept them as it would be a slight on the Gaisfords' hospitality and generosity if I were to return them, even though we both suspected the gesture was a bribe. As tempting as the offer to buy the land was, though, I refused.'

'Good. If he sees that land as valuable to him, then it is just as valuable to us. Do you think Selwyn will sell on the back of the increased offer?'

'No,' she replied firmly, to leave no doubt in his mind. 'We agreed to stand together against Miles's proposal.'

'Good. Have the Gaisfords made any other move?'

'No. Miles seems to have accepted my refusal with equanimity.' Eliza added slowly, 'But there is something else I have to tell you.'

'Trouble?'

'Well, not really, not so far as we are concerned. The mine is working well but not to full capacity. We needed more men.' She paused a moment, gathering her thoughts. 'You remember the Lowthers and the action you took there?' He nodded. 'Well, a similar situation arose. It came to my notice that a man called Jim Lund and two other Gaisford workers had been unfairly dismissed and evicted from their cottages. I got our mine manager to get them to meet me at the mine, interviewed them and took them on. They were amiable, strong, willing and grateful, and I have not had a bad report of them since.'

'Good.' He gave a little smile. 'We are doing well out of the Gaisfords.'

'I hope it continues that way.'

'You have nothing to worry about now I'm back.'

The following day, on rising, John looked out of the bedroom window. Judging the weather to be settled fair, he said. 'I'll visit the mine today and probably call in on Selwyn on the way.'

'So soon?' asked Eliza from the bed. She stretched seductively. 'You've been away so long, must you go now?'

'I'm not tied to any time,' he said quietly as he moved towards her, his eyes devouring her as she slipped the bed clothes aside.

An hour later he whispered in her ear, 'I think I must go this time,' then added. 'There's always tonight.'

She twisted in his arms and kissed him passionately. 'A reminder until then.'

Those words rang in his mind as he rode away from Penorna yet he turned his horse along the cliff track that would take him past the bay. He was still waiting for Lydia's painting of it. Did he hope that she was there now? He stopped, swung himself from his horse and ventured close to the edge so he could see the bay better. Its beauty seemed to strike him anew. The golden sand was unmarked, the azure sea lazily lapping; he knew he would always find peace and tranquillity here and it would always have a special place in his mind and heart. He swung himself back into the saddle and put his horse to a gallop, venting his unacknowledged annoyance that Lydia was not there. 'Ridiculous,' he muttered. 'There was no reason for her to be.'

He slowed his horse eventually and was deep in thought as he approached Trethtowan, a thought that still occupied his mind as he arrived at the house. The door opened as he finished tethering his horse at the top of the drive, knowing a groom would come to collect it.

'Miss Booth!' he said, a touch of surprise in his voice to see the object of his thoughts standing before him.

'Mr Mitchell!' Her voice shook; she blushed.

He noted it and liked it. He took in her high-waisted pink gown with the narrowest of brown braid trim running down the bodice in two rows from a high neck around which was set a circle of white frills. The natural wave of her short brown hair was unencumbered by a bonnet and bounced freely as she came to the top of the steps before the front door.

'Miss Booth, it is good to see you looking so well.'

'I am, Mr Mitchell, thank you. I understand you have been in Whitby. I hope your visit was pleasant.'

'Indeed it was, Miss Booth. And how is my painting coming along?'

'Very well, or at least I think so, but I would like your opinion, preferably on site so that you can compare what I am trying to achieve with the real scene.'

'Very well, Miss Booth. Which day is suitable for you?'

'The day after tomorrow is my free day.'

'Then we shall meet there at eleven o'clock.'

Lydia inclined her head in gracious acceptance but her eyes were locked on his. It was John who broke the contact and in a faltering voice which he instantly attempted to firm, asked, 'Are Mr and Mrs Westbury at home?'

'They are in the drawing room. If you'll follow me?' Lydia turned quickly back to the house and in a few moments was announcing Mr Mitchell's arrival to her employers.

'You're back!' cried Selwyn, dropping the book he was reading to the table beside his chair and jumping to his feet to greet his friend warmly.

Harriet welcomed John with a beaming smile as he took her hand and raised it to his lips. 'It's good to see you home and looking so well.' She rose from her chair. 'Let me ring for some chocolate.'

'That would be pleasant,' he replied, 'and will fortify me for my ride to the mine.'

With the chocolate at hand John asked Selwyn if he knew any more about Jim Lund's dismissal than he had already learned from Eliza.

'It seems he refused to do a dangerous job underground. The mine manager's instant dismissal of him was backed by

Jeremy Gaisford, and the same applied to two other men who sided with Lund.'

'Know anything about them?' John asked.

'When Eliza was thinking of employing them I did some enquiring. Seems they are all good workers. I never heard that there had been any complaint against them before. I gave these facts to Eliza and she acted accordingly. I could see no reason to deter her.'

'Thanks, Selwyn. I appreciate that.'

When Lydia returned outside after seeing John to the drawing room she stood on the terrace, leaning on the balustrade and gazing across the countryside while seeing nothing. Her mind was on the boldness she had displayed by suggesting that Mr Mitchell meet her in their bay in two days' time. She was hoping the weather would be as fine as it was today and that led to her picturing the meeting in her mind . . . She had to pull her thoughts together sharply. What was she expecting to happen? Had she really seen in John's eyes a personal interest in her or was that just wishful thinking on her part? Was she letting herself slip beyond the boundaries of decorum even by thinking this way? She straightened, chided herself, slapped her hands hard on the stonework in self-reproof and walked, tight-lipped, into the house.

Although when he left Trethtowan John's mind was on what Selwyn had told him, it soon became occupied with pleasanter thoughts of the charming young lady who had appeared before him a short while ago. He felt sure he had read interest in her eyes and it flattered him. But was he right or was it purely his imagination wishing to pique the interest of a younger woman? No, it was not that; he tried to convince himself Lydia really had shown interest. Then his mind began to spin in confusion as he remembered what had happened in his own bedroom but a short while ago. Eliza! If she could have read the thoughts he had recently had about Miss Booth, she would have been devastated. He should never have commissioned that painting but such things just happened and,

137

unprompted, one thing naturally led to another. Now he was to meet Miss Booth in the special place that had woven its magic around them both. He should call the meeting off, he knew. He wrestled with that thought, but by the time he'd reached the mine he knew he wouldn't.

John discussed the mine's production and men with his manager, Bert Wallace, who told him he was pleased Mrs Mitchell had approved the employing of three workers dismissed by the Gaisfords.

'They are good men, Mr Mitchell,' he said, 'and Lund is skilled with dynamite. We have had to use a small stick once since his arrival and he handled it perfectly.'

'Why Lund?'

'Our usual handler, Pat Welburn, had suffered a badly cut hand the previous day and we thought it might be an impediment if he was handling dynamite. Lund came forward and said he could do it. I hadn't any alternative so told him to get on with it. I tell you, he was most competent. No flurry. He exuded confidence, and the other men could feel that so it settled their minds. As you know, explosions underground can be tricky; nobody likes them really. I'll be using him again later this week. The section his explosion opened up looks promising but another blast will tell us if it is worthwhile pursuing further. So our expansion will not be held up by waiting for Welburn's recovery.'

Good. Then Gaisford's loss was our gain,' commented John with satisfaction. 'Will you continue to use Lund after Welburn's hand is better?'

'Yes. it's good to have two men competent with dynamite.'

'How did Welburn damage his hand?'

'He and Lund were working on a section in which some timbers needed replacing. Lund stumbled and the end he was carrying slipped; Welburn took the full weight but the trouble was his hand was trapped. Nasty, but fortunately nothing broken.'

John nodded. 'See that he loses no pay because of it.'

'He will appreciate that, sir. Thanks.'

As John rode back to Penorna he was thankful that nothing worse than a damaged hand had occurred during his absence ... and then his mind drifted to that meeting in two days' time.

Early-morning mist lay like a ghostly hand across Penorna but it was a phenomenon that John had witnessed on a number of occasions and he knew it would soon clear. Saying that he was going to visit two of his tenant farmers, he left the house immediately after breakfast.

As he'd thought the mist gradually dispersed during his walk and by the time he reached the bay had completely cleared. The wintery sun shone down from a clear sky. He stood above the bay, drinking in the colourful beauty below that was matched by the azure of a tranquil sea.

He'd started for the path down when a prick of conscience stopped him. A tight feeling in his stomach troubled him and his mind had misgivings about what he was doing here. Thoughts battled within him: to approve a painting; to meet a beautiful young woman; in friendship, nothing more; as patron of a work of art; to test himself; to purge himself of the desire he knew he had been growing; to put an end to a relationship that could only spell disaster for both of them ... But there was no relationship, not really, and did he not wish there was? He could turn back from it now, but then this place that held so much enchantment for him would be marred for him, never to be magical again, never to be filled with the joy it had filled him with from the first day he had seen it. Seen her.

He slid carefully down the slope hidden by bushes and undergrowth, negotiated the outcrops of rock successfully and dropped the last few feet on to the sand. He recovered his breath as he stood gazing across the strand to the cliffs that enclosed the bay, bringing peace and seclusion.

After a few minutes he walked slowly across the sand to a group of boulders that at some time in the past had tumbled from the cliff to lie in confusion at its foot. Reaching them, he chose a position from which he couldn't be seen but from which he could see Lydia start the first part of the descent. Only his footprints marked his passage.

Lydia felt a surge of excitement as she gathered up her artist's materials and unfinished painting. The day had developed as she had hoped, sunny but fresh with clear skies. A day to feel joy and gladness in the heart – and she was going to meet a man with whom she had fallen in love. He did not know it; she could never tell him, he was married. And yet as she reminded herself of these things another part of her did not care. She could love John from afar, but would that be enough? She told herself that it would have to be and was determined to draw joy from it.

She left the house with a brisk light step which slowed as she neared the bay. Her heart was racing. Would she be first or would John be there already? Maybe he wouldn't come? Maybe he had forgotten? There could be a thousand and one reasons for him not to appear.

There were footprints in the sand! Her thoughts went topsy-turvy and her heart raced. New sensations surged through her. She wanted to be with him, be there in front of him with his eyes fixed only on her. Without hesitation she scrambled down to join him.

He saw her! Emotions were heightened, leaving him confused. He felt as though he should hide or walk away from this situation but he knew he did not want to. Besides, his footprints betrayed his presence. He rose to his feet and automatically went to meet Lydia. At first his steps were slow and then his eagerness to see her overcame his good sense and he hurried to join her. All he could think of was seeing her again. He reached the far side of the bay before she was at the bottom of the cliff. Knowing exactly where she would emerge, he waited. The moments ticked by. It seemed an eternity. Then she was there, negotiating the last few feet and an awkward drop.

'Mr Mitchell,' she called. In that moment, with her mind diverted from her descent, Lydia stumbled. Her materials flew from her hands as she tried to steady herself and stop the painting from falling too. She managed that but did not save herself from toppling backwards and sliding the few yards to the final drop. She cried out as she plunged down. Everything seemed to whirl around her and she tensed herself against the impact. Instead she felt strong arms envelop her and a firm body take her weight. The painting slipped from her grasp and dropped to the sand.

'Miss Booth! Are you all right?' John's voice was full of concern.

She gasped for breath and struggled to hide her embarrassment. 'Oh yes. I . . . er . . . I . . .'

'Just sit quietly for a moment. You've had a shock.'

She became aware that he still held her. How comforted and protected she felt. She looked up at him. 'Oh, Mr Mitchell, I'm sorry.'

He gave a little reassuring smile that turned her heart over as he said quietly. 'You have nothing to be sorry for, you did not fall on purpose. Thank goodness you weren't hurt.' He thought he should release his hold on her but having her in his arms sent a feeling through him he did not want to lose, and she did not seem to want to move away. His eyes met hers and unspoken words flowed between them, charged with meaning that neither of them could deny. Slowly their lips came together in a passionate kiss.

When they parted, John's voice was full of embarrassment and apology. 'Miss Booth, I'm sorry.'

She put a finger to his lips. 'Don't be. I'm not. Say no more about it.'

'But . . .'

'You were going to say that it shouldn't have happened because you are a happily married man. I know that, Mr Mitchell. What has already happened, and anything that might, will always be a secret locked away in my heart.'

'I should have stopped . . .'

'No, you shouldn't,' she interrupted. 'I will be so bold as to say I've dreamed of that happening ever since the first time I met you. It is I who should have resisted such thoughts.'

'Miss Booth, there can be no future between us.'

'I know that, and would not want to break up a happy marriage.'

He looked askance at her. 'You mean, you want a relationship between us to develop nevertheless?'

'If that is what you would like and it can remain a secret, known to no one.'

'Miss Booth, you know what you are saying?'

'Yes. I cannot deny I fell in love that moment I saw you. I cannot explain why. It was as if an arrow had pierced my heart, releasing every emotion of love that was there. Don't deny me my feelings, I would be devastated if you did and I could no longer experience my love for you. I think you are gentlemanly enough not to do that.'

John hesitated, torn between what he knew he really should do and what he wanted – to love this attractive young woman who made his heart sing every time he thought about her. 'Miss Booth,' he said gently, 'I cannot deny that I was attracted to you from the first moment I saw you, but being a married man I was afraid to let such an emotion have an outlet. Yet I think you and I both sensed the attraction between us.'

She nodded but did not speak. She knew he was wrestling with his conscience. She waited, tense in the knowledge that his decision could tear her heart out.

'Miss Booth.' John's voice was quiet but she sensed the emotion in it. 'I can offer you no more than a secret love. I love my wife. I would not want to hurt her.'

'And I do not wish to usurp her place,' Lydia said quickly but with firm assurance.

'In company there must be no sign of our feelings for each other. Outside of that, perhaps from time to time we can meet here or in an old empty cottage in the little valley that lies close to the boundary between Penorna and Trethtowan Estates.'

'I know it.'

John gave her a questioning look and she nodded. There was no need for further words to seal what passed between them; the touch of their lips did that.

Chapter Eleven

The early January snow of 1786 had disappeared except for a few pockets. 'I'm going to the mine this morning,' John announced at breakfast. 'They may be going to blast, see if the seam that is being worked runs further west. If it does there's a possibility it goes even further. Another piece of dynamiting will show us everything. If it is positive it will take us into land that Gaisford wants to buy.'

Eliza came to the stable yard to see her husband leave. He was ready to mount his horse when she stopped him, kissing him on the cheek and saying, 'If you go down that mine, be careful.'

'I will,' he reassured her.

'Good morning, Wallace,' called John as he halted his horse and the mine manager came out of his hut to meet him.

'Morning, sir.' He eyed his employer with a sense of satisfaction that the good will and investment in the mine Mr Mitchell's uncle had established had been continued by his nephew. In the years since John Mitchell's arrival a good rapport had built up between himself and the miners.

'All set to blast today?'

'Aye, sir. Welburn was keen to do it, but on examining his hand I decided to leave it to Lund. The cut hasn't healed properly.'

'Was Welburn satisfied with your decision? I don't want to lose him.'

'Yes. He saw sense when I explained why I thought he should not handle explosives for at least another two weeks.'

'Good.' They started to walk towards the mine-shaft. 'Pumps working?'

'Aye, sir! That new one you had installed six months ago is a great improvement. it's pushing out about five hundred gallons a minute and enabling us to go where we would never have been able to before. Like the seam where we'll be blasting today.'

'And if we find new ones, as we hope, that will mean greater production and more profit. I'll see to it that it puts more money in the men's pockets.'

'That's generous of you, sir.'

'Not at all, they are responsible for it.'

'But it's your investment.'

'We are all in this together, Wallace.'

'It's a pity all mine owners don't share your attitude, sir. Cornwall would be a better place if they did. Exploitation of miners is rife in the county as owners line their own pockets.'

'Greed, I'm sorry to say, Wallace.'

'Aye. And it'll get worse at the Gaisford mines when Mr Jeremy takes over. I hear tell his father isn't too well again.' Wallace pulled himself up sharp then, thinking he had said too much. 'Sorry, sir, I shouldn't be criticising my betters.'

'Don't apologise, Wallace. I sympathise with your opinion.' John left a little pause and then added, 'I didn't know Mr Miles wasn't well again.'

'A recurrence of the trouble he had a while back, shortly before you went north, sir.'

John nodded and their conversation halted as they had reached the shaft head. Several miners in flannel trousers, shirts and heavy boots were already queuing to descend. Light-hearted banter passed between them to take their minds off the grim conditions in which they would work. There'd be no light except from the candles secured by lumps of clay to the convex crowns of their resin-impregnated felt hats. They would descend on wooden ladders to the first workings, about three hundred feet below, and then walk along a tunnel that gradually decreased in height and width until for the final yards they'd have to crawl. The air would progressively turn

144

fouler and the temperature soar until it became unbearable to wear their shirts, and once work started the dust would make it hard to breathe at times. Yet there was a camaraderie second to none among these men, and also among their families for many wives would be working as bal maidens at the pit head, some in the dangerous occupation of crushing the copper ore with large hammers on iron anvils, their heads protected from flying chips by large hats covering their faces.

John Mitchell's workers knew they were luckier than most, for he did his best under the circumstances to provide them with some safety measures underground, and on the surface had erected open-sided sheds to afford workers some shelter from the weather. He also gave the children easier tasks whereas many other employers gave age or sex little consideration when allotting work on the surface, and expected young boys to work hard alongside the men below the surface.

The Penorna miners valued the fact that their employer sometimes joined them below ground even though he left the active work to them. They appreciated his understanding that they were the experts in this arduous task and he was not.

The straight descent was precarious, the ladder narrow though firmly secured to the rock and every man under instruction to report immediately any loose hold he might note.

Reaching the line they would be working on today, John asked to be shown exactly what was to happen. Bert Wallace led the way along the tunnel past a line of men. They eyed John, nodded, or touched their felt hats in respect. He nodded back or gave a word of encouragement. When the tunnel narrowed he and the manager were alone until, after crawling the last few yards, they emerged into a small area that had been widened enough to hold five men and made high enough for them to kneel upright.

Jim Lund and his two assistants were already there. Bert Wallace made hasty introductions, momentarily stopping the two men who were striking the bit to make a hole for the explosive. As Art Preston and Wes Maidstone resumed their task, Lund explained what he wanted to achieve.

'I'm placing a medium-sized charge there to open suffi-cient rock face to let us see what lies beyond and what it is likely to lead to. If it is satisfactory then I'll open up a large area in which the men can work.'

John nodded his understanding. He watched, feeling all the while the choking dust rise from the continual battering the rock face was undergoing, but he was determined not to retreat until it was necessary.

After a while, covered in dust, Art raised a hand and a sweat-covered Wes stopped hammering at the bit and drew a deep breath of relief in spite of the dust-laden air. Art glanced at Jim who shuffled to the hole that had been beaten in the rock. He examined it carefully and raised his thumb. With a glance at John and Bert he said, 'I'll get it ready now.'

The other four knew this was a signal for them to retreat. This they did without any haste as that could lead to a fatal loss of concentration in manoeuvring through the narrow tun-nel back to the main hall where the miners were waiting to move in after the rock had been blasted open. The manager made sure that they were all out of danger and then waited patiently for Jim to appear after he had completed packing the explosive to his liking.

It seemed like an eternity to the waiting miners who gave a little cheer when he eventually appeared, not by way of greet-ing but as a release of pent-up tension.

Jim cast a quick glance along the tunnel and, satisfied that no one should be in danger, crawled a few feet back the way he had just come. Then he scrambled back quickly and every-one knew that the trail of gunpowder that would reach the fuse and dynamite had been lit. Men clamped their hands over their ears, some remaining upright, pressing back against the rock face, while others preferred to crouch as if to protect themselves against a foe. An uncanny silence descended on the tunnel; even the movement of dust in the air seemed to be stilled. Tension heightened. Minds queried, shouldn't it have gone off before now? Something must have gone wrong. Is Lund going to have to go back? Then all thoughts were shat-tered by an explosion that sent air-waves sweeping back through the tunnel, buffeting the men that stood there. Dust swirled and thickened until each man could hardly see his neighbour. The crash of falling rock reverberated back through the tunnel. Slowly the noise died away; dust began to settle; men looked eagerly at each other from grimy faces.

John stepped back towards the narrow tunnel that would lead them to whatever the explosion had uncovered.

Bert Wallace touched his arm. 'Not yet, sir! Lund goes first – a tradition of his that he has never broken. If things haven't gone as planned he wants to know first.'

John nodded and wiped dust from his lips.

Lund was already crawling through the tunnel. Everyone waited anxiously until his head reappeared and they saw his face wreathed in a broad smile. He scrambled to his feet and held up both thumbs which raised a relieved cheer that rippled along the tunnel. There would be hard work ahead but it meant that there would be more ore to mine and continued employment.

The manager got into urgent conversation with Lund then turned to the rest of the men. He called two of them forward and put them in charge of two gangs. The first would go into action widening the narrow part of the tunnel and then the second gang would move in as soon as was practical to clear the chamber opened up by the charge. But first he wanted to see for himself the result of the blast. He glanced at John. 'You coming through, sir?'

'Try keeping me back,' he replied with a grin. He followed his manager through the narrow tunnel to find the rock face of the chamber torn apart, but Lund's skill in placing the dynamite had made sure it had not undermined the stability of the chamber roof. Men could safely work to clear it and get to the ore that had been exposed.

'It looks to be a rich vein, sir,' called Bert with delight.

'It does,' agreed John, pleased with the way he had adapted to this life which was so different from the one he had led in Whitby.

He summed up their position underground in relation to the surface and judged in which direction Selwyn's land lay. If the ore they had uncovered now spread in that direction then Gaisford's assessment had been correct. It would also mean that if Selwyn was in agreement, he and John could join the two mines and work the new veins underground, using the present outlets, without marring the surface as Gasiford would have done.

John drew the manager and Lund to one side. 'This is a good sign. I think there might be more ore to the left of this chamber and the tunnel we will be driving now to get this ore out.'

'It is possible, sir,' agreed Wallace. 'In fact, I would say more than likely, but if we go too far that way we will be getting into Mr Westbury's land.'

'Yes, I know. There might be an advantage in joining up with him, if he is agreeable, but leave all that to me. We won't tackle the next blast until I have discussed it with him. if he doesn't like the idea we can try another direction.'

'Very good, sir.'

Already they could hear the men making a start on widening the narrow part of the tunnel.

When John and the manager finally climbed out of the shaft on to the surface they breathed heavily on the pure clean air.

John's lips tightened. 'I wish I could do more to eliminate the dust from down there but until someone invents a more powerful air pump I can't. And I don't like to see young lads of seven or eight working the pump. Get some older ones on.'

'But the families of those lads depend on their contribution to the household.'

'Give them some other work on the surface then.'

'But, sir, we are working to capacity up here.'

John cast his eyes over the constant activity: boys and girls trundling ore from the pit head to the bal maidens who wielded hammers to break it up; boys bent double jiggling large sieves, and women dressing the ore. He gave a little shake of his head. This was far from satisfactory; employment should be less exacting than this. He knew his uncle must have been a man who looked ahead. Maybe he could be the same. But he could never do what he really desired for his workers, that would cost far too much money. Still, he would do what he could. He had already seen that their cottages were better maintained and the wages he paid, while far from what he would have liked, were better than most other employers provided. It was conditions at the mine that troubled him most but there was little he could do about underground working. Maybe there was more he could do on the surface.

John screwed up his face in thought then said, 'Wallace, those boys at present employed on the air pump, set them on with some carpenters to make those open-sided sheds more weather-proof for the bal maidens. They're still exposed to driving rain and wind at the moment. And let's try and give them something more solid to stand on. It can't be good for thcm to be working on wet ground.'

'Yes, sir!' Bert's reply was brisk, indicating approval of what would be seen as revolutionary by some mine owners.

'I've heard that two of the big mines have built what they are calling drys – rooms where the miners can have a wash down and change into clean clothes before leaving for home.'

'I've heard tell of them too, sir.'

'Look into it, Wallace, and I'll do the same. We'll compare notes then and see if we can do anything similar here. I've been here long enough now to be able to make changes and hopefully improve conditions.'

'Yes sir! This is very thoughtful of you. Everyone will appreciate any changes for the better.'

'Don't say anything about this last idea until we have looked into it because it will have to be financed from the profits I can see being made if Mr Westbury and I join up below ground. But we want to move fairly quickly so that once the carpenters have finished work on those sheds we can turn them on to constructing the drys.'

'Very good, sir.'

'I look forward to hearing your calculations of the yield that was revealed today.

'I should have a good idea in a couple of days, sir.'

'Good.' John walked to his horse, satisfied with the way things had gone below ground and with the development of his ideas for improvements on the surface. He had a strange feeling that his uncle's influence was still being exerted around here and that he was only doing what Gerard would have done himself had he lived.

Bert Wallace watched him go, thankful that Mr Mitchell was walking in his uncle's philanthropic footsteps.

Eliza was pleased to see her husband riding towards the house and acknowledged his wave as he turned his horse towards the stable yard. Nevertheless a flutter of anxiety swept through her on seeing his dust-covered appearance. She knew he had been below ground and realised the danger he would have been in. She had heard people talk about conditions in the mines and was always anxious when John left to visit his even though she knew he did not always go below ground. She wondered why he had been there today.

She allowed him time to wash and change before she went into the house. He was coming down the stairs as she stepped into the hall. She sensed excitement in him as he took her hand and they went to the drawing room together.

'We discovered another good vein today,' he said, and went on to explain how this had come about. 'It seems likely it will join with Selwyn's. I'm going to have a word with him about it.'

'So Mr Gaisford was right!' commented Eliza.

'Yes.'

'I'm going to propose to Selwyn we break through. If the result is what I think it will be, we'll form a partnership in one big mine.'

'Won't new diggings mar the countryside which is the one thing you both swore to avoid?'

'I believe that if we share each other's shafts we will have enough access without making more, which is what Mr Gaisford would have done had we sold to him. I'll go to see Selwyn in the morning.'

The fine weather tempted John to walk to Trethtowan; he felt closer to the countryside and its beauty on foot than he did when he rode. It also gave him time to think. Today two things occupied his mind: the news and proposals he was bringing Selwyn, and his own relationship with Lydia Booth.

From a distance he saw Lydia leave the house with her artist's materials and canvas and judged that she would be going to their bay. Keeping to their agreement, neither acknowledged the other openly. To wave from such a distance would have indicated to others that there was a close friendship between them, and neither wanted public speculation about that.

He saw Selwyn busily poring over some papers on the terrace but when his friend looked up and saw him, he gathered the papers together and came to meet him.

'Good day, John,' he called. 'What brings you here this fine day?'

'I have news, Selwyn. Can we walk in the garden?'

'Of course,' he agreed, wondering what the news was that had brought such excitement to John's voice.

They fell into step, strolling in the rose garden down lavender-lined paths and on into the herbaceous area beyond. As they circled the lily pond John unfolded his story. When he had finished relating the facts about yesterday's blast he posed the question: 'Are you agreeable to my blasting through to your land?'

'Yes, why not?' Selwyn had become more intrigued as John's story had unfolded and he saw the possibilities of their working a large mine together. 'I suggest we first attempt a tunnel wide enough for a man to crawl down and make an examination. Then, if that proves successful, we'll move into a large-scale operation.'

'That is what I was going to propose. Do you want me to drive the tunnel from my side?'

'That would seem to be the sensible thing to do as you have been blasting there and, from what you have said, already have a good idea of the direction to take.'

'Very good. I'll discuss this with my manager and dyna-mite-handler tomorrow.'

'Then let me know when you propose to blast and I'll see my men are well clear.'

John felt that ease of mind that only comes when events fall into place. Advances at the mine heralded the possibility of greater profits. Besides that his visit to Whitby had been suc-cessful, and though it had had its nostalgic moments he had looked forward to returning to Cornwall, to Eliza and Abigail and now a third woman in his life. All was good with John's world and he strode out with a light step.

Reaching the bay, he did not hesitate but descended the steep path quickly. At the bottom he stopped and looked around him, mystified. There was no sign of Miss Booth nor any footprints in the sand. He had seen her with her art mate-rials and had felt sure she would be here. Perplexed, his heart sinking, he turned his head this way and that, searching from where he stood. No one, no sign of movement. His lips set in a line of disappointment. He shrugged his shoulders resigned-ly and had started to turn back to the path up the cliffside when teasing laughter rippled from behind him. He spun round and saw a vision of beauty emerge from a narrow cleft in the rock face.

'From the look on your face I know you care.' Her soft tone caressed him, like gentle music on his ears.

His eyes devoured her. He did not speak but held out his arms.

She came to him and let him enfold her.

There were three customers in the Waning Moon when Jeremy Gaisford, paying his weekly visit, shut the door quickly behind him to keep out the rising wind blowing in from the west. Though it howled around the eaves and corners it carried no threat of rain, but Jeremy had been glad he had chosen his long coat with its large collar which he had turned up as he crossed the high moor. Now he turned it down and shrugged himself out of the coat. He gave a brief curt nod to the three men inside, two of whom were strangers, and showed no sign of recognising Jim Lund. He was pleased to see him there, of course, for it meant that the man must have some information.

'Evening, landlord,' said Jeremy, as he came to the counter. 'A tankard, if you please.'

'Aye, sir.' He drew the ale. 'Wind rising this evening, wouldn't like to be at sea.'

'Nor I, landlord.' He took his ale and went to sit at a corner table that gave him a view of the room. He eyed the strangers and concluded they were travellers, pausing on their journey to slake their thirst. He judged they would want to be at their destination before nightfall and so would not be long in leaving. Ten minutes later he was proved right for the men put on their coats and hats, bade the landlord good night and left.

Jim Lund picked up his tankard and crossed the room to sit opposite his employer.

'Another drink each, Tom,' called Jeremy.

The landlord nodded, drew the ale and brought it to them. Jeremy handed him a coin and told him to have one himself. Tom, not invited to join them, knew something very private was about to be discussed.

'Well?' prompted Jeremy.

Jim leaned forward. 'Today we blasted in the chamber I told you about before.'

'And?'

'We uncovered a vein that looks very promising. When that has been properly opened up, Mr Mitchell is talking about blasting on its west side.'

'And if he does, that could join him up with Westbury,' Jeremy said thoughtfully.

'Aye, and if they decide to open up their mines into one and work together they can use the shafts each already has to ship the copper out. That will save expense.'

'They'll work together for certain. It will be no good Father trying to buy that land from them now they know what lies beneath the surface.' Jeremy paused, set his lips tight in thought, then slapped the table hard. 'All right, put the next part of the plan into operation as soon as you think it wise. You know what I want.'

Two days later John visited his mine again and discussed the plan to blast a small exploratory tunnel in the direction of the Trethtowan workings.

'If that is successful in telling us what we want to know, then carry on,' he instructed Wallace and Lund. 'I'll warn Mr Westbury to keep his workers clear of that particular area from tomorrow until he hears from me again.'

After he had left, the two men went below ground and planned how they would go about making the necessary blast to open up a small tunnel. Wallace left much of the actual final arrangements and placement of the dynamite to the expert – Lund.

The following day Wallace saw that the necessary area underground was clear of miners and then joined Lund and his two assistants. Preston and Maidstone were already at work making the hole Lund required for his dynamite. Wallace had little to say but observed the meticulous care Lund took. He was not surprised when later that day, after the explosion had been made, there was a reasonable hole through which he could crawl to make his examination. He re-emerged with a broad smile on his dusty face.

'It's good. Looks like a rich vein links the Penorna and Trethtowan mines.'

'Do you want us to carry on then?' asked Jim.

'Aye. Plan to make the next blast tomorrow.'

After he had gone Jim examined the chamber they were in and the tunnel he had just created. By the time he left the mine he knew exactly what he was going to do and as he walked home he smiled at the thought of the Gaisford money that would soon be jangling in his pocket.

John was on the terrace the following morning when his attention was caught by the sound of a galloping horse. When the rider came in sight he immediately sensed trouble. His fears were heightened when he recognised his mine manager's horse and saw that the rider was a grime-covered youngster.

'Mr Mitchell! Mr Mitchell!' he yelled, hauling on the reins. 'Trouble at the mine!' The horse struggled against the tight reins and the boy fought for control. 'Bad rockfall. Mr Wallace said to come at once.' The horse was still champing at the bit, seeking to free itself.

John leaped down the steps and raced for the stables, shouting over his shoulder, 'Wait for me.'

When he emerged from the stable yard a few minutes later the boy immediately turned his horse alongside John's and matched his gallop stride for stride.

'What's happened?' yelled John.

'Not sure, sir! Something to do with Jim Lund's blasting.'

'How bad? Anyone hurt?'

'Don't think so. Mr Wallace had the tunnels cleared but I think it's a bad fall.'

John realised the boy knew no more and, with the horses at full tilt, concentrated on reaching the mine as soon as possible.

Men from below ground were gathered at the pit head in groups. Surface workers stood idly by their work spots. Overall there was a buzz of speculation. John spotted Wallace and Lund, who seemed to be arguing, close to the shaft head. With concern in his eyes he rode straight over to them and dropped from the saddle.

'What happened?' he demanded.

'Explosion went wrong, sir,' replied his manager.

'How wrong? Anyone hurt?'

'No one, sir. All the tunnels were cleared beforehand.'

'Good,' John said with obvious relief. Injuries and loss of life were the last things he wanted. 'So what's the damage?'

'Bad, sir.' He hesitated a moment as if reluctant to disclose the facts, then realised he had no choice. 'Yesterday Lund opened up a small tunnel as agreed. It turned out to be as we'd hoped, indicating that there is a rich vein joining the Penorna and Trethtowan workings. We decided to open it further today.'

'So what went wrong?' John shot his question at Lund.

'After examining what we had achieved yesterday, sir, I decided that it was possible not only to open that small tunnel further but also to enlarge it into a workable chamber from which it would be easier to access the Trethtowan mine. I hoped I could at the same time enlarge the way to what was our working chamber . . .'

'But that would mean using dynamite dangerously in excess of what we have been using,' rapped John angrily. 'And what exactly do you mean by what *was* our working chamber?

Lund's lips tightened. 'It's completely blocked now, sir. The roof caved in.'

'What?' John's face showed his shock. He glanced at the manager for explanation. 'Didn't you supervise this?'

'Yes, sir! We had agreed on what should be done, and that did not include opening up the way to our chamber at this stage – that could have come later.'

John turned on Lund. 'So you went against . . .'

'Sir,' he broke in. 'I thought it safe to do so, and that it would save time.'

'You should have stuck by our original arrangements,' snapped Wallace. 'You knew that you were going to have to use more dynamite in a very restricted area.'

'All right,' broke in John. 'What's done is done. We cannot put it back to what it was. Just tell me how this is going to affect production?'

'We will have to turn men to clearing a tremendous fall if you still want to join the two mines, but that is going to take time.'

'So that will affect our output?'

'Yes. Unless you take on more men especially to do the clearing, but that would prove costly.'

John nodded thoughtfully. 'Let's just get people back to work and I'll give some thought as to what should best be done.'

'Very good, sir.' The manager hurried away and soon had the Penorna employees back at their respective jobs.

'Not you, Lund,' John said as the dynamite-handler started to walk away. 'I want you to tell me exactly what you did and what happened.'

He listened carefully to what Lund had to say and when he had dismissed him called over Preston and Maidstone. He questioned them and found their version of events corroborated Lund's.

John had much to think about as he rode slowly home.

Eliza heard him come in and left her parlour to rush down the stairs to greet him. 'What happened, John?' Seeing his distress, she led him to the drawing room where she poured him a glass of whisky. He accepted gratefully, sat down and told her what had happened.

'Let us be thankful that no one was hurt,' she comforted him.

He nodded. 'That's the positive way to look at it.'

'It's the only way. When you've made a proper assessment you'll have to decide if it is worthwhile clearing this rock fall.'

'It puzzles me why it happened at all. Lund seemed so competent. When you hired him, did you have any recommendations?'

'Mr Wallace and Mr Welburn had heard that the Gaisfords thought highly of him.'

'Then why sack him?'

'Belligerent to Mr Jeremy, it was said.'

'And the other two?

'Supported Lund.'

John played with his glass thoughtfully.

Eliza eyed him. 'You have something on your mind, what is it?'

'The circumstances of his dismissal and engagement were very similar to the Lowthers'.'

'But the Lowthers are good workers, aren't they?'

'Yes, I have no complaints against them. I was merely drawing the comparison with the way Lund came to us.'

Eliza looked puzzled.

'Supposing the Gaisfords set up the dismissal of Lund and his friends, knowing we were likely to engage them. After all, we had done the same when the Lowthers were sacked.'

'You mean, they were planting them on us for a purpose, to cause trouble because you would not sell the land?'

'Yes.'

'But the Gaisfords would know you already had a competent dynamite-handler in Mr Welburn. You weren't likely to hand that job over to Lund.'

'Right, but Welburn was injured and *that* happened while he was helping Lund.'

'You think Lund arranged that injury?'

'He could have.'

'So that he was in a position to cause this rock fall?'

'Exactly.'

'But you've no proof.'

'And never will have. They're too smart for that.'

'What are you going to do about Lund and the other two?'

'Keep them on, but keep an eye on them too. I had better appraise Selwyn of the situation. I'd rather do it before he hears about it from anyone else.'

When John had acquainted his friend with what had happened and went on to theorise about Lund's part in it, Selwyn was inclined to agree and also approved of his decision not to sack the three men.

'We'll have to assess what can be done. If we think it's still financially viable to clear the fall in order to make one big mine, we shall share the expense of the clearance even though the fall is on your side,' said his friend.

'That is generous of you. I'll arrange a meeting with you at the mine.'

Jeremy Gaisford received Jim Lund's report at the Waning Moon with delight and paid him generously. He was amazed that Mitchell had not sacked Lund, however.

'Be careful how you behave. One false step now could

158

arouse Mitchell's suspicions. See that Maidstone and Preston understand that. You might still prove useful to me.'

Jeremy rode home in good spirits but they vanished when he recounted in detail what Lund had accomplished and saw his father's face darken with anger.

'Fool! Did you countenance causing such damage?'

'I left that to Lund.'

'Did you not instruct him in what I wanted doing?'

'Yes.'

'*Exactly* what I wanted?'

'I told him to cause a rock fall that would disrupt the mine.'

'Is that all?'

'Yes. What else did you want?'

Miles scowled. His lips tightened with irritation.

'When will you learn to follow my instructions to the letter? Why don't you pay attention to detail? Why don't you listen? Are you incapable?' With each question he thumped the arm of his chair. 'I distinctly told you that any disruption was to make Mitchell think it would be better to sell to us, not to wreak such havoc that it would make him suspicious we still wanted to buy. Who would buy from him now when to put such havoc right would cost a fortune?'

Jeremy felt his pulses racing. 'Why blame me?' he snapped. 'I didn't lay the dynamite.'

'No, but it was your responsibility to see that Lund understood exactly what was expected of him. You're an incompetent fool! I wish Logan were the eldest. God knows what will happen to this estate when *you* get your hands on it. More's the pity my hands are tied by a trust that states the eldest son must always inherit Senewey. Damn whoever laid that down!' Miles was shaking as he spat the words out. He glared at his son. 'Get out! Get out now!'

Angry words sprang to Jeremy's lips but he thought better than to voice them and started for the door. 'And you're a coward! Daren't stand up to your own father, frightened to say what you think.' Stung by his words, Jeremy swung round. His face was a mask of hatred. He saw Miles's hands pushing against the arms of his chair. He was half out of his seat. Their eyes met, Jeremy's filled with enmity, his father's with disgust. 'Get out! Get . . .'

The words choked in Miles's throat and were replaced by a gurgling sound. He clutched at his chest and slumped back in his chair. His eyes widened. Jeremy felt their gaze penetrating his very soul. He stepped towards his father, then he stopped. A small smile of contempt mingled with satisfaction as he ignored Miles's attempt to reach out to him.

'My help? You want my help now?' he mocked. 'You've just been telling me how useless I am. Well, I'm not going to risk that happening again.'

He smiled as he watched his father die.

Chapter Twelve

Landowners from all over the county came to pay their last respects to Miles Gaisford. They filled the small church and filed out to join Senewey Estate workers and miners who had had to wait outside in the bleak damp March wind that blew in from the Atlantic. Not many truly mourned this man's passing but they were all there out of respect for Cornwall's foremost family and for Rowena who they noted was escorted by Logan – had Jeremy taken over Senewey completely? They knew Miles had kept a tight rein on certain aspects of his sons' lives, especially the running of the estate. Now, many of them wondered what the future held for Senewey with Jeremy at the helm. Not least among them John Mitchell.

He had paid his own respects and was turning away when Jeremy's cold voice stopped him.

'Mitchell, what a pity you didn't sell that land to my father. now you are faced with an expensive disaster. Not only that, he would still be alive today if you had obliged him.' He charged the last sentence with accusation.

It sent a chill through John. 'What do you mean by that?'

'Your refusal brought on the attack from which he never fully recovered and that finally brought about his death. You are to blame, Mitchell, and I'll not forget it.' Jeremy gave John a dismissive look and turned away to accept condolences from a sympathiser, easier in his mind now that he had put the blame on someone else.

John was tempted to accuse him of instigating the recent disaster at the mine but without proof it was too dangerous. As he left Senewey, John wondered what the future might bring. His thoughts were centred on the troubled relationship with Jeremy Gaisford, but it was another relationship that was to turn his world upside down, 10 April 1786 would always live in his memory.

Mr Mitchell, I have something to tell you but first I want you to see the finished painting.'

'Finished? I was not expecting it so soon.'

'There was a reason why I pressed on with it, Mr Mitchell.'

'Mr Mitchell?'

'A wise precaution. If we used Christian names in private then their use might become too familiar to us and we might slip up in company.'

He nodded his understanding and agreed that they should continue in the same way. He did not like the formality but saw the wisdom of Lydia's reasoning, and he wanted nothing to mar the joy of their weekly meeting in private.

'So, let me see the painting.'

With its back to him she unwrapped the canvas carefully. She was watching his face carefully when she finally turned it round and saw John's expression change to one of wonder and joy.

He stared at the painting for what seemed an age, then looked up slowly and locked eyes with her. 'That is wonderful. You have captured the very essence of our bay. It will always bring you close to me whenever I look at it.' As he was speaking he came to her. She knew exactly what was going to happen then so turned the painting to one side and allowed it to fall gently back on to the sand. He kissed her passionately as his arms enfolded her. Lydia accepted his kiss, feeling safe in the comfort of his love. When their lips parted she laid her head against his chest and shivered while his fingers gently stroked her neck. 'John, I said I had something to tell you.' She paused, half expecting him to prompt her, but lost in the joy of holding her he did not. She went on without any preamble, 'I am going to have a baby.'

For a moment his world stood still, blocking out her words, but in that moment the enormity of what had happened bit deep. He had betrayed Eliza, dear precious Eliza around whom his life had hitherto revolved. The woman who had supported him in everything he did, had borne his beautiful daughter, shared so much with him and with whom he wanted to go on sharing life. Why on earth had he allowed his interest in Lydia Booth to develop this far?

She read something in his expression that she'd hoped she would not see. 'You are angry . . . you don't want this child?' She looked up at him with accusing eyes.

He pushed her away but only far enough for him to hold her by the arms and look into her eyes. 'I'm not angry, but are you sure? I thought we . . .'

She did not let him finish. 'So did I, but it has happened.'

John shrugged his shoulders in acceptance. 'Are you happy about it?'

She nodded. 'Yes. I will always have something of you now.'

The sincerity of her reply smote his heart. 'I love you, Lydia Booth,' he whispered, drawing her close. He kissed her again, but when their lips parted practicalities were foremost in his mind. 'I must think what to do for the best. I want no scandal to fall on you.'

'It won't, and no stain will touch you if you agree to what I propose.'

'You've thought it out?'

'Yes. I love you too much to come whining to you, expecting you to solve my dilemma.'

'Our dilemma! We have caused this, we will see it through together.'

'I will leave Cornwall . . .'

'You can't!' he protested. 'I could not bear never seeing you again.'

'Nor I never seeing you! Hear me out. I will put it about that I am needed by my brother whose wife is having a baby and is extremely ill. I'll say he now lives in the North of England in a small village nobody's ever heard of, close to the Scottish Borders. No one will check that. I won't really go there; he wanted nothing to do with me when our parents died so he'll show no concern for me now. I'll find somewhere else to go to have the baby. When I return I will say that the baby is my brother's but as his wife has died and he won't take any responsibility for it, I have agreed to bring it up.'

'I don't think anyone will question that, but we do have to find you somewhere to live. I have property in Penzance but if you move into one of those houses it could look a little suspicious. You know how people speculate.'

'Then I will have to find somewhere else.'

'You will need money to buy a house. I will provide that, and make you a regular allowance.'

'That is as I expected, but there is a condition to my return that you won't like. You'd better hear it now before making any more promises.' Her eyes were fixed intently on him so that she would not miss one moment of his reaction to what she was about to say. Wary of her words, he gave a questioning frown. 'You will have no personal contact with the child!'

A chill struck at his heart. 'What?'

'You will have no personal contact with the child!' she repeated in a voice so full of determination that it shocked him.

John spun away from her in disgust. 'Impossible!'

'I insist on it or I do not come back.'

'You can't mean it?' he cried, his face darkening.

'I do. it's the only sensible thing to do.'

'It's not!' His voice was sharp, matched by an expression clouded with anger. 'I will not be denied the right of seeing my own child grow up.'

'I'm not denying you that but there will be no personal contact.'

'I won't agree,' he stated resolutely.

'If you don't you'll wreck your marriage, wound Eliza and Abigail, and destroy our love for each other.' Lydia's voice broke with anguish. 'Be sensible. If you have a personal relationship with this child, it is more than likely your wife will get to know.'

'How, if we keep it secret?'

'*We* may be able to do that, but we can't expect the child to do so. It would see you, know you, and something would slip out in all innocence.' He looked doubtful. 'How would you explain your visits to a child who would want to know who you were? And that's another thing . . . you will not be able to visit me either.'

'What?' Astonished disbelief swam in John's eyes. 'So you are putting an end to our relationship, destroying our love?'

'No, I'm not!' she cried with an urgency that pleaded with him to understand. 'You love your wife and daughter. You don't want to hurt them. In my love for you, nor do I. If our child saw you in their company and inadvertently let slip that it knew you, don't you think they would begin to wonder why?' Her reasoning held him silent. 'You can see I'm right,' Lydia went on. 'Having no personal contact would ensure that did not happen. You can see him or her only from a distance. Passing in the street, there must be no acknowledgement. it is the only way. I insist on it, for the sake of our child I will not have hurt. It is for the good of us all.'

As she was speaking, the implications behind her reasoning began to make sense. Not only did John see that but, in her frankness and concern for all, he sensed a new bond of trust would be forged between them if he accepted.

'Maybe you are right.' Though there was a touch of doubt in his voice it had all but vanished from his mind and was completely obliterated when she spoke again.

'I *am* right, John. It's the only way if we are to remain near each other.'

He gave a small nod of acceptance, drew her close and kissed her.

Lydia felt relief to her very soul.

He looked thoughtful. 'Have you thought about where you will go to have the baby?'

'No. I haven't had much time to get used to the idea myself.'

'I think I have a solution, a place I know will be reliable and not a word will ever be breathed about. The secret will be safe forever.'

She looked at him with eager expectancy. This was the one aspect of her pregnancy that had troubled her, but one that she had been determined to solve to their advantage. Now a solution might be within her grasp.

'You will go to my sister in Whitby. It is far enough away from here for no one to know. Martha and I are very close. She will help, and say nothing about you and the baby. She knows how to keep a secret even from my wife with whom she gets on well. She will know reliable people who will help with the birth and say nothing afterwards. How does that sound to you?'

'It's a gift from heaven.' Lydia's eyes shone brightly.

'Very well. I will accompany you to introduce you to my sister and offer her an explanation. You'll find her a very understanding person. I know she will not apportion blame.'

'But how will you explain your need to go to Whitby again?'

'There was some trouble in the business so I can quite openly pay her a visit again. After all, even though I draw nothing from the business, I still have an interest in it. While I am in Whitby I will set up an account into which I will put money so you can purchase a house on your return to Cornwall. It will also serve as a place to deposit your regular allowance.'

'That's wonderful.'

'But there is still the problem of where you can stay between your return to Cornwall and the purchase and setting up of your new household.'

'I think I can solve that. As you know, my family were friendly with the Westburys in Oxford. It was through that friendship that I was given the job of governess when times were hard for me. I am sure they will let me come back to them for a short while.'

'That certainly would be a solution,' he agreed.

'I can only ask. But that still does not give us a place to meet without the child knowing?'

'Hopefully one of my properties will become vacant and if it does we could have that as our meeting place. Now, the sooner we go to Whitby the better, so no one here gets any inkling of your condition.'

'We cannot be seen leaving together.'

'I know, so here's what I propose. I will go by coach from Penzance, leaving next Thursday morning. I'll go only as far as Truro where I will stay at the Lion until your coach arrives two days later. I will join you there for our onward journey to Whitby together. I'm sure Mr and Mrs Westbury will take you to Penzance.'

'I will tell them the day after tomorrow that I have heard from my brother and wish to leave their employment.'

'That sounds satisfactory, but why not tomorrow?'

'Because I am delivering the painting to you then and have no doubt that they will want to accompany me to see your reaction. We don't want to risk their mentioning my leaving then.'

'Wise,' he agreed. 'So, after your visit, the next time I see you will be a week on Thursday in Truro.'

Lydia picked up the painting. 'I think we had better go. I'll bring this to your home tomorrow to present it to you and your wife. And, remember, act as if you have never seen it before.'

'Trust me. And, Lydia, it will mean so much more to me now.'

They parted with a kiss of promise and love.

'Ma'am, Mr John is here.'

The shock of this announcement brought Martha quickly to her feet. Dropping the book she had been reading, she was halfway across the drawing room when her brother walked in.

'John! How delightful!' She embraced him affectionately. As she kissed him on the cheek her attention was drawn to a well-dressed young lady standing in the doorway beyond.

John felt Martha's surprise. He stepped over to the new-comer and said, 'Martha, I want you to meet Miss Booth.'

Lydia, who had been apprehensive about this meeting, in spite of John's continual assurances during their journey together from Truro, took a tentative step into the room.

Martha moved to greet her with one hand held out. 'Miss Booth.' Her soft voice with its gentle accent helped to ease Lydia's concern but she saw curiosity in that gaze nevertheless.

'I am pleased to meet you, Miss Mitchell.'

Martha detected nervousness marring that pleasant voice. Questions were pouring into her mind but she could not ask them now. She shot a quick glance at her brother and saw something in his eyes as he looked at Miss Booth that set alarm coursing through her. She held it in check as she said, 'And I you, Miss Booth, welcome to my home. Won't you sit down?'

'Thank you.'

Martha indicated a chair and sat down herself when Lydia was seated. 'What brings you on this unexpected visit?' she asked, turning her eyes on her brother who had remained standing.

John had rehearsed this moment many times since he had made the decision to seek his sister's help.

'I would like you to accommodate Miss Booth for a little while.' The words came out not at all as he had planned for they had a nervous timbre to them that he knew would arouse his perceptive sister's curiosity. He went on quickly before Martha could say anything. 'Miss Booth is a dear friend who needs help. I would be grateful if you could do this for her.'

Tension had seeped into the room, in spite of John's efforts to keep it at bay. Martha, sensing that her brother did not want to offer a full explanation in front of the young lady, knew there was only one way to bring him relief and took it.

'Then I had better show her to the guest room and inform the staff that we will have visitors for a few days.' She stood up. 'Miss Booth.'

Recognising this as an invitation to follow, Lydia got to her feet. As she started after Martha she cast John an embarrassed plea to make sure everything would be accepted by his sister.

Martha paused in the hall to ring a hand bell that stood on a small oak table at the bottom of a staircase whose ramped banister of fine oak resting on handsome matching balusters gave a sense of permanence and security. That feeling persisted when a maid appeared, neat in her black dress and white apron, and Martha said, 'June, this is Miss Booth who will be staying with us. She is to have the first guest bedroom and you are to give her your special attention. I will acquaint Mrs Barton.'

'Yes, ma'am,' replied June. 'I'll take that, miss,' she added when she saw Lydia go to a valise.

'Thank you,' she replied quietly.

'Mrs Barton is my housekeeper. I will introduce you later,' explained Martha.

Lydia followed her up the stairs and was glad that there were no further questions as Martha kept the conversation going about the ease of their journey from Cornwall.

'I hope you will be comfortable here,' she said as she turned the knob on a heavy oak door that opened easily.

Lydia stifled a gasp when she found herself inside a large corner room with windows that gave a view of two different aspects of the garden and landscape beyond. The room was decorated in yellow giving it a bright sunny atmosphere that was reflected in the pristine white bedclothes. A dressing table was set neatly with all the necessary accoutrements and a large wardrobe was ready to store any clothes. Martha opened a door in one wall and Lydia saw it was a toilette area.

Jane, catching Martha's small wave of dismissal, had already left the room when Lydia said, 'Miss Mitchell, thank you for your kindness.'

When she replied, 'I love my brother very much,' it carried a wealth of meaning and Lydia knew that if she hurt John she would create an enemy for life in this woman. 'Freshen up, make yourself comfortable and come and join us in the drawing room in, say, twenty minutes. I'll order some tea for then.'

Lydia gave a small nod. She offered no further explanation of why she was here; John would do that. Martha sought none for she too knew that it had to come from her brother.

She hurried down the stairs, made a quick visit to the kitchen and then returned to the drawing room. The door had hardly clicked shut behind her when she said in a demanding tone that had some anger in it, 'An explanation, John, please.'

He hesitated. This was a confrontation he had already gone over and over in his mind but now, facing his sister, he was embarrassed and all the words had fled from his mind.

'The beginning is a good place to start,' snapped Martha. The touch of irritation in her voice was accompanied by the reproach in her eyes and he knew she had already surmised some of the truth.

'I fell in love,' he said lamely.

'You what?' Her voice rose. 'I thought you loved Eliza?'

'I do.'

'So what is going to happen? Has this woman turned your head? She's a pretty little thing, I'll grant you that, but . . .'

'She's more,' he cut in.

'How can you say you love Eliza and still fall for this woman?' his sister demanded in disgust.

'I assure you it's possible,' he replied tersely but with marked conviction. He ignored his sister's protest and added, 'I'm staying with Eliza and she will never know of my relationship with Miss Booth.'

'And I suppose you are going to say she'll never know about the baby?' Martha gave a derisory shake of her head. 'Don't look surprised. These things happen, and why else would you bring her here but to avoid a scandal in Cornwall? What explanation did you give Eliza for your own visit?'

'A follow up on my last.'

'Very convenient for you,' returned Martha sarcastically. Then, regretting her tone, softened her voice as she asked, 'What do you want me to do?' She glanced at her fob-watch. 'Miss Booth will be joining us for tea in fifteen minutes.'

'I'd like you to look after her until after the baby is born.'

'You think that by your coming here, no word will ever get back to Cornwall?'

'How could it? Your servants need never know that Miss Booth's child is mine. I have merely brought the daughter of a friend here for your help, as far as they are concerned. You can even use the story we are using when Lydia returns to Cornwall.' He explained that.

'We'll see, but they can be adept at putting two and two together.'

'I know that a timely word from you will suffice to stem any gossip. They are loyal to you because you treat them well and would not want to lose their employment with you or have you spread word that would preclude them from obtaining other work in this district.'

'You are very perceptive.'

'Then you'll help?'

'Who am I to refuse my brother? And of course I owe you something in return for you saving me from Mr Horton's machinations.'

'That never entered my head.' John exchanged a small knowing smile with her.

A knock on the door heralded June and another maid with the tea. As they were leaving Martha said, 'June, will you tell Miss Booth tea is served?' A few moments later Lydia tentatively entered the room.

'Come in,' said Martha in a tone that still held some hostility. 'Sit down there,' she added, indicating a chair. She saw Lydia glance anxiously at John. 'My brother has told me everything,' she said tersely. 'You are welcome to stay here, and rest assured you will be well looked after with no scandal. I have friends who will attend the baby's birth, and all my staff know how to be discreet. I will think up a story to tell them, maybe even say your brother would not take you in after an indiscretion.'

The draining of tension from Lydia was visible. 'Miss Mitchell, how can I ever thank you – except to assure you that no harm will come to your brother's marriage. I love him too much to let that happen.'

'See that it doesn't, Miss Booth. Though I don't condone what has happened, I will have to come to terms with it and you and I will have to get to know each other better.' Martha started to pour the tea and John handed it to Lydia along with a scone and some jam. In a more relaxed atmosphere, in the

171

company of John and his sister, Lydia felt the last of the tension draining away, even though she knew she would have to work to win this woman's full confidence.

Later, after Lydia had retired, John explained about setting up an account for her, and though she knew that her brother would be cautious about how he acted, Martha issued another warning that nothing he did should jeopardise what Eliza and Abigail should have by right.

Two days later, deeming it wise to make this a short visit, John left for Cornwall.

Eight months later a baby girl was born in Whitby and Lydia christened her Tess. With her returning strength, she broached the subject of returning to Cornwall.

'You'll spend Christmas here and not return south until 1787 brings better weather for travelling. As much as John might want to see you and his daughter, he would not want you to place yourselves at risk.'

Martha and Lydia had become close by now and Martha was delighted that they would share Tess's first Christmas together. Though she wanted to see John and show him their daughter, Lydia knew the wisdom of her words and delighted in the fact that she was giving her friend so much pleasure by staying over Christmas.

Knowing nothing of what was happening in Whitby, John spent some anxious days, especially when he knew the birth would be imminent, but he submerged those anxieties in a display of love for his wife. When the time had passed and Lydia did not return he tried to convince himself that it was because of the inclement conditions and longed for the finer days and warmer weather.

He hid any anxiety and enjoyed a family Christmas with Eliza and Abigail who, now at six, was beginning to approach the festivities with an adult outlook. She eagerly helped her mother and father with the seasonal food distribution they made to their employees. It was a gay time at Penorna Manor where John and Eliza maintained the tradition set up by his uncle of a special feast for the household on Boxing Day.

Abigail willingly served the staff who had grown to admire and love this girl who showed signs of turning into a beautiful young lady, with the same complexion as her mother, deep blue eyes and copper-tinted hair, and her father's amiable disposition.

It was not until late March that Selwyn and Harriet, on a visit to Penorna Manor, unwittingly gave John the news he wanted to hear.

'You remember Miss Booth who resigned her position as governess to go to look after her sister-in-law?' said Harriet.

'Of course they do,' chided her husband. 'They have her painting hanging in the hall.'

Harriet dismissed his observation with a wave of her hand. 'We recently agreed to her coming back to us while she found somewhere local to live. Well, she arrived yesterday with a child.'

'What?' Eliza asked with surprise.

Reading the implication she supposed was there, Harriet gave a small laugh, 'Oh, not hers, Eliza. Her sister-in-law died in childbirth and apparently Miss Booth's brother wanted nothing to do with the baby, a little girl. Miss Booth agreed to take her and her brother has financed the purchase of a house and will make her a monthly allowance.'

'That's very noble of Miss Booth,' commented Eliza. 'How long will she be with you?'

'She intends to buy a house in Penzance as soon as possible.'

John's heart had been racing. Lydia and his child were close! He had to curb his own desire to ask questions.

'Has she named the child?' asked Eliza.

'She's called Tess.'

John savoured the name. He liked it. Then his mind was brought sharply back to the conversation for Harriet was continuing to speak.

'She's a beautiful baby and Miss Booth says she is so pleasant and happy.'

'I'm surprised she came back to Cornwall,' commented Eliza.

'When she left us she said she might as she had been happy here. Her brother's attitude to his daughter was such that Miss Booth thought she should move far enough away for him to have no influence over the child.'

It was a fortnight before John received further news of Lydia and Tess. It came innocently, one day after he had returned from the mine, when Eliza informed him that she had had a visit from Harriet and among the news she'd brought was the fact that Miss Booth had now left Trethtowan and was residing in a house in Market-jew Street in Penzance. To avoid any hint of suspicion, John curbed his impatience for another eight days before he went into town, ostensibly to examine his properties there. It did not take him long by casual indirect enquiries to learn where the newcomer to Market-jew Street was living.

Lydia had been adamant about him having no contact with the child but surely seeing his daughter while she was so young would not affect any future situation.

He rapped hard on the brass knocker and a few moments later the door was opened by Lydia. Her expression contained surprise, pleasure, wariness and a hint of annoyance. 'Mr Mitchell!'

'Lydia, I just had to come.'

Anxious that she should not be seen, she said, 'You'd better come in.' She moved to one side and quickly closed the door once he had stepped inside. 'What are you doing here?' she demanded. 'I told you, no contact with our child.'

'Tess,' he corrected. 'I heard about your arrival at Trethtowan and the move to Penzance. I curbed my impatience to see you and Tess then but I could wait no longer.' He reached out and spanned her waist with his hands. Lydia's annoyance because he had broken her condition melted. She relaxed in his arms and met his lips with equal desire.

When the kiss ended he said, 'Where's Tess?'

She took his hand and led him to the stairs. A few moments later he was standing beside a cot gazing at his peacefully sleeping daughter, her head on a pristine white pillow.

'She has your eyes, your hair and your nose.'

Lydia chuckled. 'You see what you want to see.'

'No. She's beautiful, just like you.'

Hearing voices, Tess twisted her head and gave them a wonderful smile. Moved by it, John reached down and touched her hand with his forefinger. Her tiny fingers came tightly round his and she gurgled at him.

'She likes you already,' whispered Lydia, pleased by her daughter's reaction. A few minutes later, when she saw Tess's eyes begin to close, she said, 'I think she's ready to sleep.'

When they went downstairs Lydia took John into the drawing room where a fire burned brightly. 'Thank you for making this possible,' she said.

'It is the least I could do,' he replied sincerely. 'Are you managing?'

'I want a maid and a cook.'

'You will engage them?'

'I have already done so. They were recommended by Dorinda whom I contacted after I moved here. They start tomorrow so it is as well you called today or I would have turned you away at the door.'

'You wouldn't!'

'Oh, yes, I would. You know the conditions I made and nothing must change them. You must never visit here again. Mrs Foxwell, the cook, and Mary Cunnack, the maid, are respectable women and have accepted my explanation that I have had to take my brother's child because he is incapable of doing so after the death of his wife in childbirth. But I would not want to try to explain your presence here.'

'Then I will have to arrange for one of my houses to become available for us.' He drew her to him and looked deep into her eyes. 'I cannot bear to be away from you too long.'

'I feel the same, John.' She hugged him. 'Oh, it is so good to see you and have your arms round me again. But we must be careful. We must avoid raising any suspicion.'

'We will, my love.' He kissed her tenderly. 'How much does Dorinda know?' he asked as they drew apart. 'You were very friendly.'

'We still are. But she knows no more than anyone else.'

'Good, keep it that way.'

'Now,' she said, 'I have a letter for you from your sister. I'm sorry I have not been able to get it to you before now, but Martha said it did not matter when I gave it to you.' She rose from her seat to get her reticule from the table.

'How is she?'

'Very well! You have a remarkable sister. I don't think she wanted us to leave. Tess became a favourite with her.'

'I know she will miss you both.'

She handed him the letter. He broke the seal and unfolded the sheet of paper.

'I'll get some tea while you read that,' Lydia offered.

24th February 1787

My Dear John,

These past months have been a delightful time for me. Lydia is a charming person and we got on extremely well after a few awkward days. I realise how much she loves you, and that in that love for you there is no rancour or jealousy towards Eliza. I believe she will do everything in her power to see that your wife never learns of this relationship. See that you keep it that way otherwise so many lives will be ruined and many people will be terribly hurt, not least the innocent Tess. What can I say but that she has been a great joy to me? I was sorry to see both of them go. Although I offered her and her mother a home here, I fully understood that Lydia wants to be near you. Even though I understand there is to be no personal contact, which I think wise under the circumstances, you can take part vicariously in your daughter's upbringing and from a distance watch her grow into the charming young woman I know she will become.

I suggest, dear brother, that you destroy this letter. If it fell into the wrong hands it could have far-reaching results. Though you may think it is in a safe place, you never know. Besides, there is no reason to keep it! Fire it.

My thoughts will often be with you and that dear lit-
tle girl.
Your loving sister,
Martha

He read it again and was tearing it up and dropping it into the
flames when Lydia returned.

'Oh, you're burning it,' she commented as she crossed the
room to place the tea tray on a low table in front of a settee.

'It was better destroyed,' he replied, straightening and turning to join her on the settee. 'It contained nothing untoward
but our relationship could have been surmised by anyone
seeking to make trouble.'

She nodded and started pouring the tea.

'Martha wrote highly of you.'

'It was she who was wonderful.'

'She wanted you to stay. Would you have liked that?'

'I wanted to be near you, and I wanted you to have Tess
close even though I still expect you to adhere to my conditions.' She saw his eyes cloud with disappointment. 'It's for
the best, John, it really is. But if you'd rather, I will go back.
Martha said I could if ever the need arose.'

'Don't think about it. We will be careful. I don't want your
life destroyed. It will be better for us once one of my houses
becomes vacant.'

'The sooner the better.'

As he walked away from the house John's mind was full of
regret that there could be no personal contact for him with
Tess, but that was dismissed in the hope that from afar he
could watch her grow up and bloom as beautifully as Abigail.

Chapter Thirteen

'Race you!' Abigail shouted as she set her horse to a gallop. Her laughter swept back to her mother and father.

'No!' shouted Eliza, but the alarm in her voice was lost on the wind.

'Let her go,' laughed John, pleased at the exuberance he saw in his daughter. 'Seventeen tomorrow, she's bound to be full of life. She'll be all right, she's a good rider.'

'I suppose so.' Eliza sighed. 'She's always been older than her years.'

'And prettier by the day,' said John. 'Some day soon a young man's going to come along and sweep her off her feet.'

'Perhaps we should be doing more to encourage someone who would be suitable,' answered Eliza wistfully, reminded of her own youth and feeling sorry that she would, in the not too distant future, see Abigail leave home.

The years had been good to them. They had had the pleasure of seeing their daughter grow up, influencing her development and view of the world. They knew they owed a great deal to Dorinda Jenkins, too, and although they anticipated the day when Abigail would no longer need a governess, did not look forward to telling her so. That task was taken from them when Abigail was fifteen and Dorinda reluctantly had to give in her notice and move to Penzance as her father was ill and needed full-time attendance.

The estate prospered and the Mitchells were liked by their tenants. When the rock fall was cleared after two years and the Penorna and Trethtowan mines joined, the yield was even better than expected and the joint business cemented the friendship between the two families.

Their prosperity was eyed jealously by Jeremy Gaisford who was thwarted at every turn when he secretly tried to cause disruption and havoc for them, even endeavouring to drive a wedge between the two families, but John and Selwyn were wise to what he was attempting. On the occasions when John was roused to anger and confronted Jeremy face-to-face, Gaisford vehemently denied that he was involved and renewed his own accusation that John was responsible for his father's death.

Because he was a Gaisford and Miles Gaisford's lasting influence was still felt by many, Jeremy relished the power he wielded in his father's stead. He regarded any challenge to it as a personal affront. Whenever their paths crossed, whether in company or not, he went out of his way to bait and insult John. By ignoring this, he only angered Jeremy all the more.

Their feud was now widely known throughout the county. Though many realised the blame lay at Jeremy's door, they dare not voice their opinion aloud for without his father's stern hand to guide him, Jeremy now ran wild. His brothers, while loyal to the family name, did not condone his unruly ways and now saw that his running of the estate would lead to ruin for he had none of his father's acumen and foresight. Though they protested at some of his decisions and offered their advice freely, they always received the same answer: 'I'm running things now, not you, and don't forget you only have your own estates under sufferance. They are part of Seneway, I can take them back any time.'

Thoughts of Jeremy were far from John's mind today as he rode along the cliff top beside his wife. Nor did his mind drift to Lydia Booth. She had made sure that her personality and charm won her many new friends in Penzance who, like her staunch ally Dorinda, never doubted that she had relieved her brother of a child he was unable to raise.

Discretion had always been foremost in their minds and in that atmosphere their love for each other had never waned. Lydia was content, in her love for him, to have it that way. She wanted nothing more than to love him and to raise their child,

179

knowing that their friendship did not intrude on his happiness with his wife.

Today, on the eve of Abigail's seventeenth birthday, all seemed well in John Mitchell's world.

Abigail urged her horse faster, enjoying the sensation of speed as she always did. In the company of her parents she kept the urge restrained but on her own the full gallop was what she liked best. Today was an exception for she was filled with excitement about tomorrow when her seventeenth birthday would be celebrated with a party at Penorna. She felt the urge to throw off the shackles of restraint and revel in her own youth and daring. Hoofs tore at the turf as her favourite horse sensed her desire. Her smile broadened and laughter rang from her lips.

She glanced back as the path twisted and saw that her parents were out of sight. She laughed louder in the joy of pounding hoofs. Ahead the track dipped into a hollow where she knew it veered close to the cliff edge, but she gave that no thought. She had ridden this way many times and had never considered the danger. The path rose slightly before it dropped into the hollow. She topped the rise and her eyes widened with horror, driving out the laughter, at the sight of a rider coming with equal speed towards her. She hauled hard on the reins, attempting to take her animal out of the rider's path and away from the cliff edge. Everything moved into a whirling kaleidoscope of horseflesh crashing against horse-flesh, but her skill had avoided what would have been a devastating head-on collision. She kept control as her horse swerved away, and brought the animal round aware of the second horse crashing to the ground, its rider thrown to the earth with a momentum that took him over the cliff edge. His scream of horror split the air. Horrified and shaken, she hauled her mount to a halt and was off the saddle almost before it had stopped. She was at the cliff edge, peering down, scared that she would see a broken body on the rocks far below. The sharp realisation that that was not the case was reinforced when she saw a figure clinging to a narrow stone

180

ledge, his legs dangling over a sheer drop. Terror-filled eyes stared up at her from a face drained of colour. Abigail dropped to the ground and flattened herself.

'Hold on!' she shouted, and inched forward until she could reach down. She strained her arm, forced her fingers as far as she could, but it was no use; the space was too much, she could not possibly reach him from here. She viewed the rock face between them. A yard down, a horizontal ledge of rock to her left offered a chance if she could lower herself down to it, but there was no way of knowing how secure it was. Any instability could send her hurtling to oblivion. But that thought was banished from her mind when she saw his fingers slip slightly, sending clods of earth tumbling past his head. 'Hold on,' she encouraged. 'I'm going to try to reach that ledge.' She saw that he knew what she intended to do.

Dismissing the terror she was experiencing, Abigail slid slowly over the edge of the cliff, sending earth spinning away. She paused, tested, and then inched down with care until she felt solid rock beneath her feet. The ledge. But would it hold? Would it take her weight and that of them both if she managed to get a hold on the man?

Abigail dampened her lips in an attempt to pluck up the courage to make her next move. She met the man's pleading gaze that was full of hope. With that strong in her mind, she gave him an encouraging smile. She focused her mind on her next move and pressed against the rock with her feet. Although bits of earth were scuffed away, she was encouraged by a feeling of solidity. Turning and lowering herself the last few feet with extreme care she lay flat on the ledge, resisting the temptation to look further than the young man who barely clung to life. She shuffled herself forward and reached towards him. Her fingers closed round the left sleeve of his jacket and even through the cloth she could sense the hope rise in him.

'I'll hold on while you reach for that rock just above you to the right,' she said. 'Test it.' His eyes flicked to the rock. She tightened her grip on his sleeve. 'Now!' she called sharply. He grabbed, she felt the extra weight shoot up her arm, then it was eased. Her eyes were intent on the rock. It held. 'Good,' she called with relief. After a moment's pause she added, 'Can you ease yourself up a little?' He swallowed hard and then, still staring anxiously at the rock, did so. It held. 'Hold tight while I get a grip on your arm instead of your sleeve.' Concern had welled up inside Abigail, for she had seen the cloth beginning to tear under his weight. 'Now!' she changed her grip and sensed some easing of the strain. 'Good,' she said encouragingly. 'Pull on the rock when I pull on your arm, and try to get your knee up on this ledge.' Realising what she was trying to do, he nodded. 'Now!'

The combined leverage drew him slowly up. Stones and earth were falling away but the rock and the ledge held firm. He drew his right knee up, felt for the ledge, then as he pressed down hard Abigail pulled on his arm. He attained the ledge and after a moment of anxiety about his solidity they both sighed with relief.

Abigail glanced at the top of the cliff. It was in reach if they could kneel. She pointed this out to the man and he nodded. 'You first,' she said with an authority that wouldn't brook opposition. He got to his knees, reached out and pulled himself up. In a few moments she was lying beside him at the top of the cliff, breathing deeply after the exertion but mostly from a sense of huge relief.

The sound of galloping horses drew them back to reality. She sat up and saw her mother and father, faces lined with worry, arriving with a riderless horse between them. They were out of their saddles and crouching beside her in a moment. 'What happened?' Are you all right?' The urgent plea for information was directed at Abigail but their eyes took in the young man who was struggling to his feet. Who was this?

Eliza frowned at her own thoughts. Luke Gaisford? What had he done to her daughter?

John was troubled too, his thoughts ran wild. He had not seen Luke for nearly ten years, not since his father had sent him away to school, but the Gaisford features were unmistakable. Why had he attacked Abigail? It was all right Jeremy directing his hatred at John, but to fill his son's mind with antagonism against all Mitchells was going too far. Such thoughts flashed through his mind in the few seconds it took to help Abigail to her feet.

'Sir, ma'am.' The young man was speaking. They both looked askance at him for his gentle voice was filled with the patent desire to reassure them. 'This young lady has just saved my life.'

They stared at him in amazement. 'What?' said John.

'If this is your daughter, as I suppose it is, she risked her life to save mine.'

John and Eliza turned their attention on Abigail to seek an explanation. She straightened up from brushing down her soiled clothes with her hands and merely shrugged her shoulders.

'What happened?' queried Eliza, her heart all of a flutter at what lay behind the young man's words.

'Let me explain, ma'am,' he said. He went on to relate what had happened and emphasised Abigail's bravery.

As Luke was speaking she had been studying him. She thought him to be about her own age. He was handsome with a strong jaw, a straight nose, eyes that held a green tinge but were sharp and bright and glistening with a love of life and adventure. She noticed his long fingers as he unconsciously adjusted his cravat while he was speaking, all nervousness thrust aside now and replaced by a confidence that was razor-sharp. At the same time his posture settled into its customary self-assurance. Abigail, still wondering who he was, nevertheless found herself attracted to him – a feeling she had never experienced before.

'Sir, ma'am, you have a brave daughter. And thank you both for returning my favourite horse.' He turned to Abigail. 'What you did showed complete disregard for your own safety. I will be ever in your debt as I do not know how I could repay you.'

'Don't try then, but come to my birthday party at Penorna tomorrow at four,' replied Abigail, hardly realising she had made the invitation.

Eliza was about to intervene when she caught her husband's slight shake of the head and said nothing. John had seen a light in his daughter's eyes that he had never seen there before and knew this was no time to intervene.

Luke picked up the reins, patted his horse with comforting hands and swung himself into the saddle. He turned his mount, checked it and said, 'Sir, ma'am.' His eyes turned back to Abigail. 'Until tomorrow then.' She smiled up at him.

They watched him ride away, upright, in command, comfortable in the saddle.

'That was a brave thing you did,' commented her father.

'You might have been killed,' said Eliza in a tone that held a touch of admonishment.

'Well, I wasn't, Mama,' replied Abigail sharply. 'I couldn't see him fall to his death. He was lucky to get the hold he did but could have slipped at any moment; there was no time to wait for help.'

'You know who he is?' asked John.

She shook her head. 'No. I wondered if you did?'

'Luke Gaisford.'

'What? Mr Jeremy's son?'

'Yes.'

'He's a lot handsomer than his father . . . must get his looks from his mother.'

'That may be,' chided her mother, 'but he's still a Gaisford, and you've asked him to your party!'

Penorna was in a festive mood. Abigail at seventeen was a beautiful and popular young lady. Many guests from all over the county remarked upon it on their arrival in the main hall where they were welcomed by the Mitchells with a glass of warming punch. Passing on, they drifted into two rooms set aside for their comfort or chose smaller ones for more intimate conversations or to renew old acquaintance. The dining room had been laid out with mouth-watering dishes of every kind to form an ongoing buffet throughout the evening. The warm balmy air had enabled the glass doors leading onto the terrace from various rooms to be opened wide, enabling the guests to mix more freely. All of them looked forward to a pleasant evening, especially when the dancing started in the large main salon that had been cleared for the purpose, leaving a few chairs round its perimeter for those who wanted only to watch and comment on who was with whom, and speculate on concealed relationships.

'I think we have met all the guests,' commented John. 'We may as well join them. Enjoy the party, you two.' He smiled at his wife and daughter. 'I'll just have a word with Albert.' He crossed the hall to the door where their head butler was standing. 'I think all the guests have arrived but if I have overlooked someone and there are late arrivals, you know what to do.'

'Yes, sir! How long, sir?'

'An hour.'

'Very good, sir!'

Abigail, disappointed that Luke had not come, wandered off and was soon surrounded by friends and well-wishers. Throughout the night and earlier today visions of him kept haunting her mind. In her thoughts she had pictured herself dancing with him, but that was not to be; he appeared to have taken no notice of her invitation.

After three-quarters of an hour the dancing started. The second dance, a quadrille, was under way when the front door was flung wide with a crash and Jeremy Gaisford strode in, brushing Albert aside without ceremony. Luke, close behind, cast the butler a look of apology and rolled his eyes skywards in a gesture of contempt for his father's rudeness. Hearing the music, Jeremy made straight for the open doors to the main room. He stood in the doorway, feet astride, arms held loosely by his sides, as he surveyed it. He then clasped his hands behind his back and rocked on his feet; a commanding presence who had already captured the attention of several people near the door. Knowing that there was no love lost between the Gaisfords and the Mitchells they were all wondering why Jeremy and his son had gate-crashed the party, for they were certain they were not there by invitation.

185

'Mr John Mitchell!' Jeremy's voice boomed across the room, reverberating off the panelled walls.

In confusion at this unexpected intrusion the musicians gradually stopped playing and the dancers, uncertain what was happening, missed their step, bumped into each other, several only saved from falling by their partner. Chaos broke out around the room followed by a tense silence.

'Mr John Mitchell!' Jeremy roared again.

Abigail saw Luke standing behind and to one side of his father. Her heart missed a beat. He had come! He hadn't ignored her! But why was his father here making such a scene?

'Here, Mr Gaisford,' John shouted from the side as he started to make his way to the centre of the floor while dancers cleared a path for him. He walked towards Jeremy with deliberate steps. 'What do you want here?' And so that everyone knew he added, 'An uninvited guest.'

Jeremy, eyes fixed firmly on John, waited until he was close, then asked in a less belligerent tone but loud enough so that everyone could hear, 'Where is your daughter?'

'That is no . . .' Before John could finish the sentence he was interrupted.

'I am here, Mr Gaisford.' Abigail pushed her way through a group of people and walked towards him. She felt his eyes fixed upon her as if he was trying to probe her very soul but did not shy away. Her footsteps did not falter. Reaching her father's side, holding herself erect and with her eyes fixed firmly on Jeremy, she said, 'What is it you want, Mr Gaisford? You were not invited, I believe.'

'Invited or not, I had to come,' he said quietly. He looked at John and was about to speak to him, when he decided otherwise. Instead he raised his voice so that everyone in the room could hear. 'Ladies and gentlemen, I want you all to know that you are celebrating the birthday of a very brave girl who yesterday saved my son Luke from certain death!'

For a moment there was a stunned silence, then a buzz of exchanges and questions rippled round the room. 'What is this?' 'What does Gaisford mean?' 'What happened?' 'Death?' What's he talking about?'

'Ladies! Gentlemen! Please, I have more to say!' Jeremy's voice brought silence to the room again. 'My son was thrown from his horse and went over the cliff side. He got a hold but could not pull himself back. He hung above a sheer drop, which would have meant certain death but for Miss Mitchell's actions. Without thought for her own safety, she went over the cliff and succeeded in getting him back.' He turned to Abigail. 'Miss Mitchell, my family will be forever grateful for what you did yesterday. If ever you need help, do not be afraid to ask us for it.' He faced John. 'Mr Mitchell, you have a brave daughter, and beautiful too. You are a lucky man. You too are lucky, Mrs Mitchell,' he added, glancing at Eliza who had come quietly to stand beside her husband and daughter. 'Mr Mitchell, we have had our differences in the past. Can we bury them now?' Jeremy held out his hand.

Detecting a sincere desire in the gesture, John took his hand in a firm grip. 'They are condemned to the grave,' he responded.

Clapping in approval of the end of this known feud broke out in the room, gathering in volume.

'Mr Mitchell,' said Jeremy quietly, still shaking hands, 'my wife is outside in the carriage. May I bring her in to make her own thanks to your daughter?'

'Of course,' replied John. 'Goodness me, you shouldn't have left her waiting outside.'

Jeremy gave a wry smile. 'We weren't invited,' he said in a jocular tone.

'Well, you are both invited now.' The two men hurried into the hall, strode outside and in a few moments were escorting Hester Gaisford into the house. She was presented to Abigail who was already talking to Luke. Eliza had called to the musicians to resume and the quadrille set people dancing again. She then took charge of Mrs Gaisford and left the men to cement the new relationship between the two families.

After the last guest had gone in the early hours of the morning, John, Eliza and Abigail flopped down at the dining-room table and ate a late supper, which, because of the attention they'd paid their guests, they had been unable to do earlier.

John gave a little laugh. 'Strange,' he said, 'how an accident can end such bitterness between two families.'

'And Abigail's bravery,' put in Eliza.

'Oh, yes, but that wouldn't have been manifest if it hadn't been for the accident.'

'And I might never have met Luke,' put in Abigail dreamily. 'He's asked me to go riding with him the day after tomorrow. I've said yes. I hope that is all right?'

Eliza and John exchanged glances and John knew that she was leaving the decision to him.

'Of course.' He'd realised from the moment they had all watched Luke ride away after Abigail's rescue of him that his daughter had grown up; she was a woman and prepared to face all the challenges that could bring, including affairs of the heart. He realised, and he knew Eliza would too when they spoke of it in the privacy of their room, that a time would come when they would have to let her go. To do so lovingly would always bring her home. In the meantime they could only warn her, advise when asked, and give her their unstinting understanding and love.

'Of course,' he repeated, and then added, 'but don't forget he's a Gaisford. That family have always had a wild streak, and none more so than his father. Beware of that in Luke. It may appear it isn't there now but these family traits can lie dormant for years before they suddenly erupt. Just beware, Abigail.'

'Does Miss Booth still visit you?' Eliza put the question when she and John were spending an evening with Selwyn and Harriet.

'Oh, yes,' replied Harriet. 'She comes once a month. As you know, I encouraged her to do so soon after she returned to Cornwall . . . when was it? Ten years ago.' She gave a shake of the head. 'How time passes! It seems but yesterday. She

188

likes to come and hear news of James and Juliana. She was here last week.'

'She is well?'

'Yes.'

John's nerves had tightened at the mention of Lydia. He concentrated on his food and avoided been drawn into the conversation lest he make some slip. It had been the same throughout the last ten years whenever Lydia's name was mentioned. They had been years of careful planning, meetings that would not attract attention, excuses made for being away from Penorna, so that two people, deeply in love, could express that love for each other. And yet throughout all that time John had found his love for Eliza had never weakened. It was a mystery to him that he could love two women with such intensity at the same time; yet he found he could and blessed his ability to do so, for it brought a richness to his life in spite of the intrigue. He drew strength from the fact that Lydia always assured him she was happy and wanted life no other way. Showing interest in Eliza and Abigail, she salved the guilt she and John shared towards them. They found reassurance together in watching their daughter grow, though he regretted having no closer contact with her. She came sharply to mind now when Eliza asked, 'How is the child?'

'Tess is a fine girl. She'll be eleven in December. Miss Booth is doing a wonderful job with her. Her brother owes her a great deal.'

John felt a flush of pride and had a sudden strong desire to admit to being her father but sensibly kept quiet; too many lives would be shattered if ever the truth came out. He changed the course of the conversation. 'Is it true that Jeremy Gaisford is not well?'

'So I've heard,' replied Selwyn. 'But what do you expect, the way he drinks?'

'I hope that is a trait he hasn't passed on to Luke,' said John with some concern.

'You are thinking of Abigail?' put in Harriet.

Eliza grimaced. 'Yes. She's seen a lot of Luke this last nine months, ever since she saved his life.'

'I suppose it was a natural coming together after that, and he is a handsome young man.'

'Indeed,' agreed Eliza. 'And always charming whenever we have met him.' She glanced at John.

'I agree. But a Gaisford is a Gaisford. What runs in that family's blood?'

'There are always good apples as well as bad ones,' said Selwyn in an attempt to reassure his friend.

'I don't think you need worry about Abigail,' put in Harriet. 'She's a sensible, self-assured young woman who I'm certain can take care of herself.'

'I hope you are right,' mused Eliza.

'Have no doubt about it,' Selwyn added his conviction. 'And if ever it came to a love match, with both of them being only children the result could be the most powerful land-owning family in Cornwall.'

These were words John was to recall in the spring of 1798 when he paid his last respects to Jeremy Gaisford. At the graveside of the man who had been his enemy first and latterly his friend, he wondered what the future held in store for eighteen-year-old Luke.

Luke watched the coffin lowered into the cold Cornish earth with mixed feelings. His father had been a hard-driving task-master but there was something about him that Luke was drawn to; that he admired and tried in some ways to emulate. As he'd moved into his teenage years, he'd found it easier to do. It stemmed from the time when his father started to treat him more as a man than a boy and shared many a fast ride with him, leading him to down a tankard of ale and swallow a dram of whisky after it. Jeremy knew if his son was like his father, other natural instincts were there too and would never be denied when they surfaced. So he was more than pleased when Abigail Mitchell entered Luke's life. He fostered the relationship through which he could see a legitimate means of achieving his own father's thwarted ambition to acquire the Penorna Estate. Luke accepted his father's ultimate aim but for himself it was only a secondary interest; he was more interested in the girl.

He glanced across the grave and his eyes rested on Abigail. The sombre black she wore did nothing to detract from the beauty of this young woman he had sworn to have. There were others among the great crowd gathered here to pay their last muted respects who Luke knew would come eagerly to his bed, some with an eye to becoming Mistress of Senewey, others simply for the fun of it. He wished Abigail Mitchell was at his side now, but that would have to wait while mourning was observed, and even then he could not be sure she would walk up the aisle with him. They had become close since she had saved his life, but she had never allowed their friendship to move beyond that.

Abigail sensed someone looking at her and, glancing in the direction of the chief mourners, saw Luke's gaze fixed on her. Their eyes met briefly and he quickly looked away but in that moment she read desire. She shuddered. It felt different from other times she'd observed that look. This time she sensed it was cold and calculating, and behind it lay the intention that one day he would break down the barrier she had hitherto held between them. That barrier had been erected on her father's warning, and though she had a great admiration for Luke, who in her presence had shown her every respect, Abigail was wary of him for at times she sensed something disturbing beneath his outwardly pleasant demeanour.

The day after the funeral Luke strode into the dining room for breakfast. He was surprised to find his mother there already, seated at the table enjoying some porridge.

'Good morning, Luke,' Hester said brightly.

'Good morning, Mother,' he replied tersely as he went to the sideboard to help himself to a glass of milk. He had no need to order porridge from the attending maid for he knew that once he appeared she would scuttle away to the kitchen to return in a few minutes to serve it piping hot. 'Too ill to attend the funeral but here you are as large as life.' His voice dripped with sarcasm.

'I had no respects to pay to your father because of the way he treated me after your grandfather's death. Until then I had

191

accorded him the dignity that went with the position of husband, but after Miles's death his behaviour ran wild. He wanted me for only one thing, and supply it I had to even if he had been with his other women.' Hester gave a grunt of contempt. 'For God's sake, Luke, don't look at me like that. It was bend to his will or be thrown out. Jeremy would have ignored the scandal, but think of the stories that would have been spread about *me*. I had to stay and give him outward respectability even though people knew how rotten to the core he was.' She looked hard at her son. 'I only hope and pray you do not turn out like him, Luke.'

He made no comment but said, 'Mr Archbold the solicitor will be here at eleven. Please be in the drawing room for the reading of the will and to hear what I have to say afterwards. Uncle Charles, Uncle Logan, Aunt Emma and Aunt Fanny have been invited to be there too.'

Hester eyed him with suspicion but said nothing. She would know at eleven what the future held for her. No doubt she would be well provided for by her husband for the help she had given him.

Uncles and aunts arrived within a few minutes of each other, were shown to the drawing room and announced by the maid delegated for the duty. Luke and his mother made their greetings amiable, and their relations showered Hester liberally with commiserations and concern.

Luke played the perfect host with a charm that did not deceive either of his aunts. Neither of them had fallen under his spell as many women of their age had done, and they had privately voiced their opinion to each other that there was more behind this gathering than the mere reading of Jeremy's will. Luke was older than his eighteen years. So far he had hidden in his father's shadow but now, as the hereditary owner of Senewey, he had real power that they judged he would be tempted to use.

They made no comment on it but shrank from the formality of the setting. Luke had supervised the seating; six straight-backed chairs faced a small table behind which stood a similar chair. There had been no attempt to make this an informal occasion. The only concession to that was when he personally showed them to the chairs in which they should sit and served them each a glass of Madeira. He also placed one on the table. It was at almost that precise moment the maid opened the door and announced, 'Mr Archbold, sir.'

A man bustled nervously in. His slight stoop, brought on by advancing years, made him seem smaller than he was. Sharp eyes darted about from one to the other as if summing them all up as he came towards Luke. The young man greeted him with outstretched hand. Mr Archbold took it and winced at his strong grip.

'Mr Gaisford.'

'Mr Archbold. You are indeed a good time-keeper.' Luke glanced at the clock on the mantel-piece.

'Eleven is eleven, sir.'

'Precisely. Let me take your coat and hat.'

The solicitor removed them and passed them to the maid who had waited to receive them. With a brief, 'Thank you, sir,' he took his document case from Luke who had held it for him meanwhile.

'You know my mother?'

'Indeed, indeed.' Mr Archbold quickly went to Hester and shook her proffered hand while nervously offering his commiserations on her loss.

'And my uncles and aunts?' Luke introduced them in turn and the solicitor renewed his acquaintances quickly.

'Your seat, Mr Archbold,' said Luke, showing him to the chair behind the table. 'And a glass of wine.'

'Most kind, sir, most kind.' He shuffled behind the table, took a sip of his wine and opened his document case. He withdrew a sheaf of papers that caused Logan and Charles to grimace in surprise at each other. It looked as if they were in for a long reading.

But their expectation was short-lived. Mr Archbold took another drink of his wine, cleared his throat and said, 'Ladies and gentlemen, this won't take long.' He picked up a sheet of paper, glanced at them all as if checking that he had their full attention, and then read: '"This is the last will and testament of Jeremy Gaisford. Being in sound mind, I leave everything I own to my son, Luke. Signed in the presence of Mark Crossley and John Golding, householders in Penzance. Dated 5th May 1797."'

The silence that filled the room was palpable. It spoke volumes. No mention of anyone but Luke. They were all in his power. How would he wield it? Their lives were almost literally in his hands. Though they were outwardly calm, Logan and Charles were quaking. They did not own their own estates; they worked them for their own livelihood and gain but the land was part of the Senewey Estate and could be taken back at any time. Father and brother had never exercised that right. What about nephew?

Emma and Fanny looked shocked and indignant. Not to be mentioned in the will they took as a slight, but worse than that they knew their destiny was now in the hands of an eighteen year old they didn't much like and definitely did not trust.

Hester sat as if frozen. No provision for her. The husband to whom she had become a plaything, suffering abuse of every kind whenever the drink took hold, had not provided one penny for her future security. Her fate now depended on a son of whom she had become wary.

'Thank you, Mr Archbold! If I show you to the dining room you will find some refreshments there. When I am ready you and I will continue with our business.'

Luke rose from his chair. The solicitor followed suit and trailed after him. Luke returned a few minutes later to be met by a buzz of indignant observations. He ignored these. He went to the chair behind the table recently vacated by Mr Archbold and held up his hands for silence. Then he sat down and looked round all the faces staring expectantly at him. He gave a little smile, enjoying the power he wielded over his relations.

'Well, there it is, I own everything,' he said smugly.

'No doubt you already knew the contents of the will and wanted to savour your triumph in front of us,' said Logan, his voice sharp with disgust.

'I did know of it, Uncle Logan, the day after Father died.'

'Eager to grab it all.' Logan did not hide his own contempt.

'Careful, Uncle.' There was a chill in Luke's words. His aunt's gesture of warning in placing her hand on her husband's arm was not lost on him. 'It seems my aunt has more sense than to rile me.' He glanced at his other uncle. 'What about you, Uncle Charles?' His uncle gave a resigned shrug of his shoulders. 'Nothing to say?' mocked Luke. 'And you, Aunt Emma?'

'What will be will be,' she replied sharply. 'What about your mother? Your father should have made provision for her after all she did for him.' She glanced at her sister-in-law who gave her a weak smile of thanks while mouthing the word silently.

'Your concern touches me. No doubt you all want to know what I am going to do about my mother.' He turned his gaze on Hester. She saw no affection there, only a cold contempt. 'I can never forgive you for not preventing Father from beating and abusing me. You will live in the West Wing on a small allowance I shall make you and will never again venture into the rest of the house. That is for my sole use.'

Words of reproach sprang to her lips but she remained silent, lanced by his hostile eyes. Besides, she knew any protests would be useless.

He turned to the others. 'Now what am I to do about you four?' He paused thoughtfully, knowing they were quaking with anxiety inside. 'As you will have gathered, I am seeing Mr Archbold again shortly. I will instruct him to assign the estates you now occupy permanently to you.' He saw relief sweep through his uncles and aunts. 'Possession of them by the Senewey Estate is hereby revoked. They will be yours to run as you please, but in future there will be no financial support from Senewey or from me.'

'But being able to fall back on support from Senewey is essential,' protested Logan.

'Now it stops. You will have to manage without that cushion.' Luke's voice was so firm, his expression so adamant, that Logan knew it was no use even trying to negotiate.

Silence fell on the room. Luke glanced at each of them in turn and then said, 'That is all. Mr Archbold will draw up the necessary documents and let you have them for signature as soon as possible.' He rose from his chair, a gesture of dismissal. 'If you wish for them there are refreshments in the dining room. Mr Archbold will have finished his. I will be busy with him for quite a while so I'll say goodbye now.'

Chapter Fourteen

Seated in the drawing room, Mr Archbold shuffled his sheaf of papers nervously. Annoyance clouded Luke's eyes.

'Get on with it, man,' he snapped irritably.

'Er . . . yes, yes.' He picked up a sheet of paper, glanced at it, and as if annoyed with himself pushed it to one side and chose another. An expression of relief came to his face. 'First of all we have the papers dealing with the farm holdings . . .'

'Mr Archbold, do we have to detail everything?'

'Well, sir, it is the only way you will know exactly what you are worth.'

'Summarise it, Mr Archbold, summarise it!' Each word became stronger as if Luke felt it necessary to hammer it into the solicitor's mind.

'You really should have all the details, Mr Gaisford.'

'Spare me those, Mr Archbold. Just tell me what I am worth and what ready money is available.'

'I am afraid there is very little of the latter. Almost next to nothing in fact.'

'What?' Luke's face darkened in angry surprise.

'Your father was a heavy spender. He got through a lot of money and in actual coinage left you little.'

'Then I will have to put that right by selling some land.'

'I am afraid you can't do that, sir.'

'Why not, it's mine?'

'True, sir, but you are prevented from selling land by an entail in your great grandfather's will.'

'What? That old bastard's tied me down?'

'If you put it that way, sir, yes.'

Luke's lips tightened.

'If you are thinking of increasing your flocks of sheep, I must tell you that when I was working out your assets and sought expert advice on the farming side of the estate, I was told that the grazing land could not sustain any more and that the flocks you have now are not in good shape.'

'Why not?'

Mr Archbold gave a gesture of helplessness with his hands. 'I am no agricultural expert, Mr Gaisford.'

The irritable shake of Luke's head dismissed that angle.

'We'll have to increase the output from the mine then.'

Mr Archbold grimaced. 'I'm afraid not, sir. Your father did that and now the copper is running out.'

'But he had another harbour built!'

'True, and that helped with his initial raised output, but he had not taken into account that the supply of copper was finite. The harbour he already had could have dealt with the copper over a longer period but he wanted to exploit it faster and thought the answer was another harbour. That harbour is about to become redundant.'

Now Luke knew why his grandfather and father had been keen to buy Penorna and Trethtowan land: copper. Their own mines were almost worked to extinction.

'I can raise rents, or are you going to tell me that can't be done either?'

'It can be done, sir, but I am afraid if you do so you will have trouble on your hands. You see, your father received a petition from his tenants concerning the state of their dwellings – they had seen what Mr Mitchell and Mr Westbury were doing for their tenants. In order to placate his own Mr Jeremy signed an agreement that rents should not go up until after repairs had been undertaken on their dwellings, and that these repairs would be completed by the end of next year.'

'My father seems to have made a fine mess of things,' said Luke with contempt. 'Any more bad news?'

'That just about sums it up.'

'He's left me in a bad way then?'

'Well, sir, the straight answer is yes, but you still have some income from the farms and rents, and a little from the mine.'

Luke looked hard at Mr Archbold. 'No word of my precarious position must get out. The Gaisfords have been an important family in Cornwall for many years; it must remain so. I will see to it that our fortunes are revived. In the meantime I must keep my word to my mother and my uncles.' He went on to instruct the solicitor what he wanted him to do.

'I am sure under the circumstances allocating their two estates to your uncles is a wise move as they will no longer be able to call on Senewey for financial help.'

'See that the necessary documents are drawn up and signed as soon as possible.'

'That will be done within the next two days, sir.'

'Good. I think you had better leave me all those other documents to peruse in my own time, see if they can help me find a solution to my precarious financial position.'

'Very good, sir! May I just remind you that much of your income should be set aside to meet the cost of renovations agreed to by your father, for replenishing stock on the farms, and to tide you over once the copper has run out.'

Luke nodded. 'Or I find a new source of income.' He smiled to himself. He had two possibilities already in mind. Maybe he would need only one of them or he might exploit them both, just for the hell of it.

Both might take a little while to accomplish but he would be patient and in the meantime exist on the income he could achieve on his current assets. Nevertheless the next day, with the weather set fair, he took a ride along the coast to the small harbour his father had constructed.

He slipped from the saddle on the cliff top, tethered his horse and walked to a point from which he could survey the harbour and its location within a sheltered cove.

The cliff dropped away sharply before him and swung round on either side into headlands that towered over the cove. His father had made use of that when he had positioned the stone harbour below with its two piers curving towards each other, offering protection from the stormy seas that could pound this jagged coast. The harbour satisfied him, but he was concerned about access to it. He strolled along the cliff edge, studying the possibilities, until he reached a position, which gave him his answer. He stopped when he realised that from here he could see winding paths climbing to the cliff top at both ends of the cove. Because of the contours they had not been noticeable from any other point but this. He felt elated. It could not have been better! He must examine the place more closely. He hurried along the cliff top to his right and was even more satisfied when the nature of the terrain hid the path from his view. He almost missed the point where it came out on top of the cliff, and this pleased him all the more.

He wound his way down to the cove and when he reached the bottom felt almost overpowered by the towering cliffs above him. He hurried on to the harbour wall that had been built into the cliff and saw that it ran in both directions to meet the paths from the cliff top so that there was one continuous route in a loop from top to ship or vice versa. He nodded with satisfaction. He made his way along the right-hand pier and on reaching the end saw what wonderful protection the two piers gave to the harbour. A vessel would be safe here from even the most monstrous waves running into the coast. But he was more interested in the shoals of rock that jutted out into the sea from the foot of the cliffs to right and left, and in the access from them to the harbour wall that ran along the bottom of the cliff. Again he nodded with satisfaction. This could be the answer to his financial dilemma and, coupled with his other idea, could make him a rich man. Visualising his future, Luke studied the scene again. Those shoals, so close to the harbour, were dangerous. He climbed thoughtfully to the cliff top and rode away.

He had ridden a mile when he checked his horse and sat deep in thought for a moment. A decision reached, he turned his mount and with a whoop put it to a gallop that he did not stop until they reached the Waning Moon. Luke swung from the saddle and strode inside. He took in the scene as he walked to the bar. Two men sat at a table in one corner of the room, deep in conversation. He did not know them but they were well dressed and he judged some trade was being discussed or a plot being hatched to outwit a neighbour. The man he took to be the landlord was rearranging some tankards behind the bar.

'Good day, landlord,' he said, his eyes summing up the man.

'Good day, Mr Gaisford.'

'You know who I am?' said Luke, a little surprised that the landlord of a lonely inn should know him.

'Tell a Gaisford anywhere. In your case I see something of your father in you so you must be Mr Luke.'

'Shrewd man. But I really shouldn't be surprised, knowing my father frequented this establishment.'

'He did that, sir, and we did business together, so if you need anything at all, you let Tom Mather know. Now, sir, welcome to the Waning Moon. Your first drink is on the house.'

'That's very civil of you, Tom. A tankard of your best, if you please.' He glanced at the two men in the corner.

As Tom placed the full tankard on the counter, he lowered his voice and said, 'They're from over St Ives way, on their way back from St Just.'

'Make it your business to know all your customers?'

'Aye, sir, I do. It pays to know who I'm dealing with.'

'Wise! Now, this business you conducted with my father, what was it?'

'A bit of all sorts, but chiefly I put men his way he could use for various enterprises. The Waning Moon was their regular meeting place.'

'So you could do the same for me, if and when the time comes?'

'Aye, I could sir. Have you something in mind? Taking up where your father left off?'

Luke shook his head. 'This has nothing to do with what my father did and it may be a little while before I can implement my plans, but when I do I will need men who can be trusted and who will keep their mouths shut.'

'You will be able to rely on the men Tom Mather gets.'

'Good. No doubt we will do business then.'

Luke was highly satisfied with his day as he turned it over in his mind on his way home. The foundations were laid for one plan, now he must implement the other.

'Another invitation?' Eliza put the question to Abigail who had just unsealed the sheet of paper one of the maids had brought to the dinner table.

She glanced quickly at the neat writing so elegantly laid out. 'From Martin Granton, a ball at Granton Manor in three weeks' time,' she replied, excitement dancing in her eyes for this meant dancing and she loved that.

'This is the fourth ball in the last six months,' observed her father. 'Sydney Leigh, George Morland, David Gillow ... you are a popular young lady.'

'Would you want me to be anything else, Papa?' said Abigail with a coy smile.

'No, but they are all cronies of Luke Gaisfords and I hear tales about their wild ways.'

'Rumours are always exaggerated. I find them most polite, especially Martin. Besides, Luke has not associated with them since his father died, and you've seen how thoughtful he is when he has taken me out riding.'

'I will grant you that, but I still think still waters run deep. And he is a Gaisford.' Seeing that his wife and daughter had finished their meal, John laid down his napkin and stood up.

He escorted them to the drawing room where they had just sat down when they heard the maid cross the hall to answer the front door. She appeared a moment later to announce that Mr Luke Gaisford was here to see them. John and Eliza exchanged a quick glance and each wondered what merited this unexpected visit. Abigail sensed her heart race a little at the mention of Luke's name and she too wondered what had prompted his arrival.

'Show him in,' John instructed.

Luke strode in, confident and in charge of the situation. There was a smile on his face yet apology in his eyes that underlay his words. 'Ma'am, Sir, Abigail.' He looked at each in turn and then included them all when he said, 'My apologies for intruding at this time of day but I thought I should waste no time. As I have now thrown off my mourning, I am calling to ask if you, sir, will give me permission to seek the privilege of escorting Miss Abigail to the ball at Granton Manor?

'You knew she would be invited?' asked John cautiously, surprised that Luke should call so soon after the invitation had been received.

He gave a little smile. 'Sir, I have been unable to attend any of the balls over the last nine months period of mourning but I hear about them all and the talk is always of how popular Miss Abigail is so I concluded that she was sure to be invited to this one. I received my own invitation this afternoon. As I wanted to be sure that no one pre-empted me, I rode over here at the first opportunity.'

'You are an enterprising young man,' commented John. 'My daughter has just now received her invitation to attend the ball, while we were dining.'

'Then indeed I am fortunate in my timing, sir. Of course, my fate hangs not only on your permission but also on Miss Abigail's acceptance.' He cast a glance at her.

She felt a thrill run through her when she read challenge in his eyes.

'I will be delighted to accept, with my father's permission.' She turned her gaze from Luke to her father who saw in it an appeal that he couldn't refuse. His daughter had always been able to twist him round her little finger, even in his sternest moments.

'Very well.'

'Thank you, sir, and you, ma'am.' Luke turned his smile on Eliza whom he knew had been studying him carefully. If there was any uneasiness in her mind he wanted to alleviate it. 'I will call for Miss Abigail and have her home at a reasonable hour. I promise she will have a splendid time.'

203

'I'm sure she will, Mr Gaisford. Though you have previously accompanied my daughter when she is out riding, a great deal will rest on your conduct at this ball for I am sure there will be others in the future.'

'Indeed, Mrs Mitchell! I understand your point. Have no fear, Miss Abigail will be well looked after. Now, I have intruded on you for too long, I will take my leave.'

'Stay, take a glass of Madeira with us before you leave,' John offered.

'That is kind, sir.'

'Sit down.' John indicated a chair as he rose from his to go to the decanter and wine glasses standing on the oak sideboard.

Luke sat down, placing his hat and riding crop on the table beside his chair.

'How is your mother, Mr Gaisford?'

'Not too well, ma'am. She has never really got over my father's death. She is turning into a recluse, confining herself to one wing of the house, not even wanting to mingle with me or any friends who call.'

'I'm sorry to hear that. Death affects people in different ways. I hope she can soon shake off her despondency and resume as near normal a life as possible.'

'Thank you, ma'am. I will convey your wishes to her.' Luke looked up and took the glass of Madeira from John who had served his wife and daughter first. 'Thank you, sir.'

John got his own glass and sat down. 'How are you settling down to running the estate? A heavy responsibility for one so young.'

'Very well, thank you, sir. When I returned home after my schooling I learned a lot from my father.'

'I heard tell that prospects were not too good at Senewey mine?'

'Rumours, sir, rumours, no doubt brought about by the fact I cut back on the workforce. My father had over-employed.' Luke hoped his excuse sounded feasible even though it was only partially true and he was in fact keeping more men on than he should to disguise the fact that the copper seams were running out. 'You seem to be running a very efficient estate, sir.'

'My uncle had left a property that was already running efficiently. I thought if I kept my tenants and workers happy they would continue to see that it did so. Which is exactly what they did.'

'You were lucky indeed to have such loyal employees.'

The conversation drifted across various topics for another ten minutes before Luke politely announced he must leave and intrude on them no longer.

As he rode away he was happy with his visit – Abigail had been invited to the ball and he had learnt much about Penorna Estate and had been able to draw some detailed conclusions about the wealth that she would inherit.

The door of the Waning Moon crashed open propelled by Martin Granton who took one step into the room and stopped. A quick glance told him what he wanted to know and he called over his shoulder, 'He's here!'

'Has he got them lined up?' Sydney Leigh almost sent Martin staggering as he pushed past him.

George Morland and David Gillow, arms round each other's shoulders, ran in and headed straight for the bar, shouting, 'Luke!' They untangled their arms and took up position on each side of Gaisford, clapping him on the back. 'Good to see you! Where have you been?'

Sydney, who had drained a tankard in one gulp, wiped his hand across his mouth and said, 'I know. That beautiful filly's got him bewitched.'

'Bewitched and bewildered,' slurred David, reaching for a tankard before Sydney could grab it.

'Keep filling them, landlord.' Sydney eyed Tom who had been forewarned by Luke about his four friends. 'They'll drink a lot, they'll get a little merry and be a bit boisterous, but they can hold their liquor. Pranksters but not troublemakers.'

'What do you want us here for?' asked Martin, eyeing Luke.

'Get your tankards and come over here.' He started for a table in one corner of the room.

The others followed but Sydney stopped and looked back. 'Remember what I said, landlord?'

'Aye, sir, no dry tankards.'

'Correct.' He turned and almost tripped but managed to keep his tankard level and not spill a drop. He staggered to the table and dropped into the only vacant chair. 'Well?' he said, shaking his head woozily as he stared at Luke.

'Sober up,' said Luke, and raised an eyebrow towards Martin who he regarded as his closest friend and who never took as much drink as the others.

Sydney sat up straight, saluted and said, 'Yes, sir.' The serious expression he had adopted vanished in a snigger which quickly turned to outright laughter. 'Thought I was drunk, Luke? You've never seen me drunk.' He looked round his companions. 'Has any of you seen me drunk?'

'No,' they all agreed in one voice.

'Good, that's settled! Now, Luke, what is this all about? Why meet on this Godforsaken moor? Never been here before.' Again he looked round. 'Anyone else been here before?'

'I have,' said Luke.

'You don't count 'cos you must have been. Must have known the landlord kept good ale. It is good ale, isn't it?' He looked around for general agreement and then eyed Luke again. 'Well, what are we here for?'

'I want you to know this place because if you are drinking with me this is where it will be done for the foreseeable future.'

'Hey, we ride the county, remember,' protested George.

'I don't until . . . well, I don't know.'

'Oh, I see, the filly's got him roped.' He gave a little grin.

The others stared at Luke, wanting confirmation or denial.

'So what if she has? There are big stakes to play for and I'm prepared to do my drinking here so Abigail doesn't hear about it. Play along with me and you won't regret it. I'm not going to be hogtied all my life. You can drink wherever you like but with me it's here. And one other thing: you keep this to yourselves. To all intents and purposes I am not riding with you anymore.'

'Ah, putting on a good show for Mama and Papa with the Penorna Estate as the prize,' said David, tapping his nose knowingly.

'Keep your suppositions to yourself, and the rest of you don't speculate with anyone. You will all benefit in the long run, I don't forget my friends.'

Martin made no comment. A vision of Abigail ran through his mind while his heart sank. To pursue her now would be to incur the wrath of his old friend, and that could be disastrous. Luke Gaisford, who always had to have his own way, would not rest until he had sated his desire for revenge on all those involved and that would include Abigail herself. Martin could never let that happen.

John let himself into the house in New Street that he and Lydia had used as their meeting place. Throughout December and January the weather had prevented him from taking Christmas gifts to her and Tess. Now, with a snap of warmer weather in the February of a new century making the ride to Penzance possible, he was taking the opportunity to do so.

He had been in the house no longer than ten minutes when he heard a sharp and persistent hammering on the front door that carried the sound of urgency. He hurried along the hall and, on opening the door, was shocked to see a distraught Dorinda standing on the step. His mind raced to consider the possible reasons she might be here. She was Lydia's friend and could only be here in connection with that. But how had Dorinda known about this house which he and Lydia had kept such a secret?

The alarm in her eyes eased a little when she saw him. 'Mr Mitchell, thank goodness you are here,' she cried with relief. 'We hoped the change in the weather would bring you to Penzance. I'm afraid I have some bad news.'

'Come in, come in,' he urged, and led the way to the drawing room. 'What is it?' he called over his shoulder as he closed the door.

'Lydia, sir. She is very ill.'

'What?' Alarm surged through him. 'I must go to her!' He started for the door but stopped and swung round to face Dorinda. 'You know about us and this house?'

'Just a few minutes ago I learned of it and Lydia swore me to secrecy. It's safe with me, sir. A promise to a dying person must never be broken.'

'Dying? Oh, my God! Quick, tell me?'

'Lydia caught a chill. It turned for the worst. She's been in bed for ten days, growing weaker and weaker.'

'Didn't she get the doctor?'

'Yes. He's called several times. He last visited about half an hour ago but gave no hope for her recovery.'

'There must be!' cried John, his face taut with anguish. 'Take me to her!'

'That's why I'm here. Lydia wants to see you.'

'Where's Tess?'

'Lydia asked Mrs Foxwell to take her out of the way, and the maid has been sent home. Lydia wanted the way clear for your visit so no one but me would know of it.'

'Come on. Let us hurry.'

Reaching the house in Market-jew Street, Dorinda led the way upstairs. At the bedroom door she whispered, 'I'll see if everything is all right, sir.'

He nodded and she slipped into the room. A few moments later she reappeared.

'You can come in, sir.'

When John stepped into the room he received a shock. Lydia lay against the pillow, her face pale and gaunt. The bloom he remembered on her face and had always carried in his mental picture of her had gone. Though she tried to muster a smile, her expression remained wan and lifeless.

He heard the door close and was immediately on his knees at the bedside. Taking her hand in his, shocked to find how thin it was as if the flesh had wasted away, he gazed into her eyes, searching for something that would tell him what he feared was wrong. 'Lydia, what has happened to you?' His voice was ragged with distress. 'Why didn't you send for me?'

'I couldn't John, that would have betrayed our secret.' Her words came scarcely above a whisper.

'I could have done something,' he protested.

'You couldn't.' The finality of her statement alarmed him and wrung his heart.

'I must!' Tears welled in his eyes.

'No, John, you can't. Mrs Foxwell has looked after me. She couldn't have been kinder.' The words croaked in Lydia's throat. He felt her grip on his hand tighten. 'I hoped and prayed that the weather would relent and I would see you one more time. God has been good and granted me that wish.' As she said those words she seemed to find a little strength. 'Kiss me, John, and then go.'

'I cannot leave you like this,' he cried, his heart rent by pain.

'You must. There is nothing you can do except what I ask.' The pleading in her eyes could not be denied.

'Anything, my love.'

'I am happy that I have seen you again and felt your lips on mine. I know that you love me.'

He was about to speak when she stopped him. 'You must keep up the pretence. Your wife must never know about us, but promise me you will see that Tess is cared for?'

'That is a promise I will never break.'

'Kiss me again and go.'

'But . . .'

'That is what I want you to do. I don't want you to see me die. I want you to remember me as I was when we shared so much joy. Don't forget me.'

'I won't ever do that, and Tess will be there to remind me.'

Her smile then was as radiant as he had ever known it. He realised she knew the end was near. She reached up and stroked his cheek, finding consolation in the contact. He leaned over and kissed her, allowing the touch to linger until she whispered. 'Go.'

He hesitated but her wisdom prevailed. Two hearts met for the last time as he glanced back and received her smile, encouraging him to face the future in the way she wanted him to.

He found Dorinda waiting for him at the bottom of the stairs and steeled himself for what he knew was to come. There were tears in her eyes as she said, 'She's not long for this world, sir.'

'I'm afraid she is not.'

'She has been happy here, sir. And I have lost a dear friend.'

'Will you take care of the arrangements when the time comes?

'Certainly, sir.'

'You know with whom she was friendly in Penzance. Please inform them. Will you also inform Mr and Mrs Westbury and let them know the date of the funeral?'

'Certainly, sir. What about her brother?'

'I will see that he is informed.'

'Very good, sir. What about Tess? I can take her until you decide what to do.'

'That is very kind of you. It would solve the immediate problem.'

'It is the least I can do. Lydia was a very good friend to me and gave me great support when my father died. I know you will want what is best for Tess but if it becomes necessary, I can take care of her.'

'That is very good of you.'

'I could not see that darling child abandoned.'

'That will never happen, Dorinda.' As he was speaking John had been fishing in his pocket. He withdrew a wad of money that had been intended for Lydia. 'This will meet any expenses. I will call after the funeral to settle anything outstanding.'

'Yes, sir.'

As he rode home John felt as if part of life had been torn from him. 1800 would be the darkest year of his life. He wept openly but by the time he reached the Manor had control of his feelings once again.

Two days later Selwyn and Harriet Westbury rode up to Penorna where they were welcomed warmly by Eliza and John.

'We come with sad news,' announced Harriet as they entered the drawing room. 'We have received word that Miss Booth, whose painting hangs in your hall, died two days ago.'

'No!' Eliza frowned. 'She wouldn't be very old?'

'No, she wasn't,' replied Harriet. 'And the child she was caring for, little Tess, is still very young.'

The words were like arrows to John's heart and it took all his strength of will to prevent a breakdown but he managed to ask, 'How did you hear about it?'

'You remember she was very friendly with your governess, Miss Jenkins? Well, they renewed that friendship when Miss Booth came to live in Penzance. It was Miss Jenkins who informed us.'

'What will happen to the child?' asked Eliza.

'The obvious thing would be for her to go to her father, but if he didn't want her when she was born, he's not likely to want her now. So it looks as if the poor little girl will end up in a home.'

The picture that conjured up in John's mind almost made him scream but he restrained himself by remembering his promise to Lydia.

'When is the funeral?' asked Eliza.

'The day after tomorrow at St Mary's in Penzance, eleven o'clock,' replied Selwyn.

'We ought to go, John. She will be part of this house as long as her painting hangs here,' suggested Eliza.

'Would you like us to bring the carriage and then we could go together?' Harriet offered.

'That would be kind,' Eliza accepted.

Two days later a sombre service was conducted by the solemn-faced rector who praised Lydia for her goodness in taking responsibility for the baby her brother had abandoned

211

at birth, and for the excellent job she had since done in raising Tess. He pointed out her involvement with church affairs and how she had enriched people's lives with her personality and their homes with her paintings.

John listened to it all with a lump growing in his throat. He stood beside Eliza and Abigail, with a heavy heart, and watched the coffin lowered into the ground. Across the grave he saw Dorinda holding the hand of his daughter, Tess. He felt certain he could see tears in the child's eyes and ached to give her comfort and tell her who he was, that he would always look after her. But he almost heard a warning word from beyond the grave: You will only confuse and hurt our daughter and shatter other lives. It will hurt me too. If you love me, don't do it.

I won't, my love, he whispered silently for answer and his grip tightened on Eliza's hand.

As people moved away, Dorinda brought Tess close to the graveside and, bending down, said something to her.

'Tess, you know Mr and Mrs Westbury but you don't know Mr and Mrs Mitchell and their daughter Abigail who live at Penorna Manor.'

'Mama used to point it out to me when we passed by on our way to see Mr and Mrs Westbury.'

For a moment Dorinda was alarmed by her use of the word 'Mama', but realised that other people would think Tess's usage the natural thing to do, the child having known no other mother.

Tess looked seriously at them. 'Mama told me not to cry because she was going somewhere where she will be happy.'

'That's right, Tess, she will be,' said John, crouching down and taking hold of her hand. Thrilled at the contact, the first he had had with his daughter since that baby grip on his finger, he looked into her eyes, so like her mother's, and a lump came to his throat. 'You are a brave girl and must go on being so. Your mother would want you to.'

She smiled at him. 'I will be, Mr Mitchell.'

'I remember you as a baby,' said Eliza.

'Do you, Mrs Mitchell?'

'Yes, I do, and you have grown into a charming girl.'

When the carriage reached Penorna, Selwyn and Harriet refused the Mitchells' preferred hospitality. John led his womenfolk into the house.

'Come down and we'll have a glass of Madeira,' he said. Five minutes later, alone in the drawing room, he was thoughtfully pouring three glasses of wine while grappling with the problem of what to do about Tess. It was something that would have to be resolved quickly. He could not rest on the good graces of Mrs Foxwell for long. The door opened and Eliza and Abigail came in. They accepted the glasses of wine and sat down.

'You know, I can't get the thought of that child out of my mind,' said Eliza. 'What is to become of her?'

'It's a problem,' said John.

'How old is she?' asked Eliza.

He looked thoughtful, as if trying to work it out. 'Let me see, I would think she'll be thirteen, maybe fourteen.'

'Fourteen,' mused Eliza, giving a little nod of her head. 'Not too young, I suppose. In some ways it could be an advantage . . .'

'What are you getting at?' asked John.

Eliza did not answer his question but put one to her daughter. 'What do you think, Abigail, would you like a personal maid of your own, a waiting maid?' The unexpectedness of the query brought a moment of charged silence then Abigail broke it with an excited cry.

'Oh, yes!' Then it dawned on her what lay behind her mother's query. 'You mean, Tess?'

'Why not?'

'Isn't she too young?'

'I don't think so. She struck me in the short time we saw her as being older than her years. My maid Sally can help to train her in the basic tasks, and any refinements you can school her in yourself.'

'Oh, yes, please.' Abigail was even more delighted now that the advantages had been pointed out to her.

'What do you think, John?' Eliza asked.

His mind had been racing. Had the answer to his dilemma unwittingly been given by his wife? Tess and he would be here under the same roof and, though he would have to be extremely careful about their relationship, he would at least be able to keep an eye on her and see that she was well cared for.

'That's sounds a feasible idea. If it is what you both want, I will arrange it with Dorinda.'

Chapter Fifteen

When John walked into the dining room the following morning Eliza and Abigail were already there.

'Are you both still in favour of the girl coming here?' he asked as he went to the oak sideboard to help himself from a silver tureen.

'Yes,' they both agreed.

'No doubts during the night?'

'No,' replied Abigail quickly.

'None,' said Eliza.

'We don't want to get her here and then either of you have regrets,' warned John as he sat down with his plate of porridge.

'What's this all about?' queried Eliza. 'Are you having doubts?'

'No,' he replied sharply. 'I just wanted to be certain you were both still in favour of having her. I shall send word to Dorinda this morning, telling her that we would like to discuss Tess's future and will send a carriage for them the day after tomorrow.'

Later that day Dorinda was surprised when a footman appeared in the shop and handed over a note from Penorna Manor. She asked him to wait and took the paper into the house before breaking the seal.

Dear Miss Jenkins,
In the matter of Tess's future, Mrs Mitchell and I believe it might be beneficial for her to come to Penorna as personal maid to Miss Abigail. Please give this some thought. I am sure you will view this suggestion with Tess's interests at heart.

If you are agreeable I will send a carriage for you the day after tomorrow at ten in the morning so that we can discuss the matter further.

John Mitchell

Reading the note again steadied her thoughts. Tess to leave her! Dorinda had grown attached to the girl during her frequent visits to Lydia and had watched with interest as she grew into an attractive, pleasing child. There would be a gap in her own life if Tess left Penzance. Dorinda brought her tumbling thoughts under control and chided herself for being selfish. She should be thinking of what was best for Tess. She knew only too well, from her own experience, that the child would be going to a well-run house and home. She would have more space there than she would have in the little house behind the shop in Penzance. Personal maid to Miss Abigail Mitchell would be a reasonably good position to have, and, though she would not know it, Tess would also be under the watchful eye of her father.

With her decision made, Dorinda folded the note, put it in the pocket of her dress, and returned to the shop.

'Please tell Mr Mitchell I will be ready at ten o'clock the day after tomorrow.'

Tess's bright smile when she came into the shop after visiting a friend touched Dorinda's heart and drove the thought of losing her to the forefront of her mind again. Could she bear to let her go? She had no need to tell Tess about Mr Mitchell's proposal, after all. She could send the carriage away without Tess even knowing, but would that be fair? Could she live with her own deceit?

'You look as if you've had an enjoyable time?' said Dorinda to postpone making a decision.

'I did, thank you. Gertrude is such fun.' Tess smiled, recollecting her friend, and then adopted a serious expression as she added, 'I think she was trying harder because she didn't want me to be sad about Mama.'

'She's a good friend,' Dorinda agreed. 'Go through and take your coat off. I'll be with you in a minute. I want to talk to you about something.'

'That sounds serious?' said Tess with a grimace.

'It is and it isn't.' Tess recognised Dorinda's reply as being one of her favourites when answering a question.

As Tess entered the house Dorinda spoke to her shop assistants, thankful that she had two such loyal workers. They had been invaluable when she had taken over Jenkins's Emporium on her father's death and set about restoring its fortunes, with considerable success.

Tess had dumped her coat in the small room between the shop and the house and was waiting in the drawing room.

'Tell,' said Dorinda, taking the girl's hand as she sat down beside her on the sofa. She knew it was no good skirting the issue so came straight to the point. 'I have had a note from Mr Mitchell who asks if you would like to be personal maid to Miss Abigail Mitchell?'

Tess stared at Dorinda in stunned silence.

'Leave you?' She frowned and her eyes pleaded for explanation.

'Well, yes. You would have to live at Penorna Manor. Miss Abigail would like you to be her own maid, but only if you would like to go.'

Tess was confused. She liked Dorinda, whom she had known for most of her life. In the days since Lydia had been ill she had found comfort and deep friendship here, a friendship that held an undercurrent of love. Now it was being suggested she should leave.

Troubled, she asked Dorinda, 'Does this mean I won't see you again?' There was a catch in her voice.

Dorinda smiled. 'No, love, of course not! You can come and visit me whenever it is possible.'

'But when would that be?'

'No doubt you will get some free time, but that can all be arranged with Mr and Mrs Mitchell.'

'But I wouldn't know what to do,' protested Tess in some distress.

'You're a bright girl, you'll soon learn.'

Tess looked at her again. 'What would you do?'

'I am not being offered the position,' Dorinda replied gently. 'You will have to decide. All I will say is that you would be going to a beautiful home with plenty of space, something I don't have in a house behind a shop. And I am sure you could be happy there. I was when I was governess to Miss Abigail. I suggest we go to see Mr and Mrs Mitchell. Mr Mitchell said in his letter that he would send a carriage for us the day after tomorrow. I agreed to go because I thought you should learn more about the position and see Penorna for yourself before you decide.'

Tess nodded. 'Very well,' she replied.

Dorinda recognised the doubt in Tess's voice, but she also knew that if she tried to persuade her, the attempt could do more harm than good. Tess was strong and sensible enough to make up her own mind.

Dorinda was thankful when she looked out of her bedroom window and saw that the morning scheduled for their visit to Penorna was bright and holding every promise of staying that way. The countryside and the house would look inviting rather than show the dour complexion they adopted when Atlantic gales drove rain and mist over them. She badly wanted Tess to gain a good impression of the place for she knew from her own experience that Penorna had much to offer. What a person took from it depended very much on them but, knowing Tess, she believed the girl could derive much from a stay at the Manor.

She was pleased when she went downstairs to find that Tess was already there and dressed carefully to present herself smartly to Mr and Mrs Mitchell.

'You've beaten me,' Dorinda said brightly. 'All ready to go.'

'I thought I may as well get ready when I got up,' replied Tess.

'Quite right! I'm pleased you chose that dress. It's as pretty as you,' commented Dorinda, admiring the pale blue, high-waisted dress that hung almost straight to the tops of Tess's black shoes. The neck-line was high and the slightly puffed shoulders lengthened into sleeves that ended tight at the wrists.

Tess looked troubled. 'You don't think Mama would mind?'

'You looking pretty?'

'Well, it's not long since . . .' Her voice faltered.

'Of course she wouldn't,' Dorinda was quick to reassure her. 'She would want you to look your prettiest.'

'And Mr and Mrs Mitchell won't think it wrong of me?'

'No, I'm sure they won't.'

The carriage arrived on the appointed minute and the coachman could not have been more polite and considerate as he saw Dorinda and Tess comfortably seated. He gave Tess a sly wink and responded with a broad smile when he saw his gesture had replaced her worried expression with laughter.

Dorinda took the child's hand in hers, thinking to reassure her but also drawing comfort herself.

'I've never been in such a carriage before,' Tess whispered, excitement in her voice. She looked around her, admiring the polished wood, the clean iron and shining leather. The sway of the carriage, the clop of the horse's hooves and swish of its tail, caught her attention. When she saw people stare at the passing vehicle with curiosity and envy, she felt like a real lady.

The route to Penorna took them at times close to the edge of the cliffs. The sea below shone blue and green, tipped with dashes of white; the horizon was far away and the sky big and blue. Tess felt almost overpowered by such space and freedom after the confines of Penzance which she had escaped only occasionally.

The coachman manoeuvred the horse and carriage skilfully through the open iron gates that admitted them to a driveway leading through a wood. The track burst out of the trees eventually into a wide-open space of manicured lawns that led gently towards a house that made Tess catch her breath.

It's size did not overwhelm, but it was large enough to impart an air of spaciousness and calm. Tess stared wide-eyed at it until her thoughts of what might lie ahead were interrupted by Dorinda.

'It's lovely inside.'

Tess merely nodded and the carriage drew up in front of four steps leading on to a stone veranda that stretched along the front of the house. The coachman was quickly to the ground, and on helping them out informed Dorinda that the carriage would be here, waiting when they were to return to Penzance. At that moment the front door opened and a maid only a little older than Tess appeared. Dorinda, knowing Mr Mitchell's meticulous timing in such matters, was not surprised.

'Follow me, please,' said the maid pleasantly while eyeing Tess with some curiosity.

She led the way along a corridor and up four steps into the large entrance hall where Tess noticed the two large doors, the upper half of which were glass, that gave out on to the veranda. She was disappointed they had been made to use the servants' entrance but then stifled the feeling; after all, Dorinda showed no signs of caring.

The maid knocked on a door, hesitated, then opened it. 'Miss Jenkins and Miss Booth, sir.' Tess now felt a flush of pride at being given her title for it made her feel like an adult. The maid stood to one side beside the door and indicated to them to enter.

Dorinda ushered Tess into a room that almost overwhelmed her with its size. Did people really need so much space to live in? The thought was forgotten almost as soon as it had come when her attention was drawn to Mr Mitchell who had risen from his chair to greet them with a warm smile. Mrs Mitchell occupied a chair next to that vacated by her husband, and Miss Mitchell was sitting in a window seat.

'Miss Jenkins, Tess, do sit down.' John indicated the sofa.

'It will have been a pleasant ride this morning,' commented Eliza amiably.

'It was, ma'am,' replied Dorinda.

'Did you enjoy it, Tess?' asked Eliza as she weighed up this girl who looked so smart in her pretty blue dress. How tragic that she should lose the person she regarded as her mother and with no loving father to turn to either.

'Oh, I did, ma'am,' replied Tess brightly.

'Good.' John had taken his seat again and Abigail had drawn up a chair beside her mother. 'Do you know why you are here, Tess?' He was finding it hard not to take this charming child into his arms and reveal the truth to her, but Lydia's words came strongly to mind.

'Yes, Mr Mitchell,' replied Tess who had seated herself prim and properly with her hands resting in her lap, just as she knew Dorinda would want her to. 'Dorinda told me.'

'What do you think to the idea? Would you like to come here and be Miss Abigail's personal maid?' asked Eliza.

John was on tenterhooks. What if Tess did not like the suggestion? She might leave and then maybe he would never see her again.

'Yes, ma'am, but I don't know what I would have to do.'

'I have given her some idea, ma'am,' put in Dorinda, 'but of course I do not know what you expect of her.'

'I am sure you will soon learn, Tess,' Eliza reassured her. 'My personal maid Sally will teach you, and my daughter will tell you what she wants.'

'It won't be hard,' put in Abigail, 'and you will have a room to yourself on the floor above mine.'

A touch of doubt floated into Tess's eyes. 'Will I still be able to see Dorinda?'

'Of course you will,' added John quickly. He sensed Tess was on the point of accepting and did not want anything to overturn her decision. He looked at Eliza. 'That will be possible, won't it?'

'Of course it will. You will have one day a week free after you have done your early-morning chores, and Sunday after morning service will also be free time for you.'

'And if ever you accompany me to Penzance there may be the opportunity for you to call on Miss Jenkins then,' Abigail pointed out.

Tess turned to Dorinda. 'What would you do?' she asked.

'I am not being offered the position,' she replied gently. 'You will have to decide. All I will say is, you would be coming to a beautiful home and I am sure you would be happy here. I was when I was governess to Miss Abigail.'

Tess nodded. 'As long as I can still see you.'

'Of course you can,' reiterated John.

She looked directly at him and from her eyes he read, Don't break your promise, but he already knew he never would. If only he could tell her the truth, he knew she would love and trust him. Tess turned to Dorinda again. 'All right, if you think that is best for me, and it is what Mama would have wanted me to do?'

'I'm sure it is,' Dorinda said. Her eyes met John's for one fleeting moment then and both knew that from afar Lydia had guided Tess to the right decision.

The carefully chosen staff at Penorna Manor welcomed Tess with open minds and helped her to settle in quickly. They liked her unassuming personality and willingness to help any of them if the necessity arose, though they were aware that, like themselves, she would eventually be guarded about her position in the hierarchy of the servants' hall. Sally, who was twenty-two and had been in service since she was twelve, coming to be Mrs Mitchell's lady maid when she was seventeen, took Tess's training seriously but imbued it with so much fun that Tess settled to it quickly. She was a fast learner and asked plenty of questions so that she was soon taking on responsibilities many of her age would have balked at.

Abigail was delighted with the way Tess kept her room spotless, cleaning the carpet with the use of damp tea-leaves and a brush, polishing the furniture and carefully dusting the ornaments. She was amused by the way Tess quickly assumed an air of authority by getting one of the housemaids to assist her in making the bed just the way that Abigail liked it. She thought her father and mother had found a gem when Tess had put away her dresses in a more orderly manner than the housemaid had previously done.

John too was delighted with the way Tess settled in, but dare not be over-enthusiastic or show her any special consideration, nevertheless, he experienced joy that his two daughters should be living under the same roof and that they got on so well, albeit as servant and mistress. As time passed he sensed a deep affection for Abigail growing in Tess, and that Abigail appreciated Tess's thoroughness and thoughtfulness.

Although initially apprehensive about moving to Penorna to work for strangers and wondering if she would really have free time to visit Dorinda, Tess soon lost her doubts. Mr and Mrs Mitchell, knowing it would enable her to settle in quickly, made sure that visits to Dorinda were encouraged, and whenever time allowed Abigail took Tess with her while visiting Penzance. Though both were unaware of it for some time, these expeditions further strengthened the bond between mistress and maid. Tess had a pleasant if small room handily above Abigail's. She was pleased that it was at the front of the house with a view across beautifully kept lawns to the small wood through which the main drive ran. The ornamental gates to the road were just visible beyond the trees. In the snatches of time she took for herself she loved to look out of this window, especially at any new arrivals at Penorna and in particular when she was able to see guests in their finest clothes, though none came close to her beloved Abigail.

But one person visited frequently and Tess took an instinctive dislike to him. After eighteen months she was clear in her own mind: she did not like Luke Gaisford. If she had been asked why she could have given no good reason, it was just a feeling. There was something about him that did not quite ring true. Could she fault his treatment of and attention to Abigail? Not really, but in her own heart she thought he was too effusive, too glib, and she did not like the way she had seen him look at Abigail. His visits to take her riding or walking became more and more frequent, and if ever there was a party anywhere in the county Luke Gaisford was always the first to ask Abigail to be his partner.

Three days before Abigail's twenty-second birthday, she and Luke rode out from Penorna Manor.

'That's a fine animal,' she commented. 'When did you get it?'

'Three days ago, from a dealer in Bosovern. Had my eye on it quite a while.'

She eyed it up and down then said with a challenging smile, 'Still not good enough to beat mine.'

He chuckled. 'We'll see,' was all he said, but his eyes told her he would rise to the challenge.

She knew she would have to be alert for the moment he threw down the gauntlet, but for the time being she would enjoy the more sedate ride. Abigail shuddered with pleasure at the feel of the gentle breeze caressing her cheeks. She loved this sort of day; small pure white clouds drifted lazily across the bright blue sky, never interfering with the sun. The gentle ride brought a feeling of contentment and she knew that an exhilarating gallop later would bring with it a sense of adventure, but no matter which she was glad she was sharing them with Luke Gaisford.

They kept to the cliff path that afforded them views across a calm sea that challenged the colour of the sky. They skirted the Trethtowan Estate and on reaching Senewey land increased their pace to a trot.

A few minutes later Abigail was jerked out of her reverie when Luke shouted without warning, 'Race you!' and put his mount into a pounding gallop.

Though caught unawares, Abigail rose to the challenge and put her own horse in pursuit. She was sure to catch him, she always did. But today she soon realised that Luke was on a very different horse from usual. She saw immense power in the animal ahead of her though she was not going to admit defeat yet. Flying hooves cut the earth and Abigail revelled in the turn of speed and the brute strength beneath her. But no matter how she exhorted her mount to greater efforts, she realised she would not catch Luke.

The track dipped into a hollow. He pulled his mount to a halt there and even before it had stopped moving he was out of the saddle and striding towards Abigail, letting his mocking laughter fill the air. Goaded by it, and filled with the exhilaration of her own swift ride, she fought her horse that wanted still to run. As she brought it under control Luke grabbed the bridle and steadied the animal.

He came to her side, laughter in his eyes. 'Beat you!' he announced triumphantly. He reached up and with his strong hands clasped firmly round her waist helped her to the ground. He did not let her go then but looked down into her flushed face. Their eyes met and held. Not a word was spoken as their lips came together sweetly and naturally. Abigail's arms slid round his neck as she returned his kiss.

'Payment to the winner,' she said softly as their mouths parted.

'I want more than that,' he whispered. 'Marry me, my love?'

She met the intensity in his eyes. A charge ran between them for an instant and then in a moment of overwhelming joy Abigail said, 'Yes, I will.'

He hugged her close; his lips found hers again and passion flared between them.

When they moved apart they automatically held hands and strolled through the hollow.

'You have made me very happy, Abigail.'

'No more than you have made me.'

'May I have your permission to ask your father for your hand when we return to Penorna?' he asked quietly.

'Of course,' she replied with an excited tremor in her voice. 'Why wait?'

Tess was at her window when the two riders burst from the wood at a gallop. Instead of riding towards the stables at the back of the house, they came straight for the front. There was joy on their faces and laughter in their eyes as they pulled their horses to a dust-stirring halt. Luke jumped from his saddle and was instantly beside Abigail, reaching up to help her to the ground. His hands closed round her waist and he continued to hold her, even when her feet were on the ground. He

225

looked down at her and she met his gaze lovingly. His lips met hers and Tess saw her accept his kiss with equal fervour. She shuddered. Something had happened today. There was a wild joy in the couple as they climbed the steps to the front door, side by side.

'Let me see if Father is in his study,' suggested Abigail when they entered the house. Luke followed her across the hall. She knocked on the door and opened it far enough to look round it. John was at his desk. He looked up and said, 'Come in,' at the same time giving a little indication with his hand, but she ignored both gestures and instead turned back into the hall. 'He's in,' she whispered, then stepped aside to allow Luke to enter the room. She closed the door behind him.

'Good day, sir. I am sorry to interrupt but may I have a word?' he began tentatively. As they had ridden back to Penorna he had wondered what would be the best way to approach Mr Mitchell. By the time they had reached the house he had nothing firm in mind and now found matters had taken their own course.

With this query John's full attention became riveted on the young man. He sensed what must be coming, or why hadn't Abigail accompanied him? 'Do sit down, Luke.' He indicated a chair on the opposite side of his desk.

Luke tried to relax as he sat down. He fell quiet and then realised that Mr Mitchell was waiting for him to speak. 'Sir, I ... er ... I would like to ask you for your daughter's hand in marriage.' The words were out before he realised it.

John held a moment's silence. 'You have asked Abigail?' he said finally.

'Yes, sir.'

'And she accepted?'

'Yes, sir.'

John looked thoughtful for a moment. 'There is no need to ask you about your prospects and whether you will be able to provide for my daughter in the way to which she is accustomed. I know Senewey, and have heard about the way you have pulled it round since your father's death.' Luke breathed a sigh of relief to himself. His efforts to hide the true state of Senewey's finances had paid off. 'There is something I must do before I give you my answer, however, and that is to have a word with Mrs Mitchell. That may as well be done now, so if you will wait here I will go to her.'

'Yes, sir.'

As John rose from his chair Luke, out of respect, did likewise. John left the room. Finding the hall empty he guessed Abigail must have joined her mother in the drawing room. He found that he was right.

'Papa?' There was a look of eager expectancy in her eyes as Abigail jumped up from her chair.

John raised one hand to calm her. He looked at his wife. 'Abigail has no doubt told you that Luke Gaisford is with me, and why?'

'Yes,' replied Eliza, her eyes fixed firmly on her husband, trying to read his decision from his expression. 'And?' she prompted.

'I haven't given him an answer yet.'

'Oh, Papa!' chided an anxious Abigail.

'I wanted a word with both of you first,' he went on, ignoring his daughter's reproof. 'Do you really know him, Abigail?'

'I do, or I would not have given him permission to ask you.'

'He's a Gaisford, remember . . .'

Abigail looked exasperated. 'You're always harking back to old times. Luke's different. You cannot judge the son by the father.'

'But blood does run deep, and who knows what hidden Gaisford traits still lie undiscovered in him.'

'Couldn't there be good traits too?' demanded Abigail.

Eliza saw that this situation could grow heated, which might turn family relationships sour. She did not want that so intervened with a question of her own. 'Do you love him, Abigail?'

'Oh, yes, Mama, of course I do.' She put such intense feeling into her reply there was no misunderstanding it.

Eliza looked at John with an expression that said, That is all that matters.

'Your mother seems convinced. I believe there are other matters to take into consideration, but if you feel so strongly about Luke then I will have to give my approval.'

'Papa!' She flew into his arms and hugged him tight. 'Thank you, thank you!'

'But you must promise us that if any doubts arise, you will tell us?'

'None will, Papa.'

He patted her on the shoulder. Abigail turned to her mother who had risen from her chair to hug her. 'Thank you, Mama.'

'Be happy,' Eliza told her.

'I will.'

'And remember your father's warning: a Gaisford is always a Gaisford.' Eliza gave a little pause, then added. 'But I pray Luke may be the exception.'

John was already at the door. Abigail wanted to rush after him but her mother laid a calming hand on her arm. A few moments later John and Luke reappeared and from Luke's nervous expression Abigail knew he still had not been told the decision.

'Good day, Mrs Mitchell,' he said politely, a gesture that Eliza acknowledged with an inclination of her head.

'Well, Luke,' said John, 'it seems you have my permission to marry my daughter.'

For one brief moment the words did not sink in then the ecstatic smile on Abigail's face confirmed what he had just heard. Luke's face lit up with a broad smile.

'Thank you, sir, thank you!' He rushed to take John's outstretched hand and then Eliza's. 'Thank you too,' he said, and she accepted a kiss on the cheek. As he turned from her mother Abigail came into his arms and they exchanged a triumphant kiss.

'I think this calls for champagne,' said John, going to the bell pull.

A few minutes later a toast was drunk to the young couple's future happiness.

Tess heard voices and went to the window of her room. She saw Luke mount his horse and say something to someone just out of sight. She guessed it was Abigail when she saw him blow a kiss. He turned his horse and in a matter of moments had put the animal into a gallop. Just before she lost sight of him in the wood she saw him sweep his hat off and wave it above his head in a way that had all the signs of someone who had just achieved something he dearly wanted.

Tess learned what that was fifteen minutes later when, having heard Abigail come upstairs, she went to help her mistress out of her riding clothes.

Hearing the door open, Abigail swung round. Her face was wreathed in a broad smile; there was joyous excitement in her eyes. She grabbed Tess and whirled her round and round. 'Oh, Tess, I'm so happy. I'm going to be married!'

She felt a nervous wrench in her stomach at the news. Abigail had her attention fixed on someone Tess did not like. Luke Gaisford! His name plunged like a spear through her mind. She wanted to cry out, No! He's not good enough for you! Miss Abigail, don't marry him! But she dare not. It was not her place to pass an opinion; it would mean nothing if she did. How could she mar the joy that enveloped Abigail? Besides, she did not want to lose Abigail's friendship and put their growing relationship on a mere mistress-and-maid level. It would sadden Tess and hurt her deeply if that happened. She quickly gathered her wits and, with fingers crossed behind her back, said, 'I'm so pleased for you, miss, and I hope you will be very happy together.'

In another part of the house two people were expressing their own doubts.

'I detect you aren't happy with this engagement, John?' Eliza put the question as he closed the door to their bedroom.

'Luke's a Gaisford, Eliza, and bad blood can run deep.'

'I know, but so far he has shown no signs of being like his father. He has always been very polite whenever he has been here, and he has always been most attentive to Abigail.'

'I agree. I cannot fault his behaviour or his attitude. He is properly considerate of our views and restrictions,' said John, but with a touch of reluctance that he had to agree there.

'And Abigail has assured me that Luke has given up drinking and no longer runs with the wild crowd he used to, although they remain friends,' went on Eliza. 'I have discreetly checked up on this when I have taken tea around the county and it seems that Luke avoids all the places he used to frequent. People say he seems to have turned over a new leaf since his father died, and is only interested in the running of the estate nowadays.'

'But he's still a Gaisford.' John's lips tightened. 'Old habits can be resurrected. I wish Abigail could see it.'

'We've pointed it out to her ever since she started seeing more of Luke.'

'I know, and short of putting an outright ban on her associating with him, we thought she would see the type he really was. Instead she seems to have reformed him.'

'We could have refused her permission to marry.'

'I don't think that would have done any good.' John gave a reluctant smile. 'You know as well as I that Abigail can be headstrong and stubborn if she wants to. She would probably have cocked a snook at convention, walked out and gone to him. Then we would have lost her for good, and we would not want that. All we can do is give her our blessing and offer her our continued love and support.'

Two days later, having helped Abigail to dress for her party, Tess remarked as she stepped back to view her mistress, 'That was a good choice of dress, miss. It suits you. You look so beautiful. Everyone will envy Mr Gaisford.'

'Thank you, Tess, and thank you for having this dress so beautifully ironed.'

Tess could not deny the happiness her mistress was feeling. She watched discreetly from a corner of the passage that led into the main hall at the moment the engagement was announced to the crowded room. It sent new joy through the guests who poured congratulations onto the happy couple.

From her position Tess caught the question that was put several times: when will the wedding take place?

As she wandered back to her room it rang in her mind and brought another to the fore. What will happen to me? Her answer was to recall that Dorinda had told her she could always go to her. Yes, that would be her best solution.

But she received a different answer the following afternoon. Abigail had slept late, and after a light luncheon with her father and mother, had gone riding on her own. Tess had taken the opportunity to straighten her mistress's room. Noticing the water jug had been chipped, she obtained a replacement from the kitchen and was returning along the landing when she heard voices she recognised as Mr and Mrs Mitchell's coming from the bedroom where the door was slightly ajar. She heard her name and halted her step.

'Tess? Well, I suppose Abigail will want to take her with her after she and Luke are married. After all, it's better to have a lady's maid she knows,' said Eliza.

Softly spoken though they were, the words thundered in Tess's mind. Go to Senewey Manor! Oh, no! As happy as she was with Abigail, she did not like the prospect of living at Senewey, nor being under the authority of Luke Gaisford about whom she was still uneasy.

'We must draw comfort from the fact that Tess will be with her. When the time comes, I'll have a word with her and ask her to report anything disturbing directly to us.'

Tess's heart was racing. It was obvious Mr and Mrs Mitchell had doubts of their own about this marriage. Why hadn't they refused permission for it? It was apparent they hadn't and that they were relying on her to stay near Abigail in case of any trouble. From loyalty to Abigail and her parents she could not refuse to go to Senewey.

Chapter Sixteen

At Luke's urging a date was soon fixed, but he had to agree with Abigail's wishes, instigated by her father and mother, that the wedding day be in six months' time. Abigail was happy enough with that because it gave her time to enjoy and savour all the parties during their engagement period and revel in the preparations for an August wedding.

Luke resigned himself to wait, soothed by the thought of the dowry which would relieve his ever-worsening financial position. But before the happy day he knew he would have to further some other schemes he had in mind.

He met his four friends regularly at the Waning Moon, sometimes more than once a week. It became 'their' place, a travellers' inn where they could have a private room for an evening's drinking, stay the night and face the world in penitent sobriety the next day.

Although Tess still harboured doubts about Luke as a suitable husband for Abigail, whom she had come to love and admire all the more, she kept them to herself. But after what she had overheard, she resolved to sharpen her vigilance when she removed to Senewey.

Unaware of Tess's misgivings, Abigail was pleased that the girl appeared to be swept up in her own joyous mood for she felt a strange affinity to her maid.

Although Eliza and John would have preferred a quiet wedding they knew it could not be so. Since coming to Cornwall their stature had grown and, though their acceptance into

Cornish society had been slow, it was founded on admiration and trust, especially after the reconciliation with Jeremy Gaisford on Abigail's seventeenth birthday. The gentry would expect a big wedding, especially as the bridegroom was from the oldest family in Cornwall on his mother's side. So the preparations were thorough. Eliza determined that everything should be stylish and correct.

The week before the wedding was one of glowering skies and rain swept in by a south-westerly wind that in the dark hours seemed to be howling a warning. At least Tess, lying awake in the darkness, took it that way. It accentuated her own troubled state. She saw nothing but disaster ahead in this marriage and feared what might happen if Abigail's deep love for Luke was betrayed, but there was nothing she could do about it.

She slipped out of bed early on the day of the wedding; there was much to get through before the ceremony at noon but the first thing she did was to go to the window. When she drew back the curtains she saw a bright morning with no evidence of the inclement weather of the past week. Was this an omen? Did the heavens shine on the wedding after all? Had her own suspicions been unfounded? She did not know the answers and there was no time to worry now with so much to be achieved before the ceremony.

Tess had done most of the packing for Abigail's immediate requirements for the two weeks she and Luke would spend at Senewey Manor before, taking advantage of the fragile peace with Napoleon, they left for a wedding trip to France. She would complete that immediately and see that all her own things too were ready to move to Senewey Manor. She had been apprehensive when Abigail had told her that Luke had agreed to her still being employed as her maid after the wedding but hid that feeling, knowing she wanted to remain close to her mistress.

When she went to Abigail's room she found her already up and arrayed in her undergarments over which she had slipped a lace robe.

'Good morning, miss,' Tess greeted her.

233

'With an exciting day ahead, I woke early, Tess, so left my bed. A day dress for breakfast, please.'

Tess quickly chose one and in a matter of minutes Abigail was on her way downstairs. Tess glanced round the room and decided to get her own breakfast before tidying up.

She was not long away and had resisted the kitchen staff's desire to know what Abigail's wedding dress was like, telling them she did not want to spoil the surprise and they must all wait and see.

By the time Abigail returned Tess had brought some order to the room and immediately turned her attention to the preparations for the wedding. Time would fly and there was the carriage ride to Penzance to consider.

When the moment came, Tess knelt on the floor and helped Abigail into a pair of pale blue shoes. She then carefully took the wedding dress from its hanger, handling the garment as if it was the most precious piece of delicate glass. They were both awe-struck by its beauty and not a word passed between them as Tess helped Abigail into the deep rose brocade silk dress. Its patterned bodice came tight to the waist and fell in smooth lines to the floor. The round neckline finished at discreetly puffed shoulders, and the sleeves came tight to the wrist. Abigail gave herself a little shake that sent the dress shimmering.

Tess stood back and looked at her with open admiration. 'Oh, you do look beautiful, miss.'

'The head-dress, Tess,' said Abigail, her voice quivering with excitement.

Tess eased the garment from its box and placed it carefully on her mistress's head. The white bonnet had a low crown, a brim decorated with intertwining green leaves and yellow rosebuds, and had a delicate white waist-length veil neatly fastened to it. It still allowed Abigail's coiffure to show, the hair swept back on either side of a middle parting.

'Just right,' said Abigail, gleefully appraising herself in a full-length mirror. 'Thank you, Tess. And thank you for all you have done to make this occasion happy for me. I hope you too will be happy at Senewey.'

'Thank you, miss,' Tess replied, though she still had misgivings about that.

'As I have already told you, a special carriage is arranged to take you there later in the day. When you arrive you will report to the housekeeper, Mrs Horsefield.'

Any further conversation was halted by a knock on the door. Tess went to it quickly and on opening it saw Mr and Mrs Mitchell.

'May we come in?' Eliza asked.

Tess glanced back at Abigail whom she knew must have heard the request. She nodded and Tess stood aside, holding the door ajar. Eliza and John stepped into the room and came to a halt. They stared in wonder and admiration at their daughter.

'Beautiful!' The word was drawn out as John stared at her in amazement.

'You look wonderful,' said Eliza, her own face wreathed in admiration.

John found himself wondering would he ever see his other daughter looking so beautiful in her wedding dress?

John was filled with pride as he walked down the aisle of St Mary's Church, Penzance, with his beautiful daughter attracting everyone's eyes. Seeing Luke's expression of adoration as he turned to greet her, he wondered if he had judged this young man too harshly and offered a silent prayer that Luke's attitude would never change. His daughter's happiness was paramount to John and he only wished he could openly express the same for Tess.

No one could fault the parson's handling of the service, and the homily he directed at the bride and groom not only expressed his hopes for their future happiness but also dwelt for a few moments on the duties of man and wife towards each other.

The church was full, with places at the back especially reserved for the staffs of Penorna and Senewey so that they could make a quick exit once the actual ceremony was over. Tess managed to gain one from which she had a good view of the ceremony which she watched with mixed feelings. She wanted to be happy for Abigail but her misgivings about Luke Gaisford had worsened the nearer the wedding day drew. She could not deny, however, that the couple looked radiantly happy and that Luke could not have been more attentive to his bride.

It was also a happy laughing pair who emerged from the church to be greeted by many casual sightseers and were soon joined by the congregation flowing out of the church to shower congratulations on them.

The carriages taking the staff back to their respective manors were already leaving, those to Penorna to be ready to serve the wedding guests on their arrival; those to Senewey to await the arrival of bride and groom later in the day.

As he came out of the church John caught a glimpse of Tess in one of the last Penorna carriages. He felt a sharp tug at his heart and a sense of his own injustice filled him. Tess should be beside him now, occupying her rightful place among the guests as Abigail's sister. The thought was driven from his mind, though, as Eliza slipped her arm under his and said, 'A lovely occasion. A pity Luke's mother was not well enough to attend.'

'Yes,' he agreed. 'Here's their carriage arriving.'

The crowd milled even closer around bride and groom. Congratulations, well wishes, advice both serious and humorous, filled the air but all were lost on the couple who had eyes only for each other. It took them ten minutes to reach the carriage after its arrival. Once it was away the other vehicles that had been lining up moved forward; the first for the bridesmaids and Martin, the best man. This was followed by one for John and Eliza, and then for the other guests.

The joyful mood continued at Penorna where no expense had been spared to make everyone feel this was a special day, one to be remembered. Wine flowed freely, there was food aplenty, and no one lacked for conversation. Inevitably bride and groom were separated as demands on their attention grew. Luke found himself confronted by Martin, Sydney,

George and David. Each in turn shook his hand, offered their congratulations and wished him well for the future.

'Will that include a resumption of our meetings at the Waning Moon?' Martin asked.

'Of course,' replied Luke emphatically. 'You'll see me turning up at the inn soon after my return from France.'

It was late afternoon when John managed to extricate himself from a conversation with two landowners from the north of the county and went in search of Eliza.

He interrupted her chat with two friends from St Ives and drew her to one side. 'It will soon be time for Tess to leave for Senewey. Should I have a word with her about Abigail?'

'If you think it wise,' she replied, but a slight nod signified her approval. 'Don't put too much responsibility on the girl. We don't want to give her the impression she will be spying for us.'

'I'll be careful.'

He found Tess in Abigail's room. She was surprised when John walked in and looked sheepish, as if she had been caught somewhere she shouldn't have been.

'I was just making a last check on some of Miss Abigail's things, sir.' Tess blushed as she added quickly, 'Er . . . I mean, Mrs Gaisford's things.'

John smiled at her embarrassment. 'That was very thoughtful of you, Tess. I'm sure everything will be in order. You learned quickly and you have always been very efficient and I am pleased with the way you have both got on so well.'

'Sir, Miss Abigail has been very easy to deal with.'

'I'm glad. Now it will soon be time for you to be going to Senewey. Robert will have a carriage ready for you in ten minutes. Before you go, I want to give you one last instruction. If ever you are worried about my daughter, in any way, come and tell me. No one else – only me, or Mrs Mitchell if I am not here. I don't want you to feel you'll be spying on her or Mr Gaisford but if you are at all uneasy . . .'

He left the sentence unfinished but from her expression knew that she had read his meaning.

'I will, sir.'

'Thank you, Tess.'

As he left the room John so wished he could turn back and tell her the truth about herself, how much he had loved her mother and now loved her.

Tess went to her room. She looked round her, sad to be leaving. She had been happy here. The Mitchells' kindness, especially that shown her by Mr Mitchell, had helped to ease the loss of her dear mama, as Tess had always called her aunt.

She picked up the valise which Dorinda had given her when she left Penzance, and went to the door. She paused, looked behind her for the last time and then left her sanctuary, determined to cope with the new life that faced her and to keep a watchful eye on Miss Abigail's welfare. She gave a little nod – yes, to Tess she would always be Miss Abigail, no matter that now she was legally Mrs Luke Gaisford.

Robert was kindness itself when he drove Tess to Senewey Manor. He kept up a light stream of chatter to try to brighten her move. He did not envy her residing in the Gaisford residence even though she was going to continue as the bride's lady's maid. He did not like the house himself but made no comment about that even though he sensed Tess shudder when it came in sight.

Her spirits plummeted but in a few moments she'd pulled herself together, determined not to let a mere house get her down, even though after Penorna this one seemed dour and dreary. It appeared to have no feeling of life about it and Tess wondered how much of that was due to the people who had lived there in the past and those who lived there now.

Robert drove into a courtyard at the rear of the house and pulled the horse to a halt at a small door. He helped Tess down to the ground and carried her bag inside.

'I've been here before. I'll show you where to go,' he whispered.

Tess thought their footsteps striking the stone floor sounded like harbingers of doom. They came to another door which he opened and Tess followed him into a small lobby which she noticed thankfully was carpeted. She didn't like the echoing sound here. Robert knocked at a door to the left and opened it on a command to come in.

'Good day, ma'am,' he said politely, 'I've brought Tess Booth, Mrs Gaisford's, that is the *new* Mrs Gaisford's personal maid as arranged.'

'And good day to you, Robert,' she said, rising from an armchair near the window that looked out on to a small walled garden. 'Ah, so this is Tess about whom Mrs Gaisford talked so highly.'

'It is,' replied Robert. He turned to Tess. 'This is Mrs Horsefield, the housekeeper.'

Tess felt uncomfortable in front of this woman who presented a formidable figure as she eyed her up and down, but ventured to say, 'I was told to report to you, ma'am.'

'You're younger than I expected,' said the housekeeper.

'I'll be sixteen in December and I'm a good worker, ma'am.'

'So I've been told. See that you remain so.'

'I will, ma'am.'

'Mrs Gaisford has told me that she wants you to devote your entire time to being her personal maid so she must think highly of you. See that you don't let her trust in you down.'

'I won't, ma'am.'

'Because Mrs Gaisford wants it that way, the only other person you will report to will be me.'

'Yes, ma'am.'

During this exchange Mrs Horsefield had gradually appeared less formidable; her features had lost their first severity and assumed a more kindly expression.

'I'll show you to your room and explain some things to you on the way.' She turned to Robert. 'You'll take a tot before you leave?'

'That is very kind of you, Mrs Horsefield. It will certainly help me on my way.'

'Very good! I'll deal with Tess and soon be back.'

As she said goodbye to Robert, Tess wondered how many tots he had previously taken with Mrs Horsefield, but what did it matter? It was none of her business and it did make the housekeeper seem more human and not the harridan that Tess had feared. Maybe it wouldn't be so bad at Senewey after all.

She followed Mrs Horsefield from the room and fell into step beside her in the corridor.

'This is the staircase you will generally use unless it is absolutely essential for you to use the main one,' the housekeeper said as they climbed to the first small landing. Here she opened a door that led on to a wide corridor, luxuriously carpeted. She crossed this and took Tess into a small vestibule that led into a big room furnished with a large sofa and four armchairs that Tess felt she would be lost in. The walls were papered with a small floral pattern against a yellow background and on each wall there was a gold-framed seascape. 'This is Mrs Gaisford's sitting room,' explained Mrs Horsefield, and then opened a door on the right. 'This is her bedroom. You will be responsible for these two rooms.' The bedroom was as large as the sitting room. Apart from the huge bed there was a wardrobe, chest of drawers, dressing table, oval card table and four chairs, two easy chairs, and small table to each side of the bed. The two large windows looked out onto lawns and flower gardens beyond which lay wild moorland.

When they returned to the sitting room Mrs Horsefield hesitated. 'That door leads into Mr Gaisford's sitting room and beyond it is his bedroom. You will never venture through that door. Tully, Mr Gaisford's manservant, looks after those two rooms. You'll meet him later, as you will all the staff. I'll take you to your own room now.'

They returned to the stairs. As the mistress's maid Tess merited a small bare room which held a single bed, small table, chest of drawers, chair and wash stand. It was lit by a sash window that looked down over the courtyard.

'Everything has been prepared for you here, Tess. Now, I will return downstairs and send Alice to show you the rest of the house. She'll be with you in fifteen minutes.'

'Yes, Mrs Horsefield. I'll be waiting.'

The housekeeper nodded. 'I hope you will be happy with us at Senewey Manor.'

Tess put her few belongings away and had just finished making the bed to her liking when there was a knock on the door.

She looked up expectantly when it opened but the person who entered was not at all as expected. In her mind she'd pictured a middle-aged woman who had worked for years as a general maid for the Gaisford family. Instead she saw a thin waif of a girl of about her own age tentatively edging into the room, as if afraid of what might confront her.

'Tess Booth?' she asked in a voice that was scarcely above a whisper.

'Yes, that's me,' said Tess brightly to reassure the girl that she was not an ogre. 'You must be Alice.'

'Yes, miss.'

Tess grinned. 'No need to call me miss, I'm only a maid like you.' She stepped past the girl to close the door.

'But you're a personal maid,' said Alice with some awe.

'I am, to the new Mrs Gaisford, but I'm still a maid like you and don't you forget it if we are to be friends.'

Alice's smile wiped the solemnity from her face. 'You want to be friends with me?' she asked eagerly.

'If you want to be friends with me?'

'Oh, I do. There's no one here of my age and it gets lonely at times.'

'Then you and I will be friends,' replied Tess, equally grateful, realising that there might be a time when she really needed a friend at Senewey. 'Mrs Horsefield said you are to show me round the house.'

'Yes, but first I have to give you these.' She thrust the things she had been holding towards Tess.

'What are these?'

'Dresses like mine,' replied Alice. 'We all have to wear the same here.'

'Oh, I didn't know that.'

'You have to try them on, and if they don't fit I have to pin them and take them to the sewing room.'

Tess shrugged her shoulders. 'In that case, I may as well try them on now and if they need altering we can take them there when you show me round.'

Tess slipped off her own frock and shrugged herself into the first of the three dresses that Alice had brought. Alice tried to hide her embarrassment at Tess's openness by saying, 'I wish I was like you.'

'What do you mean?' asked Tess.

'You aren't skinny like me.'

'Maybe you are better in other ways.'

'I doubt that. I'll never be a personal maid.'

'I knew nothing about it until I was engaged to be Mrs Gaisford's personal maid before she was married. She insisted I come here with her.'

'You were lucky.'

'I learned quickly.' Tess looked down at Alice who was deftly pinning the bottom of the dress. 'I couldn't do what you are doing so skilfully.'

'I'm sure you could.'

'No, I've never done anything like that.'

'My mother taught me. I helped her. She did some dress-making in St Just.'

They quickly adjusted the three dresses and Alice agreed that the several aprons were suitable.

'Come on, I'll show you the house, now?

They delivered the dresses to the sewing room first. The three sewing maids were friendly and Tess was told the alterations would be completed by noon the next day. The housemaids eyed her suspiciously but without any rancour; the kitchen staff were more friendly, though with all the preparations for the following day's party going on they had little time to give her. The head cook, who Tess realised ruled this domain, told her she would only be allowed in the kitchen when she was answering a request from Mrs Gaisford. She also informed Tess that staff mealtimes were to be strictly adhered to. When they left the kitchen, Alice showed her the staff dining room.

She then conducted Tess through the rest of the house, telling her where she was allowed to go and which areas were out of bounds. In the hall, which was oak-panelled and from which a wide staircase lined by an elaborately carved banister led to the upper floors, Alice indicated a long corridor leading to the right.

'Off there is the West Wing. You have no need to go there. It is where Mrs Gaisford, Mr Luke's mother, lives. You may catch a glimpse of her occasionally but she lives very much on her own and has her own maids.'

Tess looked around and then Alice lowered her voice. 'They say that when Mr Gaisford inherited, he insisted his mother should live in that wing and keep to herself.'

'Is there something the matter with her?' asked Tess.

'Not that I know of! I did meet her in one of the corridors once by accident and she asked me who I was. She seemed kind enough, but I know no more. My advice to you is, don't ask questions. Keep strictly to your work for the new Mrs Gaisford and all will be well. My only other piece of advice is, don't cross Mr Gaisford, he has a quick temper.'

'I wouldn't have thought that from what I have seen,' said Tess, hoping this would prompt Alice into saying more. But all she added was, 'You haven't worked for him and you haven't seen him at home. They tell me there's something of his father in him.'

Tess said nothing further but locked the information away in her mind.

'It's time we were leaving, love,' whispered Luke in Abigail's ear in an attempt to draw her away from conversation with Martin.

She gave a small nod as she said, 'That's a pity. I was just revelling in Martin's compliments. You must visit us soon after we get back.'

'Senewey used to be a second home to me whenever I was home from school,' replied Martin.

'You were at Rugby with Luke?'

'Yes, and Sydney and David and George. We all went there together and gained a reputation for being the Cornish Five.'

'A reputation that stuck for a while after your return,' commented Abigail with a knowing smile.

Martin threw up his arms in denial as he said, 'We reformed.'

'Reputations stick,' she teased. 'Who knows what you get up to now?'

'We really must go,' put in Luke.

Abigail took his arm, flashing Martin a dazzling smile that set his heart racing. When it became known that the bride and groom were about to leave for Senewey the guests made their way outside to give them a send off. Laughter and shouts of congratulation rang through the air as the carriage started to move. Abigail threw her bouquet in the air and a great cheer rang out when it was caught by George's sister.

The newly weds sank back on the seat with contented sighs.

'All so wonderful,' said Abigail, taking Luke's hand in hers. 'Your mother and father did us proud.'

'Thank you. I'm sorry your mother was not able to be there. I must see her before I change out of my wedding gown.'

Luke hesitated only a moment before he realised he could do nothing but comply. Besides, it would be for the best. His mother may keep very much to the West Wing nowadays but there was always the possibility that Abigail would come across her by chance, careful as she was to avoid her own son.

When word ran through the house that the carriage was approaching the staff quickly gathered in the entrance hall where they were marshalled by Mrs Horsefield to form a welcoming party.

The housekeeper greeted the happy couple and then introduced each member of the staff to Abigail. When they had dispersed she turned to Luke and said, 'Your mother?'

He nodded and led her to the door giving access to the West Wing. Here he took her through a sitting room into a medium-sized hall from which a staircase rose.

As soon as he looked inside he said, 'Mother, I've brought Abigail to see you.' He stepped to one side to allow his bride to enter. She detected delight in Mrs Gaisford's voice when she greeted her and there was no disguising the brightness that came to the older woman's eyes.

'Mrs Gaisford,' said Abigail as she crossed the room to embrace Luke's mother and greet her with a kiss.

Hester reached out for Abigail's hands and held them affectionately as she said, 'How beautiful you look, my dear.' The light in her eyes left Abigail in no doubt that the compliment was given genuinely.

'I'm sorry you were not able to be at the wedding.'

'So was I, but my health is not good and if I had had trouble during the service it would have upset everybody. I was better here, thinking of you and my son and hoping you will be good for Luke. He has a tradition to live up to, and that on top of running an estate is not easy.'

'Now, Mother, no preaching,' cut in Luke.

Abigail saw a flash of resentment cross her mother-in-law's face but as befitted a woman of breeding she brought her reaction so quickly under control that it was hardly noticeable.

But it made Abigail wonder if all was not as it should be between this proud, frail woman and her son.

Chapter Seventeen

Although she did not like Senewey Manor as much as the house at Penorna, Tess was determined to settle quickly and thankful she had already made a friend in Alice. The arrival of the bride and groom after the reception at Penorna set Senewey into a whirl of excitement that continued throughout the following day with a party that went on into the next morning. Tess was pleased to see Abigail so radiantly happy and hoped it continued for a long time.

Even though she was swept up in her love for Luke, Abigail was pleased to have Tess's familiar presence close by to negate the unfamiliar surroundings. She was also pleased and excited to tell her, 'You are coming to France with us.'

Tess stared at her with disbelief, 'Me? Going to France?'

Abigail laughed. 'Yes. Mr Gaisford is allowing me to take you as my personal maid rather than relying on hired servants there.'

'Oh, miss, that's wonderful! I never dreamed ...' Tess's words faded away. Then, with the idea sinking in, she said, 'I've never left England before.'

'Nor have I, Tess. But Mr Gaisford has been to France so he will see that we are all right.'

'I hope so, miss. I'm not sure about foreigners, but this is exciting.' Her eyes were bright at the prospect of a new experience.

When Tess broke the news to Alice, her new friend was not envious but said she would want to know all about it when Tess got back.

In the ensuing days Tess was careful to see to Abigail's every need and be meticulous about packing for the wedding trip. Throughout this time she saw little of Luke until the day they left for France when he came to see that the trunks and valises were securely packed on the coach in which Tess would travel alone during the week-long journey from Penzance to Dover.

He acknowledged her and asked, 'Have you been on the sea before?'

'No, sir.'

He grimaced. 'Well, if you are going to be sick, keep right away from me.'

'Yes, sir.'

'And make sure this luggage arrives safely.'

'Yes, sir.'

The responsibility he had thrust upon her made Tess nervous but by the time the two carriages had reached the port she had determined not to let it worry her and to enjoy her first trip abroad, though how much freedom she would have there she did not know.

The hustle and bustle at Dover took her mind off the pending crossing to France and it was only brought sharply back to mind when the ship left the harbour. Tess was thankful that the sea was smooth for the first time she left English shores and in fact found pleasure in the ship's motion.

At Calais Luke organised two coaches to take them to Paris, Tess travelling, as she had done in England, in the coach that carried their luggage. It was a lonely journey for her but she made the most of it by taking an interest in all she could see from the windows. An overnight stay in Abbeville was a welcome break, and though she became the object of curiosity when she went to dine with the servants at the establishment chosen by Mr Gaisford, she coped well in spite of the language difficulty.

It was different in Paris where they had rooms in one of the best hotels in the city for here Tess came across people with whom she could communicate more easily, though their smattering of English left much to be desired. She was pleased that she could now attend more readily to Abigail's needs for she did not like to be idle. Nevertheless her time was divided between bouts of strenuous activity and what might have been periods of sheer boredom had she let them become so. Whenever an opportunity arose during daylight she ventured out to see the city, being careful to keep to places frequented by crowds of people. She spent a considerable time in the magnificent Gothic cathedral of Notre Dame, overawed by the soaring architecture but saddened by the ravages of the recent Revolution on this holy building. She had thought that the church in Penzance was wonderful but it could not compete with this. The majestic façade of Les Invalides held her attention for many minutes, and the lively river traffic as she walked by the Seine made her think for a moment of the port where she'd grown up. Signs of the huge upheaval of the Revolution were still everywhere to be seen but she was fascinated by the work that was going on under the Napoleonic revival.

The evenings were long for her. After she had seen to Abigail's needs, before she and Mr Gaisford visited Luke's friends in the city or spent time at a theatre or restaurant, Tess's time was free. In anticipation of this Abigail had provided her with several books. She had started Anna Maria Porter's *Octavia* on the way here, and still had *The Gipsy Countess* by Elizabeth Gunning, *Tales of the Cottage* by Mary Pilkington, and *Angelina* by Mary Robinson, to start.

After Paris they moved on to Chartres where after Abigail and Luke had visited the cathedral on their first day, Abigail told Tess that she must find the opportunity to see it too. Two days later when Luke took Abigail by carriage into the neighbouring countryside, Tess quickly cleared away her mistress's clothes and tidied the room before leaving for the cathedral.

She had caught a glimpse of it as they arrived in the town but, after Notre Dame in Paris, had not expected to see another such sight. She stood for a long time taking in the carvings above the west doors above which rose three magnificent stained glass windows that were outdone only by the breathtaking rose window above them. The glory of those windows became evident when she went inside and saw the light come streaming through them. Awe-struck she just stood and stared, trying to decide whether she preferred this to the beautiful rose window in Notre Dame.

How would she ever be able to convey all this beauty and magnificence to Alice when she got home?

Tess found there was more to come when they went to Rouen where she walked in Joan of Arc's footsteps leading to the stake. Then it was on to Amiens for a few days before going on to Dieppe.

They arrived in the early afternoon and Luke excused himself to Abigail, saying that he had some business with a man who had been recommended as being able to put some business his way. Abigail decided to take the opportunity to have a rest after the bustle of the days they had spent. Seeing her mistress was comfortable, Tess retired to her room to remain on hand when needed.

'It looks as though you haven't been successful,' commented Abigail when Luke returned, wearing a puzzled frown.

'I wasn't,' he said irritably. 'I was told in England that this man would be in Dieppe, now I'm told he's in Calais.' He looked thoughtful for a moment. 'I'll have to reassess the situation when we get there.'

As Tess's coach trundled the last few miles into Calais she reflected on the master's attitude to Abigail throughout their sojourn in France. She could not fault his attention to his wife whenever she had been able to observe it. Everywhere they had been, he had commandeered the best accommodation and seen to her every comfort. He paid little attention to Tess but she knew he had observed her contributions to his wife's well-being, and, remembering Alice's warning, had given him no cause for complaint.

Riding in the leading coach, Luke took Abigail's hand in his. 'I hope you have enjoyed the last eight weeks?'

'Immensely,' she replied with a smile. 'Your arrangements have been marvellous and I have enjoyed every minute of our trip. I only wish it could go on.'

'Alas, my love, tomorrow we have to re-enter the real world.'

'Ah, well, we have wonderful memories.' She leaned towards him and kissed him. 'Thank you.'

'Abigail.' She straightened at the sound of a serious note in his voice and was disturbed to see a severe expression on his face. 'I didn't tell you this because I didn't want to spoil the little time we had left, but from what I was told in Dieppe I may have to be in Calais for a few days.'

'Why?'

'The man I had to see, Monsieur Defarge, had told a subordinate to deal with me. When I explained my business proposition he did not hold out much hope, but I insisted I should see Mr Defarge himself. I was not going to be pushed aside by a subordinate! If Defarge does not want to do business then I will have to stay in Calais a little longer and find someone who does.'

'Then I'll wait with you.'

'No! It would be far better if you went ahead. Godric will have brought the coach from Senewey to Dover and everything is arranged for our journey back. As I will not be with you, your lady's maid can ride with you.'

'But I don't like you deserting me like this.' There was a steely note to her voice and criticism in her eyes.

Luke bristled with annoyance. 'You are going to have to get used to it,' he retaliated. 'We are back to serious concerns which may take me away from you quite often.'

Abigail did not reply but turned to gaze out of the window. Their first harsh words had marred the end of what she had viewed as the perfect start to her marriage. Was reality dealing its first blow? Was a Gaisford trait revealing itself? Her father's warnings came to mind. But she knew from the harsh determination in Luke's voice that there was nothing she could do about his decision to leave her now, and it was extremely unlikely that she would be able to do anything about it in the future.

It was late afternoon when they arrived at their accommodation. Tess followed them inside and immediately sensed the tension between them. She wondered what had happened during the coach journey. Luke ordered a meal to be brought to them and, apart from arranging a room for Tess, left her to fend for herself.

'You still sulking about tomorrow?' he demanded towards the end of the meal during which Abigail had shown no inclination to talk.

'Not sulking. Hurt that you are deserting me and leaving me to find my own way home.' She cast him a withering look that condemned his ungentlemanly behaviour.

'You'll have Tess, and Godric will be at Dover. It's not as if you are going to be on your own.'

'You are my husband and you should be seeing me home.'

'Yes, I'm your husband, and the sooner you realise that I'm under no obligation to you, the better it will be. I've told you, I'm likely to be away quite a lot so you'd better get used to it. I have business to attend to.' The anger in his eyes shocked her. This was not the man who had courted her.

'What's got into you, Luke? I've never seen you like this.'

His eyes narrowed. 'You never question what I do, when I do it or what my motives are. Remember that and life at Senewey will be good.' He pushed himself to his feet and looked down at her with hard eyes. 'For now, remember we are going to be apart for a while after tonight. I'll be back!'

He swung past her and was out of the door before she could say anything, but the welcome he expected when he returned was clear to her.

Abigail sat staring at the table. What had gone wrong? What had she done? Nothing wrong as far as she knew. Since the wedding everything had seemed like paradise, but now . . . Was it the thought of their mundane life back in Cornwall that had annoyed Luke? But surely that was of his own making. Life needn't be that way after all. Had the fact that he had been unable to see Monsieur Defarge in Dieppe altered his mood? What business matter could cause such a drastic change in him?

A knock on the door interrupted her thoughts. In answer to her response Tess opened the door tentatively.

'Do you require me, miss?' she asked, seeing Abigail on her own.

'Come in, Tess,' replied Abigail.

Tess sensed the unhappiness in the room and connected it with the absent Mr Gaisford.

'I won't want you any more tonight and will manage for myself in the morning. You have been told what time to be ready to leave for the ship?'

'Yes, miss.'

Abigail did not bother to correct her. She knew that Tess still regarded her as her Miss Abigail though was always careful in front of Luke to address her as Mrs Gaisford.

'Ten o'clock,' Tess added.

'Mr Gaisford will not be accompanying,' said Abigail. Tess was aware of the catch in her mistress's voice though Abigail quickly disguised it. 'He is detained in Calais on business. Therefore you and I will travel together when we reach England.'

Though this was a plausible explanation Tess was not convinced, but it was not her place to comment.

'Very well, miss.' She started for the door.

'Thank you for all you have done for me on this visit to France. I hope you have enjoyed seeing another country.'

'I have. It has been wonderful, but I will be glad to be back in England.'

Abigail gave a little nod. 'I think I will be too.' She gave a wan smile that dismissed any excitement she might have felt about her return to Senewey.

It disturbed Tess and as she returned to her room she wondered what had happened between Abigail and Luke.

Following the instructions he had received in Dieppe and confirmation of how to find Rue de St Quentin from the concierge, Luke hurried to his destination. He found number four to be an unpretentious house that showed no evidence it harboured the headquarters of an illicit trading gang. If the luxurious trappings inside were anything to go by, though, hopefully he was going to reap the same rewards from a venture that was new to him. The servant who had admitted Luke asked him to wait in the hall and then went up a wide staircase. A few moments later he appeared on the landing and called in a thick accent, 'Will you come this way, sir?'

Luke hurried up the stairs and followed the man along the landing where he knocked on a door, hesitated a moment and then opened it. 'Monsieur Gaisford,' he announced and stood to one side to allow Luke to enter.

A small man rose from an easy chair situated to one side of a richly ornamented fireplace. Surprised that this man was not as tall as he had imagined, Luke felt he would easily be in command of their discussion, but that feeling was immediately forgotten when he absorbed the air of authority that emanated from this man. His steel blue eyes held hypnotic power as they searched Luke's face and assessed him mercilessly. This was not at all the sort of man Luke would have associated with a notorious band of smugglers operating along the Normandy coast.

'Monsieur Gaisford.' The man held out his hand and started to speak in French. He stopped and then said, 'Ah, I see from your eyes that you do not understand. I will start again and we shall conduct our business in English. I believe you were looking for me in Dieppe. Louis Defarge.'

Luke was astonished by the steely grip such a small hand possessed. 'Monsieur Defarge! You received word from Dieppe very quickly.'

The man smiled. 'No sense in setting up methods of communication if they are not efficient. The message I received was that you wanted to see me on the recommendation of a mutual friend, Joseph Boilly. Let me offer you a glass of wine.' He poured it while he listened to Luke's explanation.

'He was a friend of my late grandfather ... much younger, of course, more my father's age ... but I recalled his visits to the family home in Cornwall. I remembered hearing talk of certain activities along the Normandy coast. I also recalled the name of a Frenchman, a name that seemed unusual to a Cornish youngster. It stuck in my mind. Recent enquiries on my part have linked you with those activities.'

'Ah, monsieur, you have linked memory with diligent search. But let us not be evasive. When you speak of activities, you mean smuggling.' He left a small pause that allowed Luke to nod his agreement. 'And what is your interest?'

'I want to get involved.'

'Why?' The question was blunt.

It made Luke realise he was dealing with a man who would readily detect any lie. 'I need to increase my income.'

'You are looking at a risky trade to do that.'

'You seem to have done well out of it,' commented Luke, letting his eyes wander across the room's rich furnishings with an unmistakable implication. Immediately he realised he had made a mistake.

'You should not assume that any appearance of wealth is all derived from illegal trading,' replied Monsieur Defarge coldly. 'If you think you are going to make a lot of money by smuggling, you are mistaken. You should forget it and think again.'

'But . . .'

Monsieur Defarge held up one hand to stop him. 'I know there are already smuggling gangs in Cornwall – no, I have had no dealings with them – and you would find it very precarious setting up against them.'

'I could do it.'

'I admire your confidence if not your judgement.' Defarge rose to refill their glasses.

'I have a small harbour which would be ideal for running contraband.' Luke went on quickly to describe it and Monsieur Defarge let him.

'It is obvious you have had no previous experience of smuggling, nor have you any idea of the best situations for it. Your harbour may seem ideal to you but have you ever thought how easily it could be blocked by preventive cutters? And with preventive men in position on the cliffs, you'd have no escape but be caught red-handed. Any captives would be likely to squirm out of the noose by talking, and that would do me no good. I'm sorry, Mr Gaisford, I can't do business with you. Besides, my dealings are along the Essex and Yorkshire coasts. I don't wish to expand my English trade.'

'I can . . .'

Again Monsieur Defarge interrupted. 'No, Monsieur Gaisford, no attempt on your part will make me change my mind.' As he had made his own position clear he had seen Luke's face darkening and realised that not far below the surface of this Englishman was a seething anger that could explode. He was about to offer Luke another glass of wine but thought it wiser not to. 'But let us part in friendship.' He stood up in a gesture of dismissal.

Luke, tight-lipped and furious at being rebuffed, rose. He ignored Monsieur Defarge's proferred hand and stormed from the room.

The Frenchman watched him go and shook his head sadly. That young man's lack of self-control could be his downfall – and a threat to his associate.

Abigail spent an anxious time waiting for her husband to return. She had loved every minute spent with him until this evening and the disturbing character trait that had manifested itself. Had she caused it to emerge? But she could think of no reason to lay the blame on herself. Was it something that had happened in Dieppe? Why hadn't Luke revealed to her that their visit to France would entail business as well? Why the secret? The more she tried to unravel what had happened, the more agitated she became. She started pacing the room, twisting a handkerchief between her fingers.

The sound of heavy footsteps in the corridor froze her to the spot. Though she expected it she still jumped as the door crashed open and Luke strode in, slamming the door behind him. He was breathing heavily and she shrank from the wild angry look in his eyes. His lips were set in a hard determined line. He flung his cape to one side and grabbed her by the shoulders. She could smell drink on his breath as he bent to kiss her and turned her head away.

'Not in drink,' she retaliated, fearful and repelled to see him in this state.

He grasped her chin so that she could not escape and pulled her head round to face him. 'Any way and any time I want.'

Lips that were hard and fierce met hers. Gone were the tenderness and gentleness that she had known from him. Now they expressed only one thing. He pushed her viciously away so that she fell upon the bed. He stood over her, eyes filled with pleasure in what he would take.

'No!' she started to shout, but her cry was stifled by the blow that brought blood to her bottom lip.

'Quiet,' he hissed. 'I'll have what I want, and don't you ever refuse me.' His hands closed round her and nothing she could do stopped him from tearing her clothes from her.

The following morning Tess had seen the luggage was put on the carriage that would take them to the quay and was waiting outside when Abigail and Luke came out of the hotel. She hid her reaction when she noticed the mark on Abigail's lip and the attempt her mistress had made to hide it with an extra dusting of powder. She was also aware of a tension between husband and wife in spite of Abigail's attempt to smile as if nothing had happened. In marked contrast, Luke's attitude was one of smug satisfaction.

Their conversation on the way to the quay was stilted and Tess knew that she had only been allowed to ride with them because it was a short journey. She was glad when they reached the ship and she could escape from the tense atmosphere. She felt relief that it was an English ship and the banter between the sailors was understandable. She was able to exchange some words with them. They were helpful with the luggage and warned her that the crossing might be a little rough. She was concerned when she saw that the parting between Abigail and Luke was not as she would have expected. She felt sure that there was some resistance in Abigail's attitude to her husband's goodbye kiss. But she wondered if her imagination had been playing tricks on her when the mistress stood by the rail, waving to Luke on the quay.

Though they each kept their own counsel both women would have agreed that the arrangements for their journey to Cornwall were impeccable. That part of their return went smoothly, and they only suffered from two days of inclement weather.

Even the dour walls of Senewey seemed to offer a welcome on their return. Abigail hoped this was true and that the unpleasantness in Calais was an isolated instance due to drink. She only hoped Luke was not reverting to the reputation that had surrounded him before they met.

Chapter Eighteen

The news that the Senewey carriage was coming up the drive ran through the house like a fire-storm. Mrs Horsefield, knowing the day when Godric had expected to return, had briefed the staff to assemble in the hall immediately the carriage was sighted.

As the coach pulled up two footmen came down the steps and were on hand to assist Abigail from it. Though taken aback, they controlled their surprise to see Tess in the master's place in the coach.

Catching the merest flicker in their eyes, Abigail readily offered an explanation. 'Mr Gaisford has been delayed in Calais on business; he will be back in a few days.'

'Yes, ma'am,' they replied in unison.

While she went into the house through the main door, Tess hurried to the servants' entrance. She would be ready and waiting in Abigail's room by the time her mistress arrived.

'Ah, that is that,' she said when she did so. 'The staff all seem to be in good heart and nothing untoward has happened while we have been away.'

'That is good, miss.'

'Help me out of my outdoor clothes and find me a comfortable day dress. Then off you go and settle in. You can see to my unpacking tomorrow. I want to have a wash and a rest after those last tedious miles.'

Tess found a suitable dress, left it hanging outside the wardrobe and went to her own room, thankful that she too could now take a rest before getting back into the routine at Senewey.

Abigail stretched herself out on the bed and let the tension of the journey drain out of her, but it was not long before her thoughts were turning to the honeymoon and how the joy of it had been marred by Luke's actions in Calais. He had apologised with heartfelt repentance the next morning but that had not and could not wipe out the memory. She felt defiled and knew that regaining her trust in him would take some time, if it ever happened at all. A great deal would depend on Luke. She realised being rebuffed in business had led him to drink and that had taken effect in the worst possible way as far as she was concerned. Her mind became troubled. Could it happen again? Had his taste for drink, which he appeared to have controlled before the wedding, returned? And if it had, could the consequences be the same on other occasions? It was a thought that constantly troubled her as she awaited her husband's return.

Tess had been in her room an hour when there was a light knock at the door. She opened it to see Alice.

'Come in.' Tess greeted her with a smile that told her friend she was pleased to see her, as did her embrace when the door had closed.

'It's good to see you again, Tess,' said Alice. 'Did you have a good time, apart from work?'

'Oh, I did. We saw so many wonderful things.'

'I must hear all about them. I haven't time now, but I just had to come and say welcome back.' Alice hesitated a brief moment and her eyes brightened with excitement. 'And to tell you I have a sweetheart.'

'What?' The surprise on Tess's face was quickly suffused with pleasure as she asked, 'Tell me, quick, before you go.'

'Met him at a fair in Sennan. Leo Gurney. Three years older than me. Father's a fisherman. Leo helps him. Tell you more later! I must hurry.'

Tess hugged her. 'I'm happy for you.'

As the door closed on Alice, Tess wondered if she herself would ever feel the joy that her friend was so obviously experiencing.

Two weeks later Abigail was sitting on the terrace before the house when she heard the pounding of hooves. Looking up from her embroidery, she saw a familiar figure urging his horse on now that the house had come into view. Excited by the sight of his lithe powerful figure and thrilled by his easy control of the horse, the love for him she had felt before their wedding was revived.

Luke's eyes were bright with pleasure, laughter on his lips, as he swung himself eagerly from the saddle and swept her up in his arms. His mouth met hers in firm but gentle passion that was more like the Luke she knew and loved. She must hide any uneasy feelings from him or her marriage could be wrecked.

'It's good to be home and have you in my arms again,' he said, holding her so that he could look into her eyes.

Searching for any evidence of recrimination for what had happened in Calais, he saw none. She must have forgiven him. He was filled with joy and relief. He did not want to lose Abigail; there was too much at stake. Nevertheless he felt he had to make amends by apologising. 'I'm sorry for what happened in Calais, my love. It was the drink.'

She put a finger on his lips. 'I know.'

A groom came round the corner to take his horse. Abigail took Luke's arm and led him into the house. He was home.

While he washed and changed, he answered her question: 'Were you successful in France in whatever it was you had to do?'

'No, is the blunt reply. You may as well know, I was trying to conclude some business deals I believed necessary to keep us on a sound financial footing.'

'So does it mean we are in bad straits?' she asked with concern.

He laughed. 'It's not yet come to that, but we would have been a lot better off if I'd succeeded. Maybe we'll have to be a little bit careful until I can look into other possible enterprises here. My father spent heavily and did not leave me in such a good financial position, as people think. Don't look so worried, love.' He came to her, took her hands and pulled her from the chair. 'I will take care of things.' He kissed her reassuringly then took her hand and said, 'Let's go down.'

When they entered the drawing room he let go of her hand and went to the decanters on the sideboard, selected the one containing whisky and poured himself a good measure.

Abigail tensed. Was the old habit back? 'Don't start drinking again,' she said. The words were out almost before she realised it. She bit her lip, regretting what she had said; wishing she could snatch the words back; recalling his warning to her not to tell him what he should or should not do. She saw anger flare in his eyes but he replaced it with a mocking smile as he raised the glass in her direction. He knew she had got the message.

That evening passed pleasantly and when they went upstairs he surprised her with the present of an exquisite pearl necklace. Though it was on her lips to question the wisdom of such expenditure, Abigail knew it was wisest not to. To ask his true financial position would not be correct, it was the man's prerogative to look after that side of their lives. That night their love-making was gentle and tender.

Two days later Luke strode into the Waning Moon.

'Good day, Tom.'

'And to you, Mr Gaisford! It's good to have you back. The usual, sir?'

'Aye, Tom! A tankard of good ale, none of that French muck.'

The landlord chuckled. 'That didn't go down well then?'

'It didn't. Have my friends been coming in?'

'Aye, they have. Every Thursday without fail. Other times as well, though not always together on those occasions, but certainly they all came every Thursday, because you said you would be here the first one after your return.'

'So they'll be in tomorrow?'

'Aye. I'll be surprised if they aren't. Generally about three o'clock.'

Luke took a good draught of his ale, put his tankard down and wiped the back of his hand across his lips. 'That was good. You can be filling another, and get one for yourself.'

The following afternoon Luke delayed his arrival at the Waning Moon until four o'clock. The corner table around which his friends were grouped was already littered with empty tankards. When he swept through the door they all burst into roars of welcome which soon became ribald suggestions about the recent groom's activities.

Luke grinned but did not rise to their insinuations. He greeted each man in turn with his own barbed comments. Martin called for ale for his friend only to see that Tom had already anticipated the order and was on his way with a foaming tankard. After he had placed it on the table he cleared the empty ones away.

Luke settled himself to try to answer all the questions that were flung at him, and he in turned quizzed them all for news of events in the county.

'I heard your lady was back in residence at Senewey over a week ago, but when you didn't show up here and this lot had not heard anything I thought it must be a rumour,' said George.

'What you heard was correct,' replied Luke.

'Then what the devil kept you from the Waning Moon?'

'I was in France.'

For a brief moment silence fell as if they were trying to comprehend what he'd said.

'You were still in France and Abigail was here?' quizzed Sydney.

'I had business in France but she came back as scheduled.'

'I hope the business made the separation worthwhile,' quipped David.

Luke frowned. 'It didn't,' he snapped, irritated to be reminded of his own failure. His lips tightened. 'It was only a minor setback.'

'What were you trying to arrange?' asked Martin seriously.

'Nothing of great importance. As you all know, the mine is not as profitable as it was and I was trying to set up something else in its place.'

'Tell us,' Martin urged.

Luke gave a little shake of his head. 'No. It's over and done with.'

'All right,' said George, accepting the refusal for them all. 'Well, tell us, are you going to frequent the Waning Moon every Thursday or has the little lady tightened the knot?'

Luke threw back his head with raucous laughter. 'There's no lady that can tie Luke Gaisford down.'

'So your abstinence before the wedding was a blind?' said George.

'What do you think? A wife's property becomes her husband's. Penorna is my prize as well as the lovely Abigail!'

'You wily bastard,' rapped David. 'You loved where money is.'

'Naturally.'

'Why didn't I think of that?'

'Because you aren't sharp enough,' countered Luke, 'and you aren't as handsome.'

'You might have to wait a long while before Abigail gets Penorna,' warned Martin, upset to hear Luke's motive for marrying her.

Luke did not respond but called for more ale and then suggested that in future it would be more convenient for them to meet on a different night each week.

They did not query his reasons.

Life at Senewey settled down. Though Abigail largely left Mrs Horsefield to continue running the house as she had always done, she made some changes in its routine by subtle suggestions to the housekeeper that allowed things to alter smoothly, with the stamp of authority now belonging to the mistress of the house.

Because Luke had warned her that there were times when he might have to be absent, attending to the management of the estate and its assets, Abigail made no verbal objection when he was away from home. Besides, wasn't sharing a bed more passionate after an absence? There were times when she felt sure that drink had passed his lips but she never questioned it, for it never again reached the stage where it took him over.

Three months after their return from France, Luke made a suggestion during their evening meal. 'I think we should give a ball here at Senewey.'

Abigail looked up from her plate and saw he was watching her with interest. Her eyes widened with delight. 'Can we?' she cried with enthusiasm.

'Why not? Besides, the county will expect it. They'll have been waiting on tenterhooks to see how the new mistress of Senewey will cope with such an event.'

'Now you are making me nervous. All eyes will be on me!'

Luke smiled. 'You'll cope, my love, unless I'm very much mistaken.'

'Thank you for your faith in me! I'll not let you down. When will it be?'

He looked thoughtful for a moment. 'Though I didn't take a lot of notice at the time, I think Mother used to start about three months beforehand – there's a lot to do. Finish the meal and then we'll go to my study and fix a date.'

Twenty minutes later they were poring over his notebook that he had marked into days. As Luke flicked over the pages she noticed that there were many more of what she took to be appointments and notes than she expected to see, but she felt it was wisest not to comment. It was not her place to pry but to trust her husband to be working for their good. Luke stopped turning the pages. 'Here we are.' He stabbed a page with his finger. 'How about Friday the twelfth of March? We can dance into the next morning without intruding into the Sabbath.'

'Yes,' she agreed.

He picked up a pencil and made an entry then withdrew a sheet of paper from a drawer. 'There's no time like the present. Let me write down what is to be done. First, the musicians!'

'The same group as we had for the wedding?'

'Yes, but that was only small section of them. This will be a much bigger event. I'll send my man into Penzance tomorrow to engage them. If they can come on that date we'll go ahead with everything else. Consult with Mrs Horsefield, she's done it all before. There will be the food, the allocation of the rooms, the lay out, and the decorations to obtain. You'll probably need extra staff.' He pencilled some notes.

'But what about the expense?' Abigail asked tentatively, knowing she could be risking an outburst or at least a rebuke.

'Don't worry about that,' he replied considerately. 'Certain aspects of the estate are not contributing what they should but I have other things in mind. You are not to concern yourself. Now we must consider a guest list.' He started to write and the list grew longer and longer.

'So many?' she queried doubtfully.

'It will be expected from the foremost family in the county. We must be careful not to insult anyone by leaving them out.'

Nothing more was said until the next day when Luke announced that the musicians had been hired and Abigail could go ahead with the other arrangements. As it was late she waited until the following morning to tell Mrs Horsefield. Deeming it correct to inform the housekeeper first, she kept the information from Tess but told her to tell Mrs Horsefield she wanted to see her. 'I'll be in the drawing room.'

When the housekeeper arrived she said, 'You wanted to see me, ma'am?'

'Yes. Mrs Horsefield, we are to have another ball here at Senewey.'

Mrs Horsefield's eyes lit up. 'Oh, ma'am, it will be like old times. The house will be alive again with so many people. This is exciting.'

'I have some ideas, but I will need your help.'

'Yes, ma'am.'

'We may as well start discussing things now.'

The housekeeper drew on her past experience and also absorbed some of the suggestions that Abigail made so that by the end of the session they had a broad outline of what the arrangements would be. Abigail took Mrs Horsefield's advice on the extra staff that would be needed and left her to engage them.

Satisfied with this preliminary session, she went to her room where she found Tess putting away some clothes that had been brought by the laundry maids.

'We are going to have a ball here,' Abigail announced. 'And Mr Gaisford has said I have to have a special gown made.'

Tess caught the enthusiasm in her mistress's voice and responded with equal fervour, especially when Abigail told her, 'During the next few days I want you to help me get the invitations ready.'

Chapter Nineteen

Over the ensuing weeks excitement mounted at Senewey Manor; it meant more work for everybody. The staff enjoyed doing something different, though for the efficient running of the Manor routine had to form the basis of their lives. Abigail's enthusiasm seemed to galvanise them into wanting to make this, her first ball as Mistress of Senewey, a success. Mrs Horsefield's organising skills, as befitted a first-rate housekeeper, were even more in evidence but she was careful not to assume the authority that was rightfully Abigail's. So they worked well together.

The main worry for Abigail was not whether it would be a success but why Luke was showing so little interest. She knew he was occupied with the running of the estate and that he had some financial problems but when she broached the subject he dismissed her worries. Though she was not sure she was getting the truth she dare not pursue the subject for she had seen a spark of hostility in him that alarmed her.

As Abigail's confidante Tess became involved in much of the preparations particularly as a quick and able message-carrier for her mistress.

'Tess, the invitations all went out and we have been receiving replies, but I found this one addressed to Mrs Gaisford. It must have been mislaid in the sorting. Run with it to the West Wing now.'

Tess took the sealed sheet of paper and hurried from the room. She went via the servants' staircase to the main hall and was halfway down the corridor to the closed doors to the West

Wing when a voice she instantly recognised as Mr Gaisford's barked at her from the main hall and froze her in her tracks.

'You! Where are you going?'

She turned nervously to see Luke, dressed in his riding clothes, glaring at her.

'Well?' he demanded again. 'Tongue tied?' He stepped towards her.

'I . . . er . . . I . . .'

'I can't stand here all morning. You know you shouldn't be down here.' His eyebrows knitted together in an expression that was meant to put fear into Tess. 'Now off with you! If I catch you in this part of the house again it will be the worse for you.'

Tess bit her lip, trying to hold back the tears that threatened to flow. She seemed riveted to the spot yet knew she must go. He appeared to be barring the way though there was plenty of room for her to pass. With an effort she forced herself on. As she slid past him Luke gave her a switch with his riding crop across her back that made her flinch and released her tears.

'Remember what I said,' he rasped as she scuttled away, thankful that she had put the invitation into the pocket of her apron.

Unthinkingly, she burst into Abigail's room. It seemed the natural thing to do. Abigail swung round from the window and immediately her look of surprise became one of concern when she saw the tears of pain and terror flowing down Tess' cheeks.

'What's happened?' she cried as she rushed to the girl.

'Oh, miss, Mr Gaisford . . .' she faltered.

'Calm down, Tess,' said Abigail gently as she put her arm round her maid's shaking shoulders and led her to the sofa. 'Sit down and tell me what has happened.' She took a handkerchief from her pocket and handed it to Tess.

She sniffed, dabbed her eyes, gave a last sob and looked mournfully at Abigail. 'Oh, miss . . .' Her words choked her.

'Take your time, Tess.' Abigail rose from the sofa and went to a carafe, poured a glass of water and handed it to the girl before sitting down again.

'Thank you, miss.' Tess took a sip of the water. She swallowed hard and stiffened her back. 'I'm sorry.'

'Now tell me, quietly and calmly, what happened?'

Tess drew a deep breath and related the incident in the corridor leading to the West Wing.

'My husband struck you?'

'Across my back, miss, with his riding crop.'

'What?' Astonished disbelief showed on Abigail's face. 'You are sure? You haven't dreamt this?'

'No, miss,' replied Tess indignantly. 'Why should I make it up?'

Abigail did not reply. She knew her maid too well to doubt her. She wished she could retract the question. 'You say he told you you shouldn't be in that part of the house?'

'Yes, miss.'

'Didn't you tell him I had sent you with a message for Mrs Gaisford?'

'I didn't get a chance, miss. I had the note in my pocket . . . here it is.' She handed it to Abigail.

'All right, Tess. Say nothing of this to anyone.'

She nodded. 'I won't, miss, of course I won't.'

'I'll go and see Mr Gaisford immediately.'

'I think he'll have gone riding, miss.'

'Very well, I'll see him later. You stay here until you feel better. I'll take this invitation to my mother-in-law myself.'

Abigail was fuming at Luke's treatment of Tess as she hurried along the landing, down the stairs and across the hall. She slowed her footsteps along the corridor to the West Wing and tightened her grip on herself. She could not allow Hester to see her in this condition. What had happened had nothing to do with her. She was not responsible for her son's actions. Abigail paused at the connecting door, straightened her dress and took a deep breath. By the time she walked into Mrs Gaisford's drawing room she was in control of herself.

'Ah, my dear, how nice to see you.' Hester's smile was warm and welcoming and held genuine pleasure. It immediately made Abigail wonder if Luke's stated reasons for his mother keeping to herself was the full truth. Hester, though frail, certainly did not look ill and the greeting she gave Abigail did not speak of any desire to be left on her own. 'Do sit down. I hope this is a social visit?'

'I've brought this, Mrs Gaisford.' Abigail held out the invitation which Hester took with curiosity.

Abigail sat down opposite her mother-in-law and watched her as she opened the paper.

Hester read the words. Sat for a moment staring at them, read them again then looked up slowly. Abigail saw tears in her eyes.

'Thank you, my dear.' The catch that came into her voice after that brief moment of pleasurable excitement was not lost on Abigail. Why such sadness? she wondered. Had it brought back memories of her younger days when she herself would organise such events and be the belle of the ball? Abigail could picture this woman, whose lined face would once have been as smooth as silk, as a lively attractive person full of self-assurance. Was she sad at the thought of what had been or was there something deeper behind this?

'Had you heard about the ball?' asked Abigail tentatively.

The older woman nodded. 'The girls who look after me told me the house was buzzing with excitement that the Senewey Ball was going to be revived. They were the foremost balls in the county for many, many years. I can remember the first one I came to as a young girl of fifteen ... Oh, it was such an exciting time for someone as young as I.'

'Didn't Luke come and tell you himself?'

'Not him!' snapped Hester.

The touch of contempt in her voice startled Abigail. 'Maybe he was relying on me to do so, possibly by this invitation. I'm sorry it got mislaid,' she apologised. 'But you have it now. You'll come?'

Hester hesitated then gave a sad little shake of her head. 'I'm not well enough, my dear.'

'But you could sit down and meet people. I'm sure you would like to meet old acquaintances?' protested Abigail, feeling that Hester had made an excuse that would not stand up to scrutiny.

She gave a wan smile. 'Maybe, but I don't think so.'

'We'll see again nearer the day,' Abigail suggested, believing this was probably not the time to press the matter further.

Hester gave a small nod and changed the subject. 'Are the preparations going well?'

'Yes. Mrs Horsefield is a great help in guiding me in what should be done.'

'She always was a stalwart. She loved such occasions and knew the Gaisfords wanted to outshine everyone else. You won't be getting much help from Luke?'

Once again Abigail detected that sour note towards her son. 'He has the estate to run.' She hoped that excuse would satisfy her mother-in-law, but before she received a response they both were startled as the drawing-room door crashed open and Luke stormed in, his face a mask of fury.

'What are you doing here?' he shouted, glaring at Abigail.

Puzzled by his animosity she said, 'I came to visit your mother and invite her to the ball.'

'Did I not make it plain that she was to be left on her own?' he demanded.

'Surely you did not mean that literally?' countered Abigail.

'I did,' snapped Luke. 'In future, see that you adhere to my wishes.'

'But I see no reason . . .'

'Out!' he broke in, pointing at the door with his riding crop.

Abigail shot a glance at Hester and saw such a troubled expression in her eyes that she immediately rose from her chair and headed for the door after casting her a glance of sympathy. She heard Luke's footsteps behind her and fury at the treatment she had received boiled over when she heard the door slam behind them. She swung round to face him, anger in her eyes. 'Don't you dare treat me that way again!'

'I'll treat you how I like and don't you forget it!'

Abigail was shocked by the viciousness of his reply. It conjured up memories of Calais all over again, and that frightened her. She could feel her heart thumping, but something was telling her not to seem afraid but to keep calm. She could not do that in the face of his hostility and commanding posture, however. 'Don't you threaten me, and don't ever use your crop on Tess again.'

Luke's eyes flared into red fury. He grabbed Abigail's neck and pushed her hard against the wall. His face came close to hers as she struggled for breath. 'I've told you before, don't tell me what I can and cannot do. But I'll tell you one thing more – *keep away from my mother*. I make her an allowance and allow her to have the West Wing but she has no right to enter the main house. I have had no love for her since she refused to raise a hand in my defence. My father loved to lash out at me. Keep away from her.' He relaxed his grip on her throat and stepped back.

Abigail doubled up, gasping for breath, her hands at her throat where he had held it in a strong-fingered grip. She raised her head slowly, eyes filled with horror. 'A son in his father's image, I see. Thank goodness we have no children, nor ever will have.'

Luke smirked. He raised his crop under her chin and pushed her head back into a position from which she had no escape but was forced to look into his eyes. 'Oh, yes, my love, we will,' he hissed to burn his expectation into her mind. 'And don't you forget it!' His eyes narrowed. 'And we'll act as if none of this ever happened. We will be the perfect couple, the Gaisfords of Senewey. And Senewey will have a son and heir. In case you are inclined to forget, here is a little reminder.' He stepped back and struck her shoulder hard with his crop.

Abigail stifled the cry that sprang to her lips but could not disguise the pain on her face.

'You will act like a dutiful and loving wife to Luke Gaisford or there'll be worse to follow.' He laughed in her face, wheeled away and strode off down the corridor.

She slumped against the wall, grasped her shoulder and bit her lip, trying to stem the pain. Her eyes, fixed on Luke's retreating back, burned with hatred but she recalled the smell of drink on his breath. Had that caused his cruelty to her or was it because she had visited his mother? Or maybe something else entirely had caused his anger?

She pushed herself from the wall, tenderly touched her neck, straightened her collar and adjusted her dress. With a heavy sigh she walked slowly along the corridor to the adjoining hall. Thankful that it was deserted, she climbed the stairs with slow weak steps, her mind still trying to fathom exactly what had gone wrong within their marriage. Thankful that Tess was no longer in her room, she sank into a big armchair close to the window.

Linking what had just happened with the event in Calais, she realised that drink had been involved in both cases. That could be the immediate cause but it may not be the root of the matter. She thought back to Calais. There an anticipated business deal had not taken place and she had sensed Luke's expectations had been high. That could have led him to try to drink his disappointment away. Had some recent business arrangement here upset him or was he merely angry that he had found her with his despised mother?

Even as so many thoughts tumbled in her mind, she could not deny that her love for her husband still ran deep. She drew hope from that and believed his love for her would overcome the dangers of drink that brought out a cruel, sadistic side to his nature. She convinced herself she could fight such a foe but realised she would have to nurture their relationship subtly.

When Tess came to help her dress for the evening nothing was said about the earlier incident. Abigail tried to keep the mark on her shoulder covered but was not wholly successful. Tess's gasp made her realise that she had seen it.

'Miss, what happened?' Tess asked in horror.

'Nothing,' replied Abigail dismissively.

'But . . .'

'I tripped and fell against the wall,' she said in a tone that stated that was the end of the matter.

Tess dare not pursue it though she knew the mark on her mistress resembled that on her own back. It had been made by a riding crop.

When Tess was putting her clothes away, after Abigail had left for her evening meal, she wondered if this was something she should report to Mr Mitchell but concluded that it could only bring more trouble down on Abigail at the hands of Mr Gaisford.

The earlier confrontation in the corridor leading to the West Wing was never mentioned during their meal together. Luke could not have been more considerate and attentive to his wife. Was he feeling remorse? Was this was a way of saying sorry? But if that were the case Abigail thought he would have been more effusive, whereas tonight he was once again the Luke she had come to love and still did. She noted that there was no smell of drink on his breath and that he did not take any wine with his meal and avoided it again when they went to the drawing room.

He showed more interest in the forthcoming ball tonight. Abigail was pleased, and while they were on the subject plucked up the courage to mention the question of his mother's invitation, but not so as to confront him directly. 'I'm sorry if I misunderstood about inviting your mother.' She felt sure he would hear the thumping of her own heart.

'It's not that I object to her receiving an invitation but she really isn't well enough to attend. If she did she might be an embarrassment to herself and that would be unpleasant for everyone,' he replied quietly.

Abigail had no answer to that and was forced to let the matter drop. Luke's words had come quietly and reasonably, he seemed very much under control, so she concluded that drink had been the cause of the outburst in the West Wing. And tonight he had taken none.

Their love-making that night was prolonged and full of tenderness and Abigail knew he hoped the result would be a son and heir.

As the day of the ball drew nearer and nearer an air of expectancy seemed to settle over the house. Excitement gripped the staff; they went about their daily tasks with a new vigour so that they could get back to the preparations for the ball. Together Abigail and her housekeeper planned where to put the tables in the dining room so that the food would be easily available to everyone; which chairs should be put around the edges of the main chamber to be used for dancing; which rooms would be available for relaxation and gossip; and so many other things that would help to make this ball the talk of Cornwall.

'Another fitting day, Tess,' Abigail reminded her. 'So make preparations to go to Penzance.'

'Yes, miss. I've had it in mind. I'm looking forward to seeing how your dress looks now.'

'So am I.'

'Will I be able to see Dorinda, miss?'

'I don't see why not. We'll make it our business to see her and we'll call at Penorna on the way back. I haven't seen mother and father for a long while.'

'I think you will look lovely in that dress,' remarked Tess as their coach drew away from Penzance.

'Thank you,' replied Abigail. 'Not a word to anyone about it. It has to be a complete surprise.'

'I won't say a word, miss. Oh, I have enjoyed my day.'

'I'm pleased you have. We'll do it again next week. But we haven't finished today yet. We have time to call in at Penorna.'

Memories of her happy childhood and the joy of moving into the adult world filled Abigail's mind when the house came into view. Though she had been born in Whitby and knew her father's sister still lived there, she could remember little of it. Penorna was her real home.

She was out of the coach as soon as its wheels stopped, leaving Tess to renew acquaintance in the servants' quarters. Abigail sped across the hall to the drawing room, threw open the door and so startled her mother that she pricked her finger with the needle as she made the next stitch in the tablecloth she was embroidering.

'Abigail!' Eliza dropped her work on to the table beside her and was on her feet to exchange a loving hug with her daughter. 'This is a pleasant surprise. I'm so glad to see you. You don't visit often enough.'

'Life is so busy, Mama.'

'I know, love. It's just me wanting to see more of you. How are you? You are looking well.'

'I feel well.'

'And Luke?'

'Busy on the estate and trying to solve some problems.'

'Problems?' asked Eliza as she went to the bell pull.

'Oh, I don't know what they are,' replied Abigail, not wanting to disclose that they concerned his finances for she knew little more than that and Luke had assured her that they were not serious. 'He says there is no need to worry.'

There was a knock on the door and a maid entered. 'You rang, ma'am?'

'Chocolate for us both, please. Preparations for the ball will be keeping you busy?' Eliza said to her daughter.

'Oh, yes! It is all so exciting. I'm on my way back from Penzance where I've been for a fitting – my ball gown.'

'Oh, tell me,' pressed Eliza. 'What's it like.'

'No, Mama,' laughed Abigail. 'It is to be a surprise. Only Tess and I will have seen it before the ball.' She changed the subject. 'Where's Papa?'

'He's gone to the mine. I didn't want him to go.' A serious expression replaced Eliza's excitement at seeing her daughter. 'He hasn't been too well this past week. Off colour generally but he said he felt a little better this morning. He felt well enough to go to the mine on a routine visit. He thought getting out would do him good.'

'I hope it does,' said Abigail with concern. 'Has he had similar symptoms before?'

'Not that he has said, but you know your father – he's not one to complain about his health. Now tell me more about your life at Senewey?'

Mother and daughter spent a pleasant hour before Abigail thought it was time to be leaving. Word was sent to Tess and she was at the coach when Eliza and Abigail came on to the terrace.

'You and Papa will be coming to the ball?'

'Wouldn't miss it for the world,' replied Eliza. 'Hopefully your papa will feel more like himself by then.'

Eliza came to the coach, had a brief word with Tess, and stood watching their departure until they were lost to sight beyond the small copse.

Chapter Twenty

'Quick, Tess, quick! I can hear coaches coming,' called Abigail as Tess started fastening the buttons at the back of her gown.

Her nimble fingers sped through the remaining buttons. 'There, miss,' she said as she moved round to face Abigail with a critical eye on the dress.

'See who's arriving,' said her mistress, making swift gestures with her hands towards the windows.

Tess was there in a flash, focusing on the first of two coaches that were pulling up at the front of the house. She watched the occupants alight. 'One of Mr Gaisford's uncles in the first coach.' There was a pause as she waited for the passengers to alight from the next. 'And the other uncle in the second coach. Both accompanied by their wives.'

'I'd better hurry,' cried Abigail, finishing smoothing her dress. 'Am I all right, Tess?' she asked, patting her hair.

'You look beautiful, miss, and that dress is going to make everyone stare.'

Abigail shot to the door. She gave a brief pause and said, 'Thanks for all your help, Tess.' Then she was gone.

The maid smiled at the closed door. Her mistress was so excited, but who wouldn't be on such an occasion? Would Tess herself ever be as excited over something? How she wished she could share things with her mother, but stoically she fought that feeling as she recalled how fortunate she was to have Abigail as her mistress and to be treated by her more as a sister than anything else. She looked round the room which was scattered with clothes. She would tidy up later. Now, from a secluded corner of the landing, she watch the guests being received by the master and mistress. She hurried from the room and was in her place in time to see Abigail starting down the stairs.

She had come quietly to the top of the flight and paused there to survey the scene below. Two footmen stood beside the door and four maids hovered nearby, ready to attend to the guests' outdoor clothes or serve any other needs. Luke was greeting his Uncle Charles and Aunt Emma while Uncle Logan and Aunt Fanny waited to offer their felicitations. Luke had told her of his cold relations with his father's brothers and she had witnessed only a slight thaw at their wedding. She wondered just what the atmosphere was like in the hall at this moment. There was only one way to find out but she was not going to miss the chance to make an impressive entrance. Abigail took each step slowly. The movement caught the attention of those below. They all looked up and the conversation stopped; their attention was riveted on her. She knew immediately she had caused a sensation. Her eyes flicked over the group but settled on Luke. It was his approval she wanted. She saw it in his eyes. They not only endorsed her choice of dress, it was as if he was seeing her for the very first time. He not only approved of her whole appearance, it was as if he wished to devour her. It sent her heart racing and her mind reeling. She held their attention until she reached the bottom of the stairs and crossed over to them with a warm smile and friendly greeting. Their comments were more than approving.

Emma and Fanny were most taken by Abigail's Empire-line sheath gown. The high waist came to just under the line of her breasts and was banded with a ribbon of deep blue in contrast to the pale shade of the dress. A woven braid in a Greek key pattern bordered the hem of the gown and the small train. Tiny puff-shouldered sleeves sprang from a low, wide neckline. A single row of pearls hung from her neck to a pendant at her cleavage. Abigail carried a cashmere shawl casually draped over one arm and held an embroidered reticule in her left hand. She had taken particular care with her hair, its Grecian style, in keeping with the design of the dress, enhanced the features of her face perfectly.

Abigail could see approval in the aunts' eyes, and maybe just a little jealousy. Was it because she had outshone them or because she was mistress of Senewey? Maybe it was just because she was younger.

As more guests were beginning to arrive the Gaisfords moved off, leaving Luke and Abigail to greet the newcomers. But before that he managed to get in a quick word. 'You look lovely. What a magnificent dress!'

'Thanks to your generosity,' she said, with an inclination of her head to express her thanks.

'And what an entrance,' he chuckled. 'You stunned them. I approved of that.'

She felt his hand squeeze hers and was pleased.

'You don't look so bad yourself. I prefer the fashion for trousers though I see that not everyone has switched from breeches,' she said, noting that two of the arrivals were so attired.

There was a wide variety of fashions on display but everyone had taken care with their appearance, wanting to present themselves as well as they could. But no one received more compliments than Abigail.

As the new arrivals dwindled to a trickle she began to grow worried and Luke sensed it.

'Something wrong?' he asked.

'Mother and Father haven't arrived yet. I told you Father hadn't been well. I hope he hasn't suffered a set back.'

'There's still plenty of time,' Luke reassured her.

Five minutes later he drew her attention to the door. 'Here's your mother with the Westburys.'

The relief that swept over her was replaced by concern when she saw Eliza was on her own. 'Where's Papa?' she asked after greeting their neighbours.

'He was sick this afternoon and did not feel up to all this evening's excitement.'

'Is he all right?'

'Yes. I was going to stay but he insisted I should come. He told me to tell you that it's only a mild attack and he sends his best wishes to you both for a memorable evening.'

'Thank you, Mrs Mitchell,' said Luke. 'I hope Mr Mitchell is well again in the morning, but if there is anything we can do, please don't hesitate to ask.'

'That is kind, Luke. I'm sure he will feel better in the morning. Now, don't let this for one moment upset or spoil this evening. Your father wouldn't want that, Abigail. And let me admire your dress!'

She could do nothing but take her mother's word that there was no need to worry. She could not go among her guests with a troubled expression and was soon swept back into the gaiety of the evening. She moved comfortably among the guests who were all too ready to compare this ball with such events in the past. Opinion was generally favourable. The evening was a success.

The ball proceeded smoothly. Ladies exchanged news and gossip, men opinions on the state of the nation, the county and the ambitions of Napoleon.

At one point, with the hour heading towards midnight and Abigail dancing with Martin, Luke took the opportunity to draw his two uncles into a private room.

Not knowing the reason, Logan remarked, 'You certainly are keeping up the Senewey traditions of throwing the best ball in the county.'

'That was the idea, but it may become increasingly difficult to keep the Gaisford name to the forefront in other spheres.'

'What do you mean?' asked Charles.

'Sit down, let me charge your glasses.' As Luke went to a table on which there stood a decanter and several glasses, Charles and Logan exchanged glances in which curiosity was mingled with wariness. They thanked him when he brought them wine and responded when he raised his glass and said, 'The Gaisfords.'

Charles pursed his lips and without taking his eyes off Luke, said, 'You haven't brought us in here just to toast the family name. And I smell trouble in your previous statement.'

'The Senewey Estate is in a precarious financial position . . .' started Luke, only to be interrupted by Logan.

'Oh, come on, nephew, you don't expect us to believe that?' He gave a grunt of derision.

'It's true.'

Charles guffawed. 'With all the assets you have?'

'Look around you,' suggested Logan with a smirk. 'This ball will have cost you! Then there's your wife's dress and those pearls round her neck, your honeymoon in France . . . oh, *you* aren't short of a penny!'

'Father left little money,' snapped Luke, irritated by his uncles' attitude. 'He'd run the mine almost out; the land won't sustain more sheep; he had neglected most of his property so I'd have trouble if I raised rents. My income only just keeps us solvent but that picture will soon change for the worse.'

'So why all this show of opulence?' demanded Charles.

'To keep up the Gaisford reputation and our standing in the county.'

'So what has this to do with us?' asked Logan.

'I hear that since I gave you your estates, you've turned them round and . . .'

Charles gave a loud contemptuous snort. 'So you want us to help you out?'

'You *are* Gaisfords.'

'You didn't take that into account when you severed us from the estate,' put in Logan. His eyes narrowed. 'You'll get no help from me.'

'Nor from me,' added Charles quickly. 'What you did to us turned out to be a blessing. We both realised we had been too ready to fall back on Senewey. Cutting us off as you did made us look seriously at our situation and to make the most of our assets, some of which we had neglected to develop. Well, things turned out well, and though there is much more still to do we are at least solvent and heading for some nice profits. Thanks to you and your hasty judgement we are doing nicely and the future looks bright.' He started to rise to his feet as if that was the end of the matter. Logan followed suit.

'Wait!' cried Luke. 'You're Gaisfords. Doesn't that mean anything to you?'

'Yes, it does, but in our own way and on our own terms.' Charles's voice was cold. 'Father never really saw eye to eye with us. Jeremy was always the favourite because he was the one who would inherit. We didn't matter. He made no provision for us in his will. Oh, yes, he allowed us our small estates, but made sure that they were dependent on Senewey. You broke that yoke and,' he added sarcastically, 'we both thank you for it. But don't expect us to help *you* out.' He spun round and headed for the door, followed closely by his brother.

'You're Gaisfords!' yelled Luke, his eyes burning with anger. 'Gaisfords!'

The door slammed behind them and he was left staring at it.

'You bastards,' he hissed, anger turning to hatred. 'I'll show you. I don't need you! Senewey will survive and you'll regret it!' He started for the door, stopped, swung round and went to pour himself a full glass of wine. He drained it and poured another. His hands were shaking; wine slopped over the rim. He cursed. Fury burned deep within him. He sensed the onset of one of the terrible moods he had witnessed in his own father. Luke's mind fought against the recurring visions he suffered of those times that Jeremy, suffering some setback, had taken it out on him, a child or youngster unable to defend himself. He drained his glass and placed his hands firmly on the sideboard, needing the sensation to strengthen his will against the red mist that threatened to spin him into the same hellish regions that had consumed his father.

Abigail, in light-hearted conversation with some guests but alert to what was going on around her, had noticed Luke draw his uncles aside. The move puzzled her for she knew that her husband was not on the most friendly of terms with them. She had heard that his father's death had brought about a rift within the Gaisford family and that there was little communication nowadays between uncles and nephew. In fact, it had only been at her insistence that they had been invited to the Gaisford Ball. So now, as the door closed on them, she wondered what was afoot; what could have drawn them together? A reconciliation? She kept her attention on the door as she moved among the guests.

It opened. Abigail, in conversation with George Morland, tried to read something into the fact that Luke had not come out with his uncles and that they both emerged talking earnestly. There was about them an air of smugness that spoke of victory. She excused herself from George and started over to the side room. Why was Luke still in there? She was halfway to it when the door opened. She stopped, eyes fixed firmly on her husband. Alarm coursed through her for she was sure that he was struggling against anger. As he stood and surveyed the room and put his hand on the door jamb as if to steady himself, she sensed drink was behind the movement and there was still a long night ahead of them. She saw him set off in her direction and his step was steady, but was he keeping himself in check?

The fury that had contorted his expression when she first saw him had been almost disguised by the time he reached her, but what lay beneath? And, smelling drink on his breath, she inwardly shuddered.

'Shall we dance, my love?' he asked.

She took his arm, a signal of assent. As they walked to the main hall they nodded or passed a few words with their guests without stopping. She could tell Luke did not wish to be drawn into talk at this moment. Throughout the cotillion she realised he was using this interlude to calm his reaction to whatever had happened with his uncles behind the closed door. When the dance finished he escorted her over to her mother who was talking to the Westburys, and then excused himself. She saw him beckon to one of the manservants and take a glass from the proffered tray before going in search of George Morland.

Though she danced with other guests, exchanged gossip, enjoyed the refreshments, accepted compliments about the success of the ball, Abigail's eyes kept drifting to her husband. Misgivings began to grow in her at the amount of drink he was consuming. That it showed no sign of taking effect made her even more uneasy for beneath his seemingly ice-cold attitude seethed a volcanic temper. What might lie in store if someone, even she herself, upset Luke tonight? She tried to keep her mind off the possible consequences but they still haunted her when, after the departure of the final guest, with the cold streaks of dawn heralding another day, she made her way to her room.

During the last twenty minutes she had not seen Luke at all and was ill at ease when, on passing his door she heard angry mutterings and curses within. She did not pause to try to make sense of the words but moved quickly and silently to her own room. After locking the door she leaned back against it with a sigh.

Gathering herself together, she walked across the room. She felt a strong desire for Tess's companionship and wished she hadn't told her maid that she would not be wanted until later in the morning. As she started to undress, her mind turned to her father. She hoped he would soon recover from his indisposition. She recalled her mother's reassurances but still wondered about the extent of her father's illness and hoped that nothing was being kept from her. She would go to Penorna later in the day.

Abigail started, the run of her thoughts interrupted by a faint sound from the door. She swung round and stared at the moving handle. Her heart started to thump. The door resisted the attempt to open it. Though she knew she had locked it there remained the fear that it would open. There was a harder tug at the door followed by a low curse.

'Abigail, open this door!' Luke's voice was low but commanding.

'No,' she returned, her voice trembling.

'Open it!'

'No. Not now, Luke.'

'Open it!' The command was followed by a thump on the door.

She did not answer.

'Do it or it will mean deep trouble for you.' This threat held a note of menace that she feared would mean worse for her than she'd suffered in Calais.

'No.' She tried to sound confident. 'You've had too much to drink.'

Luke fumed. His hammering on the door made her recoil. 'Don't criticise me! Open this door! Immediately!'

'No!'

The silence was intimidating, a portent of what tomorrow might hold.

'Bitch! You'll pay for this!' His fist drove at the door one more time then she heard his footsteps move away, the curses he rained down on her fading into the distance.

As she turned towards the bed she found herself trembling, whether with rage, fear or both she did not know. A lovely day, concluding with a splendid ball for which she had been showered with compliments, had been ruined. She flung herself on the bed and sobbed herself to sleep.

She woke five hours later and immediately recalled how that locked door had saved her from a catastrophic encounter with Luke. She shuddered. Yet still beneath her feeling of loathing lay love for her husband. How could such extremes exist side by side? Drink, she supposed. But she knew the habit, which he had allowed to slip back into his life, did not always precede violent conduct towards her. There had been times when his loving had been tender and considerate despite his drinking, and at those times hers in return satisfied them both. So why had that violent outburst threatened her a few hours ago, and previously in France?

She suddenly realised she must look a sight. Tess must not see any evidence of her tears. She sprang from the bed and, knowing that Luke would not dare to cause a scene now, unlocked the door and started her toilette.

A familiar knock sounded on the door.

'I hope you slept well, miss?' said Tess brightly, entering the room.

'I did, thank you.'

'It was a splendid ball,' her maid commented. 'And you looked so beautiful, no one could match you.'

Abigail laughed softly at the adoration in her voice. 'I don't know about that, everyone had made a special effort to look their best.'

'I was sorry that Mr Mitchell wasn't there.'

'He was not well. I must go to see how he is after I have had something to eat. When we have finished here, will you inform them in the kitchen that I will be down in a few moments and also tell Godwin to have a carriage ready to take me to Penorna?'

'Yes, miss. I hope you find Mr Mitchell recovered.'

'I hope so too.'

Tess glanced around the room to make sure her mistress had what she wanted. She would come back to straighten everything later. She started for the door.

'Tess, do you know if Mr Gaisford is up yet?'

'I saw him riding away about half an hour ago.'

Abigail felt some relief at this for it meant there would be a short interlude before she came face to face with him.

As soon as he left the stable yard Luke stabbed his horse into a gallop. He had been curt with the maids when he'd snatched a quick breakfast and the grooms were not sorry to see him ride away. Something had upset their master and they preferred him out of the way at such times.

A problem he'd thought would be solved last night was still with him. He cursed his uncles. Had they no care for the Gaisford name, which would be stained if his financial position were not regularised? Precarious as it already was, it would be worse when the debts incurred by that lavish ball were added to it. The weather matched his mood. Glowering clouds were swept eastwards by a strong wind that buffeted the rider and rippled the pools of rain left in the rutted track. He took a narrow bridle path that led to the cliff-top a mile away. High above a sea churned into whitecaps by the wind he gentled his horse to a walking pace and rode on until the harbour built by his father came in sight. Luke stopped his horse and controlled its restlessness in the pummelling wind. He sat in the saddle for a few minutes, contemplating the scene, before his attention was held by the fast-running sea, pounding the cliffs and sending spray high in the air. Its vicious unrelenting power seemed to surge through him, filling him with a sense of excitement and mastery of his own destiny. Harness such power and he could solve his petty problems. His eyes narrowed in resolve; a faint smile lifted the corners of his lips. He slipped from the saddle, tethered his horse and walked along the cliff edge. He turned off the track along the headland that sheltered the harbour from the brute force of the sea. Reaching the end, he stopped to survey the scene. The headland dropped away before him. To his left the sea swirled into the harbour; to his right the cliffs swung down but a hundred yards into their descent to the sea were broken into a series of huge step-like sections that finally gave on to a strand of sand stretching another hundred yards or so before it ran into a barrier of soaring cliff. He studied this area carefully for some time before he was satisfied that it would be possible to negotiate a way from the sea to the top of the cliffs via the step formation. The thoughtful mood held him until he reached his horse again and swung himself into the saddle.

Exhilarated by the plans that had formed in his mind, he spurred his horse on urging it to go faster and faster, enjoying the pounding of its hooves and the sweep of the wind through his hair. Luke let out a whoop filled with excitement even though he knew that what he had in mind still needed much careful planning. He would take the first tentative steps when he reached the Waning Moon.

Chapter Twenty-One

Though there had been a touch of anxiety in her mind as the carriage left Senewey, memories of a happy childhood and growing up in the beautiful setting of Penorna Manor flooded back to Abigail when Godric guided the horse up the long drive. The house seemed to send out a welcome stability in contrast to the uneasiness Abigail was beginning to feel at Senewey. But now there was her concern for her father, to shadow this homecoming.

She entered the house unannounced and went straight to the drawing room. Finding it empty, she climbed the stairs quickly and hurried to her father's room. She gave a light knock on the door and tentatively began to push it open as she called out, 'May I come in?'

'Of course,' came the reply.

She recognised her mother's voice and detected a note of relief mingled with joy.

'Oh, we are so pleased to see you,' said Eliza, hurrying to hug her. She kept hold of her daughter's hand as she turned back to the bed.

Alarm surged through Abigail when she saw her father's pale, drawn face. 'Hello, Papa.' She took his hand and leaned forward to kiss him on the cheek.

'Hello, love.' John mustered a smile and his eyes brightened a little but his voice lacked its usual strength.

Abigail glanced at her mother. 'How long has he been like this?'

'Nearly three weeks.'

'What?' Anxiety bit deep. 'Why didn't you let me know?'

'Your father forbade me. He knew you were embroiled in all the preparations for your first ball at Senewey and did not want to distract you,' Eliza explained.

'That was naughty of you, Papa,' Abigail rebuked him mildly. 'You'll have had the doctor?' she asked her mother.

'Oh, yes, he's puzzled by your father's illness, though, particularly as it is persisting and does not seem to be responding to the medicines prescribed. So all we can do is to keep him warm in bed and give him plenty to drink.'

Abigail saw that her father was making an effort to keep his eyes open. When, a few moments later, she saw them shut, she took her mother's hint that they should leave him.

On the way to the drawing room Eliza ordered chocolate to be brought in a few minutes. As they settled Abigail realised that, until now, she had not noticed the worried lines on her mother's face; last night she had disguised them with powder and paint. Now in the harsh daylight they were newly noticeable.

'Mama, you are worried. Is there something you are not telling me?'

'Not really. It's just that this illness is dragging on and your father seems to make no progress. He's failing daily. I'm hoping now he's seen you he will improve. When you walked in I thought he might be revived, but you saw he was soon drifting into sleep.'

Abigail saw her mother was fighting back tears. 'Mama,' she said firmly, 'when I've had my chocolate I'll go back to Senewey, collect a few things and return to stay with you.'

'But you can't leave Luke.'

'I can and I will. This is an emergency. If it helps Papa to get better then it will be worth it. Besides you need my help.' As she added, 'Luke will understand,' she wondered if he really would after what had happened last night.

'Well, it would be a great comfort to me, if you are sure?' replied her mother gratefully.

'I am,' said Abigail forcefully. She gave a little pause then added, 'Luke was out when I left but as soon as he returns I'll come back here. Will it be all right to bring Tess in case I have to stay awhile?'

'Of course! You must have your maid with you. She can have her old room; it's not in use. I'll have it made ready.'

'Thanks, Mama.'

'No, it is I who should thank you. I'm sure it will do your father the world of good to have you here.'

As soon as she had had her chocolate Abigail left for Senewey. She instructed Godric to keep the carriage in readiness to take her back to Penorna, and summoned Tess.

'Make ready to go with me,' she instructed. 'My father is not well and I must be at Penorna. You are to come too. You'll have your old room.'

'Yes, miss.' Tess felt a surge of excitement at the prospect of returning to the house she had come to love, but it was tempered by the bad news of her old master's illness. 'I hope Mr Mitchell will soon recover. I'm sure it will do him good to see you.' She went about her task of packing quickly and efficiently, consulting her mistress about what she would like to take. With that seen to Tess hurried to her own room to gather her clothes then went in search of Alice.

'I'm going to Penorna,' she informed her.

Alice looked glum. 'How long for?'

'I don't know, it will depend on how long Mr Mitchell is ill.'

'I'll miss you, Tess.'

'And I'll miss you, but you'll have Leo Gurney.'

'Aye, when I can manage some time off and that isn't often. I'm frightened he'll find someone else.'

'I'm sure he won't.'

'I hope you are right. And I hope Mr Mitchell recovers so that you will soon be back here.'

They hugged and then Alice went off to resume her tasks. Tess, after reporting to Mrs Horsefield, went to busy herself in Abigail's room while awaiting their carriage trip to Penorna.

Abigail hoped that they could leave soon but knew she should wait until Luke returned. She was thankful when she heard him enter his room in the mid-afternoon, and hastened to knock on his door.

When he opened it he showed surprise. 'Abigail! Come in, come in.'

Relief swept over her. His expression was amiable and his tone lacking in animosity.

He closed the door behind her and before she could speak, said, 'I must congratulate you, my dear, on the splendid way you organised the ball.'

'I had Mrs Horsefield's experience and advice to guide me.'

'Nevertheless you had the final word and I know there were certain things you instigated. Everyone was talking about it. Thank you for keeping up – no, improving on – the Gaisford tradition. I am grateful to you.'

Abigail was astonished, though she kept that hidden. This was not the Luke she had expected after she had refused him last night. She could smell drink on his breath still but his demeanour was pleasant and the light in his eyes held no animosity. Something must have pleased him this morning.

'Thank you, Luke, I am happy it was a success.'

'Indeed it was. Some guests were expressing the hope we could hold another one before the end of the year.'

She gave a little smile. 'That's a good recommendation, if they want more.'

He laughed. 'Aye, but they don't think of the expense. We'll see.'

'Luke, there's something I need to ask you.'

'Oh? That's a serious expression,' he broke in lightly.

'I'm afraid it's a serious matter. You were aware that my father was not well enough to attend the ball?' He nodded. 'I have been to Penorna this afternoon. He's not at all well. I know Mama is terribly worried though she won't admit it. I said I would go over to be with her until Father is on the mend.'

'Of course you must go.'

Abigail was so taken aback by the quickness of his assent that she had to stifle a gasp. 'Oh, Luke, you don't mind?'

'No. You must be there.'

'What about you?'

292

'I'll be all right. I hope it won't be for long and that your father is soon well again.' He came to her and took her in his arms. 'Don't worry about me. Just get your papa well. Until then I'll miss you.' He kissed her gently on the lips.

She looked up at him. 'Thank you,' she said quietly. Her eyes became coy. 'I think you had better have something better than that to remember me by.' Her lips met his with a passion that promised much on her return.

He came to see her leave, sending his good wishes for a speedy recovery to her father. As the carriage drove away she looked back and saw him still standing watching it. She waved and he raised his hand. Abigail settled back on the seat wondering at Luke's enigmatic personality. He had not mentioned last night; it was as if it had never happened. The person who had hammered at her door and shouted curses was no longer evident. In his place was the kind and considerate Luke she had known before their wedding. His violent mood swings seemed to be linked to drink, but also to unexpected bad news. As much as she loved her husband she dreaded his reaction to the next problem he encountered.

After the carriage had disappeared Luke, lost in thought, strolled slowly into the house. He really did not like Abigail leaving Senewey for an unknown length of time but at present, after his walk on the cliffs and visit to the Waning Moon, it would at least give him time to himself to lay plans for what he had in mind.

The coastal location he had examined would suit him ideally for it presented the situation he wanted and was handy for Senewey, which would be central to his scheme. His visit to the Waning Moon had proved satisfactory for, without Luke's revealing anything of what he had in mind, Tom had assured him that he could recruit five trustworthy men who for a price would do any job asked of them and keep their mouths shut. Luke would meet them tomorrow afternoon at three o'clock on the cliffs above the harbour.

On an afternoon when a strong wind had abated to a pleasant breeze and the sun shone from a sky strewn with puffy white clouds that obeyed the whims of the breeze, Luke arrived on the cliffs an hour before the meeting. He tethered his horse and spent the time surveying the area again, analysing its potential and weighing advantages against disadvantages so that by the time the five men arrived he had made his decision.

They came on foot, a rough-looking crew with only one small man among them. Luke judged him to stand at five foot six whereas the rest were no less than six foot and burly with it, not that the small man lacked strength; he looked as powerful as his companions.

When they came to a stop in front of him one man stepped forward.

'Mr Gaisford?' he asked, his tone suspicious.

'Yes,' replied Luke, eyes boring into the man, exerting his authority, letting him and his companions know who was in command here and would be ruthless with them if his instructions were not carried out to the letter. 'You the leader?'

'Aye, sir, Josh Ebbs.' He touched his forehead with the broad forefinger of his right hand. He held himself erect, with a wild defiant air that Luke reckoned had led him into many a scrape, evident from the scar down his left cheek and a nose that had been clumsily set after a fight.

'Right, Josh, name the others.'

'Harry Leland.'

Luke was pleased at the way this man met his scrutiny without dropping his own eyes, a strength of character that Luke hoped would be matched by his loyalty. He stood as tall as Josh and emanated the same strength but there the comparison ended; Harry's face was unmarked except for the lines beginning to age him.

'Wes Outhwaite.'

Luke nodded at a man who was only slightly smaller than the first two. His face was leathery and deeply tanned, marks of toil in the open, farmwork or fishing, it didn't matter to Luke. What did was the pose the man adopted which was that of a man alert and ready to give a good account of himself if the necessity arose.

'Pete Masters.'

Luke was looking at the youngest of the group. He reckoned him to be in his twenties but he had an air of strength and willingness to use it on command, whatever that entailed. His eyes were sharp and his ready smile made Luke wonder if he could ever be fired to anger.

'Titch Vasey.'

The small man who stood in front of the others grinned, touched one finger to his forehead and did a little jig by way of introduction. 'Ready, Mr Gaisford, sir! I can be in and out where these monsters can't get, and as quick as a flash of lightning.' He puffed out his chest, proud of what he could offer. Luke knew he would be the joker of the party and that if caught in any misdemeanour would turn his round face into a picture of cherubic innocence.

'That's us, Mr Gaisford,' Josh concluded the introduction.

Luke eyed them all for a moment, taking in their thick jerseys, woollen trousers tucked into heavy boots, and woollen caps clamped to their heads. 'You look as though you will be capable of the job I have in mind. Tom will have told you that I require the utmost loyalty and tongues that don't wag. If they do you'll feel the long hand of punishment, but holding them still and doing a good job will render you well paid. Don't doubt me on this. I never go back on my word.'

'We understand, Mr Gaisford.' Josh spoke for them all. 'You can depend on us. What is it you want us to do?'

'That will come later. For the moment, come with me and I'll tell you what I want you to do during the next two weeks.' As they walked along the cliff above the harbour Luke told them something about it. Then he led them towards the headland where he stopped.

'There is a shelf of rock running a short distance out to sea and back towards the harbour. That makes gaining access a little tricky but a good boatman will soon master what is required without mishap.' He turned along the coast and pointed out the run of rocky terraces that descended to the strand of sand. 'What I want you to do during the next two weeks is to explore them and find two ways that can be used to reach the top of the cliffs from that stretch of sand. Then I want you to do the same from the harbour.'

They all would have liked to know what lay behind this command but knew they should follow Josh's example and ask no questions.

'There is one other thing. You have seen that entering that harbour from the sea will require skill. Do you know of two men who could handle that?'

Josh did not hesitate. 'Wes has two brothers, both fishermen, skilled with boats. They'll go anywhere.'

Luke nodded and looked at Wes. 'That right?'

'Aye, Mr Gaisford.'

'Can they keep their mouths shut?'

'They can be dumb like me.'

'A boat?'

'Two if required, sir. They'd rather use their own; they fit them like a pair of gloves.'

'Excellent. Names?'

'Andy and Morgan.'

'Recruit them.'

'Yes, sir.'

'Good. I'll meet you here in two weeks. Same time.' He strode away, and as he passed each man touched his forehead. Luke liked to exert his authority on his subordinates.

Tess felt a sense of coming home when the carriage drew up at Penorna. When she'd left Penzance for the first time she was very apprehensive but he had settled here quickly thanks to the kindness and thoughtfulness of the Mitchell family and their staff. Now she looked forward to meeting Mr and Mrs Mitchell again and to being in her old room. She hesitated when she got out of the carriage and watched Abigail hurry up the steps.

Her mistress stopped and turned to her. 'Come along, Tess.'

'But, miss . . .' It was obvious that Tess was thinking she shouldn't be using the main entrance even though she was with her mistress.

'Come along, you aren't at Senewey now.' Abigail's smile of encouragement held a touch of amusement when she saw Tess's doubt turn to pleasure.

'Yes, miss.' She hurried after Abigail with a light tread.

Eliza, who had heard the approaching carriage, was hurrying down the stairs when Abigail and Tess entered the house.

'Wonderful to have you,' she said, grateful to have someone else to share the responsibility of nursing a sick man. She hugged her daughter and then turned to Tess who had stood back modestly. 'Welcome back, Tess.'

'Thank you, ma'am. I was sorry to hear about Mr Mitchell.'

Eliza smiled an acknowledgement and said, 'You are in your old room.' She linked arms with her daughter and set off up the stairs.

'Yes, ma'am,' returned Tess, and turned her attention to the luggage that was being brought in from the carriage.

Finding her father asleep, Abigail stayed a few moments watching him and then went to her own room where Tess was already unpacking. An hour later her mother appeared to tell her that John was awake.

'Hello, Papa,' said Abigail as she entered his room.

'Abigail, it is good to have you here. Your mother tells me you are staying awhile?'

She was shocked at the effort it took him to say these few words, but pleased that his eyes were brighter and he'd mustered a smile, faint though it was.

'I'm here to help out and give Mama some rest. And to get you better.'

He reached out and took her hand but there was no strength in his grip. 'Have you brought Tess?'

'Yes,' replied Abigail.

'Good. She shouldn't be left alone at Senewey and you need her here.'

'It's all taken care of,' said Eliza reassuringly.

John gave a little nod of satisfaction. 'Bring her to see me sometime, she was part of this household.'

'All right, Papa.' Abigail could see that the effort her father had had to expend had drained him. 'Rest awhile. I'll sit with you.'

He nodded, gave a wan smile and adjusted his head more comfortably on his pillow. As his eyes flickered shut Abigail glanced at her mother and mouthed quietly, 'Go and have a rest.'

Eliza slipped from the room.

John remained stable for three days. Fully conscious, he could speak to them but it was an effort and each conversation was short-lived. On the fourth day, when Abigail was sitting with him, he became restless and tossed his head on his pillow, grimacing and muttering as if he was searching for something.

Abigail went closer. 'Papa, Papa,' she said quietly with a touch of alarm and urgency in her voice. 'What is it?' His words in reply were indistinct. She leaned closer, looking into his eyes. They were wide open but he did not seem to see her. Instead he appeared to be looking beyond her as if seeing something she could not. His lips moved. 'What do you want, Papa?' Muttered words came fast. Abigail frowned as she strained to catch their sense. What was that? Tess? Was that what he had said? It couldn't be. Was that the same word? Tess. But why should he mention her? She could think of no reason. John's mutterings faded away to nothing and he lay at peace.

A short while later Eliza came into the room and saw her husband peacefully asleep. 'Has he been all right?' she asked quietly when she joined her daughter, sitting in the window catching the sunlight of a bright day while she read *The Farmer's Boy* by Robert Bloomfield

'He's been tossing and turning a bit. Not for long, but he was muttering which he has never done before.'

'What was he saying?'

'It was difficult to make out but I think I caught the name Tess.'

'Tess?'

'Yes, but I couldn't be certain and I can see no reason why Father should mention her name.'

Eliza looked thoughtful. 'Remember when you arrived he asked if Tess was with you, and seemed relieved that she would not be alone at Senewey?'

'So he did. I wonder why he was concerned?'

Eliza gave a little shake of her head. 'I don't know, unless it was that he thought it would be better for you to have her here.'

'Maybe in his delirium that thought had come back to him and he was wondering again if Tess was here?' Abigail suggested.

'We'll say nothing about what has just happened but I'll make an excuse to bring her in to see him.'

'She asks after him each day so you could use that as your excuse.'

The following day Abigail was once again sitting with her father when her mother came into the room.

'How are you feeling, John?' she asked as she came to the bed.

'A little better, thank you, now that I have my two lovely ladies with me.'

Eliza sat down on the opposite side of the bed to Abigail and took his hand. 'Flatterer,' she said, pleased that he was interested enough to make such a comment.

After a few minutes she let go of his hand and said, 'I'm going to leave you, John, I'll be back in a few minutes.'

He nodded and she left. When she returned she ushered Tess into the room. With one hand on the girl's shoulder she led her to the bed.

Tess was shy about seeing Mr Mitchell in bed and showed her unease.

'Mr Mitchell,' said Eliza, using the formal code of address in front of a servant, 'I have brought Tess to see you. She is always asking after you.'

'Ah, Tess, how nice to see you.' John's eyes brightened as they rested on her. He reached out to her.

Tess, wondering if she should take his hand, looked up at Mrs Mitchell with query in her eyes. Eliza read her dilemma, smiled at her and nodded. Tess took his hand and had the strangest sensation that he was comforting her rather than she consoling him.

'Is it pleasant to be back at Penorna, Tess?' he asked.

She nodded. 'Yes, sir.'

'Good, good.' He managed a smile but his mind suddenly cried out for her to say 'Father' instead of 'sir'. His lips trembled, about to say the word, but he forced it away; there were two other people here who should never know. 'I am pleased you have come to see me.'

'Thank you, sir.'

He looked hard at her. 'When you go back to Senewey, continue to look after Abi . . . Mrs Gaisford.'

'I will, sir.'

'Good. That pleases me.'

Tess, not knowing how to reply, merely nodded.

He let his hand slide from hers. Eliza smiled at her. 'Off you go, Tess. You have done well.'

'Yes, ma'am.' Tess looked back at the slight figure in the bed. 'Goodbye, sir.'

'Goodbye, Tess.'

Abigail's eyes were on her father. She saw him watch Tess every step of the way across the room until the door closed behind her. Did she see a flicker of interest in him? Of pride or admiration? It must have been her imagination; there was no need for him to feel anything for Tess. But hadn't there been times when she herself had felt closer to this girl than the mistress–servant relationship warranted? She dismissed such fanciful wanderings when her mother spoke. 'Abigail, I'll sit here awhile if you would like a walk in the garden. The fresh air will do you good.'

'Thank you, Mama, it will.'

She left the room after giving her father a kiss on the forehead and telling him she would not be long. Collecting a light cloak, she strolled on the terrace where she paused to breathe deeply of the crisp air and admire the well-kept gardens that had always captured her attention. She left the terrace and crossed the lawn towards what was known as 'the hidden garden', an expanse of grass paths and small individual garden 'rooms' with seats surrounded by tall yew hedges, making the whole area one of seclusion and peace. She had almost reached its entrance on the north side when she heard the sound of a horse's hooves. She stopped and looked towards the drive, awaiting the appearance of the rider who would come into sight once he had ridden out of the wood.

He came riding at a trot. Her heart skipped a beat. Luke! He had been once before and promised to come again soon, but as whole days passed her disappointment had grown. Now it was banished. There was joy in her heart as she hurried in his direction. He saw her and waved, slowing his pace until they met on the drive. He was out of the saddle and sweeping her into his arms almost before she realised it.

'It's so good to see you, Abigail,' he whispered close to her ear as he hugged her. Before she could answer their lips met and passion, heightened by absence, soared between them.

'I've missed you, Luke,' she whispered when their lips parted.

'How's your father?' he asked, leaving the next obvious question unspoken but knowing she knew that he was really asking, When are you coming back to Senewey?

'He's not really any better. He has his good days but mostly they are bad.'

Luke looked glum but said, 'You must stay if you think it helps.'

'I'm sure my being here gives him heart, and I know Mama is grateful for my presence.'

'If that is the case then you certainly must not think of coming home yet.'

Abigail, a little surprised by his easy compliance, said, 'You are so understanding. Thank you. I will make it up to you as soon as I return.'

He smiled, a twinkle in his eyes as he said, 'I'll see you do. Were you going for a walk?'

'Just in the hidden garden.'

'May I accompany you?' he queried light-heartedly.

'I'll think about it,' she replied coyly.

'Don't think about it too long,' he teased, taking her arm. 'Tell me what you have been doing.'

'My visits haven't been as frequent as I wished but I have been working on something I think will solve most of Senewey's problems.'

Her eyes brightened with excitement. 'Tell me.'

He shook his head. 'No, not until I think it's the right time.'

'Luke!'

He shook his head. 'No, and none of your charming wiles will make me talk.'

Try as she might, she was no wiser when he'd left Penorna than when he'd arrived but she was pleased to see Luke in such a good mood and hoped that whatever his scheme was, it would bear fruit to keep him that way.

Chapter Twenty-Two

As he rode home Luke was not sorry that Abigail would be absent from Senewey for a while longer. It would give him continued freedom to concentrate on his plans.

At his second meeting with Josh Ebbs and his gang he had met Wes Outhwaite's brothers Andy and Morgan. He was impressed by them, for they had chosen to arrive by boat to demonstrate their skills in the fast-running sea that made entry to the harbour tricky. They made it look easy but he knew it was not.

They left their boat in the harbour and climbed the cliff to join the others. Wes introduced them.

'Andy.'

The fisherman touched his forehead and stuck out his hand. There was only a moment of reluctance on Luke's part before he shook it, feeling a strong grip, fingers callused from working oars and lines. He saw a face weathered by wind and sea, and strength in the thick neck set on broad shoulders.

'Morgan, youngest of the family,' said Wes when he saw doubt in Luke's eyes. 'He may be only seventeen but he'll do a man's job and more if required.'

'Aye, I will that, sir,' said the youngster eagerly.

Luke saw the enthusiasm of a boy desiring to enter and be part of a man's world.

'See that you do,' he said, 'and even if your brother has already told you I'll repeat it: not one word of what we do and what you see must pass your lips.'

'They are sealed, sir,' replied Morgan emphatically.

The men then reassured him that they had planned routes from the strand and harbour to the cliff top, and on examining them Luke was pleased with what they had done. Both ways were usable but would not be obvious to anyone on the cliff top. As curious as the gang was to know what Mr Gaisford was planning, he would not reveal anything to them then. 'You will know more when you meet me at the Waning Moon four nights from now,' he had told them.

He had one more essential part of his plan to fit into place and as he rode home from Penorna he hoped that would be settled tomorrow.

Luke turned the collar of his coat up against a wind driving threatening clouds that as yet had not decided whether to douse the warm earth. He eased himself in the saddle and turned over in his mind what he had chosen to say to his friend. Martin Granton lived at Granton Manor, a small Elizabethan house that had come into the family in the early-seventeenth century. It had suffered mismanagement later in the century, from which it had never truly recovered. When Martin was left as sole heir on the death of his parents he had struggled to maintain it, but pulling the estate round was a hard task when financial resources were limited. It was this latter fact that Luke hoped to turn to his own advantage.

He eyed a building that was showing marked signs of needing repair. He felt sorry for his friend and hoped he could stem his own slide towards a similar penury. He halted his horse at the side of the house and tethered it to a wooden railing placed there for this purpose. At one time a groom would have hurried out to see to it. Luke patted the animal as he walked past and up the stone steps to the terrace. The balustrade was badly weathered and in some places the stonework showed signs of imminent collapse unless something was done soon to save it. Reaching the front door, he pulled hard on the metal bell-pull. A few moments later the door was opened by a manservant. At least Martin was managing to keep up some appearances.

'Good day, Mr Gaisford,' the man greeted brightly.

'And to you, Roger! Is Mr Granton at home?'

'He is, sir,' replied Roger and stood back to allow Luke to enter. 'He's in his study, sir.' He started across the hall from which all the furniture but two chairs had been sold to raise money.

Luke halted him with, 'It's all right, Roger, I'll announce myself.'

'Very good, sir.' He turned in the direction of the servants' quarters at the back of the house.

Luke tapped on the door and hearing the call of 'Come in', entered the room.

Martin, who was sitting behind a large oak desk, jumped to his feet when he saw his friend. 'Good to see you, Luke,' he said with a smile as he came over to shake hands. 'Glass of Madeira?' he asked, starting towards a sideboard standing near a large window that looked out on to the garden in which one man was battling to curtail the prolific growth.

'Not for me, thanks.'

Martin stopped in his tracks and swung round, surprise on his face. 'What, Luke Gaisford refusing a drink?'

'Just this morning.' Luke smiled, sitting down in one of the two armchairs drawn up opposite each other in front of an ornate fireplace.

'This must be a serious occasion?' said Martin, taking the other chair.

'It is,' replied Luke. 'Are you still in need of financial help?'

Martin gave a grimace. 'You know I won't accept charity.'

'I'm not offering it,' replied Luke. 'What I am about to tell you is strictly between us. We have been good friends all our lives. I'm closer to you than to the others. You I trust implicitly.'

'You are right there, but what's this about? You know whatever you tell me will go no further.'

'I am not as well off as I appear.'

'What?' A puzzled frown betrayed Martin's disbelief.

'It's true,' said Luke.

'But the expense of the ball?'

305

'Oh, yes, that's cost me dear, but the county expects it of the Gaisfords.'

'But . . . your other assets?'

'Very precarious.' Luke went on to elaborate.

'If things don't turn for the better you are soon going to be in the same position as I am,' returned Martin.

'Yes, but I am going to do something about it. In fact, I have laid plans already.'

'Why are you telling me all this?' asked his friend with marked curiosity.

'Because you could benefit too from what I have in mind.'

'Me?'

'Yes. But once again I want you to swear that you will not tell anyone, even if you turn my proposition down.'

'I'm not likely to if it is going to make me some money. You can trust me to keep my lips sealed. But why are you offering whatever it is to me?'

'You need money. You and I have shared a few adventures together, ridden hard, drunk hard. You have never been afraid of a fight or of danger.'

Martin gave a laugh as memories came to mind. 'That's true. So what have you planned?'

Twenty minutes later a tense silence had come over the room. Martin stared at his friend. His mind was in turmoil as he grappled with Luke's proposition. Something warned him not to become involved, but the enticement of easy money was strong and Luke's scheme piqued his taste for adventure, especially when he would be involved in it with his friend. If this worked out he could be looking at a much brighter future for Granton Manor.

'Wait a minute, Luke.' He held up his hands to stop Luke saying anything more. 'I hate to bring this up but I think it is better to do so now rather than later. I hear Mr Mitchell is not well. Suppose he dies. Aren't you likely to come into a size-able fortune then through Abigail?'

Luke gave a wry smile. 'I must admit the thought has crossed my mind, but I have already gone a way down the road I have described and been bitten by the adventure of it.'

'So what is the next move?'

'Are you in?'

Martin nodded. 'Yes.'

'Good.'

When Luke stood up, Martin did likewise. They clasped hands, sealing their pact.

'We meet on the cliffs above the old harbour four nights from now, seven o'clock,' Luke declared. 'Come by way of Senewey. We'd better go together the first time you meet the men I've recruited.'

'Are they trustworthy?' asked Martin cautiously.

'They know what will happen to them if they aren't,' replied Luke, his voice cold and menacing.

A shiver ran down Martin's spine as he realised this was also a warning to him.

The men were already on the cliffs when Luke and Martin arrived. They stared in silence as the two riders slid from their mounts.

'You all doubtless know Mr Granton by sight but he won't know you.' Luke went on to introduce each man in turn. 'Mr Granton will be working with us and providing some of his buildings for storage. We also have mine on Senewey and some at the Waning Moon, as well as the caves accessible from the harbour.'

'This sounds like a smuggling job?' said Josh, making his comment a query.

'No, it's not. That would have required a much bigger and more detailed organisation, involving more people and increasing the possibility of betrayal. What I am about to reveal to you involves only us and you all know what will happen if you break your word to me to keep silent. What I have in mind will leave no trace apart from a few broken timbers.'

'Wreckers!' More than one man gasped at the idea.

Luke nodded. 'Aye, it's been done before, so tradition tells us. I'm reviving the practice for our benefit. We'll all make money from it.'

'You'll want no survivors?' queried Joss, having heard tales of the brutality of previous wreckers.

'That's right,' replied Luke, committing these men to something they had not thought about when they assembled on the cliff a short while ago. 'Is anyone against that? If so, let him go now! But woe betide him if he betrays us later.'

The men looked uneasy, whether at the thought of leaving no survivors or the threat to themselves neither Luke nor Martin could be sure, but no one walked away.

'Good,' said Luke. 'We will place lights on the main headland and a minor one high above the far side of the harbour. Ships thinking there is a safe passage between them are likely to sail closer to the brighter light and that will put them in danger from the shelf of rock that runs out from the foot of the cliffs. The Outhwaite brothers will be stationed in the harbour ready to row out to the wreck, take on board what they can and ferry it back to the harbour. The rest of us will be at the foot of the cliff ready to exploit the strand and the ways you have explored of climbing the terraces.'

'How are we to know what cargo a ship will be carrying?' asked Titch.

'Doesn't matter! Ships heading for the south coast and the Thames always carry valuable cargoes. After each wreck we'll store the goods and wait awhile before gradually disposing of them. I will make out that I've set up a trading company, but that part of the operation needn't concern you, except for transporting the goods to their destination when I have concluded a transaction with an interested party.'

'How do we know what you receive in payment?' queried Andy, a touch of suspicion in his voice.

'You'll have to trust me, just as I have to trust you not to talk. Any more questions?'

'Are we to be here every night?' asked Pete Masters.

'No. Once we have taken a ship we will lie low until I deem it safe to operate again. You'll get a message via Tom at the Waning Moon. We can't guarantee when a ship will be lured by the lights, it will depend what is happening on board and on the gullibility of the captain. I believe we are more likely to be successful in foggy or stormy weather. Any of you expert weather readers?'

'Aye,' said Wes Outhwaite, 'brother Andy's an expert. Needs to be as a fisherman.'

'Right, Andy, you read it for us.'

'I'll do my best, Mr Gaisford. How should I let you know?'

'Granton Manor will be nearer you. Let Mr Granton know and he'll inform me. You can tell the rest of the men, and that night we'll meet on the cliffs here at dusk.'

'Right, Mr Gaisford!' He glanced skywards. 'Now we are all here, I suggest we meet in two days' time.'

Martin raised an eyebrow in surprise. 'You think the weather will be to our advantage then? It looks so settled.'

'Trust me, Mr Granton.' Andy gave a little smile.

'It will be interesting to see if you are right,' countered Martin amicably.

Two days later in mid-afternoon the sun was still shining when Martin arrived at Senewey Manor.

'Looks as though Andy will be proved wrong,' he said with a grimace as he joined Luke on the terrace.

They settled down with their whiskies and an hour later went inside for a meal. They were halfway through it when they both paused while cutting at a slice of beef. They exchanged glances, querying what they had heard.

'Is that the wind?' said Martin tentatively.

The windows rattled for answer.

'That was sudden,' said Luke. 'It was so calm when we came in and there was no sign of a change.' He got to his feet and went to the window.

Martin had to allay his curiosity and left the table to join him. They did not speak as they stared unbelievingly at the dark clouds rolling towards them across a sky that but a short time ago had been clear. As if to prove this was reality a streak of lightning seared the horizon and thunder rumbled threateningly. The wind would not be left out and shrieked at the house, trying to batter a way in.

'Extraordinary,' muttered Martin. 'There was no sign of this when we came in.'

'Has Andy got a sixth sense?'

'Else he's a magician.'

'It's uncanny but it's exactly what we want. That wind will be turning the sea into a maelstrom. Come on, let's finish our meal. We'll need to eat our fill for what this night holds ahead.'

With black turbulent clouds filling the sky, darkness came earlier than expected. Luke and Martin wrapped themselves up to contest the wind and rain that had started to lash land and sea. The wind seemed to be angry at their intrusion when they stepped outside and went for their horses. Hunched in the saddles against the bruising weather they kept their animals to a walking pace, only breaking into a trot when Luke, who was leading the way, felt it was safe to do so.

There was no sign of anyone when they reached the cliff above the harbour and tethered their horses in the shelter of a huge boulder. Leaning into the wind, they hurried towards the headland. They had almost reached it when a figure stepped into their path.

'Here, sirs.' Josh's words were torn away by the wind. As he turned from them, Luke and Martin knew the others must be seeking shelter in a hollow to their right. So it proved but any protection from the elements was minimal.

'We've a good night for it, sir,' said Josh as they joined the others. 'The sea's running high. Any vessel driven on to that shelf won't last long in this.'

Luke nodded, sending water streaming from the hat crammed tight down on his head. 'Andy, are you a wizard or something? A short time ago there was no sign of this weather.'

'I feel it in my bones.' Andy grinned, pleased that he had been proved right, though he'd never doubted he would be.

'Let's get organised,' said Luke, stamping his authority on the situation. 'Morgan, you get off to the cliffs at the far side of the harbour, light the lamp and then join your brother at the boat in the harbour. You both know what to do from then on.

The light on this headland will be lit when we see Morgan's light, then take up your positions as planned. From then on you'll have to use your own initiative but you know where to conceal any goods. Don't forget, don't take everything – leave something as evidence that the rest could have been swept out to sea. And remember, no survivors live to tell the tale. The whole crew could easily have been lost in the wreck and drowned.' He emphasised the last word to remind them of what should be done.

Morgan hurried away around the cliff top. His brother Andy accompanied him until he took the path to the harbour and the boat. Everyone else waited until they saw Morgan's light appear then occupied themselves as pre-arranged. Josh lit the light on the headland then joined the others who were making their way to the strand to take up position close to the foot of the headland. Luke and Martin remained on the cliff top so that they could oversee operations even though the driving rain made visibility poor. But watch they must, for theirs was a vital role. The minutes ticked by and ran into half an hour and still they waited, buffeted by the wind and slashed by the rain. Only the thought of the rich pickings to come kept Martin from walking away as his conscience pricked him with the thought of no survivors . . .

'There!' Luke's cry startled him.

Martin's eyes strained to penetrate the blackness that had intensified with the merging of sea and sky, with only the sound of the sea pounding at the rocks and swishing up the sand to indicate that they were not one.

'Where?'

'There!'

He followed Luke's raised arm and pointing finger. A light! Then it was gone. He held his breath. Visible again, he realised it was swaying, dipping and rising. A light on a mast-head? In that direction it was all it could be. 'A ship!'

Luke was already bending to the lantern. Sheltering as best he could, he managed to light it at the third attempt. The note of triumph in his voice was unmistakable. He picked up the lantern and held it high, a signal to the Outhwaite brothers in their boat in the harbour and to the man whom they knew Josh would have set as a lookout. From their high vantage point they could now signal the ship's progress to the waiting men until it came into sight.

Time seemed to drag and the light at sea did not seem to move any nearer. It would disappear and then reappear in the same place as the powerful waves dictated its progress.

'It's closer!' cried Martin.

Luke trusted his judgement and swung the lantern twice. They could still not be certain that it was heading for the coast to seek shelter from the driving sea and the striving wind.

The minutes passed. 'It's running in!' shouted Martin.

Luke swung the lantern three times, paused, and seeing the light seeming suddenly to sweep nearer, raised his lantern and swung it quickly three more times. He put the lamp down. Now it was up to his men to pick up the ship which he was certain was running for the safety the two lights on the cliff falsely offered.

The ship's hull took on a solid shape surmounted by masts and rigging that pierced the dark sky. A sail hung torn and bedraggled, evidence that the crew had not been able to deal with it before the storm struck. Lifted by an enormous wave, the ship seemed to be thrown into a deep trough, but by skilful seamanship or a miracle it survived only to be pounded anew by the sea, angry that it had not gained a victory, and the wind screeching at its escape. Their anger turned to triumph when the ship lurched as if struck by a huge hand. There was the tearing sound of timber as the hull hit the underwater rock. The vessel attempted to go on only to drive the wound deeper, allowing water to pour in. The ship reeled and tilted. A sharp cracking sound penetrated the maelstrom of noise and a mast broke, toppled, and dragged the tattered sail with it. It fell with a crash into the sea, dragging the ship further over and more quickly to its doom. Cries of horror and pleas for help were torn away by the howling wind as the merciless wreckers moved in to take their booty.

The ship broke in two. Half of the main mast was swept out to sea then beaten back by the current towards the strand. The rest was breaking up on the rocks. The Outhwaite brothers dealt with that section, loading their fishing boat with cargoes as quickly as they could in the circumstances, but their sailing skills enabled them to make three runs before the break up of the ship made any more impossible.

From the sand Josh directed the operation of getting as much booty as they could on shore before the stern broke up completely and was swept away to deeper waters. Before the goods were taken up the cliff, he ordered his crew to make sure no one had survived the doomed ship, just as the Outhwaite brothers were doing on the other side of the headland.

Martin had been mesmerised by the spectacle of the ship's death throes. He felt chilled by it but also triumphant for they had accomplished what they had set out to do. Now all that remained was to see what goods it had been carrying and to hide the cargo as quickly as possible.

Master of the whole operation, Luke had not only felt excitement but been gripped by the immense power that was his. He could send ships to their doom and men to their deaths. In his frenzy of excitement, he had an ungovernable urge to act as executioner himself. Standing high on the cliff, unsubdued by the howling wind, unbowed by the lashing rain, he felt like a god.

'Come on.' Martin broke the spell but it had left a deep impression on Luke.

They hurried along the cliff top and awaited the arrival of the first man from the beach. Harry Leland appeared, carrying a wooden case on his shoulder. He dropped it to the earth with relief and drew air deep into his lungs. Martin was quickly on his knees, prising the lid open.

'Brandy!' he called triumphantly.

'There's a few more cases like that,' cried Harry. His exhaustion forgotten, he hurried to return to the sand.

Before dawn the storm had blown itself out; all the cases and boxes had been hidden in prearranged places to be removed at a time and date when Luke gave the order. Little evidence that a ship had foundered was left. Whether it was found sooner or later it would only be regarded as a ship lost with all hands in foul weather. The storm would have been reported and the ship's owner would presume it was to blame.

Luke told the men to meet him at the Waning Moon the following night, an order Martin had to turn down due to a prior commitment.

The following evening Luke made sure he was first at the inn and occupying the back room, telling Tom to direct the others there and to keep the ale flowing. Discussion of their first venture as wreckers was filled with triumph, hilarity, analysis, and suggestions for improvements, though all realised that much depended on how events turned out on the night. All the men were relieved that all hands had been lost when the ship broke up and no one had had to commit the ultimate act, but Luke warned them that in future they must not turn away from it. If they did it could scupper the chance of any future operations and endanger their own lives. The sombre mood that his warning brought was dismissed in a moment when he announced that they would move the goods in two days' time to destinations from which he could set about arranging their sale and disposal. After which their pockets would jingle.

They were all in a more than amiable mood when they left the Waning Moon, and took no notice of the other people in the bar. Two sat deep in conversation at one of the tables, talking no notice of them, and two at the bar appeared to take only a mild interest in the men loudly enjoying themselves in the back room.

Chapter Twenty-Three

During the next three weeks Luke visited Abigail three times. On each occasion, fearing his arrival would signify an insistence it was time for her to return to Senewey, she was pleasantly surprised to find that he was in an amiable, in fact buoyant, mood. Curious, she probed him about this when they were alone but he refused to be drawn, merely saying, 'All is well, you have nothing to worry about. My financial problems are taking a turn for the better.'

His euphoria was the result of being able to dispose of the looted cargo under the guise of a trading company he said he had founded, explained away to people in the county by the fiction that he was diversifying and expanding his assets. He was generous in his payments to Martin and his 'employees', knowing that this was the best way to keep their tongues silent.

As he rode home after a fourth visit, Luke's thoughts drifted back to the night of the wrecking and he felt an urge to feel that fierce excitement again. Knowing from which cove the Outhwaite brothers operated their fishing enterprise, he rode there on the off chance that he would find them. He was rewarded by seeing them checking their lines.

After greetings had been exchanged, Luke put the important question to Andy. 'Can you predict the weather pattern for the next few days?'

Andy looked thoughtful as he glanced at the sky, studied the clouds and wind direction. He scratched his head. 'Signs are a bit confusing, as they have been over this whole week. I've seen them like this before then give way to fog.'

'So you are saying that we could expect fog in the next few days?' asked Luke eagerly.

'Aye, could be.'

'Then I think it's time to light the lamps again. Will you spread the word to meet at the Waning Moon tomorrow night?'

Andy glanced at his brother. 'Morgan, you can do that.'

'Aye, I'll away.' The youngster was off, driven by the excitement of what he viewed as a new adventure.

The following night plans were made, though they all agreed there was little new to do to improve the operation. Much depended on how the next ship reacted when it struck the rocks. Following Andy's new prediction that fog would roll in over a calm sea, they met on the cliffs two nights later.

Because of the fog Luke employed two lights close together, hoping they would entice a captain looking for a safe passage closer to the coast. It was shortly after midnight that his judgement paid off. One moment they were staring into a clammy blanket of fog; the next a dark mass visible through the night sent their pulses racing: a ship was heading to its doom.

Timbers ripped apart; masts shattered, broke and crashed to the tilting deck. Cries of horror and shouts for help were muffled by the fog as confusion reigned on board. Sailors who had not been killed by the initial breaking up were thankful for the calm sea. If they could escape the jagged rocks there was still hope for them. But that hope was short-lived. Powerful grips held their heads below water until they were pushed away to their end in a watery grave.

Luke, Martin and their gang worked hard to hide the cargo. Finally they left for their respective dwellings with instructions to meet at the Waning Moon two nights later. Everyone was highly satisfied with their night's work.

When he parted from Martin and rode to Senewey, Luke experienced once again that euphoria that had gripped him on the cliffs as he'd watched a ship come to an inglorious end at his command. Once again he had wielded the power of an executioner.

The meeting at the Waning Moon, where they used the back room as usual, was one of jubilation. They had high expectations of the cargo's value, enhanced by much hard drinking and hilarity.

As they left together, Luke made an observation. 'You were a bit subdued tonight, Martin. Something troubling you?'

He was silent for a few moments then let his doubts be heard. 'Is it really necessary to get rid of the survivors?'

'What else are we to do?'

'I don't like this killing.'

'Getting cold feet? Think of the money that will save Granton Manor.'

'Is it worth it? And I shudder at the way the others joke about holding a man under water.'

'You aren't actually doing it so shut it out of your mind. Besides, you are in too deep now to get out.'

Martin shrugged his shoulders. 'I suppose so.'

Luke did not like the tone of regret in his voice. 'And don't think of going to the authorities.' He made sure his words carried a chill warning.

The next day Luke was still in a euphoric mood when a hard-ridden horse disturbed the silence around Senewey. Luke, who was on the terrace blindly staring across his land while reliving the sight of the ship breaking up, recognised one of the grooms from Penorna.

The rider spotted him and turned his horse to bring it to a halt at the foot of the steps. Breathing heavily after his fast ride, he swung from the saddle and thrust a letter at Luke, 'From Mrs Gaisford, sir,' he said as he removed his hat.

Luke said nothing but broke the seal and read the few words quickly. 'Tell Mrs Gaisford I'm on my way.'

'Yes, sir.' The man turned back to his horse and galloped away as Luke hurried to the stables before briefly returning to his room in the house. A few minutes later he was back at the stable and mounting the horse that stood ready for him. Without a word, he left Senewey at a gallop. Abigail's brief message, 'Father died last night' was imprinted on his mind.

How much had Mitchell been worth, and how much would Abigail inherit? Maybe there had been no need for him to become the leader of a gang of wreckers after all.

The sound of the galloping horse brought a groom hurrying out to take charge of his horse. Luke ran into the house. 'Where's Mrs Gaisford?' he called to a maid who was crossing the hall towards the kitchens.

'Upstairs in Mrs Mitchell's room, sir.'

Luke raced up the stairs and knocked on the third door along the landing. It was opened by a red-eyed Abigail, her face drawn and pale with the expression of someone overwhelmed by circumstances.

'Oh, Luke!' Her wail sounded like a deep cry for help as she flung herself into his arms.

He held her tight. 'I'm here, love, I'm here.' He saw beyond her. In the room a man was standing by the bed.

'Your mother?' he queried.

'She's so ill,' Abigail whispered as she took his hand and led him into the room.

The man at the bed turned to them.

'Doctor Fenchurch,' Luke acknowledged in a low voice.

'Mr Gaisford,' returned the doctor. 'I'm so glad you are here, for your wife's sake.' His sombre expression struck Luke then.

'Mrs Mitchell?' he queried anxiously, glancing towards the bed. He saw a woman aged before her time, a face so pale that a arm coursed through him. Eliza's eyes were closed, her breathing shallow. He felt Abigail's grip tighten on his hand.

The doctor nodded. 'On one of my early visits to Mr Mitchell, Mrs Mitchell told me she too was experiencing some pain. I examined her and the diagnosis was not good, but she made me promise to tell no one while her husband was ill.' He glanced at Abigail. 'She did not want to add to your worries.'

'Why not?' cried Abigail. 'I could have helped.'

'I pointed that out,' the doctor went on, 'but she insisted and I had to respect my patient's wishes. The strain of the succeeding weeks took its toll in spite of your insistence, Mrs Gaisford, that she took more rest.'

'I thought her deterioration was caused by worry over Father's illness and that she would recover in time,' sobbed Abigail.

The doctor grimaced. 'I'm afraid not, Mrs Gaisford. On top of her illness, the shock of losing her husband has been too great even though she'd begun to expect it. We cannot tell how much her mental attitude has contributed to what we see now. Thankfully she is unconscious and will have no pain that I can tell. I'm afraid there is nothing more we can do.'

'Oh, no!' Abigail wailed and sank against Luke's side. His arm came round her to offer support as the tears flowed and sobs racked her body.

'Nothing?' he queried.

The doctor shook his head. 'Sadly we do not yet know enough about our mental composition and how to treat its reaction to severe trials. The desire and will to live depends largely on the individual. I'm afraid with the death of her husband, Mrs Mitchell appears to have given up.'

'Mama!' Abigail slipped from Luke's arms and went to her mother. She took Eliza's hand. It was so cold. She was aware that her mother did not even know she was there. The hand went limp; Eliza's breathing became shallower and then stopped completely. The doctor stepped to the bed and felt Mrs Mitchell's pulse, then laid her hand gently back on the bedclothes. 'She's gone,' he said quietly.

'Oh, no!' Abigail collapsed sobbing on the bed, her arms reaching out to her mother as if she would prevent her journey in death.

Luke started to go to her but Doctor Fenchurch raised a hand to stop him and mouthed silently, 'A moment or two.' Luke waited until the doctor nodded and then went to his wife. He put his hands on her arms and gently prised Abigail from the bed and on to her feet. 'Come, love,' he said gently, and led her, weeping, from the room. They waited on the landing for the doctor.

He came out a few moments later and, glancing down into the hall, was thankful that Mrs Downing, the housekeeper, was there awaiting news. They went down and when he had informed her of what had happened and she had passed her commiserations to Abigail, assuring her that she was willing to do all she could, the doctor said, 'Will you look after Mrs Gaisford while I have a word with Mr Gaisford?'

'Certainly,' she replied, and accompanied Abigail to the drawing room.

The doctor and Luke went into the study. 'Two deaths on the same day is bad enough, but when it is your father and mother it could be devastating. Mrs Gaisford will require every care and attention, especially from you, the only relative she has left. She should not have the worry of the funeral arrangements which I suggest are made as quickly as possible. If it will help, I will set them in motion today. It is a matter of where you would like the burial to take place? I would suggest the little church at Sandannack. It is the estate village and I'm sure Mr and Mrs Mitchell would like to be buried there, but of course that decision rests with your wife.'

'I will have a word with her and let you know later today.'

'Do that and I will put things in motion.'

Luke saw the doctor out and went to the drawing room. 'Give me ten minutes, Mrs Downing, and then come back.'

'Very good, sir.' She left the room.

He sat down beside Abigail whose distress showed in a face drained of all colour, the pallor of exhaustion evident in her eyes. He took her hands in his. 'What can I say, love, what can I do?'

She looked pleadingly at him and whispered hoarsely, 'Comfort me.' She fell into his arms, sobbing. He held her until the tears eased, then gently pushed her away so he could look into her eyes. 'I will have to leave you for a short while.'

Before he could say any more, she grabbed his arm and cried out, 'No, Luke, no!'

'There are things I must see to,' he explained. 'Mrs Downing will be here. I won't be long.'

She bit back the tears, and when Mrs Downing appeared Luke left immediately.

He rode swiftly to Granton Manor where he was immediately admitted to Martin's study. After acquainting him of the situation at Penorna and receiving his friend's commiserations, Luke asked him to take charge of the storage and disposal of the cargo from the wrecked ship. He rode back to Penorna where he found Abigail composed if subdued.

Finding that she had drawn on her inner strength and seemed determined to cope, he put forward the doctor's suggestion and received her agreement that the funeral should be at Sandannack. Luke left to see the doctor, calling on the way to arrange a date with the parson. The doctor had already informed the undertaker who was always engaged for the Gaisford funerals.

Though the following week was a trial for Abigail she came through it remarkably well, and believed she had done so because of the support she had received from Luke. They rode back to Senewey together. Luke had arranged for her father's will to be read there once the last of the sympathisers had paid their respects. With that completed they led the solicitor, Mr Wagstaff, into Luke's study. He poured each of them a fortifying glass of Madeira.

The solicitor cleared his throat, glanced at the papers in front of him and said, 'Because Mrs Mitchell died as well there are certain bequests made to her in Mr Mitchell's will that are no longer applicable. She was not entitled to make a will unless her husband approved, a right which was not pursued, so everything will be regarded as being disposed of by Mr Mitchell's. Which means, everything will go to you Mrs Gaisford.'

At this announcement Luke's pulse raced. His financial problems were solved at a stroke for what a wife held was by rights her husband's and could be disposed of or used as he wished. He heard the solicitor speaking again.

'But it is not as straightforward as that. Mr Mitchell made everything over to his wife, with the proviso that she could not dispose of any of the assets but only enjoy the interest on them for life. It would have made her a good living, I must say. That condition would have continued to operate until her death. Once that occurred all assets were to go into a trust for his daughter.'

These words numbed Luke. He was well and truly tied. He could not now lay a finger on any of the Mitchell assets, which he would have diverted to uphold the Senewey Estate.

'Under the terms of this will,' the solicitor went on, 'Mrs Gaisford has the use of the income from the Penorna Estate, but only in set yearly amounts. It will provide Mrs Gaisford with a good living similar to that her mother would have enjoyed. I think your father saw it as a nice addition to anything Mr Gaisford allows you, ma'am.' He cleared his throat. 'Before I conclude, I must add that Mr Mitchell made some bequests from the ready money available which he saw was sufficient to cover them. These bequests are in varying amounts to members of the Penorna staff. There is only one person who isn't, though she was at one time and continues to be Mrs Gaisford's maid. To Tess Booth Mr Mitchell left the sum of five hundred pounds.' He looked down at a document and quoted, '"in recognition of her faithful duty to my daughter"'. He paused and then glanced at them. Letting his eyes rest on Abigail, he said, 'Will you inform her, ma'am? And I think you had better advise her what to do with the money. It is a considerable sum for such a person.'

'I will, Mr Wagstaff.'

Luke said nothing. His silence concealed an intense fury. His dreams lay shattered. He said very little as he saw the solicitor from the house then stormed into the drawing room, slamming the door viciously behind him. Abigail flinched then swung round from the window where she had gone to stand when the solicitor left. The crash eliminated all thoughts of why her father had left so much money to Tess. She saw Luke's face darken with anger.

'That damned father of yours!'

'Don't you talk of him like that,' snapped Abigail, drawing herself up boldly. She guessed what Luke was hinting at and had it confirmed when he hissed, 'Tied everything up so I couldn't get my hands on it!' There was hatred in his tone.

Now she saw a Luke she did not recognise. Gone was any consideration for her in her bereavement. In these circumstances she had to stand up to him. She was alone now. There was no one else to help her and she had experienced his dark side in the past. Now he was heading for the decanters on the sideboard.

'And would you have taken it?' she demanded. His answer would show where Luke's real loyalties lay.

'Damn right I would. Senewey is what matters!'

'I thought you told me things were turning out better for you?'

'Penorna would have made sure of that.'

'Then I'm glad my father protected it. Penorna means so much to me.'

He drained his glass and poured another.

'Luke, don't!'

He glared at her in fury. 'I've told you before, don't tell me what to do!' He drained his glass at a gulp and in defiance of her wishes filled it again.

Abigail knew where this could lead and was pleased when he announced he was going out. She was even more relieved when, from the window, she saw him ride furiously from the stable yard. She felt sorry for the animal for in his rage Luke would ride it hard. She hoped that by the time he returned he would have ridden the anger out of himself. But in case he hadn't, tonight she would lock her doors as a precaution. Abigail rang for a maid and asked her to find Tess and tell her to come to the drawing room.

She was sitting on the sofa when Tess arrived. Her mistress asked her to sit on the chair opposite hers, saying, 'I have something to tell you.'

Tess sat down, placing her hands primly in her lap. Wondering what this was about, she looked straight at Abigail.

'As you probably know, Tess, the solicitor has been here to read my father's will.'

'Yes, miss.'

'Well, in it my father left you five hundred pounds.'

This was almost beyond Tess's comprehension. She just stared at Abigail,

'Do you understand what I have said?'

323

'Er . . . yes, miss.'

'Well?'

'So much money!' gasped Tess.

'It is indeed.' Then Abigail had to put the question that had been puzzling her. 'Do you know why he should do this for you?'

Tess shook her head, 'No, miss. The master was kind when I first came to Penorna, but so was Mrs Mitchell.'

Abigail said no more about it but in her mind linked this with the name her father had muttered when he was ill. The association puzzled her.

'What do you want to do with the money?' She asked.

'I don't know, miss. What can I do?'

'Would you like me to see to it for you?'

'Oh, please, miss.'

'I'll ensure that Mr Wagstaff puts it into a reputable bank.'

'Thank you, miss. Oh, could I give a hundred pounds to Dorinda? She was always kind to me, especially when poor Mama died.'

'That is a kind thought, Tess. I'll arrange it and then you and I will go together to tell her. And, Tess, it might be as well to keep word of your good fortune to yourself. Some unscrupulous people might try to play on your good nature.'

'I will, miss.'

Tess lay on her bed, snatching some time to herself before she prepared Abigail for bed. She was bewildered by her good fortune and found it hard to believe that she now possessed so much money. One question haunted her: why had Mr Mitchell done this? She could find no answer.

A knock on the door interrupted her thoughts. She swung off the bed, straightened her clothes with a swift brush of her hand and opened the door.

'Alice! Come in.' She closed the door behind her friend. 'Come to tell me what you've been doing on your free day?'

They sat down side by side on the edge of her bed.

'I met Leo.' Alice's eyes brightened at the memory. 'We walked on the cliffs and down to the beach where his father keeps his boat. The fishing has been good lately and they have been asked to supply fish to the Waning Moon, an inn on the moors used chiefly by travellers though some of its former reputation still clings to it.'

'What was that?' asked Tess.

'I can only tell you what Leo told me. It seems it was a rough place frequented by a gang of smugglers. It has brushed off that image lately but Leo wonders if it has quite disappeared.'

'What do you mean?' queried Tess, who loved listening to Alice's tales.

'Well, Leo told me that on one occasion, when he and his father had delivered fish and had stayed for a tankard before setting off home, a gang of men in very high spirits came from a back room. They had to pass through the bar to get out. A rough-looking crew, said Leo, all except one. He was much smarter than the others and that is why he caught Leo's attention, though it was only for a moment as he led the others out.' Alice paused.

Tess could tell that she was dying to tell her something so prompted, 'Well, go on?'

'Leo said it was Mr Gaisford.'

'What?' Tess frowned. 'It couldn't be.'

'Leo said he would swear on the Bible.'

'But Mr Gaisford wouldn't associate with such men.'

'That's what I said, but Leo would have it that the man he saw was Mr Gaisford.'

'Did he know any of the others?'

'A man called Josh Ebbs and two fishermen. Not personally, but he recognised Ebbs as a man he saw get into a fight in St Ives. Apparently he has an unsavoury reputation. Leo said that if the others were running with him they would be up to no good.'

'So why was Mr Gaisford with them?'

Alice shrugged her shoulders. 'Who knows?'

'If you hear any more, you will tell me?' pressed Tess.

'Of course! You are my friend.'

This conversation drove all thoughts of her own good fortune from her mind and, in her concern for Abigail, remained to haunt Tess.

As he rode hard for the Waning Moon, Luke sent curses ringing to the heavens that would have doomed John Mitchell to hell had Luke the power. A fortune snatched from his hands by his cunning father-in-law! He would now have to endure the sight of Penorna prospering under the efficient manager John had left in place. The only way Luke was ever likely to get his hands on it was through a son. Abigail was sure to make her child her heir, and with her out of the way the child would be under Luke's influence. But he needed money now and wanted something else to take his mind off the blow he had been dealt by a measly-mouthed lawyer.

He burst into the Waning Moon, startling Tom who was behind the bar drawing two tankards of ale.

'A tankard and a bottle,' Luke shouted as he blundered to a corner table. Chairs clattered as he flung himself down on the corner settle.

Leo Gurney glanced at his father who raised an eyebrow in contempt for Mr Gaisford's boorish behaviour. Leo locked this away in his mind. Here was something to tell Alice, and he noted more when the innkeeper took the tankard, a bottle and a glass to Luke.

'Pass the word for a meeting. Tomorrow night, Tom.'

The landlord was surprised that this order was so openly given, though it would mean nothing to the other occupants of the bar.

It might mean nothing but it had raised Leo's curiosity, especially as he assumed that the meeting would be with Josh Ebbs and the others he had seen in their company. He could have a fine tale now with which to impress Alice!

The following afternoon Leo told his parents he was away to Sennen and might be late back. Instead he arrived at the Waning Moon shortly before dusk, ordered a tankard of ale and took it to a corner table from which he could observe the door without being too conspicuous. Two other men came in and settled themselves at a table. Ten minutes later a man came in, took a tankard from the landlord, and made his way to the back room. Leo was alert; he couldn't be sure if this man was among those he had seen before but things were definitely beginning to happen. Three men came in together then, two of them the fishermen he knew by sight. He recognised the next man to arrive – Josh Ebbs. Now he was certain something was afoot, especially when Ebbs too disappeared through the same door. Two more men arrived, one much smaller than the others. He did a little jig at the bar while he called for two ales and enquired if they were the last to arrive.

'Two more,' Leo heard the landlord reply, and guessed one of them would be Mr Gaisford.

He was proved to be right a few minutes later when Luke Gaisford arrived and went straight towards the door to the back room. Tom immediately placed a bottle and two small glasses on a tray and filled two tankards. Leo guessed this was their routine. He saw Mr Gaisford open the door, momentarily halt his step and say, 'Open a window and get this damned fug out of here!' He heard a chair scrape as the door closed behind Mr Gaisford. The landlord put the two foaming tankards on the tray and went to the back room. When he returned Leo noticed he carried one glass and a full tankard. Leo took it that the second man must not be coming. He finished his own drink, bade the landlord goodnight and left the inn.

Once outside he allowed his eyes to adjust to the darkness and then made his way quietly round the building. As he had hoped and expected, the sash window of the back room had been raised. He crept quietly to it but was disappointed that a curtain had been drawn across, however that mattered little; what he wanted now was to hear what was said.

Ten minutes later he had heard enough to shock and leave him bewildered as to what he should do next.

If he told his mother and father it would brand him as a liar, for he had not been to Sennan and they would never trust him again. If he went to the authorities, would they even believe him? If they investigated further, Mr Gaisford would be in serious trouble and that could lead to ruination for Leo's own family, such was the power of the local landowner. He had told Alice about his first sighting of Mr Gaisford at the Waning Moon, maybe he should confide in her?

He was no nearer a decision by the time he reached home but after a restless night decided that, because he was meeting Alice the next day, the last option was the one he would implement.

Chapter Twenty-Four

Tess, her arms full of clean clothes from the laundry, staggered when Alice raced round the corner of the corridor leading from the domestic wing and bumped into her.

'Alice!' she gasped irritably, just saving the clothes from falling.

'Oh, sorry, Tess. I was miles away, wondering how I was going to tell you . . .'

'Tell me what?'

Alice glanced up and down the corridor. 'Not here, Tess.'

'Why?'

'Leo and I have a problem.'

Tess stared at her. 'You're not . . .' She let her words trail away but the inference was not lost on Alice.

'Of course not,' she snapped. 'I'll come and see you this evening when I finish,' she said, and hurried away leaving Tess staring after her wondering what that was all about.

She found out later when Alice recounted what Leo had told her when they'd met the previous evening.

Tess was flabbergasted by the story. 'This can't be true,' she said doubtfully while at the same time finding no reason for Leo to make up such a tale.

'That was what I thought but he swears it is. He doesn't know what to do about it.'

Tess looked thoughtful. She had never really conquered her dislike of Mr Gaisford and still wished Abigail had never married him, but she had and if Tess went to her with this story, what sort of reception would she receive? A wife would not tolerate such accusations against her husband, not without proof. But how to get it? And did Tess really want to act? Wouldn't her mistress's life be shattered if Tess were able to prove that her husband was the leader of a gang of wreckers? Maybe it would be better if she left well alone.

She pondered a few moments longer while Alice watched her anxiously. Then, a decision made, Tess said, 'Let's not do anything at the moment. Give me a little more time to decide what is best. Tell Leo to keep what he heard a secret, and if he finds out any more to let you know. We need proof. I think if the three of us witness a wrecking we stand a good chance of convincing Mrs Gaisford. Ask Leo if he can find out when there is likely to be another attempt, and warn him again not to say anything about this to anyone.'

When Alice saw Leo and told him what was wanted he wondered how he could find out when the gang would be active again. Then he remembered something he had overheard but had regarded as insignificant at the time. He had heard Andy Outhwaite being congratulated on his weather predictions.

The next morning Leo walked in the direction of the beach on which he knew the Outhwaite brothers kept their boat. Seeing them working on the timbers, he wandered over and after exchanging greetings, said, 'Repairs? Did you run into trouble?'

'Caught a rock,' said Andy. 'That young brother of mine wants to learn to avoid them,' he added with a touch of light-hearted contempt.

'He shouldn't have told me to go in closer,' Morgan retaliated.

'Will you have it ready to sail later this week?'

'Must fish tomorrow. We'll not get out for two days after that. Fog will be rolling in.'

How innocently information can be given away. Leo, who guessed that fog could provide good conditions for the wreckers, had got what he wanted but stayed chatting for another ten minutes.

After he had sauntered out of sight he quickened his pace and headed for Senewey Manor. He knew he could be rebuffed when he made a request at the servants' door to see Alice, but he had to take a chance.

His enquiry was passed to Mrs Horsefield who, when he reassured her it was a matter of urgency and that he would not make a habit of calling at the house, sent for Alice and allowed them five minutes. It was all he needed.

Alice was surprised to see him but his news that a suspected wrecking might take place the day after tomorrow alarmed her.

When Alice passed on this message, Tess battled with a dilemma. She knew the authorities should be informed of any law-breaking, but would they believe the word of a working girl against that of a landowner, a member of Cornwall's respected family? If they did, disgrace would come upon the Gaisford family and that would include Abigail too. Could she do this to the young woman who had befriended her?

Early that evening she was going to the mistress's room to turn down the bedclothes for the night when raised voices beyond the door brought her to a halt.

'You'll do as I say!'

'Not when you're saturated in drink!'

'Whenever I want!'

'Why are you drinking more these days?' There was open criticism in Abigail's tone.

'I'll drink if I want to.'

'What's made you do it this time?'

'What do you mean, this time?'

'It always seems to be when something has upset you . . .'

'And hasn't your damned father upset me? Not even a mention in his will.'

'So that's it? Money. You thought Penorna would rescue Senewey.'

'Why else did you think I married you?'

'Luke!' There was horror in her voice. 'You don't mean it! You can't?'

'I do!'

331

'It's the drink talking . . .'

'It's me. There's only one thing I want from you now – a son.'

'No, Luke!'

The sound of a vicious slap followed by a hard blow resounded through the door. Tess stiffened. Her hand flew to the door-knob but never reached it. If she opened that door the consequences could be far worse. Mr Gaisford would know what she had heard and could easily blacken her character so no one would believe anything she said. She closed her ears to the cries and protestations of her mistress and walked away, but her resolve to find proof of what Leo had heard hardened.

She spent a miserable hour before she returned to tap lightly on the door and await permission to enter.

'May I turn down the bed, miss?' Tess asked as she walked in, noticing the bed clothes in a dishevelled state.

'Yes,' called Abigail who was sitting in front of her dressing table, wiping her face and peering in the mirror. Though there was an attempt to give the usual bright reply, Tess noted the catch in Abigail's voice. That, together with the evidence she saw through the mirror, alarmed her. Abigail was trying to disguise some marks on her face with powder but she could not obliterate the cut on her forehead.

'Miss, are you all right?' cried Tess. 'You're cut. What happened?'

'It's nothing, Tess. I fell and knocked myself on the bed,' replied Abigail, trying to dismiss her concern. 'I grabbed the bed clothes to save myself, but didn't.'

Tess did not accept what she saw as a poor excuse for the state of the bed but it was not her place to comment. 'Miss, those bruises are . . .'

'Forget them,' snapped Abigail.

'I can't. I was in the corridor and heard . . . oh, if only your father was still alive!' cried Tess, the words blurted out before she could control them.

Abigail swung round on her stool. 'What do you mean?' she demanded.

For a moment Tess looked embarrassed then she knew there could be no holding back; it would be better if the truth came out. 'When we left Penorna after your wedding, your father asked me to report to him anything untoward that happened at Senewey.'

'He did what?' Shock ran through Abigail.

'He wanted me to look out for your welfare.'

'How could he do such a thing?'

'He was only thinking of you, miss. I don't think he was too keen on Mr Gaisford, and nor am I.'

'What tales have you carried to him?' cried Abigail in disgust.

'None, miss,' Tess protested quickly. 'I thought if I did it might make things worse for you with Mr Gaisford.'

'That was thoughtful of you,' replied Abigail sarcastically.

'But now, miss, after what I heard tonight, and judging by your face, I wish your father was still here.'

Abigail looked sharply at Tess and hardened her stare. 'You must tell no one, understand? No one!'

She shrugged her shoulders, a gesture of hopelessness. 'Who is there I can tell?'

'So that solves your problem.'

'Not entirely, miss.'

'What do you mean?' asked Abigail suspiciously.

Tess hesitated nervously.

'Out with it,' demanded Abigail, irritated by this.

Tess went on to relate her suspicions about Mr Gaisford's activities. As her story unfolded doubt filled Abigail's expression.

'Rubbish, Tess,' she finally exclaimed. 'These are just fanciful ideas that a young man has dreamed up for some reason of his own. Mr Gaisford wouldn't even go to a place like the Waning Moon.'

'But Leo swears he did overhear these things. He is sure the wreckers will be on the cliffs above the Gaisford harbour that has never been used, the first night there's fog.'

'Tess! That's enough! I don't know why you have got caught up in these foolish accusations. Now, let me hear no more of this nonsense.' Abigail turned back to face the mirror.

'Yes, miss.' The mistress was subdued and did not speak again as Tess went about her tasks. She left the room without a word.

Abigail sighed as the door closed. She stared at herself in the mirror but her mind turned elsewhere as thoughts came crowding in. Could there be some truth behind it? What had Tess to gain? In fact, how could Alice and Leo profit? They would only bring down Luke's wrath upon them, and she well knew that it could be of a terrible nature. If they were planning to attempt blackmail they would never have drawn Tess into it; involving a third party would have been too risky. She wondered what they would do now that she had told Tess to forget everything? Was Luke really capable of the desperate action Tess had mentioned? Abigail was sure he had financial troubles but would he resort to wrecking to solve them? She fingered her bruises and shuddered at the thought that he could be capable of anything. She spent an uneasy night as she battled with thoughts of what she should do next. By daylight she had decided that her only possible course was to seek help from Martin Granton. Close as he was to Luke, she did not believe that he would be involved in such a scheme and she knew he could be relied upon to give her sound advice.

When she'd left Abigail Tess sought out Alice. 'I've told Mrs Gaisford,' she said, but nothing about what she had overheard from the corridor or about Abigail's facial injuries.

'Oh, Tess, what will she do?'

'She doesn't believe me, said it was nonsense and I should forget it.'

'But Leo wouldn't lie to me,' Alice protested.

'I know he wouldn't,' soothed Tess.

'What can we do? Should we forget it? I don't know whether Leo will. He may go to the authorities.'

'He can't!' Tess was alarmed by this possibility. 'Tell him not to. Well, not yet. We need proof. We'll have to witness a wrecking ourselves.'

'What?' Alice was alarmed by the prospect.

'It's the only way,' Tess insisted. 'What did Leo say? Clear day tomorrow then fog the next two days?'

Alice nodded.

'You see him tomorrow and arrange that if it is foggy the following night, we'll meet him. Get him to arrange the place.'

Abigail avoided Luke at breakfast, and when she heard him go out, ordered the groom to get a horse ready for her. In doing so she remarked on the absence of Mr Gaisford's horse.

'He left for Penzance, ma'am,' came the information.

Abigail was pleased for it meant that the way would be clear for her to visit Martin.

She rode quickly to Granton Manor and was relieved to find him at home.

'This is a pleasure,' he remarked with a warm welcoming smile when she was shown into his study. He came from behind his desk, took her hand and raised it to his lips. 'You are looking particularly charming this morning.'

'I don't feel it,' she returned, and the worried expression that crossed her face then troubled Martin.

'Something on your mind?' he asked with concern as he indicated a chair.

Abigail bit her lip. 'It concerns Luke.'

'Luke?'

'Yes. I don't know whether to believe what I have heard or not. You are his best friend and a dear one to me. I could think of no one else to turn to, as you will soon realise ...' She paused as if gathering her thoughts.

'Begin at the beginning,' he prompted gently.

'Tess, my personal maid, is friendly with Alice, one of our house maids. Alice is courting Leo Gurney.'

'I know the Gurneys – fishermen, I believe.'

'That's right. Well, Leo told Alice that he had seen Luke at the Waning Moon with a gang of undesirable men he later learned were wreckers.'

'What?' Martin showed outward disbelief while his mind was racing with the possible consequences of this. He had never expected that a casual sighting could be their undoing.

'That's exactly how I reacted. But I cannot see what Leo has to gain by spreading false information. No one would take his word against Luke's.'

'So you think there could be some truth in it?' Martin still seemed surprised.

'Well, it seems Leo delved some more and swears that he overheard them plotting to cause another shipwreck. What am I to do, Martin?'

It was a plea for help he could not sidestep. Could he use it to try to turn his friend away from this nefarious trade that could only lead to doom for them all?

Martin gave a little shake of his head. 'Why would he get involved in something like this?'

'I know he's had some financial worries. Maybe he saw this as a way of solving them.'

'Surely not. He would know it was a dangerous game?'

Abigail gave a grimace. 'He's not been himself lately. Gets very irritable easily, as if he has a mountain of worries. Do you know anything?'

Martin shook his head. 'Luke always was a volatile person. He would take risks at school, and that was what endeared him to us, but they were calculated risks. He always liked activity and excitement. Whenever a new escapade came to mind he was charged with an energy that was almost over-whelming. We all saw that you had a calming effect on him and hoped with that and maturity he would settle down. Now it seems that for some reason he hasn't.'

'Can we save him from himself?' Abigail queried uneasily.

Martin hesitated. 'That could be difficult. If he is the leader of a wrecker gang he has stepped beyond the law, and with a number of men involved it will be difficult to do what you ask.'

'We must try,' she cried.

'I think for the time being you mustn't approach him or tell anyone else. Instruct the others who know to say nothing at this stage. I will see if I can find out anything more.'

She nodded. 'If you think that is the wisest thing. You are a good friend, Martin.'

'Go home and try to lead as normal a life as possible. Don't let Luke suspect that you know anything about his activities. Such knowledge could spell danger for you if it is true.'

He led her outside. When they reached her horse Abigail turned to him with tears in her eyes. 'Thank goodness you are here, Martin.'

He smiled, overwhelmed with guilt at the trust he saw in her eyes.

Wondering what she would think if she knew how he too had been sucked into Luke's scheme, he watched as she rode away.

Afterwards he walked slowly back into the house, knowing that he was faced with momentous decisions that would shape not only his future but that of others. But one thought began to predominate: Abigail must come out of this unharmed.

Two days later Tess spent an uneasy time closely watching the weather. It appeared to be settled as it was a calm sunny day but she felt almost relieved when in the late afternoon wisps of fog started to curl in from the coast. When it started to thicken about five o'clock, she quietly sought out Alice, helping in the kitchen.

'Tonight, ten o'clock,' she said and received a nod in acknowledgement.

As the hour drew near Tess spent an anxious few minutes after preparing Abigail's bed and room for the night, hoping she would not be wanted any more. She was relieved when the mistress dismissed her and she was able to hurry back to her own room. After donning suitable footwear, she fastened her cape around her shoulders. Careful to ensure that there was no one to see her, she hurried down the back staircase and out of the servants' door. She was pleased to see that Alice was already at the corner of the house. There would be no time lost in waiting. The girls fell into step and took the path that led to the coast. The fog was thick but they knew their way and reached the fork in the track, where Leo had said he would meet them, without mishap. They were disappointed to find that he was not there and spent some anxious moments stamping their feet to keep warm in the damp clinging fog.

'Where is he?' muttered Alice between teeth chattering with cold and nervousness.

The fog swirled and broke a little. In those few moments Tess's eyes tried to pierce the gloom but the fog closed in again, seeming denser than ever.

'We'll see nothing in this,' moaned Alice. 'He could walk past us and not see us.'

'I can see you.' A voice, ghostly through the fog, startled them.

They spun round, grasping at each other for reassurance. No one there! They stared into the fog that swirled, anew mocking them.

'Here.' The voice, muffled by the fog, seemed to come from another direction.

They whirled round again. A dark outline began to emerge. They felt relief when it took on human form and with one more step revealed itself to be Leo.

'Where have you been?' snapped Alice, realising that he had come from an unexpected direction.

'Been scouting around for an hour. Thought it best I be knowing something definite before you got here.'

'Have you learned anything?' asked Tess.

'Aye. They've lit lamps on the headland and two others on the cliffs at the opposite side of the harbour. Two men are ready with a boat in the harbour, two are on the headland – Mr Gaisford and one other I couldn't identify. His back was to me. The rest have gone down to the beach to the right of the headland.'

'What do we do now?' asked Alice anxiously.

'I've found a place where we will be sheltered and yet be able to see if a ship is lured in. Come on.' Leo led them along the headland turned on to a rise on their right and then down into a small hollow facing out to sea. 'Settle here,' he advised.

Pulling their capes around them, they sought a comfortable place.

'How long are we likely to be here?' asked Alice, beginning to think this was not a good idea.

'Who knows?' said Tess. 'Be patient.'

Abigail looked out of her bedroom window. Fingers of fog swirled, thinned, and disappeared to leave only ghostly moonlight. Her thoughts turned to what Tess had said. Could she be right? The fog rolled in towards the house, turning the moonlight into an eerie glow and gradually obliterating it; an ideal night for wreckers if the old stories were true. But these days? There was doubt in her mind but still the possibility tormented her. Martin had told her to do nothing, to wait to hear from him. But she hadn't so far and this waiting was too hard. She had to do something. She had to know. If Tess was right, this was likely to be a night for wreckers to go abroad.

There was only one way to find out; only one way to lay that ghost. Abigail stepped quickly to her wardrobe. She grabbed a thick cape which she flung round her shoulders; wound a kerchief round her neck and tucked it inside her cape which she fastened at her throat. Outside the house she recalled that Tess had mentioned the Gaisford harbour that had never been used so hurried in that direction, thankful that the fog had thinned a little by now. She heard the slap of the sea against the cliffs before she could see it and slowed her steps to orientate herself. She felt sure she was not far off where she wanted to be, but what should she do now? Where should she go? She tightened her lips in annoyance. What on earth was she doing out here? Why had she come? She should be fast asleep, safe in bed. She started to turn for home then stopped. A rent in the fog exposed a light further along the cliffs. Beyond that moonlight for a brief moment flirted with the water in the harbour. Was that new light there for some nefarious purpose? Did Tess's story have some foundation? If there were to be a wreck then the wreckers would be looking somewhere near the bottom of those cliffs. Could she find a way down?

She sought about her in desperation and in so doing noticed a second light along what she knew to be a rocky headland.

She recalled seeing a small stretch of sand to the right of it. Could that be where she would find the wreckers? Was that where she would discover the veracity of Tess's story? Abigail started off quickly but soon slowed her steps, reminding herself that she should be careful. There might be men posted on the cliff top. She must not be caught.

Twenty cautious steps later she received such a shock that she would have cried out but for the strong hand that had come from behind to clamp itself on her mouth. The other arm had closed round her waist in a firm hold.

A voice close to her ear said, 'It's all right, Mrs Gaisford, I'm a friend – Leo Gurney. Tess and Alice are with me. Don't make a sound or we'll all be in trouble.'

Abigail relaxed her stiffened body and gave a little nod of understanding.

Leo released his grip and whispered, 'This way, ma'am.'

In a few steps she was beside Tess and Alice.

'Miss!' Tess greeted. 'Thank goodness Alice saw you. If you had gone much further you might have run into Mr Gaisford.'

'What?' Abigail gasped, not wanting to believe this confirmation of what Tess had told her.

'I think he's nearer the end of the headland,' said Leo, 'and there's someone else with him.'

'Who?'

'I don't know. Never saw his face.'

'Then it's true?' said Abigail, sinking into despair. 'I must stop him!'

Leo grabbed her. 'Sorry, Mrs Gaisford,' he apologised. 'I had to stop you for your own sake and for ours. Show yourself even to Mr Gaisford and I reckon you'll not see the light of another day.'

'What?' cried Abigail, indignant at the implication behind his words.

'Mrs Gaisford, your husband may be the gang's leader. If he won't sacrifice you for the safety of all, the rest of the gang will turn on him and then it will be the worse for everyone. These men will be desperate to silence tongues. We've got to let matters take their course for now, and then if we want to go to the authorities we can all bear witness to the truth.'

'But I can't see my husband commit . . .'

'Miss,' broke in Tess, 'let's wait a while. It's the only thing to do.'

'Martin! There!'

He glanced in the direction in which Luke was pointing. He could see nothing but fog. 'You must have damned good eyesight.'

'There!' Excitement raced through Luke. His whole body felt a feverish thrill at the power that swelled in him. He could douse the lights now and the ship might alter course; leave them and it would surely sail to its doom. He had power over life and death, power to which he must keep returning, power which would condem some but which, if wielded wisely, would save others from the gallows. 'There! See it now, Martin?'

'Yes.'

They watched in silence for a few moments.

'She's coming our way!' said Luke, grabbing Martin's arm. 'It's a watery grave for her and her crew. No survivors!'

Martin was shocked by the glee in his friend's voice for it confirmed his inner suspicions: Luke was delighting in the murderous side of their venture as well as its financial rewards. Martin was overwhelmed by a desire to walk away from this whole filthy enterprise but he knew he could not. If he attempted it, it would be he who ended up with his head held under the sea until he drowned.

The ship came on towards them, looming larger and larger.

'She's going to founder nearer the beach!' called Luke. 'Come on, we'll get down there.'

Realising the implication behind his words, Martin was reluctant to follow, but he had to otherwise he would be a marked man. They were soon at the terraced face of the cliff that would give them ready access to the beach and to the men already there, awaiting the vessel fast sailing towards her end.

Not far from Luke and Martin four figures stood as if in a trance. Each one felt the urge to shout out and halt the ship in its tragic course but they were rooted to the spot by the spell of doom. A movement close by startled them and they saw two figures suddenly materialise and climb quickly along the cliff to their right.

'They're going down,' said Leo, knowing the lie of the land from his earlier foray.

'Are we going too?' asked Tess.

'We'll have to if we want full proof of what is happening.'

But no one moved. It seemed as if the three friends had silently relinquished authority to Abigail, and she knew it. She appreciated their concern for her and for what the expected discovery could do to her. She sensed that if she called a halt to this they would respect her decision, leave her to deal with it privately and say not a word. But she could not walk away from what would happen on the beach; she had to know the truth. 'We must go down,' she said.

'Very well, ma'am, follow me,' said Leo. 'Keep close and be careful. The descent can be tricky in parts. Don't make a noise . . . and, whatever you do, don't be seen.'

They slipped away into the fog, their attention divided between finding footholds and observing the ship. It was momentarily cloaked by the mist that soon drifted away, allowing them to see the vessel on course for destruction. It was close to them by the time they'd reached the beach without mishap. Leo ushered them into the shelter of some rocks from which they could see the ship only as a darker mass in the fog that had thickened round it again. They saw figures moving about near the cliff face. The ship was looming over them now and they froze. The next instant the vessel foundered and brought with it the splintering sounds of timber and the crashing of masts as she heeled over. Shouts rent the air. Cries for help dwindled from the helpless vessel as it broke up.

Figures moved from the foot of the cliffs, ran along the beach to the vessel and clambered on board, risking being lost themselves as it made a last attempt to right herself. The fog swirled away from the moon, allowing it to bathe the scene in a white light.

Abigail gasped to see the frenzied activity and had to stifle the cry that sprang to her lips when she saw fighting break out. There was no attempt to rescue the crew. Instead she saw men forcibly dragged into the sea and held under. She wanted to intervene but then was struck dumb in horror as she recognised Luke among the attackers, urging the others on, fending off an assault that resulted in his heaving his attacker overboard and then jumping in after him to make sure he drowned. Shouts of triumph, alarm and terror filled the night air. Not even the rolling fog could muffle them nor hide the horrific sights. Abigail shuddered. She felt Tess slide a hand into hers. Alice trembled in Leo's arms.

'Abigail!' A whisper so close by startled them all.

They swung round in alarm.

'Martin!' Abigail's soft exclamation was filled with horror. 'You and Luke?' They must be together or why was Martin here? When she had spoken to him at Granton Manor he had not revealed that he was a member of Luke's gang, yet here he was at the scene of a wreck. The thought almost overwhelmed her. She had betrayed what she knew and suspected; now no doubt Luke would come to know of it and she feared the consequences. 'Martin! You've betrayed me!'

Shocked by her accusation, he stepped forward and grabbed her by the shoulders. 'I haven't. There's much to say but you are all in too much danger now.'

'It'll be worse when you expose us.'

'Never!' he cried, desperately wanting her to believe him.

'If you aren't in league with Luke, why are you here?'

'It's a long story, but I want no part of what is going on now. The gang will be coming this way to go up the cliffs. I know another path further along the beach which they don't. Trust me! Come on . . .' He took Abigail's arm and hustled her away. The others followed. They kept as near to the rising land as they could, using it as camouflage to lessen discovery, but the wrecker gang was too preoccupied to think that anyone else might be on the beach.

'Why did you . . .'

Martin halted her. 'We'll talk later. Another two hundred yards and we'll be clear of the route they will take to the top.'

When they'd passed that mark he still urged them on. Another two hundred yards and they came to a cleft where the cliffs started rising again at the end of the strand.

'It's a bit of a stiff climb but manageable,' he informed them. 'I'll go first to show you the best way. You, young man, bring up the rear.'

'Yes, sir! Leo, sir.'

'Right, Leo, make sure no one falls.'

'Won't you be missed?' asked Abigail with concern.

'It's easy to go astray in a mêlée. I'll think of some explanation later.'

'What's Luke doing?'

'Talk later,' he said. 'We must get . . .'

'Wait!' Tess urged. 'I heard a cry! Listen.'

Above the surge of the sea on the beach they heard splashing.

'Someone's floundering,' said Leo quietly.

They listened with deep concentration. The splashing sounds continued and then they heard a gasp for breath followed by a scrambling across shingle and the sound of someone falling to the ground, followed by a groan.

'There!' whispered Tess.

They saw a figure struggling to get up.

Martin and Leo rushed forward.

The figure started and dropped to its knees, as if giving up. 'No! No!' He shuddered and threw up one arm to ward off the expected blow.

Martin was kneeling beside him. 'We are friends,' he said vehemently. 'Friends!'

The man stared at him in disbelief.

'Come on.' Martin got one arm under his right shoulder and Leo supported him on the left. They stumbled up the beach to join Abigail, Tess and Alice.

The man started in bewilderment on seeing three females.

'No time for explanations now,' said Martin. 'You are safe. Can you make the top? That's a nasty gash on your forehead, and there's another on your thigh.'

'Not surprising after being held under water and being left for drowned. I fooled them into believing it. But don't worry, I'll get to the top. I'll do anything to escape that murderous crew and see they get what they deserve.'

His remark sent a chill through Abigail. Here she was, helping a witness who could condemn her own husband to the gallows.

Chapter Twenty-Five

The climb was hard but the sailor met the difficulties resolutely, ignoring the reopening of the wound on his thigh. Aided largely by Leo while Martin helped the ladies, he reached the top. They all collapsed on the grass, drawing gulps of air into their heaving lungs. Silently they fought to steady their nerves and forget the horrors they had witnessed.

After a few minutes Martin had scrambled into a sitting position when he heard Abigail say, 'What are we going to do now?' Sensing her helplessness before the dilemma that faced her, he said in a comforting tone, 'We'd better get away from here before we decide.' He got to his feet and helped her from the ground. The others followed suit. He turned to the seaman. 'I'm Martin Granton,' he said, then introduced Abigail who took over to give the names of the others.

'Noel Ford, Captain of the *Lady Jane* – the vessel you saw lured to her doom by that pack of scoundrels!' Anger and bitterness resonated in his voice.

'Captain?' asked Martin.

'Aye. You think I'm too young? Maybe, but I've been at sea since I was ten. I worked hard, determined to become captain before I was twenty-five. I succeeded. At twenty-three this was my first command. Now I'll have to prove I was not to blame for losing my ship. Thank God I have you all as witnesses.'

'We've got to find you a safe hiding place,' put in Martin quickly before anyone could comment on Ford's remark. 'The wreckers will soon be swarming all over this area.'

While Leo took the lead, Abigail dropped back to walk with Martin at the rear. She touched his arm and slowed her pace to open up a gap between them and the others.

'Where are we going to hide him?' she asked anxiously.

'Senewey and Granton are out of the question. Penorna is a possibility but I'd rather the hiding place were more remote. Maybe Leo can help.' He called softly to the fisherman who dropped back. 'Leo, we need to decide where to hide Captain Ford. It will only be a temporary measure. We can't go to Senewey, Granton or Penorna. Have you somewhere where you keep your boat?'

'Aye. We have two boathouses on the beach, little more than shelters for the boat. Nobody else uses them. I'll put it right with Father.'

'Good. It will only be for a short while, to give him a chance to recover and for us to decide what to do because his first reaction will be to go to the authorities. Take him to the beach and wait with him there until I return from escorting the women to Senewey. Don't tell him anything until I get there.' After another half-mile he halted the party at a fork in the track. 'Captain Ford, I want you to go with Leo. He'll shelter you until I get back. I'll explain everything then, but for now I must see the ladies get home safely.'

The seaman nodded. He must bow to Martin's superior knowledge of the district. He did not want to stumble on the wreckers and was besides drained by his terrible experiences. After witnessing his crew being murdered and having been on the verge of death himself, he felt both physical and mental exhaustion.

Martin left Abigail and her maids at the servants' entrance to Senewey, warning them to say nothing to anyone and await word from him.

Reaching the beach used by the Gurneys, Martin saw that the two buildings were in a dilapidated state but would at least provide shelter. Double doors hung limp on their hinges, stonework was crumbling. In a corner of one shed the roof had fallen in. Leo was standing close to one of the doors. When Martin went inside he saw that the young lad had made the seaman as comfortable as possible, propping him against a boat and covering him with a piece of old sail.

Thinking him asleep, Martin asked Leo quietly, 'How is he?'

Captain Ford caught the words and replied, 'Safe, thanks to you.'

'Tess should take the credit,' said Martin as he and Leo came to the sailor. 'She was the one who heard you in the sea. No one else did.'

'Then I am grateful to her. I hope we shall meet again.'

'We must see to your recovery first,' said Martin gently. 'That is a nasty gash on your forehead but at least it has stopped bleeding. How is your leg?'

Noel Ford winced as he sought to ease it. 'Hurts like hell after that climb, but it has stopped bleeding since Leo got me here. I think you'll have to get a doctor, though. The sooner the better. Then I can call those blackguards to justice and prove it was not my own incompetence that caused the wreck. I must clear my name and save my career.'

Martin hesitated then said, 'I have some explaining to do myself. It is important that you listen carefully.'

The serious note in his voice caught Captain Ford's attention.

'We were not on the beach by accident.' Martin's bold statement alarmed him.

'You weren't part of that gang?' he asked, a tremor of fear in his voice.

'Please listen,' Martin requested, and went on to explain why exactly they were at the scene of the wrecking. When he had finished his story, he added, 'So, you see, there is more at stake here than merely bringing these men to justice. For my part I regret ever becoming involved, but rest assured I took no part in what happened tonight after your ship struck. I was sickened by what was going on and sought to leave the whole vile undertaking.'

Captain Ford nodded. 'You are an honourable man, Mr Granton, otherwise you would not have committed yourself to my rescue. With my death there would have been no one to bring an accusation against the wreckers, and you could have resolved your problem with your friend without anyone else knowing. I also see that if I pursue my quest for justice, with support from you and the others, I will be endangering all your lives and Mrs Gaisford's name will be besmirched forever. I need to consider my next move carefully. Why not leave me here and come back in the morning?'

'I'll stay with him, Mr Granton,' offered Leo.

Ford smiled. 'You needn't do that. I couldn't get far in my present state.'

Leo looked askance at Martin, but seeing him nod knew that he too had to trust this man.

When they went outside the fisherman said, 'I'll bring him some breakfast in the morning, sir.'

'Good. What about your parents?'

'I'll fix it with them.'

'Very well. I'll be back in the morning.'

As he made his way to the cliff top where he and Luke had left their horses, Martin was still wary of running into one of the gang.

Luke leaped from rock to rock until he reached a position from which he could survey the beach. The breeze that had made itself felt in the last few minutes was beginning to tear rents in the fog and reveal the whole scene bathed in ghostly moonlight. He stood with feet apart and body braced, revelling in the knowledge that he had been responsible for such destruction and killing. He chuckled deep in his throat then threw back his head and laughed aloud, letting the sound fill him with the sweetness of success.

He watched his men moving the cargo along the beach and up the cliff towards its allotted hiding places. He surveyed the wreck, lazily swaying in the sea, and knew that even if it were seen before the waters claimed it as their own, it would merely be regarded as an unfortunate casualty of the fog. No evidence of deliberate wrecking would remain. Satisfied that all was going to his liking, he wondered where Martin was. No doubt he would be taking care of the salvage.

Luke climbed steadily to the cliff top, pausing frequently to look back on the scene with a high degree of satisfaction. Reaching the horses, he hoped nothing had happened to his friend in the general mayhem. He was sure it hadn't; Martin was capable of looking after himself. Well, there was no point in waiting, he would see him tomorrow.

He climbed into the saddle and urged his horse recklessly along the track.

At Senewey he quickly unsaddled the horse himself, as was his practice when he had been out late, threw a blanket over it and went into the house. He hung his redingote and hat in the lobby and went quietly up the stairs. He had taken two steps along the corridor that passed Abigail's room to his own when he stopped. His eye had caught a mark on the carpet. Annoyance tightened his lips. Someone wasn't keeping the place clean. About to move on, he dropped to one knee instead to examine the mark more closely. He reached down and fingered it. Damp! It had been made recently. And something in it felt rough. He brushed his hand firmly across it. Sand! Who had been out tonight? And then he wondered where, and what exactly they might they have seen. He straightened up thoughtfully and went to his room.

Tess sat on her bed, wondering how Abigail was reacting to the knowledge that her husband was the leader of a band of wreckers. She glanced at the coat she had thrown on the bed and thought she had better put it away. As she picked it up she remembered being a little way behind Abigail on their climb up the cliff and seeing a neckerchief lying in front of her. It must have come loose in the effort of the climb and slipped unnoticed from Abigail's neck. She remembered picking it up and stuffing it into her own pocket where it had lain forgotten until now. She must return it at once. Abigail might be wondering what had happened to it and worrying it was lying somewhere, evidence of where she had been.

Tess slipped from her room and hurried quietly through the house. Turning into the corridor that led to Abigail's room, she pulled herself back instinctively. Her heart was thundering. Mr Gaisford was in the corridor! She should get quietly away, she knew, but what was he doing on his knees, examining the floor? Tess peeped round the corner again. He was rubbing his hand on the carpet. He rose slowly, muttering to himself. She wished she could have heard what he was saying. He paused a moment and then continued on his way. When she saw him enter his own room Tess breathed more freely. Though she knew she should return to hers, curiosity got the better of her. When she reckoned Mr Gaisford was settled, she moved silently to the spot he had been rubbing and ran her own hand over the carpet. Sand! It must have come from Abigail's shoes. Could Mr Gaisford be wondering how it came to be there? Could he possibly think his wife had been at the scene of the wreck? Alarm coursed through Tess. Abigail must be warned!

'I must see you, miss,' whispered Tess, tapping at the mistress's door.

The note of alarm and concern in her voice made Abigail unlock the door.

'What is it?' she whispered.

'I brought you this. You dropped it as we were climbing the cliff.' Tess held out the neckerchief which Abigail took.

'Oh, my goodness. A good job you saw it. But by the look on your face there's more to this visit than that?'

'Yes, miss. It's what I've just seen and discovered.' Tess went on to relate her experience of the last few minutes.

'Oh, no!' gasped Abigail when she had finished. 'I never thought of that.'

'Mr Gaisford can't know it's you.'

'But as the mark is in this corridor, he may conclude I left it.'

'Give me the shoes you were wearing. I'll clean any sand off them then there'll be nothing to link you to it. Other people could have used that corridor. Me, for example. We must be careful not to give him any reason to suspect you.'

'I must warn Mr Granton of this latest development and find out what he's doing about that unfortunate Captain Ford.'

'In the morning, miss. You can't do anything now.'

351

When Tess came down the following morning to attend to Abigail she found her, in spite of yesterday's revelations, in control of her self. Nevertheless Tess felt duty bound to warn her, 'Miss, if you are going to see Mr Granton today, be careful, Mr Gaisford may want to see him too.'

'I shall, Tess. Thank you for your concern.'

With those words in mind Abigadil paused at the door to the dining room, wondering if Luke was there. She drew herself up. He had to be faced some time and the outcome of their meeting could have a profound effect on her future. She opened the door and went in.

Luke rose politely from his chair, looking rested and composed. 'Good morning to you, my dear! I trust you had a good night?' He flashed her a dazzling smile.

Abigail almost overreacted. Was this the same man she had seen on the beach? 'I did, thank you. I trust you did too?' She sat down and a maid immediately came forward to pour her coffee as she always did.

'I had a splendid night. Don't think I've ever slept better.'

Abigail glanced at the maid. 'I'll have my usual, please.'

'Yes, ma'am.' The young woman left for the kitchen.

As soon as the door closed, Luke directed his attention to his wife. 'I have a problem for you to solve, my dear.'

Abigail cocked one eyebrow at him as she took her first sip of coffee.

'When I came home last night, I found some sand on the carpet in our corridor. You know I don't like such sloppiness. I want you to find out who made it and why they hadn't cleaned it off immediately.'

'Sand? Well, I'll see it's dealt with but is it worth all the fuss of finding out who left it?'

'I want to know.'

'It may be difficult to discover. Whoever did it may not even know they did so.'

'You investigate and find me the culprit!' His eyes narrowed and she could not evade his scrutiny as he declared. 'I will expect an answer when I get home.'

'Very well.' Abigail nodded. 'Will you be late?' she added casually, hoping he would not sidestep the question.

'I have to see Martin this morning and then I must go to St Just and St Ives on business so may not be back until the day after tomorrow. You'll have plenty of time to solve our little puzzle.' He laid his napkin on the table and stood up just as the maid returned with Abigail's breakfast. 'I must away, my dear.' He came to her and kissed her on the cheek.'

When the door closed she sagged with relief. She knew who had unwittingly made that mark – she had herself. Thank goodness Luke had automatically thought it must have been a servant. She would have to make a pretence of questioning them all but could not throw the blame on anyone. But if she had no evidence to lay against anyone, might Luke suspect her? If so then she was in great danger for he would fear that anyone abroad that night might have witnessed the wreckers at work. She was relieved. She still had some time to play with but could not make her first move until this afternoon. She must give Luke time to be clear of Granton Manor before she sought out Martin.

Martin was heading for the stables when he heard the sound of an approaching horse. He went to the front of the house and saw Luke. His lips tightened. Damn! How long would he stay? Martin needed to see the captain of the *Lady Jane* as soon as possible.

'Morning, Martin,' called Luke as he brought his horse to a halt. 'What happened to you last night? Your mount was still there when I left.'

'Didn't think to wait, did you? Anything could have happened to me in that affray,' he muttered sarcastically.

'I knew you could take care of yourself.'

Martin ignored the remark and said, 'For all you knew a knife might have split me open.'

'Apparently it didn't, so stop being grumpy. It was a good night's work.'

'Was it?'

'You should have been there to see the cargo. You'd be dancing a merry jig now if you had. We'll make a lot of money out of this one and that should make you happy.'

Martin's face took on a grim expression. 'I don't like this slaughtering of the innocent.' The words were out before he realised it. He silently cursed himself for being a fool. Luke would not tolerate a weak link.

His friend's eyes narrowed.

Martin had seen this look in them before. He knew he should take it as a warning. A break with Luke now could prove catastrophic. He had to be sure he didn't endanger other people.

'Sick of it?' Luke queried. 'You know why we could leave no survivors.'

Martin held up a hand. 'Yes, I know. But I thought some of the men got too carried away last night.'

Luke laughed out loud. 'Squeamish now, are we? I can't restrain them, Martin, it's part of what makes them such good wreckers. You and I don't have to kill like they do so take no notice of their handiwork. Just think of the money which will save Granton Manor.'

Martin was almost on the point of saying, 'You *did* kill, I saw you. And I've seen the blood lust in your eyes before. I've seen the demons take over.' But he held his tongue. To speak now would to betray everything, and he knew if he did so he would not live long. Instead he asked lamely, 'Why are you here this morning? I thought we were not to meet again for a week?'

'Friendly concern, old boy.' He clapped an arm round Martin's shoulders. 'I wondered what had happened to you.' Luke glanced curiously at his friend. 'What *did* happen?'

'I was in the sea, fighting one of the sailors. We were getting deeper and deeper into the water and he was getting the better of me when a hand grabbed him, pulled him off and pushed him under. The tide swept me away then and I came ashore further down the coast.'

Luke nodded. 'Thank God you made it safely back. I can't afford to lose my old friend. Now that I'm satisfied you are all right, I must be on my way. Off to St Just and St Ives.'

Martin had no need to ask him why. He knew that when they met in a week's time Luke would have buyers lined up for the commodities he would pass off as the fruits of legitimate trading.

As soon as Luke had gone Martin hurried to the stables and in a matter of minutes was riding for the Gurneys' boathouse. He was thankful when he saw Leo talking to his father outside the shelter.

'Good day, Mr Gurney,' he said amiably.

'Good day to you.' He eyed Martin. 'I don't like what my boy has got himself into, sir, I'll tell you straight, and all I can say is, I think you should go to the authorities immediately.'

'If we do that, Mr Gurney, innocent people will be hurt and lives will be shattered. All I want is time to work this out. If I can't, I'll lay everything before the authorities myself. Please, Mr Gurney, bear with me.'

'Pa, please do as Mr Granton asks. Alice is one of the people who would be affected.'

Mr Gurney pondered his son's plea. 'What about him in there?' He indicated the shelter. 'He's calling for justice for his crew.'

'I explained things to him last night when we brought him here.' said Martin 'I'll have another talk with him. How is he?'

'I don't like the look of that leg,' put in Mr Gurney. 'He needs proper care and attention.'

'Right, I'll see to it,' said Martin, not knowing what he would do but realising that he had to put on a show of authority and reassurance. 'Now I'll have a word with him.'

In spite of the captain's pleas for him to go to the authorities, Martin persuaded him to wait a few days. He agreed on condition that if Martin couldn't find a solution by then, he would seek official help.

It was an anxious ride back to Granton Manor but he was still no nearer solving his problem by the time he walked into the house.

He was still battling with it when Abigail arrived.

'Thank goodness you are here,' she said when she was shown to his study and they were alone. 'I have a problem.'

'So have I,' replied Martin.

'Did Luke visit you this morning?'

'Yes.'

'Did he say anything about what he found at Senewey last night?'

'No?' Alarm came into Martin's eyes.

Abigail quickly told him about the mark on the carpet. 'I can't blame any of the staff and that will lead him to one conclusion – it was made by me.'

'We've got to do something to dispel that idea.'

'We have time to think of it. He's likely to be away until the day after tomorrow.'

'Oh, thank goodness.' Martin heaved a great sigh of relief. 'He didn't tell me that. Meanwhile I've got to decide what to do about Captain Ford. He needs medical attention and can't get it where he is. I've got to move him, but where to?'

They turned over some possibilities. It was only when they were trying to keep their spirits up with a cup of tea that Abigail had an idea.

'I know someone in Penzance who might help.'

'Who?' asked Martin.

'You probably don't know her. Dorinda Jenkins was my governess until she went to look after her ailing father, a shopkeeper there. After he died she kept the business on. When she was my governess she became friendly with another one at Trethtowan named Lydia Booth. Miss Booth left her situation there when her sister-in-law was ill in childbirth. Alas, she died. Because her brother would have nothing to do with the child, Lydia brought her back to Cornwall and settled in Penzance. Dorinda and Lydia renewed their friendship then and Dorinda grew fond of the child too. Unfortunately Lydia died and it was thought it might be a good idea for the child, who was nearly ten by then, to go into service. She came to Penorna as my personal maid. You've met her – Tess.'

'The girl who was with you last night?'

356

'Yes. She alerted me to the whole sorry tale when Leo told her friend Alice. Oh, I didn't believe it at first, but there were certain things that made me wonder.'

'So that's how you came to be on the beach?'

'Yes. Now I can see a possible solution to helping the captain. I think Dorinda might do it, especially if we take Tess along to ask.'

Martin got to his feet. 'You and I will ride into Penzance now and see Miss Jenkins.'

'No, Martin, that could be a waste of time. You take a coach and pick up the captain. I'll go to Senewey to prepare Tess. You come via the house and then we'll all go to Penzance together.'

'But what if Miss Jenkins won't agree to help?'

'Then we'll just have to bring him back and think again, but I think she will.'

Within the hour Abigail and Tess were climbing into the coach at Senewey.

The captain remembered them. After they had settled down he addressed Tess directly. 'I believe I have you to thank for my survival.'

'Me?' She looked puzzled.

'Yes. I'm told if it hadn't been for your sharp ears, I might not be here now. No one else heard me in the sea.'

Tess blushed at the warmth of his glance. 'That was nothing.'

'It was a great deal,' he said. 'Thank you.' His thoughts were responding to the attractive girl whom he judged was only a year or so younger than himself.

'You'll not do anything to betray my mistress, will you?' she cried.

'I'll have to explain the loss of my ship and clear my own name of any blame, but for your sake I'll try to avoid any mention of your mistress,' he replied quietly.

The ride to Penzance was not an easy one for the captain; the movement of the carriage jarred his injured leg and sent pain shooting through him. At the particularly rough sections of road it took all his willpower to stop himself from crying out. At one point it was so bad he instinctively grabbed Tess's hand for support. For the briefest of moments she was inclined to pull it away but instinct told her he needed her help. She held his hand tightly, sensing his suffering. Even under these circumstances his touch brought feelings to her she had never experienced before. Though she knew that the sooner they reached Penzance, the better it would be for the sailor, still a part of her was wishing this journey could go on forever.

Although Martin needed to concentrate on handling the horse he managed to carry on a low-voiced conversation with Abigail who was sitting on the box beside him.

'Knowing what you do now, will you return to Senewey?'

'What else can I do? I am Luke's wife. He does not know I witnessed the wrecking and appeared perfectly normal this morning.'

'Be careful, Abigail. You may not have experienced it yet but Luke is highly volatile.' He glanced at her as he spoke and caught a grimace on her face that alarmed him. 'You have already seen his unpleasant side?'

Denials sprang to Abigail's lips but she held them back, realising that Martin had guessed the truth and knowing in her heart of hearts that she badly needed a confidant she could trust. She felt a closeness to this man despite his long association with her husband.

She nodded.

'Has he mistreated you?'

Abigail bit her lip. 'Yes.'

'On more than one occasion?'

She nodded, tears welling in her eyes. She wiped them away. She must not break down now. She glanced through the coachman's window and saw that Tess and the captain were engrossed in conversation inside the cariage.

'Abigail, you can't go back to Senewey.'

'I must. I'm his wife.'

'Then you will be in danger. I've seen blood lust in Luke's eyes recently. It's a heightening of a trait I have seen in him before, even when we were at school. I'm worried for you, Abigail.'

The tremor in his voice reflected the feelings he had kept hidden from her; it made her wonder if deep down there had been reciprocal feelings within herself. She automatically laid her hand on his arm as she said, 'And you will be in danger too. He will learn of your part in saving the captain, I'm afraid.'

'I can take care of myself. It is you I'm worried about.'

They fell into a charged silence.

The coach rumbled into Penzance. Following Abigail's directions, Martin brought the vehicle to a halt outside Miss Jenkins's shop.

'Come on, Tess,' called Abigail as she eased herself down. With a reassuring smile at Captain Ford, Tess slipped out of the coach and followed her into the shop. Within a few moments one of Dorinda's assistants had brought her from the house. She expressed delight at seeing her friends and quickly ushered them into her drawing room. She realised from their serious expressions that something was troubling them.

'Dorinda, we need your help ...' Abigail explained the captain's plight as clearly and concisely as possible. 'He needs to be kept hidden otherwise he could be in great danger. Can you help us?'

Dorinda glanced from one to the other. She could not avoid the pleading expression on Tess's face. 'I'll do what I can. Bring him in.'

Relief swept over them all. Tess hugged Dorinda and said, 'Oh, thank you,' with such heartfelt meaning her old friend wondered what lay behind it.

'Wait a moment!' Dorinda called them to a halt. 'I'll send my assistants to the storeroom then they won't see anything from the shop window. When the way is clear, bring him to the side door.'

They made a show of saying their goodbyes to Dorinda in the shop. Outside they awaited her signal and then quickly took Captain Ford to the side door where Dorinda awaited them. She assessed his condition at a glance and led the way upstairs to one of her spare bedrooms. They left Martin, who had brought clean clothes from Senewey, to attend to the captain and see him comfortably to bed.

Back in the drawing room, Abigail further explained their reasons for bringing the captain to Dorinda and swore her to secrecy.

When Martin came downstairs he announced, 'Captain Ford is going to need a doctor. Do you know of one who can be trusted to keep his presence here a secret?'

'I will attend to that,' said Dorinda confidently. 'I'm friendly with Dr Bushell who was widowed four years ago. I can trust him.'

Tess remembered Dr Bushell and was pleased at the implication she read behind this, but made no comment.

'Good.' Martin addressed Tess. 'Captain Ford was asking to see you before you left.'

Her blushes did not go unnoticed by Dorinda who looked enquiringly at Abigail when the door had closed behind Tess.

'It was Tess who saved him from the sea,' she explained. 'She was the only one who heard him.'

Tess knocked tentatively at the bedroom door and then entered shyly. Captain Ford smiled and held out his hand. 'I want to thank you again for saving my life.'

She took his hand and felt the same sensation as she had experienced in the coach. 'I only said I'd heard something.'

'No one else did,' he pointed out. 'And if you hadn't, I might have perished there. I will always be in debt to you.'

'You can repay me by getting well and not endangering the lives of my mistress and friends.'

'I must clear my own name but I'll do it without implicating them, I promise, though I might need a witness . . .'

'Then use me, not them.'

He looked at her with open admiration. 'You are such a loyal person.'

Her face reddened as she met his gaze. 'I must go.' She let her hand slip from his.

'Please come and visit me again?'

'I will,' she promised with an encouraging smile.

On reaching Senewey Manor Abigail invited Martin to partake of some refreshments and he accepted readily. Tess hurried away to her own room then went to find Alice to reassure her that Captain Ford had been taken care of and she herself had nothing to fear so long as she told no one of what had happened.

As they settled at the dining room table the contrast between this quiet domestic scene and the enormity of the dilemma that faced her was almost too much for Abigail to bear. Her world, the one she had dreamed about when she'd married the handsome heir to Senewey, lay in ruins around her. She felt bereft, with no one to turn to who could truly help her unless it was this man, the one who had saved her last night. But Martin had his own problems to contend with too. Luke would see any help he offered her as a betrayal of him, and Luke's machinations could be deadly.

The question that occupied both their minds was voiced by Abigail. 'What should we do? Face him with the truth or say nothing and hope he never learns of it?'

'I think both of those would be dangerous. You would be on a knife-edge all the time, and I know Luke would be sharp enough to detect it and want to know why. You already know what *that* could mean for you.'

'I'll have to risk it. I can't walk out on my own husband. Think of the scandal.'

'Isn't that better than what you may suffer at his hands?'

Abigail shrugged her shoulders as if resigned to staying and accepting the consequences. 'What about you? You've been part of this horrible affair. Luke is not just going to let you walk away. You would be too much of a threat to him. And I think, in clearing his name, Captain Ford is bound to reveal so much of the truth that the finger will be pointed at Luke. That could implicate you too.'

'I can only think it would be safer for me to leave. Come with me, Abigail, don't try and outface Luke.'

'But he might never know I witnessed what happened. And if I left too, it could look like marital desertion. That you and I were lovers.'

'Oh, that we were!' Martin immediately made a gesture as if to pluck back these words. He knew he should never have uttered them, but they were out and in a way he did not regret it for he saw sympathy in Abigail's eyes and knew that she had guessed something of his feelings before now.

She reached out and took his hand. 'Another place, another time, who knows? But we must play the cards we've been dealt. I cannot run away even under these circumstances.'

'Luke will not be back until the day after tomorrow,' Martin pointed out, then added a final piece of advice. 'In the meantime, think things over very carefully.'

Chapter Twenty-Six

When he had gone Abigail felt very alone. She needed some-one to talk to who wasn't directly involved in what had happened. How she wished her parents were still alive! Had her father seen traits in Luke that she, love-struck, had been blind to? Had the old rivalries between the families still troubled him even though there had been that reconciliation on her birthday? And had this led him to ask Tess to contact him if she observed anything untoward? Why hadn't she herself heeded her parents' doubts? Why hadn't she been aware of Martin's feelings towards her – if only he had pressed his case then, what might have been … She realised it would have made no difference, though. Her love for Luke at that time had been all consuming. Now she was lost without that certainty in her life.

By late afternoon she was no nearer solving her problem but then a name began to impinge on her mind – Mrs Gaisford. Luke's mother might help her. Abigail knew all was not well between mother and son, but would Hester talk against him? She recalled Luke's behaviour when she had visited his mother. Shuddered at it, in fact. Once again she wondered what lay behind his isolation of Hester, his reason for forbidding his wife to talk to her. There was only one way to find out. Abigail made her way to the West Wing.

'Ah, my dear, I'm so pleased to have your company,' Hester greeted her warmly.

'And I am pleased to see you, Mrs Gaisford,' replied Abigail, taking a seat opposite her mother-in-law.

'How have you been?' asked Mrs Gaisford.

'Very well.'

Hester gave a little knowing smile. 'Maybe, but I think something is troubling you.'

'Very shrewd,' said Abigail with a grimace.

'And that look tells me it concerns my son. You can tell me, if you like?'

Abigail did not answer immediately.

'It is best to begin at the beginning. Don't spare my feelings. I know what my son can be like.'

Almost before she knew it, the words were pouring out of Abigail and the sordid story lay before Mrs Gaisford.

Hester shook her head sadly. 'I feared things would go this way. I hoped not. But I have seen much of my husband's character reproduced in Luke, and unfortunately all his worst traits. I suffered greatly at his hands, both physically and mentally. Oh, Jeremy was the catch of the county when I was young – he was a Gaisford, after all. I soon realised he had married me only to outdo his rivals.' Hester gave a wistful smile. 'I used to be the belle of every ball then. You would not think so to look at me now, but young men courted me in droves and Jeremy did not like it so swept me off my feet, and up the aisle. The biggest mistake I ever made! My life became a misery to me. I had to be there whenever he wanted me. I had to do his will. He would mock me and flaunt his liaisons with other women, knowing I dare not do anything about it. I tried once. That's when the beatings started. They were worse when he was in drink, and at those times he was cruel to Luke too.'

She shook her head sadly at the recollection and dropped it in shame as she added, 'And I did nothing about it, frightened to turn Jeremy's wrath even more fiercely against me. I turned Luke away when he sought protection in front of his father and afterwards he did not even seek it in private, thinking I was privy to all that was happening. And that is why I am here now, shut away from everyone except the two servants charged to see my basic needs. Luke is punishing me for not lifting a hand to save him from his father. I could see the ill

364

treatment was having a marked effect on him, but hoped you would have a steadying influence on him and make him into the man I always believed he could be. And now he has revived the notorious trade of wrecking and taken lives to line his own pockets. He has sunk too far. His father was bad but would even he have done this?'

'What should I do, Mrs Gaisford?' Abigail pleaded.

She hesitated only for the briefest of moments. 'Leave! Go, my dear, go!'

'But I'm his wife.'

'Give that no countenance. If you stay, your life will be a misery to you as mine was to me. In fact, I believe in your case it would be worse. My husband never killed, but from what you saw Luke do on the beach there's no telling how far he will go. He could harm you. Leave him to take the consequences once this sea captain sees justice done.' A catch came to her voice as she added, 'I wish I'd had the courage to leave my husband. Don't make the same mistake.'

'Thank you for listening, Mrs Gaisford, and I'm sorry to bring you such news.'

Hester dismissed the apology with a wave of her hand. 'I'm pleased you did. I see my son at his true worth. I long ago stopped trying to make excuses for him.'

'And thank you for your advice.'

'Heed it, my dear. Go and don't look back. Only remember me.'

Abigail hugged and kissed her, and said, 'I will, Mrs Gaisford. Goodbye.'

With a saddened heart, Hester watched her daughter-in-law leave.

Abigail's new determination quickened her step as she returned to her room. Mrs Gaisford had made her see that the only course for her was to leave. She called for Tess and was already changing into her riding habit when the girl appeared.

'Tess, I want to pack our essentials. You and I leave here tomorrow morning.'

The order set Tess's mind into a whirl. 'Where are we going, miss?'

'I don't know. I'm on my way to see Mr Granton now to discuss that. Unless this trouble blows over very quickly we won't be coming back here. At least, not for a considerable time.'

Tess sensed urgency in her mistress's words. In a way she was not surprised they were leaving; she knew there would be danger here after what they had witnessed, and was glad that they would not be under Mr Gaisford's continued scrutiny, but her heart was wounded by the thought that she might not see Captain Ford again.

'Tell no one about this, Tess, no one! Just have everything ready.'

During the few minutes Abigail had to wait impatiently while the under-groom prepared a horse for her, she fought to keep her mind focused on the decision she had made. She rode fast to Granton Manor and was quickly shown into the drawing room to await Martin.

He hurried into the room at the servant's summons. 'Abigail, what brings you here so soon?'

'I'm leaving, Martin, early in the morning. I thought you should know.'

'I'm glad. I think it's the best course for you.'

'What about you? I feel I'm deserting you.'

'Don't think that.'

'But it worries me to think about what might happen to you.' She caught his gaze and added impetuously, 'Come with me, out of danger.' He hesitated. 'Why not?' Abigail prompted.

'There is no reason why I shouldn't . . .'

'Then do it. Don't leave yourself at Luke's mercy.'

'Where have you planned to go?'

'I was at a loss at first but on the way here an idea came to me. I have an aunt in Whitby, father's sister Martha, of whom I have only faint memories. Whitby's on the Yorkshire coast, surely far enough away from Luke.'

'But does he know of her?'

'I don't think so. He took little notice of the wedding invitations, only providing a list of the people he wanted inviting. Aunt Martha was ill at the time so could not come. When Father and Mother died I wrote to her at our old home Bloomfield Manor, but of course the letter did not reach her until after the funerals. My aunt replied but as far as I know Luke did not see the letters.'

'Was she never talked about?'

'Luke was never interested in my background. I was only five when we came here and I think he regarded me as virtually Cornish. His only concern was for the Gaisfords.'

'I must admit that, though I knew your mother and father were not from these parts originally, I never knew their origins.'

'Then we shall go to Whitby and seek help from my Aunt Martha.'

'No one must know where we are going. We must make our departure as secret as possible. I'll take my two-horse carriage and drive it myself. We do not want to make your leaving Senewey obvious so I propose I come to the servants' entrance at ten tonight and bring you here so we can set out early in the morning. I have had to deplete my staff and those still in my employ I can trust implicitly.'

'I will have to bring my maid. I cannot possibly leave Tess behind with no protection when Luke realises I have left.'

'His actions would be too terrible to contemplate. You must bring her, of course.'

'What about the captain, the Gurneys and Alice?'

'We are going to have to let matters here take their course. Captain Ford knows the full story. We must trust to his discretion in whatever action he takes. I'm sure the Gurneys will look after Alice.'

She nodded, realising there was nothing more they could do. Now all she wanted was to get as far away from Senewey as possible.

On reaching the Manor, Abigail quickly informed Tess of their plans.

Though she was in full agreement that her mistress should

seek safety from her husband, Tess's heart sank: she would not see Captain Ford before they left. The thought brought such a sense of loss she was bewildered. Such feelings to be caused by a stranger.

'What about the sea captain, Miss? And Dorinda and Alice and Leo?'

'There must be no communication with any of them. We two and Mr Granton are in grave peril from Mr Gaisford. I believe it will be better for the others concerned if we leave here and they do not know where we have gone.'

'But Captain Ford will be in danger!'

'Only if Mr Gaisford discovers him. With us out of the way there's little chance of that.'

Martin was on time and they loaded the carriage quickly with Abigail and Tess's belongings, which they had kept to a minimum. Though they couldn't be absolutely sure, they thought no one had observed them.

When they reached Granton Manor, Martin summoned Mrs Duckworth, his cook housekeeper, and instructed her to see to the immediate needs of Mrs Gaisford and her maid.

'I will see to it, Mr Granton. I'll call Marcia.'

'She's the only maid we have,' he offered by way of explanation to Abigail.

Mrs Duckworth hurried from the room and returned in a few minutes with the maid who knew which rooms were to be given to Mrs Gaisford and her maid.

Mrs Duckworth was following them out when Martin called her back. 'I will be leaving early in the morning with Mrs Gaisford and her maid. I don't know how long I shall stay away but I want you and Marcia to look after the house until I return. I am sure you are wondering what this is all about. You are a trustworthy person, Mrs Duckworth, so I think you deserve an explanation. Because of certain events, which I need not go into, Mrs Gaisford is in great danger so I am taking her where I hope she won't be found. You must tell no one of this, especially Mr Gaisford. If he or anyone else comes looking for me, you do not know who was here or where I have gone.'

'Very good, sir! You can rely on me.'

'Instruct Marcia and I will tell Roger.'

'Will he be staying on as groom while you are away, sir?'

'Yes, the horses will still need attention.'

'Of course.'

Martin hurried to the stables where Roger had taken the carriage. He was already taking the horse from the shafts.

'Roger, I want the two-horse coach ready for seven o'clock in the morning. I will be driving it myself.'

'Yes, sir.' The groom was surprised. It was very rare for Mr Granton to drive the coach, though Roger knew he was capable of doing so. It looked as if this might mean a long absence.

His supposition was confirmed when Martin added, 'See that the valises in the carriage are transferred to the coach and leave space for mine also. And make the inside comfortable for Mrs Gaisford and her maid.'

'Yes, sir! Will you be gone long?'

'I don't know. And listen, Roger – you know nothing if anybody comes questioning you. I've gone away, you know not where, and on no account reveal that Mrs Gaisford and her maid have been here. There is a perfectly good explanation, you will hear it one day when I return.'

'Yes, sir! My lips are sealed.'

'You are a good man, Roger. See to things here while I am away.'

'I will, sir.'

At seven o'clock the next morning, Martin took up the reins. He nodded his thanks to Roger, Mrs Duckworth and Marcia. The four servants were all that remained of a once grand household. They and their master held each other in mutual esteem. It was a sad parting but they trusted him to return one day when it was safe to do so.

Luke rode up the drive to Senewey highly satisfied that he had received orders for most of the goods salvaged from the *Lady Jane*. There were always customers for brandy, wine, lace and tobacco, the goods shipped to Spain and from there to

England. Though there had been rumours of ships wrecked on the coast recently no one treated these as being deliberately caused; the days when ships were lured to their doom were thought to be long since gone. No one questioned the trading venture that Luke had set up, either. His enterprise was proving highly profitable so far. There would be other ships heading up the Channel, other nights spent watching men fighting for their lives while he held their fate in the palm of his hand. Now, home again after two nights away, there was only one thing he was in need of. He went straight to his wife's room. No one there!

His lips tightened. He swung out of the room and down the stairs. The drawing room was similarly empty. His examination of the study, dining room and ground-floor reception rooms proved unfruitful too. Abigail was not on the terrace, so where was she? She should have been here awaiting his return! He stormed through the house to the servants' quarters and Mrs Horsefield's room.

Luke flung the door open, startling the housekeeper who sat at her desk sorting some bills for payment. 'Where's my wife?' he demanded angrily.

Mrs Horsefield rose from her chair. 'Sorry, sir, I did not know you were back.'

'Well, I am,' he snapped. 'Where is she?'

'I thought she had gone to join you, sir.'

'Join me? Well, she didn't. Did she not tell you where she was going?'

'No, sir. I didn't know she intended leaving. It was only after her bed had not been slept in for two nights that I thought she must have gone to join you.'

'Not slept in?' Luke frowned. 'Does that maid of hers know anything?'

'She's not here either, so I conclude she has gone with Mrs Gaisford.'

Luke's face darkened. 'Where the devil are they?'

'Could the mistress have gone to Penorna, sir?'

'She isn't in the habit of doing so.'

'I have known her ride over there on the odd occasion.'

'Have you?' Luke looked thoughtful. 'But never taking her maid?'

'No, sir. Maybe because you were away she thought to stay over.'

Luke nodded. Calmed a little by this possibility he left the room without another word. He hurried to the stables and rode from Senewey as if the hounds of hell pursued him. But the manager and skeleton staff at Penorna knew nothing.

Anger seethed in Luke. Where was she? Why take her maid? That seemed to indicate she intended staying away, unless she had gone to Penzance taking her maid to help with some shopping or whatever. But all the Senewey carriages were at the Manor. He had subconsciously noted that when he went to the stables. She could always have been picked up by one of the Westburys. She had not seen a lot of them since her marriage but occasionally one of them visited, clinging to the friendship of childhood days.

In a state of pent-up anger he rode quickly to Trethtowan Manor, only to be told that none of the family had seen Abigail for two months.

Luke fought to conceal his rage. He turned for home but, when he came to the fork in the track pulled hard on the reins, bringing the animal to an earth-tearing halt. He was not far from Granton Manor; he may as well tell Martin that his share from the last wreck would go a good way to solving his financial problems.

The house looked dejected; it certainly needed restoring. Luke strode through the yard, seeking some sign of life. There was none visible and because of it the house seemed to have a forlorn air. Luke tugged at the metal bell pull. A few moments later a maid timidly opened the door.

'Mr Gaisford to see Mr Granton,' he stated.

'Mr Granton is not at home, sir.'

Luke's lips tightened. 'Where is he then? When will he be back?'

'I don't know, sir.'

'Useless girl,' he snapped. He pushed past her and said, 'Get your housekeeper, she may know.'

Marcia scurried away, glad to leave the matter in Mrs Duckworth's hands.

She appeared in the hall. 'It is as Marcia said, sir,' she got in before Luke could question her. 'Mr Granton went out early. He did not say where nor when he would be back. I'm sorry I can't help you further, sir.'

Luke cursed, ignored her courtesy and stormed out of the house, slamming the door behind him. Fuming, he stopped at the top of the steps, slapping his riding crop against the palm of his hand. Didn't anyone ever tell their servants where they were going?

He strode to his horse, climbed into the saddle and rode to Senewey.

There was still no sign of his wife there, nor was there the following morning. Frustration did not help Luke's temper and his staff suffered the lash of his tongue anew when they could provide no answers. Where was Abigail? How could anyone disappear so completely?

He rode to Granton Manor where once again Marcia told him that Mr Granton was not at home.

'Did he return yesterday?' Luke demanded.

'No, sir,' replied Marcia automatically, then feared she had innocently imparted information she should have kept secret.

Luke paused when she'd shut the door, realising for the first time the fact that his wife and friend had disappeared at the same time. Could there be anything in that? Making sure the groom wasn't around, he went to the carriage house. He knew Martin's carriages. One was not there! Luke frowned. Was that significant? He gave a little shake of his head. A missing carriage did not mean the missing pair were together, yet it was strange that both had left their homes about the same time. He sought out Roger. 'Your master took the coach. Was anyone with him?'

'No, sir.'

'So why did he need it?'

'Don't know, sir. He did not say.'

'Did he tell you where he was going or when he would be back?

372

'No, sir.'

Luke gave the groom a curt nod and left. If the man knew anything he was not saying. Luke was reluctantly beginning to believe that Abigail and Martin were together.

He must find them, deal with Martin and bring his wife back – no scandal must be allowed to besmirch the Gaisford name.

He searched Abigail's room for something that might direct him to her whereabouts but found nothing. It was an angry and frustrated man who went to bed that night. His sleep was disturbed by haunting dreams. Faces swirled under water, came close to condemn him and floated away; waves broke, their spray merging to form female flesh. She turned her head. Abigail was accusing him! Luke sat up in bed, sweat pouring from him, shouting her name. Moonlight streamed through the window. Wide-eyed, he swept his gaze around the room but he was alone.

Shaking, he slipped from the bed and went to the window. What was the meaning of his dream? He drew the cool night air into his lungs and focused his mind. Men he had killed. Abigail on a beach with accusation in her eyes. Was she haunting his conscience? Or had she been on the beach? That mark in the corridor near her room. Sand . . . was that why she had fled, knowing what would happen if he found out the truth? Had she gone to Martin for help and he, knowing her fate if he confided in Luke, could not bring himself to betray her? To track Martin ought to be the easiest option as they'd been friends for so long but since his parents had died he seemed to have no close relatives in the county and his friends were all Luke's too. He wouldn't approach them. Luke was at his wit's end.

With daylight he was in the saddle and riding to see George Morland but a casual query about Martin's connections drew no response. It was the same with David Gillow and Sydney Leigh. It seemed that Martin's wider connections were a mystery.

Fury stalked Luke for two days; he was making no progress. It seemed Abigail and Martin had disappeared off the face of the earth. Martin knew the truth about those wrecks. Even if he hadn't revealed it to Abigail, Luke sensed that somehow she knew of it too. They were both a danger to him. He must find them.

Dorinda came up to Captain Ford's room with his breakfast tray. She found him out of bed fully dressed.

'Captain Ford, what are you doing?' she cried. 'Get back into bed at once.'

'I'm so much better, Miss Jenkins.' He smiled as he took the tray from her and placed it on the table. 'I'll enjoy that,' he added, eyeing the bacon and egg and wedge of white bread.

'You know what the doctor said, a full week in bed,' she admonished.

'But that was at the start of my illness when he did not know how well I would progress.' Before she had time to protest any further he went on, 'I have to find Tess. She said she would visit me and she hasn't.'

'Maybe she hasn't had the opportunity.'

'Perhaps, but I have a feeling it's more than that. I have to find out. I know from what Mr Granton told me that she works at Senewey Manor for Mrs Gaisford. Tell me how to get there?'

'I will not. I know what you were told. It is too dangerous for you, as you are well aware. I thought you wanted to see justice done?'

'I do, and I will.'

'You won't if you confront Mr Gaisford.'

'But I must see Tess.'

'You can thank her again for saving your life when you have brought those wreckers to justice.'

There was a knock on the house door. 'I'll have to go,' Dorinda said.

She admitted the doctor with the news that Captain Ford was out of bed, fully dressed and wanting to know the way to Senewey Manor.

He hurried up the stairs followed by Dorinda. 'What's this nonsense?' he demanded as he burst into the room.

'Good morning, doctor,' Captain Ford greeted him pleasantly. 'I'm glad you are here. You can confirm that my leg is very much better.' He stood up and started to unbuckle his breeches. Dorinda gasped and fled from the room.

Ten minutes later she came back in answer to the doctor's call.

'Captain Ford is right. His wounds have healed remarkably well. A strong constitution always helps. He can go about his business.' The doctor halted Dorinda who was about to speak. 'I don't want to know what that is. I have kept, and will continue to keep, his presence here a secret since it was you who asked me. I don't need to know anything else.'

Dorinda blushed. 'Thank you.' When the doctor picked up his bag she added, 'I'll see you out.' When they reached the front door she added, 'Come and dine with us this evening.'

'It will be my pleasure. Thank you. You are a remarkable woman, Miss Jenkins. Oh, by the way . . . you were governess to the present Mrs Gaisford, I believe?' Dorinda nodded. 'There's a rumour going round that she and her maid have disappeared and that Mr Gaisford is almost out of his mind with worry looking for them. There's another curious thing. I had reason to see Mr Granton, but when I called at the manor I was told he was away and it was not known where he had gone nor when he would be back. There may of course be no connection between the two events . . .' He gave a little grunt. 'I shouldn't be spreading rumours but I knew you use to work for the Mitchells.'

Panic was rising in Dorinda. Had Luke Gaisford discovered his wife knew the truth and taken steps to silence her and Tess, and maybe Mr Granton as well?

She hurried up the stairs and found Captain Ford in high spirits, consuming his breakfast with enjoyment. 'There, I told you I was better, Miss Jenkins.' His voice trailed away when he saw her concern. 'What's the matter?'

'The doctor has just told me it is rumoured Mrs Gaisford and Tess are missing.'

'What?' Captain Ford was on his feet, food forgotten.

'And when the doctor called on Mr Granton, he was told he was away as well and the housekeeper did not know when he would be returning.'

'You mean, they are together?'

Dorinda shrugged. 'I'm not saying that, but it seems strange that they are all missing at the same time.'

Noel Ford started for the door. 'I must find Tess before she comes to harm.'

'Wait!' Dorinda's sharp tone stopped him. 'Where are you going?'

'To find Mr Gaisford.'

'And what will you gain by that?'

'I'll throttle the truth out of him.'

'And gain nothing. Don't go rushing blindly into this. By confronting Mr Gaisford, you'll be revealing who you are and then he'll make sure you don't live to bring evidence against him.'

The chill that brought over him made the captain realise that Dorinda was right. It would be foolish to dash into this situation without thought.

'You fear for Tess?' she continued.

'Yes. And the others, of course.'

'Then, let's approach this sensibly. If, as it seems, Mr Gaisford is looking for them, then they have as yet come to no harm. They had good reason to flee.'

'But where? They could be anywhere.'

'True, but let's try and reason this out.'

'What do you know of them? If Mrs Gaisford and Tess are with Mr Granton, isn't it likely he would take the lead? Do you know of any connections?'

'Not really.'

Noel threw up his hands and looked heavenwards in despair.

'That may not be a bad thing.'

'But . . .'

'Hear me out,' interrupted Dorinda. 'Being in service as a governess and then running my shop, I hear a lot of chatter.

Few people know anything of Mr Granton. It seems he has no close family left. He came into Granton Manor after his parents died and spends all his time there. He has few friends within the county apart from those of his schooldays. That was all he wished for.'

'I can try them.'

'No! Mr Gaisford was one of that close circle so there would be danger for you in contacting any of the others. Because there seems to be little to lead us further after Mr Granton, we must think about where Mrs Gaisford might take them, to whom she might turn. Besides, that's the line you must follow in case Mr Granton isn't with them.'

'So where?' said Noel, desperation in his voice.

'Mrs Gaisford would want to get as far away as possible.' Dorinda paused thoughtfully. 'I went to be governess to Abigail just after Mr and Mrs Mitchell came to Cornwall. Abigail was five . . .'

'Where did they come from?' asked Noel, grasping at what might be a possible lead.

'Whitby in Yorkshire.'

'Might she have gone to relations there?'

'It's possible. She had an aunt there.'

'Is she still alive?'

'I don't know. It's a long time ago.'

'What's her name?'

'I don't know. All I do recall is that she was Mr Mitchell's sister. It's possible she is still in Whitby, if she is alive. But even then, she may have married and have a different name by now. Oh, there are so many imponderables.'

'But if this is my only lead I must pursue it,' replied Captain Ford determinedly.

'How will you travel?'

'I'll go to Falmouth, find a ship and work my passage to London. I'll sail onward from there to Whitby or one of the ports nearby. If there's the opportunity in London I'll give the owner of the *Lady Jane* a shock; no doubt by now she will have been declared lost with all hands.' He looked at Dorinda with admiration in his eyes. 'Thank you for all you have done. I will be ever grateful to you. Wish me luck.'

'I'll do more than that. I'll pray for your success, and that you'll find Tess again.'

'I promise I will, and bring her back to you.'

Chapter Twenty-Seven

Though he did not believe that Martin would betray him, because if he did he would only be implicating himself, Luke still felt uneasy about his friend's absence, especially as the housekeeper at Granton Manor insisted she did not know when her master would be returning. He did not want to link Abigail's disappearance with Martin's but suspicion nagged at Luke and the possibility of Martin and Abigail being together held the prospect of calamity. His need to find them was desperate.

He paid a second visit to the Westburys.

When the door was opened by the maid at Trethtowan Manor, he said, 'Mr Luke Gaisford would like to see Mr and Mrs Westbury.'

'One moment, sir,' she replied. 'Please step inside.' She held the door for him before hurrying to Mr Westbury's study.

A few moments later Selwyn greeted him, privately wondering what brought Luke Gaisford to this house again so soon. After all, it wasn't as if the two families were on the best of terms and the disputes he had had with Luke's father still rankled in his mind.

'Mr Gaisford,' he greeted Luke without noticeable enthusiasm. 'What brings you here so soon?'

'I am pursuing a new line of enquiry about Mrs Gaisford's absence.'

'You've had no news of her?'

'No, and it's most worrying.'

'I'm sure it is. But why come here? We told you only days ago that we knew nothing.' There was a note of irritation in Selwyn's voice now.

'I know, but it might help me if I learned something of her origins.'

'Then you had better come into the drawing room.' Selwyn led the way. 'Harriet, Mr Gaisford is here seeking our help again,' he said as they entered the room.

She looked surprised. 'What more can we possibly tell you than we did on your last visit?' she said coldly. She had never been an admirer of Luke, nor indeed of any of the Gaisfords. She wished John Mitchell had forbidden his daughter's marriage but Abigail had been a head-strong girl and, as her father had said at the time, it was better to keep her love rather than suffer an estrangement.

'Do sit down,' said Selwyn.

As Luke took a chair, he said, 'I know nothing of my wife's origins and if I did it might help me to find her. I was only very young when the Mitchells came to Cornwall so did not take much notice of any talk at the time. Abigail was only two then, I believe, and I suppose could not remember much about life before coming here. I know you were friendly with the Mitchells when they arrived and wondered if you knew where they originated?'

'You think Mrs Gaisford might have returned to her roots?'

'It is a possibility. I've got to search everywhere. I know an aunt was invited to our wedding but was ill and could not come. I know nothing more about her or where she was living at that time.'

Hester eyed her husband. She wondered if they would be doing Abigail a disservice if they divulged the little they knew. But she did not catch his eye and Selwyn was already answering Luke.

'The Mitchells arrived here from Whitby when Mr Mitchell's uncle left him the Penorna Estate. That would have been in 1782.'

Hester kept her annoyance hidden but from the look of satisfaction in Luke's eyes she knew he had grasped the information that had slipped out so easily. Whitby.

Seeking to elicit more, he asked, 'Did this aunt live in the town itself?'

'We don't know,' put in Harriet quickly before her husband could speak. Almost too quickly for Luke's liking.

'Do you know if she was married? It is no good my looking for a Mitchell if she was.'

Once again Harriet quickly answered, 'We don't know.'

'Mrs Westbury,' said Luke smoothly, 'did you ever hear of Mr and Mrs Mitchell being invited to a wedding?'

'No,' she replied haughtily. 'Though for all we know she may have married before they came here. We have told you all we know.'

For a brief moment Luke's lips tightened. He realised he had been politely told to leave. He said in a tone that matched Hester's for coldness, 'Thank you, Mrs Westbury. You have both been most helpful.'

He rode home already planning the details of his journey north tomorrow.

About the time Luke was leaving Senewey, Noel Ford was claiming a berth in the fo'csle of the *Sunbeam*, a brig heading for London. She had put into Falmouth with a sick crew-member and her captain was only too pleased to find a sailor willing to fill his place. Noel kept his true identity a secret, willingly serving as a deckhand to get a passage to London. In favourable weather the brig made good progress up the Channel. He felt exhilarated by the sway of the ship, the wind in his face, the slap of the sails and the creak of the ropes. This was where he belonged, and this was where he would be once again, back in command the next time, his name cleared of the taint of negligence.

The Thames was heaving with shipping. Masts seemed to terrace the sky everywhere he looked. Ships were unloading goods from all over the world, stevedores straining their muscles to stow cargoes in time to catch the tide while lighter boats were ferrying passengers to and fro across the navigable river that made London the commercial capital of the world.

Work finished, paid off, an offer to sign on refused, Noel Ford paused at the top of the gangway. The quay was overflowing with people pursuing their everyday jobs amongst the array of warehouses and jetties. Passengers were hurrying to their ships, pickpockets eyeing up their next victim, girls seeking another customer. The smell of dung from the dray horses was added to the smell that rose from the murky waters of the river, to mingle with the stench from the factories, breweries and tanneries belching smoke to join that of the multitude of domestic chimneys covering the city in a cloying black soot. Noel shuddered; the sooner he was out of this filth and on the open sea the better.

He hurried along the quay, seeking the offices of shipping companies that sailed north from the Thames. His enquiries at the third one proved successful; he could work his passage on a collier due to call in at Whitby on its way to Newcastle for its next load of coal. The ship would sail in three hours and the captain expected him to be there an hour beforehand.

Noel was thankful that he still had time to visit the offices of Harland Shipping. He ignored the two clerks who stared at him open-mouthed when he walked in and went straight to the door of an inner office where he walked in without cere-mony.

The portly, red-faced man seated behind his oak desk looked up, scowling at the intrusion. Words of admonishment died on his lips unspoken. He gaped at Noel in utter disbelief. 'Captain Ford!' The words came in a whisper.

'You are not seeing a ghost, Mr Harland,' Noel announced. 'I'm very much alive.'

Mr Harland swallowed hard. 'What . . .' He choked with emotion, took a deep breath and then the words poured out. 'The *Lady Jane* was reported lost with all hands on the Cornish coast, evidenced by a piece of wood that drifted ashore. What the devil happened? Why were you so near the coast? Incompetence, I assume, Ford. Sheer incompetence on your part!'

'No, sir,' Noel broke in sharply to stop this tirade. 'We were lured on to the coast in fog by wreckers, sir.'

'What? Don't try to cover your own stupidity by telling such tales. Wrecking was suppressed decades ago.'

382

'It's back, sir. The villains murdered my crew in cold blood. I nearly lost my own life, but managed to fool my would-be killer and was helped to escape. It is a long story, sir, one I cannot disclose in full now. I'm on my way to Whitby where I hope to trace some witnesses to the wrecking and so prove my innocence.'

'Whitby? You talk in riddles. How can Whitby be connected with a wreck in Cornwall?' grunted Mr Harland with disdain.

'I'm not sure it is but I have hopes.'

'A wild goose chase, more like. I should have you arrested for incompetence leading to loss of life . . .'

'Give me a chance to prove my innocence first?'

'What, and let you walk out of here never to return?'

'Sir, I needn't have come here at all but thought you should know the truth before you took further action with your insurers. I want to prove my innocence and to captain a ship for you again.' The light in Noel's eyes spoke of his sincerity.

'And you believe you can find the truth in Whitby?'

'I hope so, sir.'

'It seems a tall order to me.' Mr Harland eyed him for a moment. 'Very well! I'll retain my faith in the man I promoted to captain before his time. See that my faith is not misplaced.'

At about the same time as Captain Ford was sailing down the Thames as a deck-hand on the *Pelican*, Luke Gaisford was riding north and a coach was approaching Whitby.

The journey from Cornwall to Yorkshire had been made with little difficulty, though it had been long and tedious. Martin had handled the horses well and been solicitous for the comfort of both Abigail and Tess at every nightly stopover.

Having shared the horrors on the beach, the tension and uncertainties of the aftermath and their closeness in the coach, Abigail and Tess were by now far closer than they had been previously, more like friends than mistress and servant, though Tess did not presume upon Abigail's kindness.

They had reached York one late afternoon and Martin decided it would be better to stay the night there and face the rest of the journey refreshed. Upon making enquiries he was directed to the tavern in St Helen's Square. Here they found the comfortable accommodation they sought and stabling for the carriage horses. After a hearty breakfast the next day, they set out for Whitby, each entertaining their own hopes and thoughts.

They were thankful that the day, though somewhat cloudy, did not threaten rain, especially when the trackway took them on to the high wild moors. Anticipation mounted as they twisted and turned their way through the valley of the Esk, following the river down to Whitby where it ran between high cliffs into the sea. Red-roofed houses climbed skywards. Ships lay at quays on the east bank; hammers resounded from the shipbuilding yards; the whole town alive with activity as people hurried about their final tasks before heading for home or the many inns.

Martin enquired for the best coaching inn and was met with a choice when the man eyed his coach and informed him, 'White Horse in Church Street for the horses; Angel across the river for the ladies.'

Martin did not hesitate; he negotiated the coach through the crowds flowing across the bridge in both directions. As he turned into the Angel's yard an ostler and his assistant were instantly at the horses' heads, steadying them as Martin brought them to a stop.

'Stabling for the night, sir?' came the enquiry.

'Not sure. It may be longer.'

'Very good, sir! They'll be well looked after.'

Martin turned to the coach but already two liveried boys had hurried from the main door and were assisting Abigail down. One of them escorted her to the inn with Martin accompanying them. The second boy smiled at Tess and took one of the cases with which she was struggling.

Tess felt important when he said, 'Follow me, miss. I'm sure you will be comfortable at the Angel.' As they entered the inn he called to two younger boys, 'Bring the rest of the luggage from the coach.' They scampered off. 'Have to tell them 'everything,' he whispered confidentially to Tess. He put her case down near a desk at which Martin was speaking to the landlord.

'That will be ideal,' said Martin gratefully. He turned to Abigail. 'I have booked you a room which has an adjoining one suitable for a personal maid. I will be three doors away.'

This was much better than she had expected and Abigail thanked both Martin and the landlord.

'Will you require a meal this evening, sir?'

'Yes,' replied Martin.

'We have a special room for travelling servants so . . .'

'No.' Abigail halted him. 'Tess will dine with us.'

'But, miss, I . . .' Tess started, but was cut short.

'We have shared so much over these last few days, you will not dine alone.'

Tess glanced at Martin who smiled and approved of Abigail's action. 'Of course you must, and whatever happens from now on we will see it through together.' He turned to the landlord. 'You may be able to help by telling us if anyone called Mitchell still lives at Bloomfield Manor?'

The landlord hesitated thoughtfully. This was a strange travelling party. The gentleman had booked in as Mr Granton, he had booked the lady in as Mrs Gaisford, but the younger female who had been given a room for a maid had addressed her mistress as 'miss' and the three of them were going to dine together. They did, however, *look* highly respectable.

'Yes, sir! There is a Miss Mitchell in the town. Bloomfield is a modest estate but she also runs a merchant business in Whitby quite successfully.'

Abigail felt a tremor of excitement run through her. This must be her aunt. Never married and still lived at Bloomfield Manor. Did this signal a change in their fortunes?

'Can you direct us to the Manor?' Martin asked.

'Certainly. You will be going tomorrow, sir?'

'Yes, I suppose so.'

'I think the best thing, if you are agreeable, sir, would be to send this boy to direct you. Billy's father is one of the gardeners there.'

385

The lad grinned, pleased he would be relieved of other duties for a while tomorrow.

'That's very good of you, landlord.' Abigail turned to the boy. 'Very well, Billy, be ready at half-past nine.'

The following morning, with Martin driving the coach and Billy sitting beside him, they travelled south along the coast road from Whitby. After about four miles Billy indicated some ironwork gates ahead. 'Bloomfield Manor, sir. The house lies nearer the coast. Stands on the cliffs with wonderful views out to sea.'

'You seem to know it well?'

'Been up here with my father, sir.'

When the house came in sight they saw that it was of only medium size but had the appearance of being loved and well cared for.

'Look after the coach and horses, Billy,' Martin instructed him as he drew to a halt in front of the main door. Abigail alighted from the coach. As she cast her eyes over the building, she had a strange feeling of coming home. She turned to Tess. 'You are to come in with us.'

Martin tugged at the bell pull.

Each of them wondered what awaited them when that door opened.

At that very moment a ship was beating in towards Whitby. Noel Ford surveyed the old town clinging to the cliffs, its red roofs climbing towards the venerable church and ruined abbey, and wondered if it was here that he would find those who could prove his innocence, and also the girl who had tugged at his heart strings.

A neat little maid looked askance at the three people standing on the steps of Bloomfield Manor attended by a boy she recognised as the son of one of the gardeners.

'We would like to see Miss Mitchell, if she is at home,' said Martin pleasantly.

'Whom shall I say is calling, sir?'

'Mrs Gaisford, Mr Granton and Miss Booth,' replied Martin, finding that the easiest way to make it known who they were. To try and explain that Tess was Abigail's personal maid would only complicate the situation and he wanted to keep it simple for Miss Mitchell.

They were soon admitted for she was especially curious about the names Gaisford and Booth.

While she was crossing the hall Abigail's sense of recognising her surroundings became sharper. They walked into a comfortable drawing room and she knew she had been there before.

A well-groomed, immaculately attired elderly lady rose from her armchair. She held herself erect, someone clearly in charge of her every emotion. Her eyes were piercing. She looked the visitors over, quickly summarising them, confident in the knowledge that her first impressions were generally correct. She could not fault what she saw as the gentleman introduced them, but was caught by the expression on Mrs Gaisford's face. It was one of extreme curiosity, as if she was trying to recall the dim and distant past and match it with the present.

'Do sit down.' Martha indicated some chairs. 'You'll take chocolate?'

'Thank you, ma'am,' replied Abigail politely.

Before Martha took her own seat the door opened and the chocolate was ordered. She was aware that Mrs Gaisford had surveyed the room quickly and was now looking at her with even deeper curiosity.

'Miss Mitchell, it would appear even from here that you enjoy a marvellous view from that window. Do you mind if I take a look?'

Though she was struck by the unexpected request and wondered why this question had come before the purpose of their visit was revealed, Martha agreed. Sensing that Mrs Gaisford's companions too were surprised, she watched Abigail go to the window. No one felt inclined to break the atmosphere that descended over the room. Abigail stood perfectly still, gazing out of the window, then slowly turned round. She fixed her eyes intently on Martha. 'I remember looking out of that window. I have lived here,' she said quietly. Her eyes never left the lady before her. 'I believe you are my Aunt Martha.'

Martha frowned for answer then said tentatively, 'Abigail?'

'Yes.'

'But . . . Gaisford?'

'You were invited to my wedding.'

Martha was lost for words. She held out her arms. 'I was ill,' she recalled in a falling voice. 'Then your father and mother . . .' Her eyes filled with tears. 'It was too late to come. You poor child, I should never have left you unvisited.'

She hugged Abigail lovingly. There was a knock on the door. Martha straightened up, drew a deep breath and, taking a handkerchief from her pocket wiped her eyes. Abigail realised she did not want the servants to see her so moved.

'Come in,' she called.

A maid appeared with the chocolate and placed it on a low table in front of Miss Mitchell.

Once the door had closed again, now totally in command of her feelings, Martha asked, 'What brings you to Whitby?' She started to pour the chocolate.

'It is a long story, Aunt, but first I must properly introduce my travelling companions. Mr Martin Granton, my very dear friend, and Miss Tess Booth, my maid.' She notice her aunt start at this. Assuming she was surprised to have a servant sitting with them, Abigail quickly added, 'She is more than that, she is a friend as well.'

Realising how her niece had viewed her response, Martha inclined her head in acceptance of this explanation whereas her real reaction had been one of suppressed shock. Tess Booth! This must be the child who'd been born in this very house, her brother's child! A young woman. She was maid to Abigail, her own sister, yet first she had been introduced as a servant and then as a friend. It hit Martha like a thunderclap then. These two young women did not know they were sisters! Martha stiffened, holding back the revelation that sprang to her lips. Why did they not know? John must have had his reasons for wanting the relationship kept secret. Now she was the only one who possessed that secret. Her mind was spinning when Tess came to her side to help hand out the chocolate and sweetmeats.

Once Martha was settled back in her chair, she said, 'Now, tell me why you are here?'

'We need your help, Aunt,' said Abigail. 'I fell in love with a handsome young man named Luke Gaisford, heir to the biggest estate in Cornwall. Father and Mother had their doubts about him, I believed at the time because of hostility Father had experienced at the hands of Luke's father. There was a reconciliation when I saved Luke's life in a riding accident when we were seventeen. But he always had a wild reputation.' She glanced at Martin, wanting him to endorse that.

'It's true, Miss Mitchell. Five of us went to Rugby from Cornwall. Oh, we certainly acquired a reputation there and Luke was a natural leader. That reputation clung to us all when we left school but it held most tenaciously to Luke, who seemed to want to carry it on. We all thought when he met Abigail she would have a calming effect on him, and she did for a while, but a leopard doesn't change its spots. The unsavoury side of Luke which he inherited from his father soon emerged.' He glanced at Abigail whom he wanted to take up the story, for he did not know how much she wished to reveal to her aunt.

Abigail explained how the relationship had deteriorated, how she came to hear of Luke's activities but would not believe that he was a wrecker until she saw the evidence for herself, what that had led to and how they were now in danger for their lives. 'We hope that Luke will not be able to trace us and that the sea captain Tess saved will bring my husband to justice.'

'You wish that on your own husband?' asked her aunt.

Abigail hesitated, battling with the feelings this question had aroused. 'He should be tried,' she said slowly, 'but I don't wish him to hang.'

'Why didn't you go to the authorities in Cornwall?'

'If I could explain,' put in Martin. 'The Gaisfords are extremely powerful there. Their word is far more likely to be believed than ours. We saw that our lives were threatened and would continue to be until Captain Ford had recovered and laid his allegations. We had no idea when that would be and thought it best to leave Cornwall in the interim.'

'You are far enough away here but determination has a long arm. You must stay at Bloomfield with me out of danger.'

'Oh, Aunt, we are so grateful!' cried Abigail. 'I did not know to whom I could turn, then I thought of you and hoped we might find you still here.'

Martha dismissed that observation with a wave of her hand. 'I'm very glad you did. Now I'll have the opportunity of getting to know my niece. I'll ask my housekeeper to have rooms prepared. Mr Granton, will you and Tess see to the transfer of your belongings from the Angel?'

'Certainly, ma'am! It is most kind of you to offer me accommodation as well but I can easily stay at the inn.'

'No, I won't hear of that. I think it best if all of you remain together.'

When Martin and Tess had left Martha said to Abigail, 'Tell me about Tess. You introduce her as your friend and personal maid. Those terms seem somehow incongruous.'

'When her mother died and her father would have nothing to do with her, Tess was brought to Cornwall by an aunt who was once governess to our neighbours' children. I don't know whether Tess even knows the true story because she always referred to Miss Booth as her mother.'

The truth? Martha thought. How near Tess was to that by calling Miss Booth her mother! And Martha knew how Lydia would have relished being called that. Her respect for her old friend grew now she knew that for John's sake Lydia had kept the truth a secret.

'When Miss Booth died, Father suggested that Tess should come to me as my personal maid,' Abigail explained.

Martha nodded. The reasons behind John's actions were clear to her.

'Tess fitted in very well and we became close. I found she was very easy to confide in. In fact, there were times when we seemed more like sisters.' Martha tensed at that but Abigail did not notice. 'She looks after me wonderfully well and I'm glad she was with me at Senewey.'

'Good, good,' was all the comment Martha offered. She was left wondering what her best course of action might be. To reveal the truth might destroy Abigail's opinion of her father, but didn't Tess have the right to know the truth? Martha would battle with these questions further.

Noel Ford stepped ashore oblivious to all the activity of the busy port. He eyed the people going about their daily lives. At that moment a young man carrying a sheaf of papers was hurrying past him. Noel grabbed his arm, bringing the man to an unexpected halt. His face clouded with annoyance and he was about to confront Noel when the seaman spoke first.

'The best inn in the town?' he asked.

'For what?' demanded the young man.

'Rooms where the best people would stay,' said Noel, having reasoned that if the people he sought had come to Whitby, they would seek the best accommodation.

'The Angel, across the river,' replied the man, anxious to be on his way to deliver the papers for his employer.

'Thanks.' Noel released his arm and the man hurried away to be lost in the crowd.

Noel crossed the bridge and entered the Angel. 'Good day, landlord,' he said heartily to the man behind the counter who was examining the visitors' book.

He looked up enquiringly at the man who confronted him.

'You may be able to help me,' Noel went on. 'I am looking for a gentleman and two young ladies.

The landlord eyed him suspiciously. 'I am not in the habit of imparting names or information about our guests.'

'It is imperative that I trace them,' pressed Noel. 'I can give you their names. Mr Granton, Mrs Gaiford and ...' He stopped. He realised he did not know Tess' surname. 'Oh, I don't know the other surname, I only know her as Tess.'

The landlord looked thoughtful, uncertain about disclosing their whereabouts. The door opened then and he felt a surge of relief when he saw Mr Granton coming in.

'Sir, this man . . .'

His words faded when Martin, looking surprised, greeted Noel. 'Captain Ford, what on earth . . .'

The question was cut short by Noel's exclamation of: 'Tess!'

She stopped in her tracks. A moment's disbelief was dismissed in her cry of, 'Captain Ford. What are you doing here?'

'I need my witnesses so I came to find you.'

'How did you know we were in Whitby?' asked Martin.

'When Mrs Gaisford's family first came to Cornwall, Miss Jenkins was appointed her governess. She remembered that they had come from Whitby where she seemed to think there could be an aunt. It was the only lead I had. I thought I'd try my luck and it has proved to be correct.'

'Then you had better come with us,' said Martin. He told the landlord, 'We are leaving. Make out our bill while we collect our things. I am most obliged for your help and for making us so comfortable.'

'All part of the service, sir. I am sorry you are going, but maybe we will see you again sometime.'

Twenty minutes later he was driving his coach back to Bloomfield Manor.

Inside the coach Tess and Captain Ford sat in a strained silence in which each of them could only guess what the other was feeling in the shadow of the unknown future that hung over them all.

Abigail was more than surprised when Captain Ford walked in. After his introduction to Martha he told his story. When Noel had finished explaining how he had found them, Martin came out with the ominous observation that if Captain Ford had found them so easily, so could Luke.

Chapter Twenty-Eight

In the gathering darkness the rising land beyond Pickering seemed to present a formidable barrier to Luke Gaisford as he approached the market town from York. He knew from previous enquiries that he faced a journey across wild moorland so, as much as he would have liked to press on, deemed it wise to stay in Pickering for the night rather than face unknown hazards in the dark. He was pleased with the good progress he had made and estimated that if his quarry had used Martin's coach their journey would have been much slower than his. He felt sure he must have closed the distance between them considerably.

The next morning, fortified for his ride, he left Pickering in high hopes that his quest would soon be brought to a satisfactory conclusion. Abigail would return with him, a chastened wife subject to his rules and whims, and Martin with his lips sealed by the threat of being named the leader of the wreckers, for who would not believe the word and integrity of Luke Gaisford, head of the foremost family in Cornwall?

Reaching Whitby, he followed his instinct that Martin would choose the best inn to house Abigail. A stable boy raced out of the stables when he heard the clop of horses' hooves in the yard. A few moments later, his horse taken care of, Luke entered the inn, booked himself a room for a stay of unknown length and then made his enquiry.

'I am seeking a gentleman accompanied by a lady and her maid. It is a matter of life and death that I find them as soon as possible. Have they stayed here recently?'

As soon as Luke had made his reservation, the sharp-minded landlord had connected his name with that of the lady accompanied by another gentleman. His mind was filling with possibilities, foremost among them was that this man was a husband pursuing an absconding wife and her lover. He might be able to make something out of this. After a few moments of thoughtful consideration, he made the standard reply that he used until he saw how a situation might develop. 'I am not in the habit of revealing what I know about my clients, sir.'

'It sounds to me as if you are confirming these people stayed here.'

'I did not say that, sir.'

Luke gave a little smile. 'I rather think you did. Maybe that will help you to recall?' He pushed his bribe discreetly across the counter.

The landlord quickly slid it out of sight. 'Well, sir, I do remember three people who would fit your description. They stayed here for one night.'

'Recently?'

The landlord pursed his lips. Luke slid another coin to him.

'Two nights ago.'

'Are they here now?'

'No, sir.'

Luke's eagerness was dampened but he put another question. 'Do you know where they went?' He did not wait for further pondering; another coin was proffered.

'Yes, sir, Bloomfield Manor.'

'Bloomfield Manor?' said Luke, looking puzzled.

'Yes, sir! Miss Mitchell's place.'

Luke grasped at this information. Mitchell? Abigail's maiden name! So she must have known about and found a relative. 'Where is this manor?'

'South of Whitby, about four miles.'

'You can direct me to it?'

'Of course, sir.' The landlord's hand covered another coin and he went on to give Luke the directions.

Luke thanked him and said, 'My room, landlord.'

A few moments later, ensconced in his room, he was considering his best course of action.

When Martha sat down to breakfast with Abigail, Martin and Captain Ford, Tess having resumed her position and duties, she asked if they had any plans.

'No,' replied Abigail. 'If Captain Ford's observation of yesterday is correct, maybe we had better move on.'

'That won't solve your problem for good. Your husband may still keep up his pursuit and you would always be looking over your shoulder then,' Martha pointed out.

'I can't keep running,' put in Captain Ford. 'I came to find the witnesses who will prove me innocent of negligence and save my career at sea.'

Abigail looked worried; this could mean facing Luke again with all that entailed. She looked appealingly at Martin.

Seeing she was going to abide by his opinion, he said gently, 'We can't keep on running, Abigail. I think it would be better to face Luke here where we know we have the support of your aunt.'

'You can count on me in anything you decide. I would like you to stay. I think it is the best course for you,' Martha confirmed.

'Don't desert me now,' pleaded Captain Ford.

Abigail, whose first instinct had been to keep as far away as possible from Luke, saw it was not the answer. She nodded. 'But what if he does not come?'

'I daren't consider that,' replied Captain Ford. 'I think he will.'

'So do I,' agreed Martin. 'We are a potential danger to him and always will be while we are alive.'

'You think he will go that far?' asked Abigail in alarm.

'As far as I am concerned, yes,' replied Martin. 'After all, I was part of his gang. In your case, Abigail, he does not know you were a witness to the wrecking, and the same applies to Tess, so he may conclude that we are together as lovers. He does not yet know that the captain of the *Lady Jane* is alive and that could be a great asset to us.'

'So all this puts you in a strong position when he finds you,' said Martha. 'I think you've got to let that happen.'

The morning sunshine was warming the gentle breeze blowing from the sea when Luke rode boldly up the drive to Bloomfield Manor. He viewed the house's exterior derisively, thinking it small compared to Senewey, but it looked well cared for and spoke of money not being a problem. His enquiries had elicited that Miss Mitchell, apart from her servants, lived alone and ran a successful merchant's business in Whitby. An unusual woman then, he realised.

That proved to be true. He recognised from the way she held herself and her delivery when she greeted him that here was a strong personality.

Martha Mitchell was alone when she came into the drawing room where he had been shown by a maid.

'Mr Gaisford,' she greeted Luke as she pushed the door to behind her.

'Miss Mitchell,' he returned, meeting her searching gaze calmly.

'Do sit down, sir, and tell me the purpose behind this visit from a man who is a total stranger to me. And one who, from his accent, is not from these parts?'

'Miss Mitchell, I will not bandy words with you but confront this delicate matter head on.' He saw her give a little nod of approval and recognised that she was a person who liked straight talking, no doubt from her years spent working in what was almost exclusively a man's world. 'I believe you recognise my name and that you have my wife, your niece, staying with you.'

'And I will give you a straight reply, Mr Gaisford. Yes, Abigail is with me.'

'Then I am relieved to have found her and hope I am in time to save her mental condition from worsening. I must take her home immediately to familiar surroundings which will help her to a full recovery.'

'Mental condition, Mr Gaisford? I can see nothing wrong with my niece's state of mind.'

'But to leave her own husband without a word! And after the strange way she has been acting lately, that does seem to signify an upset mind. I would be most grateful if I could see her.'

'All in good time, Mr Gaisford. At the moment Abigail is walking on the cliffs with a friend.'

'A friend?' He made his query sound surprised.

'Yes. A Mr Granton.'

'Ah, Martin, my oldest and dearest friend! Now, Miss Mitchell, does that not indicate to you the instability of my wife's mind? Why else would she leave Cornwall accompanied by a man who has been my loyal companion since boyhood?'

'It would indicate to me that she was seeking a trustworthy person's protection.'

'Protection? What tales has she been telling you?'

'Of cruelty. Of beatings.'

'What?' Luke feigned surprise and shock. 'Miss Mitchell, do I look like a man who would risk bringing scandal on the family name?'

'Ah, Mr Gaisford,' said Martha with a glint of triumph in her eyes, 'you are just the sort of man to risk anything – if you think you can get away, with it.

'Miss Mitchell, I resent that implication.' A note of hostility had entered Luke's voice. 'And I demand to see my wife.'

'I have told you, Abigail is not in.'

'Then I shall have to find her.' He was out of his chair and striding towards the drawing room door when it opened.

Martha was also on her feet and seized control of the situation immediately. 'Ah, Captain Ford, meet Mr Gaisford. Mr Gaisford, Captain Ford of the *Lady Jane*.' She saw the Captain stiffen but immediately respond to her frown and slight shake of her head, an indication to him to do nothing. He merely acknowledged Luke's terse greeting as he pushed past, intent on finding Abigail and Martin, and stormed out of the room.

Luke came out of the house and was about to mount his horse when he saw her. Tess. She had emerged from a door at a lower level of the house near the corner and was carrying a basket, its contents covered by a white cloth. A picnic? Was she taking refreshments to Abigail and Martin? If so, then she must be going to a pre-arranged rendezvous. Not realising she was being observed, she headed for a path that disappeared into a wood. Beyond he could hear the distant sound of the sea.

Luke followed and, because the path was quite overgrown, was able to keep a discreet distance away without losing sight of her. He was halfway through the wood when he pulled up and stood stock-still. His mind whirled and then focused on the words that now rang like a death knell in his ears: 'Captain Ford of the *Lady Jane*.' The *Lady Jane*? It couldn't be! Impossible! None of the crew had survived. But now there was doubt in his mind. Martin was here, too, and he was implicated in the wrecking. It could not be coincidence that these two men were together. But how, and why were they here? Did this give him the reason for Martin's departure from Cornwall? Had he now two threats to deal with or were there more? But if the two most closely involved witnesses, Captain Ford and Martin Granton, could not testify, the second-hand nature of the evidence of the others would count for nothing, he reflected. Luke continued along the path. He had lost sight of Tess but it was obvious that she would have gone this way.

'Miss Mitchell, if that was the man behind the loss of my ship, I want my revenge as you well know. Why stop me?' raged Captain Ford, as the door slammed behind Luke.

'Because he would simply have denied every accusation you threw at him. It would have been his word against yours. There could well have been violence done here in this room which would have got you nowhere. Besides, he might well have dealt finally with you and then me there and then, which would have left no one to alert the others. I let slip that my niece and Mr Granton were walking on the cliffs. He showed no sign of connecting you with the ship he wrecked, though I deliberately mentioned her name. Off with you, then, and follow him! I have a hunch that it may work strongly in your favour as he tries to persuade my niece, one way or another, to return with him to Cornwall.'

Noel did not wait another moment and was just in time to see Luke disappearing into the wood.

'Martin, where is this all going to end?' asked a distressed Abigail. 'We are walking these cliffs as if all was well with the world and yet our future is overshadowed by a dark cloud which we can do nothing about.'

'We are waiting for a development that will dispel that cloud forever.' He tried to sound reassuring, to promise her that all would be well, even though he privately harboured doubts about the outcome.

'You really think there will be a reckoning here? That Luke will find us?'

'Yes.'

'Then let it be soon.' Abigail's plea seemed to be thrown to Heaven. Then she added, 'I hope it will not be too dreadful.' Distress and despair at the thought of the outcome turning in favour of her husband made her blanch and shudder.

Martin instantly took her hand, offering comfort. 'I wish I had opposed Luke from the start, pursued you for myself, but I was weak, too ready to bow before his dominant personality, so I stepped aside. I have loved you since first meeting you. That is why I never looked elsewhere.'

She met his admiring gaze frankly and there was a touch of regret in hers as she raised a hand to his cheek. 'You are a dear friend, Martin. Who knows what might have been?'

They heard a rustling sound and turned to see Tess emerging from the wood fifty yards away. Her face broke into a broad smile when she saw them. She thought what a striking couple they made and wished with all her heart that her mistress had chosen this man instead of Mr Gaisford.

'What's this?' asked Martin, noting the basket Tess was carrying.

Abigail smiled. 'I arranged a picnic for us and asked Tess to bring it here about this time. That is why I manoeuvred our walk to end here where the path from Bloomfield meets the one along the cliff edge.'

'Splendid,' said Martin enthusiastically, 'and what a wonderful view. How did you know about it?'

'A childhood memory. When I mentioned it to my aunt she brought me here to show me that memory had served me well.'

'Your picnic, miss,' said Tess.

'Thank you, Tess, I'll take it,' said Martin.

'Everything is in order at the house?' asked Abigail as she turned along the cliff path.

'Yes, miss. Enjoy your picnic.' Tess hurried away.

'Thank you,' Abigail called after her.

Tess raised her hand in acknowledgement without looking back.

'You have a truly devoted servant there,' commented Martin.

'She's more than that,' replied Abigail. 'She is a true friend, though she never oversteps the mark.'

'Where are we going to have this?' he asked.

'There's a hollow a few yards along here.' Abigail started along the cliff path to reach a depression in the ground close to the cliff edge which gave them views of the sea breaking on the rocks far below. Today they swelled gently, washed towards land by an undulating sea that stretched to the horizon in a dazzling expanse of blue.

They settled themselves comfortably with Martin dancing attendance on Abigail, and she wondering how she had ever mistaken Luke's attentions for a proof of love.

Tess made for the house, wishing such trouble did not hang over them. She should not be entertaining dismal thoughts on such a pleasant day. She thought instead of Captain Ford. She sensed that he had some feelings for her, but did they purely stem from the fact that she had saved his life? She found herself hoping not, which made her examine her own feelings. He was a handsome man, engaged in a trade that carried a thrill of adventure which automatically gave him a dashing aura. She smiled to herself; she should not become carried away. Nevertheless she allowed her thoughts to develop. What if their feelings towards each other were to be spoken aloud? What if he proposed? How would she answer? Could she really say she was in love with him? Was she?

Her happy speculation was interrupted by a noise ahead. She stopped. Who could it be? Caution took hold. She stepped away from the path and quickly sought cover in some bushes. A few moments later a figure appeared. Mr Gaisford! He had found them! Panic gripped Tess. How did he come to be on this path, one that would lead him straight to her mistress? What had happened at the Manor? Her every instinct was to warn her mistress but now Mr Gaisford was between them. If she crashed through the undergrowth he would hear her, yet she had to do something. Panic was rising in her when she heard the crack of a twig. Someone else was coming! She crouched lower, then relief surged through her when she saw Captain Ford. She rose from her hiding place and the sight of her stopped him in his tracks. He raised a finger to his lips and then held out his hand in an indication for her to come to him.

Tess stepped lightly on to the path and he came to stand beside her. His hand automatically sought hers to offer reassurance as he asked, 'What are you doing here?'

'I brought a picnic for Mrs Gaisford and Mr Granton.'

'You know where they are?'

She nodded.

'You saw Mr Gaisford?

'Yes. Are you following him?'

'Explanations later! Come on.' Still holding her hand, he led the way forward.

They reached the junction of the paths and he looked askance at her.

Tess indicated the way she had gone to meet Abigail and Martin. He nodded and gestured again for quiet. They moved on cautiously until they heard raised voices. Another five yards made the voices more distinct and they rounded a bend in the path to see Luke standing on the edge of a hollow overlooking the sea.

401

'. . . and such a cosy setting,' he said in a mocking tone. His voice turned cold and threatening then. 'Try to steal my wife, would you, Martin?'

'No, I . . .'

'Or were you running away from something else? Well, both issues can be settled as one.' He jumped down into the hollow. Though Martin had half expected this he was surprised by the swiftness with which Luke acted.

Luke's blow took him high on the cheek with such force that it knocked him to the ground. His head stuck a stone and he lay still, close to the edge. Luke, eyes wild with the lust to kill, let out a cry of triumph as he moved towards the inert form of his former friend. His intention was clear and Abigail grasped his coat.

'No!' she screamed.

He glared at her with eyes blinded by blood lust. It was a look she had last seen on that beach in Cornwall. He tried to shake her off but she held on to his arm. 'You are coming home with me to act the dutiful wife, and woe betide you if you don't. He knows too much. He'll never see Cornwall again.' Still held by Abigail, he struggled towards Martin.

'If you kill him, you'll have to kill me too,' she yelled. 'I was on that beach!'

Luke stared at her. Suspicions that he had tried to suppress were now confirmed. 'Then you'll have to die too!' He swung round on her so forcefully that she was forced to drop his arm. She tripped over Martin's outstretched hand and fell. Gloating triumph fired Luke's eyes. All reason was gone.

'And you'll have to kill me too!' a voice boomed behind him.

Luke swung round. 'Ah, the captain who managed to survive. Well, this time you won't,' he yelled with a wild laugh.

Noel jumped at him but Luke stepped aside just as Noel hit the ground. He swung a vicious kick at the captain that brought a gasp of pain from him as it took him in his ribs. He fell back against the side of the hollow. Luke moved in, planning that in a few moments three bodies would lie broken on the rocks far below, waiting for the sea to take them.

Abigail, still dizzy from the vicious blow he had dealt her, was struggling to get to her feet and screaming at him to stop.

He reached out to grasp Noel's shirt.

The rock struck his forehead. Taken completely by surprise Luke staggered backwards under the severity of the blow, lost his balance, and with arms flailing felt the ground crumble away under his feet. With a scream he fell to the fate he had intended for the others.

It was a dishevelled and wounded party that reached Bloomfield Manor, shocking Martha by their appearance. Once she had seen to their needs and they were seated in the drawing room with a reviving drink, she heard all the details of what had happened.

'You were right, Miss Mitchell, to stop me from confronting Mr Gaisford here,' said Captain Ford. 'Although it was a tragic end, I think it was probably the best one. With respect for your loss, Mrs Gaisford.'

'And no doubt best for me too, the way my life would have gone if Luke had survived.' Abigail rose from her chair. 'I must bring Tess in and reassure her that I attribute no blame to her.'

She returned with a tearful Tess, still murmuring apologies.

'Come and sit here with me,' said Martha, who occupied a sofa on her own. She took Tess's hand in hers. 'From what I hear you did a very brave and necessary thing. You should not suffer any regret.' She patted the girl's hand comfortingly and continued to hold it for a minute. Then she fished a handkerchief from the sleeve of her dress and handed it to Tess who wiped her eyes, stopped her tears and smiled wanly.

'Miss Mitchell is right, Tess. If it hadn't been for you I would have lost my life,' said Captain Ford. You saved me, and not for the first time.'

Martha, who had held Tess moments after she was born, felt anew a sense of responsibility for her. Realising the feeling behind Captain Ford's words she asked him, 'What will you do now?'

'If you will all give me written statements, I will go to London and clear my name with my employer. In order to spare Mrs Gaisford, I shall request that none of this is made public and that the owner merely reports that the wreck was caused by inclement weather. I am sure he will agree. I will request another command and ask him to allow it to sail out of Falmouth so that I will be near Tess, who I suppose will be returning to Cornwall with Mrs Gaisford?'

Tess's heart leapt. Captain Ford wanted to be near her! She wanted to be near him too.

'Is that what you will be doing, Abigail?' asked Martha.

'I think so, Aunt.'

'You know, you can stay here with me if you think Cornwall will hold too many bad memories for you.'

'I know, but it holds happy ones too. After all, I have lived in Cornwall for most of my life. I know it's a little soon after what has just happened, but in Cornwall I will be close to the man I should have married in the first place.' Her eyes met Martin's and she saw there the answer she wanted. 'There will be three estates to administer once we are back,' she went on quickly, 'and I must bear the responsibility of breaking the news to Luke's mother.'

'From what you have told me I am sure she will understand, though that will not ease the loss of a son for her.' Martha paused a moment then, looking at her niece, said, 'Abigail, come and sit the other side of me.' She did as she was bidden, and when she'd sat down Martha took her hand. 'Before you go back to Cornwall there is something you and Tess must know.'

They all looked at her curiously.

'What I am going to tell you is a secret that I have kept for a long time. Before I tell you, I want you to promise me that you will not think less of a certain person I shall name.'

Abigail said, 'I promise.'

Tess nodded.

'Good. From what I have seen of you both in the short time you have been here, I know you will keep your word.' Martha went on to tell them the whole story of her brother

404

and Lydia Booth. 'He thought no less of your mother, Abigail, and did the right thing by your mother too, Tess, who demanded nothing. From what I saw of Lydia who stayed here with me while she awaited her confinement, she was a kind and loving woman. To save you and your father from public censure, Tess, she pretended she was your aunt. I am pleased to hear you always addressed her as Mama, which indeed she was.'

There was a charged silence as each of them tried to take in this revelation.

Abigail was stunned. Her father had betrayed her mother! How could he have loved someone else? Her mind set against him, but then she remembered he had never altered in his affectionate behaviour towards her, he had always been the kindest, most considerate and loving husband and father. She could not fault him in his paternal duties so she really had no cause to condemn him. How must he have felt, having Tess in his household yet never being able to acknowledge her as his daughter? Now she understood why he had asked to see her when he was dying.

Tess was bewildered. The man who supposedly would have nothing to do with her was not her father after all. The man who was had been kind to her. Now she knew why. How she wished she had just once been able to call him by his proper name, but she understood why it hadn't been possible – too many people would have been hurt, too many lives shattered. Her dear aunt had in reality been her mother, and now Abigail was not just her mistress but also her sister.

When Martha rose from her chair to announce she was going to sit on the terrace for a while before getting ready for the evening meal, Captain Ford and Martin tactfully followed her.

Speechless, the meaning of their aunt's words sinking in, Abigail and Tess stared at each other. Then as one they held out their arms to each other, realising now why they had often felt a special bond between them, one they were both determined to make even closer now, as they knew their father would have wished.